FURBIDDEN ATTRACTION

R. O'LEARY

Copyright © 2019 by R. O'Leary

All rights reserved.

No part of this book may be reproduced in any form or by any electronic or mechanical means, including information storage and retrieval systems, without written permission from the author, except for the use of brief quotations in a book review.

Editing by Suzanne Johnson

Cover Design by The Book Brander

❦ Created with Vellum

For Mom and Dad
(Please skip the sex scenes)

1

Oh shit.

Pain exploded across his side, rippling in excruciating waves. The crash of each labored heartbeat pounded in his ears. A crust of grit ground deep into his back, shards of gravel burrowing and needling their way into his skin.

He was going to die.

He was going to die alone, lying on an empty stretch of backwoods road.

He had failed.

A savage rage burned through his veins, choking a howl of despair in a ruthless grip. Teeth slammed together with a click. The Den must be warned. He could *not* fail. He rolled onto his stomach, tucking his legs beneath him. Sharp rocks nipped at the pads of his feet as he pushed against the ground. His legs straightened, forcing himself upright.

Ignoring the blare of a car horn behind him, he took a step. And another. And promptly crashed face first back onto the ground.

Darkness crowded him, creeping across his vision. He closed his eyes and let the nothingness envelope him.

She needed chocolate. Sighing, Louisa dropped into a desk chair. The day was rapidly circling the drain. Who did she think she was kidding? Her whole life was circling the drain. She yanked open a drawer and fished blindly for her hidden stash of candy. Fingertips brushed foil. Bingo.

She yanked out an errant truffle and popped the chocolate into her open mouth. Dark chocolate dissolved against her tongue, bitter and rich, as the wrapper sailed into the trashcan.

Ever since Louisa had moved to Raven Falls, things had gone from bad to worse. No, more like bad to unbearable. Her apartment looked nothing like the pictures the landlord had posted online. Mystery stains dotted the carpeting. The walls remained a dingy yellow despite the numerous buckets of bleach Louisa had splashed on them, and the shower. Louisa shuddered. Good god, the shower was horrifying. Seriously, it was a damn wreck.

The used car she bought barely made the trip to Maine before growling ominously and demanding three thousand dollars' worth of work from the local garage. Louisa was fairly certain they were ripping her off, but of course it happened to be the only garage in town.

And worst of all, every single resident of Raven Falls had been treating her like some kind of deranged serial killer.

Louisa had been in town for two months, and still people were glaring at her in the grocery store. She had no idea why. Maybe it was her hair, or the way she dressed? Hell, it could just be plain old small town paranoia.

Yesterday, a young mother actually dragged a toddler

across the street to avoid her. She didn't want to seem whiny, but, damn, this little town was going to give her a complex.

She had moved to Maine to get away from people, but this was getting ridiculous. Well, not all people. Just her shitty ex, and her boss, and everyone she'd ever met. Okay, all people.

Louisa tugged the hair band loose from the knot of curls at the back of her neck and scrubbed her fingers against her aching scalp.

Raven Falls was supposed to be a new beginning, but it was quickly becoming the cherry on a lonely, twenty-five-year sundae. She just wanted somewhere to belong, especially after the gut-wrenching nightmare that New York had turned into.

She'd really thought this place would be different, and she felt like she was giving it her best shot. Early this morning, she had woken up with a warm, fuzzy feeling. Filled with determination that things were going to turn around. As though today was going to be different. As though her life was going to change for the better. Yeah, frickin' right.

She'd sipped her coffee on the drive to the office, contemplating a new area rug. Anything, really, to cover the unidentifiable stains in the middle of the living room floor.

Louisa had made it less than three steps into the office before Dr. Adler had descended on her like some mutant shark scenting happy, optimistic blood. The hag could sniff out joy like a bloodhound.

And that had just been the beginning of the death spiral. A lovely orange tabby with the most spectacularly fluffy fur had thrown up on her pants mid-exam. The sweet little white rabbit with an ear infection had taken a chunk out of Louisa's finger for breathing in its vicinity.

She glared down at the pink bandage wrapped around the tip of her middle finger. Precious little bastard.

But worst of all was the sweet, sandy-furred dog that had come in covered in blood. Her sandwich, halfway to her mouth, had dropped back onto the desk with a sad thump when the two boys had run in, dragging the dog between them.

The air had seized in Louisa's lungs when she saw his beautiful fur stuck up in sticky bunches—rusty patches of blood dried by the warm afternoon sun. He lay limp in the stained blanket, struggling for each breath. She had barely glanced at the pale faces of the two boys hoisting the dog between them before wheeling him away.

The boys... who had no idea where the dog came from. Louisa's mouth twisted severely at the memory of that conversation. So much teenage disdain.

Someone had to be wondering where their dog had wandered off to. Or not; maybe they didn't want him. Maybe she could keep him. Louisa snorted around her truffle. Her landlord would just *love* that.

She'd always wanted a dog, or a cat, or any type of pet, really. None of Louisa's foster parents had been animal lovers, though, and no amount of begging had budged them on the matter. A quick shake of her head sent the memory back into the shadows.

Some things Louisa avoided thinking about: the endless string of foster parents, hauling her things from home to home in a garbage bag, her whole childhood, really.

Maybe if things turned around here, she could get the puppy she'd always wanted. No, an older dog, a rescue. Louisa smiled as the thought tumbled through her brain. A rescue would be perfect, something unwanted and unloved for her to cuddle and pet. But a dog would need a yard.

Maybe she could rent a house after her lease ran out next spring.

A steady tap sounded behind Louisa's chair, ripping her away from her daydreams. She spun around, barely stifling the frustrated groan in her throat. Dr. Adler stood, skinny-bird arms crossed over her chest, her impractical stiletto tapping sharply against the tile.

"If you have time to stare at the wall, you have time to inventory supplies." Her toes continued their incessant tapping.

Louisa sighed. That's what she got for letting her guard down in this snake pit. She started to push herself out of her chair.

"I'll get started inventorying the meds."

Dr. Adler waved a hand, cutting her off. Her droopy buzzard-eyes narrowed.

"No, I want *all* the medical supplies inventoried," she snapped.

Louisa's jaw dropped open. A full inventory would take all night. The old battle-ax couldn't possibly expect her to stay here sorting supplies hours after her shift had ended. She studied Dr. Adler's icy demeanor, her foot still tapping impatiently. Yes, yes she could, apparently.

Louisa took a deep breath.

"Dr. Adler, I have plans tonight," she reasoned. "I couldn't possibly stay tonight and sort the whole office. I can come in this weekend and get it done much more efficiently."

The only plans Louisa had that night involved a pint of ice cream, her couch, and a few hours of reality TV, but she wasn't about to tell that to the old witch.

The harpy waved her hand, dismissing Louisa's objections. "The inventory will be done by tomorrow morning, or else you'll be hunting for a new job by dinnertime."

Louisa sighed. Tonight was going to suck.

"Alright, I'm just finishing up some paperwork and then we can go get started."

Dr. Adler's brittle smile set Louisa's teeth on edge and soured the lingering chocolate on her tongue.

"Unfortunately, I have a previous engagement," she sneered. "But I'm sure you'll have no problem getting it done."

Louisa ground her teeth together as Dr. Adler clicked away. If she didn't need this job, Louisa would have tipped her coffee over the bitch's head a dozen times over the past couple of weeks. Dr. Adler was the embodiment of this town —frosty and unfriendly.

Louisa sighed as her chocolate buzz deflated. This was going to be one hell of a long night. She glanced at the empty coffeepot. Better start chugging some caffeine.

Louisa blinked her weary eyes at the glowing clock on the wall. She'd run out of coffee sometime around her seventh hour of inventory and was rapidly losing her ability to keep her train of thought chugging in a straight line.

Flicking off the office light, she shuffled down the narrow hall. The office sat empty, the monstrous Dr. Adler and Jessica, the evil minion receptionist, had abandoned Louisa hours ago. One quick round to make sure all of her furry buddies were tucked in, and then she would be free to stumble into her own bed.

Light shone from underneath an exam room door. Louisa frowned. She'd thought Jessica had closed everything up for the night hours ago. Louisa nudged the door open. Her favorite furry patient for the day was tucked in the pen they used for anesthesia recovery. Jessica was supposed to have moved him to the kennels for the night long before she took off. Sterile plastic bags had been casually tossed across the table.

Poor baby. The beautiful brown dog was sprawled on a nest of blankets. His bandages glowed stark-white against the warm brown of his downy chest.

Louisa slipped the plastic bags waiting on the exam table into the deep pocket of her scrub pants. Her hand flicked, the bright-pink bandage flashing, and unlocked the gate of the pen. Louisa settled herself on the floor, legs folded into a neat pretzel.

Louisa's hand lifted hesitantly, fingers stretched. She ran her fingertips through the fluffy fur dusting the crown of the dog's head. Her fingers drifted, floating the length of his large ear. Louisa smiled as the ear twitched against her fingertips.

She'd always loved animals. There was something innocent and kind about them that humans lacked. Probably a soul, Louisa snorted.

As her hand moved down the length of his soft nose, Louisa blinked at the unusual bottle-green eyes staring back at her.

"Hello. You had quite the adventure today," she whispered soothingly.

Her fingers continued their descent along the bridge of his nose. The green eyes stared at her face, glazed in drug-induced confusion. His head lifted incrementally. A quiet whine slipped from between his lips.

"Somebody shot you, and you were hit by a car. Then a ditzy idiot left you in here all alone."

Louisa could practically see the unasked questions shining at her from green depths.

"You're going to hurt for a little while."

Her free hand crossed her body and dug through her pocket. With a sharp tug, the two bags slid free. Louisa held the smaller bag up to the light, studying the metal fragment inside. It was clearly a bullet. Or it had been, anyway. Now it was a malformed hunk of nothing.

Blood still congealed on the odd gray metal. Her eyes narrowed. It sure didn't look like any bullet she'd ever seen. Because she was such an expert on weaponry. Louisa shook her head.

She tossed the bag back on the floor and scooped up the larger bag. Louisa gripped an edge between her teeth and tugged it open. Her hand dipped inside and grasped the collar inside. Flapping her hand, Louisa whipped it back and forth to free it from the bag. She studied the silver tag.

"Jack," Louisa read aloud.

She glanced at the green eyes still calmly watching her as his nose nuzzled her hand.

"I like it. Simple. Masculine. Jack."

Louisa flicked her hand, flipping the silver medallion. She squinted at the string of numbers neatly printed across the back. So small. She really needed to see about getting a set of reading glasses.

Louisa began to untangle her fingers from the mass of fur when Jack growled quietly at her. She blinked at him. Pushy monster.

Louisa balanced the collar carefully on her knee and fished through her pockets for her cell phone. She hesitated as the screen lit up. It was late, extremely late. Calling right now would just wake someone up and get Louisa yelled at.

She bit her lip. If her dog were missing, she would want

to know right away if he were found. Steeling her spine, Louisa punched in the phone number. She pressed the phone to her ear. It rang. Twice. Three times. The loud beep pressured her to leave a voice mail, the lack of prompt throwing Louisa off-balance. Who doesn't have their outgoing message set up in this day and age? Weird.

"This is Louisa from the Raven Falls Animal Clinic. Your dog, Jack, was in an accident earlier this afternoon."

Jack's ears pricked up at the sound of his name. Louisa pet a hand soothingly over his head. He settled his chin on her knee and watched her mumble into the phone.

"He's being treated for various injuries, but he should be stable enough to take home in a day or two. Please stop by the clinic or give us a call as soon as possible."

Jack whined softly. Louisa set her phone on the floor beside her and stroked his ears. Where were his people? She glanced back at the odd bullet. Her blood froze in her veins. What if they had been the ones who shot him?

Louisa peered into the green eyes watching her. No, monsters who shoot dogs don't raise kind fluffballs like Jack. Kind fluffballs who needed to rest.

She yawned loudly, her mouth dropping open. A wave of dizziness passed over her in a rush. If Louisa didn't get some sleep ASAP, Dr. Adler was going to find her here, passed out on the floor.

"Time for bed, buddy," she said, stifling another yawn.

Louisa stumbled to her feet and heaved Jack into her arms, carefully avoiding the bandages enveloping him. Carrying him out the door, she winced when her foot connected with the doorjamb. Louisa grumbled as she walked him down the hall to the wall of kennels.

Jack whined in her arms the closer they got to the empty cage. Ooph, arrow straight to the heart.

Don't look in his eyes. Whatever you do, don't look in his eyes.

Louisa settle him inside and stepped back. His anxious whine halted her in her tracks. His luminous eyes stared at her, wide and begging. Fuck.

"Don't give me that look," Louisa scolded. "You need to stay here tonight and I am far too tired to argue with you about it."

Jack's paw scooted across the floor of the kennel and nudged the door. He eyed her, whining pitifully. *Oh no, don't even try it.*

"I'll be back first thing in the morning...unfortunately," she mumbled.

Louisa turned to leave, his soft whines following her footsteps. A steady ache settled in her chest. The urge to turn back and cuddle the beast against her was nearly overwhelming. She was such a softy; if he got any more pitiful she would absolutely shatter.

Louisa forced herself to put one foot in front of the other. As her fingertips brushed the doorknob, the wall of kennels erupted into whining and panicked squeaks. She jumped, her heart pounding wildly. The hell?

She studied the wall over her shoulder. Nothing seemed wrong. Maybe the animals just needed to adjust to their new friend. Turning back to the door, Louisa jumped even higher as the first howl cut the air. The whining quickly reached an earsplitting crescendo and dissolved into terrified screeching. She clapped her hands over her ears.

"Stop it!"

Animal after animal hurled itself at the door of its cage. Claws hooked in the metal, rattling doors on their hinges. Except for Jack.

He still lay where Louisa had placed him, eyes wide and begging as he pawed weakly at the front of his prison. What the hell kind of trickery was this? His eyes grew wider under her scrutiny.

"Fine!" Louisa threw her hands in the air.

Surrendering to the twinge in her chest, Louisa stomped back to the kennels and ripped Jack's open.

"This is all your fault," she growled into his fur as she scooped him back up.

The remaining animals quieted to gentle whining and huddled in the corners of their kennels as Louisa turned to walk away. She frowned at them. Maybe...?

Louisa hopped a few more steps toward the door, stopping when the whining faded into silence. Jack watched her through his cracked eyelids. Her foot slid backwards in an experimental step. Soft growls swelled behind her, sending the fine hairs on the back of her neck to attention.

She slid forward again, Jack's fuzzy, brown form clutched tightly to her chest. The room quieted. Well, that was frickin' weird.

Louisa's eyes dropped to his upturned face. Little troublemaker. Maybe she could tuck him somewhere in the office tonight? Far, far from the rest of the kennels.

As though sensing the direction of her thoughts, Jack gave Louisa's neck a delicate swipe with his tongue. A final, pitiful whine slipped from his chest. He closed his eyes, exhausted, and nestled into her arms. Oh, the devious little rat.

She was such a sucker. This is exactly how she had ended up staying with her cheating waste of an ex for months longer than she should have. Well, not exactly the same. Jack was much cuter, after all.

Fuck it. Louisa sighed. "I guess you're coming home with me tonight."

2

Jack licked Louisa's nose in a gentle kiss as she leaned over him. She deserved it, after all, for bringing him home. The thought of staying in that kennel surrounded by the stench of fear pouring off those animals made Jack shudder.

Louisa gently scooped him out of the backseat of her car. A whine escaped from between his lips as the pressure of her touch sent lightning bolts through his abused ribcage. They sloshed through the downpour. Louisa clutched him to her chest, shielding his body with her hunched shoulders. Water dripped down her face as she tore across the parking lot.

Louisa stepped into the cover of the entry. She gave her curly head a shake, sending droplets flying into the air. Cool drops splashed across Jack's face. He barely blinked as the water soaked his fur, failing to make a dent in the drug-induced haze smothering him.

"We have to be quiet," she whispered in his ear. "I'm not allowed to have pets in the building."

Jack gifted her another lick. You got it, babe. Silent as a church mouse.

Louisa trudged up the stairs. Jack's teeth clenched tightly as he fought back a pitiful howl. He'd promised after all. Each bounce exacerbated his agony.

Hurry up, Jack growled to himself. Tiny black spots were beginning to swarm his vision as the pain crescendoed.

"Holy shit," Louisa gasped as she crested the stairs. "Either you need to go on a diet or I need to work out more.

Jack turned his eyes to her. Louisa's cheeks glowed pink from exertion, her forehead glistening. Too tired to lift his head, Jack narrowed his eyes. A diet? She was tossing his poor, battered body around like a paint shaker and she had the nerve to call him fat? Rude.

Jack huffed into her elbow. Clearly, she needed more cardio in her day.

Louisa stepped up to the door and froze. She glared down at him.

"I don't suppose his majesty could unlock the door?"

Jack growled softly. This chick was batty. What was she expecting? He had a bullet hole in his shoulder and no thumbs. Jack gifted her a light lick on her arm and closed his eyes. She'd figure it out. Hopefully sooner rather than later.

He heard her sigh softly in the silent hallway. She lowered Jack gently, carefully laying him on the doormat. He cracked one eye open. Louisa shook out her arms with a grunt and went fishing in her bag. A handful of keys flashed in her hand. She stepped over him and unlocked the door.

She's an odd one, but at least she was entertaining.

Jack opened his eyes fully as the mat beneath his back slid haltingly. Louisa was crouched next to him. Her arms

Furbidden Attraction

were straining, her jaw clenched. She was tugging hard, trying to drag Jack through the open door. His eyes rolled.

He carefully pushed himself to his feet. A surge of nausea crashed through Jack as he forced his body upright. Choking it back, he limped forward. He stepped off the slowly inching mat and settled on the floor.

The doormat jerked into Louisa's chest. She fell back and landed on her butt with a thump. She looked between the doormat and Jack's crumpled form. Her eyes narrowed. Louisa toed off her soaked shoes, cursing under her breath.

He watched her blearily from his new spot.

"Sassy dogs don't get dinner," she sniffed as she pushed herself to her feet.

"Just something you might want to keep in mind," Louisa called over her shoulder.

Jack huffed as she slipped out of the room. No dinner? He was a fully grown male, perfectly capable of foraging for food after she went to sleep if it came to it.

Or not. He winced at a new twinge creeping along his side. Maybe if he looked pathetic enough, she'd slide him another pain pill.

Louisa padded back into the room, heavy sweatpants swishing against her legs. She walked into the kitchen and poked her head into the fridge. Good, maybe she'd bring him something tasty.

Jack hungrily followed her progress as she crossed the kitchen with two paper plates clutched in hand. Louisa set one plate on the floor beside him and plopped herself on the couch. He nudged it with his nose before nibbling off a bite.

Sweet and nutty notes mixed with an unfamiliar vanilla hit Jack's tongue. Peanut butter and jelly and Louisa, yum.

A low moan perked his ears. Louisa was devouring her

food with enormous bites, small, happy noises squeaking out of her as she chewed. Jack huffed softly into his sandwich. She was fucking adorable.

He abandoned the rest of his sandwich and looked around the tiny apartment. The walls were an odd shade of yellow, and the carpet had an alarming number of stains. Despite the shabbiness, the apartment was immaculately clean.

Louisa stared at the far wall. Jack followed her eyes and growled quietly. A framed photo of an ad featuring a backyard barbeque hung on the wall. Faded lines crisscrossed the picture where it had been folded and unfolded, over and over again. The edges were ragged, no doubt torn from a magazine.

He looked between her and the photo. Louisa's heart-shaped face was twisted, her dark eyebrows wrinkled in thought. She looked sad.

Jack pushed himself onto his paws, a twinge in his side charging through the muddled haze of painkillers. Louisa jumped in surprise as Jack's tongue swiped her bare ankle. She smiled at him. Her hand dropped to his head, giving him a thumpy pat between the ears. Louisa tottered to her feet and slipped out of the room.

Jack waited impatiently. He wanted more pets. A needy desire swirled through him; he needed her warm scent floating around him, cutting through the ache radiating beneath the bandages. He whined softly.

Louisa floated back into the room, something clutched in her arms. A heavy blanket tumbled to the floor beside him. Jack glanced between her and the blanket. What?

Louisa knelt down and patted the thick pad.

"Come on. Bedtime." She patted the bed insistently.

Jack stared back at her. This was just insulting. Had she

seen what this carpet looked like? Blanket or not, he'd probably pick up some form of hepatitis from the stains.

"Please, I'm tired. Just go to sleep," Louisa begged, exhaustion mingling with frustration.

He blinked back at her, unmoving in the face of her disappointment.

"Fine!" She threw her hands in the air. "Sleep on the floor if you want."

Louisa stood in a rush, mumbling as she strode out of the room. Jack listened to the sounds of water running in the bathroom as she got ready for bed. He waited patiently in the living room, studying her décor for more hints at her life. A formation of Pez dispensers lined the windowsills, their bright, cheery faces creepily stared back at him. Pez dispensers? What a weirdo.

Louisa flicked off the light and shuffled into the bedroom. Jack padded to the bedroom door and waited as she folded herself into a nest of blankets. Stepping quietly, he slipped into the bedroom. Jack leapt onto the bed. His shoulder exploded with pain. He choked down a sharp whine and settled on the bed.

Jack's nose poked into Louisa's nest of blankets, his nose bumping her shoulder. She cracked open a tired eye. His tongue flicked across her nose. Jack's chin dropped to her shoulder as his weary eyes drifted closed.

"Just for tonight, Jack." Louisa yawned.

JACK BLINKED AWAKE. A heavy curl of Louisa's hair drifted across his nose. He buried his nose in his paws and sneezed. The sleeping lump beside him shifted. Jack studied her in the pale, morning light.

She was pretty. Especially asleep, when she wasn't

frowning at everything. Louisa's wild cloud of hair swallowed the pillows. It was easily his favorite thing about her. As annoying as it may be, Jack thought, puffing another dark curl away from his face.

The fog had lifted from his mind as the pain meds wore off in the night. A fresh wave of pain inched along his side. Jack started to rise but dropped back down as pain spiked through his shoulder. A disgruntled growl rumbled in his chest. Alright, take it slow.

His toes flexed, one paw at a time. Jack cycled through his body, systematically testing for injuries. Paws, good. Legs, fine. Right shoulder, burning like a motherfucker. Ribs, sore and aching with each breath. Tail, intact. Thank god.

Definitely wouldn't be chasing his tail anytime soon. He'd have to get Nate to cut him a break on patrol duty. Jack chuffed quietly. As if the grumpy bastard would even consider it. He'd just tell him he had it coming with that annoyingly dead expression on his face.

Jack scowled. He wasn't supposed to be here. He was supposed to report to the Den...but report what? There was something important that Jack needed to tell them. Something life or death. He whined as his mind betrayed him. The knowledge was there but dancing seductively just out of reach.

Okay, fuck this. Time to go home.

Jack leapt painfully to the floor. Spots spun all around him. The soft carpet cushioned his footfalls as he stepped lightly into the living room. Time to blow this popsicle stand.

Jack closed his eyes and reached for the power that burned deep inside... and couldn't find it. Oh shit. He was trapped. He was freakin' trapped!

Jack closed his eyes and tried again. It was there, still burning quietly and winding through him like trickling water. He just couldn't reach it. It slipped through his mind like wind through his fingers. How the hell was he going to get out of here?

Oh god, he was going to live the rest of his life in this form. He was going to have to eat dog treats and play fetch. Jack's breath came in whining pants as panic settled on his chest like a ten-pound weight.

A familiar scent wafted through the room. Jack cracked his eyes open and stared at the curly mane moving toward him. Louisa dropped a clumsy pet between his ears. He took a deep breath of her calming scent and watched her sleepily shuffle into the kitchen.

Okay, new plan. Stick with Louisa until he could contact the Den. She would take care of him. Jack padded into the kitchen. Louisa spread cream cheese on an untoasted bagel, her toes curling away from the cold tile.

Yeah, stick with her. Jack snorted. Girl couldn't even toast a bagel, clearly she needed him more than he needed her.

Jack nudged her bare leg with his nose.

"Eh?" she mumbled around a bite of bagel.

Another quick jab and pointed glance at her bagel. Louisa stared blankly as he warmed her icy toes with his paws. *That's right, babe. See how useful I am?*

She ripped off a chunk of bagel and tossed it to him. Victory!

Louisa stumbled away to shower while Jack gnawed on the cream cheese-slathered rock. Stale as fuck. He braced it between his paws for another angle. How the hell was his bushy-headed girl managing to chew through this? Jack growled ferociously. He'd eaten Frisbees more appetizing than this.

Louisa walked out of the bedroom. She buried her hands in her damp mass of hair and twisted her curls into a knot with a deft flick of her wrists. Jack cleaned the cream cheese off his paws as she straightened her scrub top and tied her shoes. Double-knotting her laces, Louisa gave him a stern look.

"We're going to behave ourselves today, yes?" Her eyes narrowed. "It would be a shame if you embarrassed yourself with another tantrum."

Louisa crouched in front of him and ran her fingers along his nose. She leaned in close. A few rebellious curls liberated themselves from her bun and brushed the tips of his ears.

"What would the other dogs think?"

Louisa shot a conspiratorial wink his way and straightened. She tossed the rest of her things together and waved Jack toward the door.

Slip some real food his way, and she wouldn't hear a peep out of him for the rest of the day.

Louisa threw Jack a disgusted look. This morning she'd tried, rather selfishly, to tuck him away in the kennels again. Thanks to the animal kingdom's natural aversion to his kind, he was now sprawled in the corner of the office on a pile of towels.

The howling had been loud enough for the neighboring restaurant to send a lanky, pimpled waiter over to complain. Jack had tried to warn her, he really had.

Louisa turned her glare back to the mountain of paperwork spread in front to her. She poked at it with a hiss. Poor thing, maybe if she gave him some pets she would feel better.

The grating ring of the phone forced an end to her staring contest. She reached for it, sighing for the seventeenth time in the last hour. Jack knew, he was keeping count.

Poor Lou, she clearly hated this job. And yes, Jack had decided to call her Lou. Louisa was such a serious name for someone so damn cute. Those wild curls? And the way she nibbled on her pouty bottom lip? Goddamn adorable.

"Raven Falls Animal Clinic," Louisa recited tonelessly into the phone.

Jack looked up as she replaced the phone and stood up. He scratched absently at his ear. Louisa straightened her scrubs and walked out the door. Arranging her armor. She had performed the same routine every time the phone rang. It wasn't even lunchtime and the phone had been ringing all morning.

Maybe she'd bring back snacks. Four of her last missions beyond the office had included returning with food. Jack's paws were crossed for a fifth.

He dozed as he waited for Louisa's return. His feet hung in the air, twitching occasionally as he lolled in his nest.

"Behold and tremble at the formidable might of the Den's guard dog, renowned for his ferocity."

Jack's eyes snapped open. A voice as familiar as his own laughed. A pair of gray eyes floated above his face. Jack struggled to roll onto his feet, the remains of quiet laughter still lingering like tendrils of smoke in his head.

Alice! Thank God. I thought the Den might be cutting its losses and leaving me here. He rolled his eyes. Yeah, right. He was too awesome for that.

Alice carefully schooled her face into a serious expression as she pet his ears.

Right, she couldn't hear him. Shit.

Her eyes twinkled with composed mirth. Jack wagged his tail furiously. It felt so damned good to see someone who actually knew that he was not, in fact, a dog. He'd been on the brink of barking out a message in morse code, desperate for any kind of intelligent understanding.

A serious, Hispanic man walked into the office, talking to Lou over his shoulder. Connor. If anyone could figure out what was going on, it was the solemn-faced cop.

"What happened, Jack?" Alice whispered to him.

Jack dragged his eyes back to Alice's concerned face.

"Oh, right. You can't talk."

He whined softly. Jack couldn't remember anything but pain... and feeling an urgent need to get to the Den... but he couldn't remember why.

Alice glanced at Connor, concern painting her features. He turned toward the two of them, crouched in the corner.

"When can we take him home?" Connor's deep voice boomed through the small office.

Louisa blinked at what must have been a sudden change of subject.

"He needs another couple days of observation, Mr...?"

"Flores."

"Mr. Flores," she continued. "Your dog had extensive surgery yesterday. He is healing much quicker than expected, but he still needs to be watched for complications."

Jack tuned out their argument. Lou was going to win. Connor was stubborn, but Lou had grit. Alice continued to watch them volley back and forth.

"Can I have a moment alone with my...uh...husband?"

"Sure," Louisa sighed. "Kick me out of my own office, but sure take a moment," she grumbled under her breath.

"We need to get you home." Connor turned to him as soon as the door clicked shut. "Why haven't you shifted?"

Jack whined. He shook his head violently side to side, his big ears swaying.

"You can't?" Connor and Alice looked at him in shock.

Alice's delicate, red eyebrows soared. "At all? Not even partially?"

Jack whined and gave his head another shake.

"Okay, tap your paw once for yes, twice for no, okay?"

Jack tapped his paw. Aww, sweet communication.

"The batty lady said they removed a bullet, right?" Connor asked. "Did you see the bullet?"

Jack stared at the lumbering idiot. Seriously? *Well Connor, I was unconscious when they ripped it out of my shoulder. So that's a definite no.*

Jack tapped his paw twice. Dumbass.

"If it contained silver, it would have been slowly poisoning you until it was removed. Your body might still be getting rid of the excess," Alice mused.

Understanding flooded in a wave of helplessness. Fuck.

"We're taking him home," Connor growled. "Right now."

Jack tapped his paw twice.

Alice and Connor raised their eyebrows simultaneously. They were going to be soooo mad.

"Funny," Connor deadpanned.

Jack tapped his paw again twice, his paw thumping harder.

Connor glared sharply at Jack, still huddled in his nest.

"You can't tell us how you got shot, or who shot you, and you want to *stay*? Unprotected? Did the bullet pass through your tiny, useless brain?" Connor scrubbed a frustrated hand over his short buzzcut.

Jack nodded his head, tapping his paw once as an after thought. He wasn't ready to leave yet. Louisa's scent drifted over him as she came to knock on the office door.

"Everything alright?" she called through the door.

"Just fine, thanks!" Alice called back.

Connor regarded Jack seriously. "You're sure about this?"

Jack tapped his paw firmly. He was staying until the silver poisoning passed. Louisa needed him.

3

Louisa rolled over, her blankets tangled around her in a dense cocoon. She was way too comfy to be awake and far too cozy to get out of bed. One blurry eye cracked open and searched for the red glow of the alarm clock on the nightstand. Twenty-seven minutes left.

Her eyelid thumped shut with weary satisfaction. Louisa pulled the blankets tighter around her. A little wiggle and she was settled back into the cloudy comfort of the mattress. A blanket of sleep eased slowly back over her. Louisa had just begun to drift back into nothingness when something nudged against her ribcage.

"I'm sleeping, Jack. Go away." Louisa pressed her face into the pillows.

They'd gotten in late last night. The Evil Dr. Adler had demanded she clear the backlog of filing twenty minutes before the office closed for the day. Jessica and Louisa had been sorting patient files late into the night, Dr. Adler nowhere to be seen, of course.

Another nudge against her side. She reached out to

shove Jack away. Her fingertips brushed skin. Louisa's eyes flew open. There was someone in her bed.

Her heartbeat was deafening in her ears. Oh shit, oh shit, oh shit. Air froze in her lungs as Louisa looked over her shoulder.

Nestled on the other pillow was one of the most handsome faces she had ever seen. Sharply chiseled cheekbones framed by a strong jaw dusted with golden stubble. Long, golden-brown eyelashes lined eyelids closed peacefully in sleep. Gorgeous...and a complete stranger.

A scream burst from her chest, piercing the morning tranquility. There was a stranger *in her bed!* Louisa leapt from the bed, or tried to anyway. Bedding tangled her limbs as she flailed unsuccessfully.

The angelic creep woke with a jerk. He jumped off the bed and landed in a crouch, his head swiveling as he scanned the room. A frown crinkled his brow as he watched Louisa's panicked struggle through bleary eyes.

Oh no, he was naked. Like super naked. Louisa's eyes tracked from his handsome face down his carved chest. A light dusting of hair sprinkled across his chest, trailing down his rock solid abs to his... *fucking perfect dick*. Holy hell.

Louisa jerked her eyes away. Not that it mattered, the image of that monster would be forever burned in her mind. With a hard twist, Louisa tumbled off the bed in a thrash of blankets. She hit the carpet with a dull thud. Struggling to free herself, she rolled onto her knees.

Her mind whirred with terrifying scenarios as she untangled her legs. There was a strange man in her apartment, possibly a serial killer. A naked serial killer who clearly had a gym membership. And she was going to be murdered because she liked to sleep under a mountain of blankets.

Louisa poked her head up over the edge of the bed. Her unwelcome visitor straightened from his crouch, his head cocked to the side as he watched Louisa with wide green eyes. He took a step forward and pitched sideways, nearly falling flat. He caught himself on the footboard, a large, tan hand gripping the bedpost. Pulling himself upright, he raised his hands to touch the lines of his face. His fingertips traced the shape of his mouth and trailed along the bridge of his nose.

"Yes! Finally!" he shouted, triumphantly punching a fist into the air. He winced at the motion.

Louisa watched him warily as he probed his shoulder. Dark lines webbed from his muscled pec outward. His frown slid back into place as he studied the area.

She dropped onto all fours and inched toward the door, her traitorous blankets abandoned. Forcing herself to take slow, calm breaths, Louisa silently crept forward. A shadow blocked out the faint morning light. She froze. He stood over her, staring with a perplexed expression on his face. Shit.

Louisa lunged to her feet and dashed across the remaining distance between her and the living room. Years of paranoia had pushed her to keep a baseball bat by the front door. If Louisa could just get her hands on it, this guy would be toast. She scrambled across the small apartment, twisting around cramped furniture. With every step, she could hear the echo of his feet behind her.

Louisa slammed bodily against the front door, her hands frantically grasping for the bat tucked to the side. Her fingers wrapped around the handle. Louisa spun, whipping the heavy, wooden bat between them. The bat shook in her hands as adrenaline coursed through her body.

He leapt back as she brandished it threateningly in front of her. Louisa gave it a few test swings back and forth, just so he'd know she meant business. Now who's in charge, jackass?

He reached out a hand in a placating gesture, his pale-green eyes calm. Louisa swung the bat again, wood whistling through the air as it sailed perilously close to his face.

"Get the hell away from me!" her screech cut through the awkward silence. She took a deep breath to steady herself against the wall of terror in front of her.

"I don't know who you are, but you need to get the hell out of my apartment."

He raised his hands slowly and took another step away from her. Louisa shuffled her feet backwards until her shoulders thumped against the door.

"My name is Jack," he said soothingly. He had a great voice. Warm and deep, like a really good dark chocolate.

Louisa had a brief image of his sexy abs covered in melted chocolate. Like a chocolate-dipped Norse god, just for her. Mmmm....if only he hadn't broken into her apartment.

Pull your head out of your panties, moron.

"What are you doing in my house, Jack?" Louisa waved the bat in his direction.

"You brought me here."

Her mind spun. Did she bring someone home last night? That didn't sound like her. Louisa had had a single one-night stand in all of her twenty-five years on Earth, and it was absolutely terrible. She had been avoiding a repeat performance ever since. And quite frankly, Louisa was pretty sure this chunk of man was miles outside of her league.

"You brought me home two days ago... I was just a bit more furry at the time," Jack continued.

Jack...as in Jack?

Her jaw gaped open. This guy thought he was a dog twenty-four hours ago... He wasn't just a possible serial killer, he was seriously unhinged.

Louisa's jaw clicked shut as she shook her head. Just get him out of here and call the police. Then she could call out of work and spend the rest of the day huddled on the couch in a tangle of frayed nerves. There may even be a scoop of ice cream left.

"While I find it doubtful that you used to be a dog, I'm going to humor you," Louisa said gently.

She took one hand off the bat and slipped it behind her, blindly groping for the deadbolt. Almost got it. Her fingers locked on the knob and twisted it awkwardly behind her.

"Since you're naked, I think it would be unsporting of me to bash your head in with this bat, Fido," she started. "But I will if I have to."

Jack looked down in surprise. As he took in his nakedness, color flooded his cheeks. He glanced around, clearly looking for something to cover himself with. Nothing close at hand, Jack turned back to her and shrugged in embarrassment.

Now that Louisa had pointed out his nakedness, it was exceedingly difficult not to look down and admire his... assets. He really was disgustingly handsome. Right down to his deliciously carved abs and his—

She jerked her eyes back to his face and felt heat rising in her own cheeks. Louisa focused hard on the space between his eyes. Anything to stop her gaze from trailing lower...and lower.

"I'm going to open this door, and you're going to walk

right out of here and we'll both pretend this never happened. Clear?" Louisa gave him a hard stare.

Her hand closed on the doorknob. And then she would call the cops and have the clown picked up and hauled off to a psych ward. But he didn't need to know that.

Her thoughts must have shown on her face, or maybe the bastard was psychic, because he lunged forward just as the door began to swing open. A flash of undiluted panic pulsed through Louisa, freezing her in place. She had a fraction of a second to recognize her failure in the face of danger before he closed the distance between them.

A muscled arm wrapped around Louisa's waist and heaved, dragging her away from the swinging door. She swung the forgotten bat wildly, trying to connect with every inch of him that she could. Jack twisted behind her, his arm still iron against her abdomen. Louisa slammed her bare heel on top of his foot.

He grunted in pain as he struggled to keep a hold on her wriggling body. Still whipping the baseball bat around, Louisa managed to bring it down hard on his left kneecap. Jack howled in her ear, her back pressed into his chest. He caught the wooden bat in his bare hand and ripped it out of her hands.

"Will you hold still, for fuck's sake?" he hissed in her ear.

His arms blurred, jerking up quickly to pin Louisa's attacking hands beneath the band of his arms. She threw herself side to side. Anything to wiggle free of this creep.

Jack's arms were firm against her ribcage, refusing to give a fraction of an inch as she fought. Do something, anything! Stomach-curling fear closed in around her. He was bigger than Louisa in every way. She was slightly taller than average for a woman, but the big bastard had to be nearly a foot taller still. He was wider and stronger.

Louisa pushed feebly at the prison his carved, muscular arms had created. She threw her weight back against him. His chest was warm against her back...and naked. Louisa froze, the full extent of his nakedness pressed against her.

Any other time, a naked, gorgeous man pressing up against her would be cause for celebration. But not like this, not today. Louisa looked down at the meaty arms criss-crossing below her breasts. Well...that might work.

She opened her mouth as wide as she could and bit into the thick flesh. Jack yowled in pain. A satisfied smirk tweaked Louisa's lips, her teeth still sunk deep into his skin. One of his arms disappeared before a sharp thunk rang in her ears and shadows crept up around her.

JACK CURSED QUIETLY under his breath and dropped the lamp on the floor. Louisa's limp body draped over his arm. She was gonna be so pissed when she woke up.

He hadn't meant to scare her. Hell, Jack had probably been more surprised than she was when he woke up in his human form. He hadn't changed in his sleep since he was a little kid.

Pain radiated across Jack's chest and shoulder. The wound might have healed on the outside, but the muscles beneath were still trying to regenerate the cells that the silver had killed. He groaned. There were still several days worth of healing to be done and this little tussle wasn't exactly speeding it along.

Not to mention the skin where Louisa had sunk her little teeth was now tender and red.

"She bit me. She fucking *bit me*! Who the hell does that?!" He looked around the room, his eyes wide with shock.

He dragged her over to the lumpy couch, still grumbling bitterly.

The front door burst open, banging against the wall. A tall figure in a black hoodie stood silhouetted in the doorway. Jack froze, Louisa's unconscious form partially lowered onto the couch.

He couldn't protect her like this. Not while she was vulnerable.

The power locked carefully away in his mind swirled. Jack gripped it tightly in hand and pulled gently. His teeth began to lengthen and sharpen, his jaw stretching uncomfortably as he lowered Louisa on to the couch. Shifting sideway, Jack planted himself between her and the stranger and let the shift take me.

"You wanna put some pants on?" an amused voice rang out from the shadows of the hood.

Jack halted mid-shift. His muscles relaxed, his claws reflexively returning to human flesh. He smiled, flashing his fangs as they receded to human size.

"I would if I had any, Connor," Jack grumbled.

Connor stepped into the apartment and shut the door firmly behind him. He tugged the hood back and looked around the room. His eyes danced over the chair lying on its side and the various wreckage from Jack's dance with Louisa. Connor focused on her unmoving body and quirked an eyebrow.

"Did I interrupt something?" A knowing smile curved Connor's face. "She was shrieking something awful, but I didn't think it was that kind of screaming, ya know."

Jack frowned and observed the chaos strewn around them. Oh, she was gonna be really pissed. He reached over and righted the chair.

"Funny," he deadpanned. "You're a real comedian."

Connor shrugged and watched Jack move around the room, reassembling the natural order. He crossed his arms and stared, no doubt waiting for some sort of explanation. Jack plugged the lamp back in and straightened with a sigh.

"She woke up to find a strange, naked man in her bed." He looked over at Louisa, curled silently on the lumpy couch cushions. "She panicked, and I hit her over the head with a lamp."

Guilt prowled deep in his chest. Jack hadn't wanted to hurt her, but she hadn't left him much choice. His hands twitched as the urge to stroke Louisa's curls surged to the forefront.

"You hit her with a lamp?" Connor cut through Jack's self pity.

His fingers thrust through his hair. This really wasn't going to help Jack convince her that he wasn't a monster.

"She wouldn't stop screaming and then she bit me and, I don't know. I just picked up the lamp and..." Jack trailed off.

Connor's mouth gaped. "She bit you? What is she, some kind of animal?"

Jack nodded his head, relieved. "Thank you! I mean, who does that, right?"

Connor's head shook in disgust.

"Well, we need to get going. So find something to wear and we'll get out of here." Connor turned his back and started walking toward the door.

Jack looked back at Louisa. He couldn't just walk away. She had been kind and gone above and beyond to make sure he healed. And she smelled so very nice...

"We're not going to leave her here," he said to Connor's retreating back.

Connor stopped in the doorway and turned.

"Dude, there is no way that her neighbors didn't hear

that banshee scream of hers. We need to go before you're hauled away in handcuffs."

Jack crossed his arms over his chest and planted his feet.

"I can only pull so many strings before people get suspicious, Jack." Connor narrowed his eyes. "And Nathan is going to be livid if he has to dip into the bail fund again."

Jack resisted the urge to snort. What's a bail fund for if not bail? Their fearless leader could be so whiny sometimes. He reached out and tucked a curl behind Louisa's ear.

"Lou could have a concussion." His voice was heavy with finality. "I'm not going to abandon her after I might have caused permanent brain damage."

"Lou?" An odd look passed over Connor's face. He deliberated for a moment before sighing loudly. "Fine. She comes too."

Jack grinned at him. He was such a pushover.

"Find me some pants, I'll pack her a bag. We leave in five."

Connor nodded and walked out, the front door swinging shut behind him.

Jack ran into Louisa's bedroom and started rifling through her closet. He hissed quietly to himself as the movement pulled on his abused shoulder. Hurling aside shoeboxes, he found an empty duffel bag. He ripped clothes off of hangers and stuffed them into the bag. Dragging the bag over to the dresser, Jack started opening drawers.

A sea of brightly colored lace filled the first one. In an attempt at being a gentleman, Jack averted his eyes and blindly fished handfuls of lace out of the drawer. Patting himself on the back for his chivalry, he shoved them into the bag as he darted back into the living room. Jack zipped the bag shut and veered off into the bathroom.

Toothbrush, toothbrush, where did she keep her damn

toothbrush? Almost out of time, Jack quickly pawed through drawers before ripping open the cabinet and shoving random cosmetics into the already tightly crammed bag. With a final shove, he managed to wiggle Louisa's errant toothbrush into nonexistent space.

Jack ran back into the living room as Connor slipped back into the apartment, a gray bundle in his arms.

"These were all I had in the car," he apologized.

The bag dropped to the floor as Jack caught the bundle of clothes. He tugged on a pair of gray sweatpants, slightly short in the leg, and pulled on a white T-shirt that had clearly seen better days.

"Shoes?" Jack tugged the hem of the shirt lower. Connor was several inches short than his towering six-foot-five.

Connor shook his head. "Couldn't find any. You'll have to go barefoot."

Connor turned and poked his head out the door. He waved his hand for them to hurry.

Jack tossed Louisa's bag at Connor's feet and moved to the couch. Her face was serene. Her dark eyelashes were stark against her caramel skin. A horrible thought drifted through his mind. His fingertips pressed against her neck, hunting desperately for a pulse.

Air whooshed out of his lungs as her steady heartbeat thumped beneath his touch. That could've been terrible. Jack's guilt twinged again. It never should have been necessary.

Jack put a stopper on his well of blame and grabbed a blanket from the arm of the couch. Wrapping it tightly around her, he scooped Louisa up, one arm tucked beneath her knees.

He quickly crossed to Connor and stepped out the door.

Connor shut the door firmly behind him and directed him down the hall.

"We have less than a minute to get out of here," Connor hurried them along. "One of her neighbors called it in. Someone will be here any second, and I don't have an explanation for why I'm at the scene of a domestic disturbance."

Jack moved faster, speeding up into a run. His shoulder burned as Louisa's slight weight pulled at the healing bullet wound. They sprinted down the stairs, cold pavement nipping at his bare feet.

"If I lose my badge for you, I'm going to be pissed," Connor huffed beside him.

They slowed as they stepped outside and started across the parking lot. The hair at the back of his neck stood at attention, forcing tingles up Jack's spine. Someone was watching them. He moved slower, striving for an air of nonchalance. He glanced around the parking lot.

The sharp bite of sirens cut the silence of the empty morning. They broke into a run, long legs eating up the last few feet of pavement. Connor whipped open the back door of a nondescript car and hurled the duffle in.

Jack climbed into the backseat as Connor sprinted to the driver's side. Louisa carefully settled in his lap, Jack stretched the seatbelt over the both of them. Her safety came first, after all.

Connor shot him a look in the rearview mirror as he threw the car in gear and pulled out into morning traffic.

4

A dull ache pounded through her skull. Louisa groaned, hugging her pillow tight to her face and letting herself sink deeper into the cloudlike mattress. She was not getting up. Ever. This bed was sheer heaven. Her headache pulsed again, mocking her hopes and dreams.

Louisa pushed herself onto her elbows and cracked open her eyelids. Sunlight drilled into her eyes like daggers. Her hand slapped over her face, blocking out the light. So it was gonna be one of those days, huh? She forced one eye open and glared around for the alarm clock.

This was not her apartment. She bolted upright, ignoring the pain in her skull. How did she end up here? More importantly, where exactly was here? Louisa kicked her legs free of the blankets and pushed herself off the bed.

Looking around the room, there wasn't a single clue how she had come to be here. Large bed, soft green comforter. Solid, masculine furniture. Nice, but a little spartan. It could use some photos, definitely more knickknacks.

Her eyes rolled. Really? Criticize the kidnapper's decorating choices?

The motion shot little spikes of pain through her temple. With a shaking hand, Louisa prodded along her hairline. Her fingers skimmed over a raised lump just above her ear. Everything was a little hazy, memories dancing just outside her grasp. Where the hell had that come from? Did someone jump her on the way to work?

Louisa looked down at her soft pajamas with a wince. Yeah, probably not. Squinting into the sunlight, she studied the scene outside the window. Trees. Lots of trees.

Louisa sighed. There was no doubt in her mind that she was going to end up running for her life through that stretch of endless forest. That's how it always turned out in those horror movies, the kind that made her want to leave the kitchen light on at night.

A frown crept along Louisa's lips. She hoped the neighbors found Jack before he got too hungry. Jack... she scrubbed a hand through her tangle of curls. Something about Jack... Soft, fluffy Jack with those big green eyes... and ripped abs. Oh. My. God.

The morning's events crashed through her head, cascading and unstoppable. Handsome, alarmingly naked Jack. Well, handsome, alarmingly naked man who *thought* he was Jack. Louisa's fingertips gingerly poked at the lump beneath her curls. That jerk had knocked her out. In her own apartment, no less! He'd wish he'd never climbed into her bed by the time she was done with him.

Growling, Louisa turned back to the room. She padded across the floor on bare feet and paused in front of the door. Her hand hovered over the doorknob. Annnd this is how the first girl would die in this horror movie.

Louisa's hand dropped to her side as she backed away

from the door. She couldn't go out there without a plan, Not-Jack would just crack her over the head again and toss her back in here.

She turned and started to hunt for a weapon, her eyes flitting from corner to corner. Louisa hurried to the dresser and jerked the top drawer open. Shuffling through it, there were boxers, just endless boxers.

Louisa popped the drawer shut. Useless. Dozens of pairs of superhero undies, but not a gun in sight. Maybe the nightstand? As she crossed the room, her foot snagged on the end of the footboard and she tumbled face-first to the carpet.

Motherfuuuu.... Hello. A large, black toolbox peeked out from under the bed. Louisa pushed herself to her knees and hauled it out in front of her.

Footsteps rang out down the hall. Shit, out of time. Flipping the lid off, she fished blindly through the toolbox and pulled out a large wrench.

Louisa hobbled to the door, her heartbeat thudding in her ears. The muffled footsteps moved closer. She waited. Her breath caught in her throat as the doorknob started to turn. The wrench raised above her head, Louisa stepped behind the door as it began to swing open.

A dark head of hair poked through the gap. Louisa threw all of her weight into the swing of her arms and the wrench met flesh with a sickening crunch. The dark haired man dropped to the floor with a crash. She winced at the sound. Hopefully, no one heard that.

Louisa stuck out a foot and nudged the shorn head of hair with a toe. His head dropped to the side. The hell? It was the scowly jerk from the office, Connor something or other. The one who wanted to take Jack home right away... Jack who turned into a large, naked man.

She shook the thought away with a jerk of her head. Nope. Not even gonna consider it.

"Right. Escape now, freak out later," she murmured.

Louisa clambered over the unconscious body sprawled in the door and darted into the hallway. She glanced back at him. He'd be fine. Just a little headache later. Louisa scowled. Not like she didn't know a little thing about that right now.

Mile-long legs stuck out into the hallway, blocking the door open. Well, shit. She looked down the hallway. It would take just one person to come across him and put a stop to her grand escape attempt. Ugh.

Louisa slipped back into her prison and hooked her hands in the giant's shirt. Heaving with all her weight, Louisa dragged the body a few inches farther. Jeez, this guy weighed a ton.

After folding his legs through the door, she swiped her hand at the sweat that had begun to form on her forehead. With one last quick peak to make sure the coast was clear, Louisa closed the door behind her with a soft click and tiptoed down the hall.

"What happened?" Nathan asked, settling behind his desk.

Jack scrubbed a hand through his damp hair. A dull ache lingered in his shoulder, even though the wound had fully closed during his last shift.

"I don't remember." Jack rubbed at his aching shoulder. "I was leaving the Den and then I woke up at the vet clinic."

Nathan's eyebrows soared.

"You don't remember where you were going or why?"

Jack shook his head, frustration weighing at him.

"No, it's like a huge chunk of time has been scooped out." A whimper echoed in his words.

Nate stood up and started pacing the length of the office. He'd always been like this. Couldn't form a thought without moving some part of his body. Finals had been literal hell, trying to focus while Nate's long legs ate up laps around the room.

"How long was I missing?" Jack asked his back.

"You left Saturday morning to investigate whether the Blight had any connection to the missing women. Today is Friday."

The Blight, of course. Jack's lip curled. The worst of their kind, the Blight had no regard for justice or human life. Driven by their basest urges to eat and mate, they killed and raped indiscriminately until someone intervened.

Some were too weak to control their monster, other simply didn't care enough to try. Allowing the curse to take control of their soul and become Blighted was the most dangerous choice a supernatural could make. A crime punishable by death in some clans, including their own.

The frown pulling at his mouth was starting to make his face ache. It figured that the missing women would be tied to the Blight...missing women?

Jack slammed the brakes on his contemplation.

"Missing women?"

Nate stopped abruptly and turned to him with a quizzical look curving his brow.

"You're missing more than a few days."

Nate picked up a newspaper off of his desk and tossed it to him. Jack looked down at the face of a young, cheery blonde smiling off the front page of the paper. Nate continued his pacing as he explained.

"She's the sixth woman to go missing in the last month,"

Nate explained. "The police have no evidence, no leads, nothing. None of the women have been seen since, dead or alive."

Jack tossed the paper back on Nate's desk, skewing the tidily stacked paperwork. Nate scowled and crossed to his desk to straighten his papers into perfect stacks. Oh no, there goes the meeting.

"I was looking for a connection between the women and Blight activity," Jack prompted.

Nate nodded absently, his focus still directed at adjusting his paperwork.

"You left to survey known Blight hives. When you failed to check in halfway through the list, I withdrew all Den members from their day-to-day roles. Your new friend called us Wednesday night. Connor and Alice went to collect you yesterday morning." Nate glowered up at him, his chiseled cheekbones sharpening. "And then you chose to ignore protocol and hang out with your little girlfriend instead."

His deep voice rumbled in his chest. Only twenty plus years of friendship clued Jack into how deep his worry and rage truly ran. Nate was holding it together by a thread.

He sighed. "Oh good, I was worried you'd be upset about that."

The muscle above Nate's eyebrow twitched. He was seconds away from picking up his desk and beating Jack into a bloody pulp with it.

"Shall I begin begging and groveling at your feet?"

Nate snorted, his sharp frown relaxing.

"You'd rather eat glass." Nate shook his head. "Why did you bring her into our world? It's against the Pact's most important laws."

"I didn't really have a choice when I woke up naked in her bed," he said drily.

"You know there will have to be consequences, Jack."

Jack glanced out the window. He knew, and he was prepared. Louisa was worth it. He nodded.

"I'll come up with something after you're done solving your own disappearance." Nate rubbed a hand wearily over his face. "Why did you have to bring her here, of all places?"

"Bring who here?" a small voice asked from the door.

They both turned as a dark head bobbed into the room.

"Uncle Jack!" A small body exploded the last few steps into the office and leapt into his arms. Enormous blue eyes stared back at Jack from a small, round face.

He hugged her tight. "Did you miss me, Abbycakes?"

A chubby hand tugged sharply on his ear.

"You were gone forever," she scowled with all the admonishment her five-year old body could muster at him.

"It was less than a week, Abby."

Her scowl grew more fierce. Jack sighed as Nate chuckled at the exchange.

"Maybe I'll take you for ice cream this week..." he whispered in her ear.

Abby nodded seriously, her mouth pursed. "I guess."

"You guess?" Jack laughed. Turning her upside down, he mercilessly tickled her tummy. Nate sighed dramatically as he watched Jack dangle his daughter upside down by her ankles.

"Aren't you supposed to be practicing your reading with Miss Alice?" Nate interrupted.

Abby looked up at Jack, eyes wide. He flipped her upright and set her down on stockinged feet. She shuffled up to the desk; her father watched her seriously.

"Miss Alice said she had to help Mr. Connor find something and to come find you."

Nate raised an eyebrow. "Is that so?"

Abby nodded emphatically, her dark ponytail bobbing.

"That's what she said, Daddy. Promise."

"Mmhmmm," he growled skeptically at the innocent look unconvincingly plastered across her face. Sensing a lecture, Abby quickly skipped around the desk and climbed into Nate's lap. He looked down her dark head, barely poking over the edge of his desk and struggled not to laugh.

"Who's Uncle Jack's friend?" she asked from her new perch.

Nate and Jack blinked at each other in surprise.

"How do you know about Uncle Jack's friend?" Nate raised his eyebrows.

"I saw Uncle Jack and Mr. Connor bring her in," Abby said, bouncing with excitement. "She's pretty. Are you going to marry her, Uncle Jack?"

Jack choked on air as Nate burst out laughing. His lungs burned while Abby looked back and forth between them, her little brow twisted as she tried to understand the joke.

Nate stood up, scooping Abby into his arms. He dropped a kiss on top of her head and set her down at the door.

"Okay, you go back upstairs and finish your reading," Nate said, wiping a tear from his eye. "I'll be up in a few minutes to play."

He gently scooted her out of the office as she squawked her protests. Nate shut the door firmly behind her. They listened as her little stomps faded away.

Nate turned back to Jack with a sigh. "I envy her energy."

"We were never that excitable when we were kids," Jack agreed.

"I wasn't. I'm not so sure about you though," he snorted.

The levity faded as he watched Nate's pacing resume. The brief respite in this ass-chewing was about to end.

"Why did you bring her here?" Nate rubbed a hand over

his face. Poor guy probably hadn't gotten a wink of sleep since Jack had missed his check-in.

Jack chewed his lip. How to explain this to Nate without sounding like an idiot? His oldest friend, the closest thing to family that he had. And never had there been such a hard, unrelenting prick.

Nate was not prone to emotional displays; he had considered everything to the point of a migraine ever since he was a little kid. And Jack had to justify his actions without Nate considering it the beginnings of a psychotic break or as a massive breach in security.

"She'd seen too much. We couldn't just leave her behind to talk –" Jack started.

Nate waved a hand to cut him off.

"Don't lie to me. It's insulting."

Jack's teeth ground together. Damn it, he was positive security would have been the safest approach. He started again.

"Well, she was very kind and I had to knock her over the head pretty hard," he rambled. "We couldn't just leave her on the floor. She could have had a concussion!"

He gestured wildly. He really hoped Nate was buying this.

"She could have died, Nate!"

Nate rolled his eyes. "You're getting warmer, but still a lie."

It was all Jack could do to choke back a growl as Nate continued pacing. He could practically hear his own teeth grinding away as he clenched them together. Nate paused in front of the windows. He stared into the gardens, his hands clasped behind his back as he waited.

"I don't know, okay?" Jack finally burst out. There was no

explanation, not really. He pictured Louisa's raven curls and flashing smile.

"There's just something about her. I couldn't leave her lying on the ground like that. Lou was just too... I don't know."

Jack's hands scrubbed through his hair until it stuck up like a pissed-off porcupine. His control was on its last thread, the stress of the week bearing down hard. Skin prickling painfully, Jack ran his knuckles down his arm. It was taking everything he had not to change forms and curl up in a sunny spot on the floor to sleep away the rest of the day.

"We need more allies. Maybe I can explain things to her," he tried, despondent.

"Explain *things*?" Nate stared at him in disbelief. "Things like how we shift into animals and giant hellbeasts? How we're not the only things in the shadows? How her world is a lot more terrifying than she realizes? There's a reason we don't involve humans in our world, Jack."

Jack winced. Nate knew that better than anyone.

"I think Louisa will handle it pretty well. She won't even be here very long," he sighed. "You won't even know she's here."

"Is that so?" Nate stared out the window.

Was he...caving? Grasping for the line dangling in front of him, Jack scrambled to pull it together.

"She'll be like a ghost. Utterly invisible," he nodded. Jack could still turn this back around. "She won't be any trouble at all."

Nate laughed drily. "I highly doubt that."

Jack blinked. "Why's that?"

Nate finally turned away from the window. His eyes were laughing as he fought a grin.

"Because she's crawling through the flower beds in what I can only assume is an escape attempt."

Oh shit. Jack leapt out of his seat and bound to the window. He scanned the scene in front of him. Louisa on her hands and knees, crawling through the rosebushes alongside the house in her ridiculously bright pajamas.

"No trouble, huh?" Nate chuckled.

"Shit," Jack cursed, turning and sprinting out the door.

5

Louisa hugged the side of the house. Dirt stained the knees of her thin pajama pants as she ducked and crawled through thorny rosebushes. She moved slowly, making every careful inch count.

A steady ache formed in her neck as she turned, for what felt like the thousandth time, to look over her shoulder. Louisa paused to rub at the stubborn knot.

She glanced at the window above her head and winced. Please don't let anyone choose this moment to pop open a window for some fresh air.

How many people were even in the monster of a house? There'd been the tall man she'd left crumpled on the bedroom floor. And of course the crazy, naked guy who thought he was a dog.

Hopefully he wasn't planning on popping out of a rosebush. Louisa wasn't sure she had it in her to crack yet another nosy onlooker over the head... at least, not without a serious dose of caffeine and a handful of painkillers.

And to think that just a few days ago, she had thought that things were going from bad to worse. New York was looking better and better. Sure, her ex-boyfriend had cheated on her... and stolen her savings... and slept with her boss, but at least no one had tried to kidnap her. The idea that her petty problems had been the "worse" was feeling pretty laughable right about now.

Louisa poked her head around a particularly magnificent rosebush. She scanned the yard. A wide expanse of neatly cut grass and colorful flowerbeds opened up to a wall of towering maples. Her eyebrows soared. These people might be kidnap-y, but they sure had some lovely landscaping.

Louisa followed the line of trees with her eyes. A couple of dozen yards to her left, trees gaped around a paved driveway. The beginnings of a plan started to form in her mind.

Get to the road. Flag a car. Call the police on these weirdos. Go home and curl up in a ball and hyperventilate. Piece of cake...right? Louisa groaned. She just had to get to the road... across the wide open lawn... overlooked by a dozen windows from which she could easily be spotted. Right.

Taking a deep breath, Louisa shot one last uneasy look over her shoulder. Worst plan ever. She took a tentative step away from the bushes and burst into a run. Louisa sprinted across the yard. The afternoon sun beat down on her shoulders, drying the morning dew still clinging to the grass and slicking her bare feet.

A shadow loomed over her, blocking out the sun. Louisa stumbled to a stop. She turned her face up toward the clear, blue sky in confusion. Dread curdling in her belly, she turned slowly in place.

A T-shirt, stretched across a wide, muscular chest, hovered mere inches from her face. Louisa swallowed as her eyes traveled north to a familiar face.

Crazy, naked guy was back... and clothed... and standing far too close. How the hell had he gotten so close without making a sound? Louisa studied his bemused smirk. His green eyes twinkled at her from his tan face.

He might be a delusional nutjob who thought he could turn into a dog, but he really was handsome. With his sandy hair haphazardly sticking up and mischievous dimples dotting his cheeks, Jack had a roguish, overgrown schoolboy thing going on.

Not that she was into that kind of thing. Nope. Louisa jerked her eyes back to his, her heartbeat thudding in her ears.

Yeah, definitely not into that kind of thing.

"Going somewhere?" Jack's mouth twisted into a cheeky grin.

All traces of attraction evaporated in the face of Jack's knowing smirk. The nerve of the bastard. Louisa's head was still pounding from Jack's earlier attentions AND he'd kidnapped her. He'd actually kidnapped her! And now he had the balls to try and *flirt* with her?

Rage crashed through Louisa like an avalanche battering a mountainside. Her hands clenched at her sides, her nails biting into the meat of her palms. No. The pompous pretty boy did not get to win. Savage will warmed her from the inside out. Jack had no idea who he was messing with.

Maybe she could still salvage her glorious escape?

Louisa quickly reworked her plan. She could swing it, but only if she was prepared to be very, very bold. Resisting the urge to mess up his pretty face with her fist, she arranged her face into a mask of wide-eyed innocence. A smile stretched her lips.

"I'm just admiring the scenery." Louisa waved at the overflowing flower boxes against the side of the house.

Jack quirked an eyebrow.

"Uh-huh," he said slowly. "So crawling along the side of the house...?"

Jack waited, staring at her expectantly. The smug jerk probably thought he was sooo tricky. Well, Louisa could play this game too, and she would play it a hell of a lot better.

"I was just trying to get a closer look at the flower boxes." Louisa batted her lashes at him. "I'm a big fan of roses."

Inching closer, her breasts swayed, braless beneath her thin pajama top. Scant inches from his chest, Louisa took a deep breath. She smothered a giggle as Jack's eyes dropped to her expanding cleavage. So predictable.

His breath hitched in his chest. Shifting nervously from foot to foot, Jack uncrossed his arms. Louisa squashed the eye roll that was struggling to escape. This was going to be easier than she'd thought.

"So, definitely not trying to leave without, uh, thanking us for our hospitality and, uh, top-notch first aid skills?" Jack stammered.

He must be awfully hard up. Louisa was well aware that her breasts were on the small side; they'd never gotten such an enthusiastic response before. If Jack had been a little less kidnap-y and a lot less crazy, she might actually be flattered.

The grin twitching on Jack's lips vanished as Louisa's cleavage bobbed closer. His glazed-over expression was even a bit of a turn on. She almost felt bad for him. Almost.

"Because that would be impolite," he finally finished.

Louisa nodded in agreement as she shifted even closer. Breasts brushed lightly against Jack's heaving chest. With a mind of its own, her hand floated up to rest on his solid shoulder. He really did have a great chest. Fingertips trailed downward, dancing along his muscular pec.

"So impolite," Louisa breathed in his ear.

Time to bring it home. Scraping the bottom of her toolbox, Louisa bit her lower lip in what she hoped was a seductive pout. Jack inhaled sharply, his pithy response disintegrating at the sight of Louisa's teeth teasing her plump lower lip.

Holy shit. It was actually working. Jack leaned forward, her kissable pout drawing him in like a moth to a flame. Louisa held her breath. She was sorely tempted to let him kiss her. It would be an outright lie to say that she hadn't imagined what Jack's lips would feel like pressed against her own. Or that the thought made certain bits tingle in a very distracting way. Maybe just one kiss... for research purposes, of course.

Louisa banished the traitorous thought as Jack's lips closed the distance. She had something much better in mind. Well, maybe not "better" per se, but definitely effective.

As Jack's eyes fluttered shut and his breath brushed against her neck, Louisa lunged. No longer teasing Jack's ribcage, her hands planted themselves against his chest. Louisa heaved, throwing her weight behind it.

Green eyes blinked in surprise as Jack's ankles tangled on the foot Louisa had oh-so-carefully maneuvered behind his own. Windmilling his arms in alarm, Jack tumbled to the lawn. He met the ground with a painful thud. Air exploded out of his lungs in a rush.

Without sparing a fraction of a second for a triumphant fist pump, Louisa turned and ran. Her bare feet skimmed the ground as she flew across the lush, green lawn. As her legs ate up the sprawling yard, Louisa reflected on her life.

How did she end up in these situations? Had she been cursed at birth? Maybe she had pissed off a witch doctor in a former life. Surely, normal people did not end up kidnapped by weirdos who thought they were werewolves, or whatever? And on a Thursday, no less.

Pain prickled up her side as the treeline loomed closer. Louisa's breath came in sharp bursts as the stitch traveled along her ribcage. Shit. She really needed to work out more, maybe join a gym.

A shadow came hurtling from behind. Louisa groaned internally and altered her course. Weaving in a crooked zigzag, she kept her eyes locked on the cover of the trees. That was what you were supposed to do when fleeing an attacker, right? Zigzag? Or was that only when they had a gun?

A soft chuckle slipped through the deafening pound of her heartbeat in her ears. Thick arms wrapped around her waist and jerked her to a stop. Wet grass slid under her feet. Louisa had a half-second of realization to clench her eyes shut as the ground rushed up to meet her.

Louisa flopped down on her back, the ground surprisingly soft beneath her spine. One eye warily cracked open to peek at her surroundings. Louisa blinked her eyes open.

A cloudless expanse of sky stretched above her. She sat up. Or at least she tried to. Louisa thudded backward as a hard restraint locked around her chest.

The ground chuckled beneath her. Louisa glared at the tanned arm holding her hostage. Well, that explained why the ground had been so soft. She elbowed the human mattress stretched beneath her.

"Was that supposed to hurt?" Jack laughed against her ear.

Louisa pinched Jack's wrist and smirked at his surprised yelp. The smirk vanished as the sky pitched and her face pressed into the grass.

Jack rolled her facedown on the ground, his weight pinning her. Louisa spit out a blade of grass. A string of curses sprang to attention at the tip of her tongue.

"I think that's going to bruise," Jack pouted at his wrist.

"Boo-hoo," she hissed.

Louisa tested her prison. She couldn't move one frickin' inch. Arms pinned at her side, legs trapped beneath his. She wriggled with all her might, fighting for any bit of give.

Jack choked behind her. Great, with her luck, the big weenie was probably dying from her little pinch and she was going to be stuck here, pinned beneath his stupid corpse. Louisa doubled her efforts, squirming with all her worth. No one would ever call her a quitter.

"Honey, you've got to stop," Jack groaned against her ear.

Louisa froze as his words registered. A hard bulge pressed firmly against her ass. No fucking way. On one hand, she was flattered as fuck. On the other? Fuck him. Serves the jerk right, Louisa smirked into the grass.

A small spark of satisfaction curled through her belly. She wiggled her hips against the straining denim between his legs, dragging another quiet groan from the man at her back. Louisa frowned.

Why did the sound of Jack's groan make her girly bits get all tingly? It hadn't been *that* long since she'd had sex. Good sex, though? Ages, it had been ages. And if Jack's dick was anything to go by, sex with him would be *so, so good*.

Slamming the door on her neglected libido, Louisa stuffed the alarming reaction down into the shadowy place deep inside to be examined at a safer moment. One where she was alone, behind a locked door. Maybe with some chocolate. And something that vibrated.

"I'm going to let you up," Jack growled against her neck. "Be good."

He pushed to his feet, trapping Louisa's hips firmly between his ankles. He gripped her waist with surprising gentleness and flipped her onto her feet. Jack spun her around. Before she could squeak a protest, she was hanging upside down over his shoulder.

Louisa's stomach churned as the world flipped upside down.

"Put me down!"

Hands smacked helplessly at the back of his legs. Maybe she could trip him if she got a good grip on his pant leg? Jack placed a hand firmly on her round bottom as he set off across the grounds. Louisa sputtered.

"Get your hand off my ass, you fucking perv!" she yelped at him.

Louisa gripped the waistband of his jeans and pushed herself up. While she appreciated the generous view of his muscular ass, she had no urge to be hauled around like some helpless damsel. She batted at the hand cupping her cheek. Jack chuckled.

"Now as much I approve of the cardio, Lou, which quite frankly you need, I can't have you running off quite yet." He gave her buttock a firm squeeze. "As for your ass, which is quite lovely if I may say so—"

"You may not," Louisa interjected. "And stop calling me Lou!"

Jack ignored her, carrying on as though she had never spoken.

"—obviously, I need a firm grip so that you don't fall."

"You're the devil," Louisa hissed into his jeans.

Jack's laughter carried them all the way up the front porch.

6

Louisa gritted her teeth. Jack could practically hear them cracking from where her head bobbed over his shoulder.

"What if I promise to behave?" she ground out. "Then will you put me down?"

Jack snorted. He was not falling for the sudden change in attitude, not again. The grass stains all over his clothes were all the reminder he needed not to trust the wily vixen.

Hopefully, none of the clan had seen the little lawn incident or the jokes would last for weeks. At least his shoulder had finished healing before they had taken their tumble across the grass. Outsmarted *and* injured? He'd never hear the end of it.

"Sorry, Lou." Jack hauled her through the front door. "I just can't take that chance."

"Fucking caveman," she hissed like an angry cat.

He trudged through the tasteful foyer, edging around the intricately woven throw rugs. Jack was careful not to track dirt onto the polished wood floors. God knows he had enough on his plate without putting himself on the housekeeper's shit list too.

"And I'm *not* falling for the flirty attitude." Jack smacked her ass gently. "Besides, what are you going to do? Outrun me? You made it like twenty yards on that last go."

He dropped Louisa into an armchair, but not before delivering one last healthy pat to her delectable ass. Fierce, little Lou would probably punch him for it later; better to make it count now. She really did have a nice ass... and breasts...and really everything else.

Louisa leaned back and crossed her arms over her chest, drawing his eye like a laser. Jack winced as his dick rushed to stand at attention. Damn it, he'd just gotten the last erection under control.

How the hell was Jack supposed to question her when all the blood in his brain kept rushing to join his dick in a happy dance? And Louisa was fully clothed! What was he going to do if he saw her naked?

A naked Louisa danced through Jack's head as a surge of heat rushed to his throbbing groin. She'd look great in his bed... or against the wall. Hell, even bent over this chair.

Struggling to form coherent thoughts, Jack scowled up at the elegant, vaulted ceiling. Surely he had a sweatshirt somewhere that he could swaddle her up in.

"You're an asshole." Louisa glared at him.

Jack winced and tugged the hem of his T-shirt a little lower. He had no doubt that if Louisa caught an eyeful of his predicament, her insults would get much more colorful.

He stifled a snort as he got a good look at her scowl. A smudge of dirt ran across her chin and streaked down her neck. Grass stains coated the ragged knees of her pajama pants. There was a particularly nice tear in her tank top, giving him a peek at the golden skin of her belly.

A chuckle slipped past as he studied her hair. Black curls tangled in a chaotic nest. Twigs and a dusting of grass clippings poked out of the tangles. A few more pieces of greenery, and she would be beating nesting birds away.

"Hold still."

Louisa jerked back as his hand reached forward. Jack cringed. Of course she was afraid of him. After being bashed over the head and kidnapped, he wouldn't be in a trusting mood either. Louisa would be an idiot not to be wary of him, and his Lou was no idiot.

Jack moved more slowly, giving her plenty of time to lean away from his touch. Gripping her chin gently, he started freeing pieces of the lawn from her hair with the other. Jack kept his eyes firmly planted on Louisa's curls.

The weight of her wide-eyed stare was burning into his face. Jack was sorely tempted to meet her gaze, but he had a bone-deep feeling telling him that if he started staring into those chocolate-brown eyes, he'd never stop.

Or he'd get caught looking at her cleavage again. Either way, Jack would be in deep shit.

He wasn't sure why he was so drawn to her. It wasn't like Louisa was his mate. Shifters didn't have mates; that was strictly a wolf thing... right?

Despite the rational arguments forming in his head, Jack knew with every fiber of his being that that pull wasn't going anywhere soon. Maybe he could convince her to go to dinner. Was that bad form? Asking your captive on a date?

Jack leaned back, flicking the last piece of grass to the floor. Louisa's hair was a tangled disaster, but at least no one would be picking through it for mulching supplies. Bending at the waist, he swept the little pile into his hand.

A quiet squeak caused his ears to perk up. Jack glanced over his shoulder and grinned. Eyes glazed over, Louisa was staring intently at his denim clad butt. *I guess the attraction is mutual.*

The little sneak wasn't nearly as horrified by him as she pretended to be. Resisting the urge to throw down the grass and burst into a victory dance, Jack composed his face. Perhaps dinner wasn't as far off the table as he'd thought... unless Lou pinched him again. That shit seriously hurt.

Louisa dropped her eyes to the floor, her cheeks flushing a brilliant red, as Jack straightened. He tucked the grass into his pocket and let his arms and chest flex... to no effect. A frown turned the corners of Jack's mouth. Nothing. Drool had practically been running down her chin as she admired his butt, but not even a polite dribble for his biceps? Maybe she wasn't an arm gal?

Jack gave his muscles another quick flex. Louisa didn't even blink. In fact, Louisa wasn't even looking at him. She was glancing around the room under her eyelashes... looking for another escape.

Jack sighed.

"It would hurt a lot more to be tackled on a wood floor," he said drily.

Louisa looked up at him. Her eyes widened, the picture of innocence.

"And we are absolutely not going through that little show again." His eyes flashed her a warning.

A ghost of his earlier embarrassment at their tussle made Jack cringe. Maybe he could wipe the security cameras before Connor saw the footage...

Louisa narrowed her eyes and crossed her arms.

Movement danced in the corner of his eye. Jack spun, using his body to shield Louisa. A small, balding man stood in the doorway on the far side of the spacious hall.

It was just Tony. Jack relaxed, his arms falling back to his sides. Fingertips tingled as his claws shrank. Jack studied his hand. His claws only sprang out in response to a threat.

Except Tony wasn't a threat. He was a raccoon shifter and a phlebotomist. Even in his fiercest form, Jack could still tear him apart with his bare hands. Was he losing control?

The thought settled in his gut like a rock. To lose control was to die, and Jack had things to do. Like winning over a girl who smelled like peanut butter cookies.

Something brushed against his leg, snapping Jack out of his crowded mind. Curled into a ball on the chair, Louisa tucked her legs against her chest. A perfume of fear floated off of her, choking him. His jaw popped uncomfortably as fangs dropped into Jack's mouth.

Aw. It was Lou. Somehow, she was sending his protective instincts into overdrive. Jack rolled his jaw, forcing his fangs away. He moved next to the chair and dropped his hand onto her shoulder. Louisa leaned into his touch.

Across the room, Tony's eyes lit on her curled form. He turned back through the doorway and shouted, his voice echoing through the hall.

"Found her!"

Louisa cringed farther back into her chair. Jack squeezed her shoulder comfortingly as more people shuffled into the room, heads poking around doorways. A dozen pairs of eyes landed on her curled form.

"Yes, you found her. It was such a challenge," Jack drawled at the crowd. "She was so well hidden... sprinting down the driveway."

Connor stomped into the room, an ice pack clutched to his head. Sharp eyes searched the room. He took a step forward as they landed on Louisa.

"We should eat her."

Louisa's eyes widened. She sank back into her chair, no

doubt hoping that if she tried hard enough, she would sink right through it.

"Seriously," Connor growled, glaring at Jack. "I'm going to have to eat her. She hit me with a wrench."

If Louisa weren't shaking beneath his hand, the whole situation might be laughable. But her fear was starting to claw at Jack's iron control. He glowered at Connor, a silent warning in his eyes.

Alice breezed into the room, her eyes rolling behind her dainty, round glasses. Oh great—fire, meet gasoline. Jack was seconds from throwing Louisa back over his shoulder and charging out of the room.

"You're a vegetarian, moron," she reminded him.

"I'll make an exception." Connor glared at her.

Jack rolled his eyes. God save them all from two-hundred-pound drama queens.

Alice looked pointedly at Louisa's cowering form and delivered a well-placed elbow to his rib cage. Connor glared down at her. He pulled the dripping ice pack from his scalp and dropped it square on top of Alice's head.

A wet thwack echoed through the silent hall. Water dripped lazily down her neck, plastering her hair to her face in sticky strands. Connor smirked. Alice's eyes burned with icy fury. A dozen pair of eyes flicked between the pair.

Jack sighed. Another showdown, great. If they broke another antique, Nate was going to kill them with his bare hands... or bear claws. He really wasn't too picky.

Jack shifted closer to Louisa, shielding her from the rest of the room. She leaned cautiously around his hip as Connor and Alice squared off. Teeth bared, Alice leapt at the hulking mass in front of her.

An earthshaking roar shattered the fragile tension in the room. Louisa clapped her hands over her ears. Nate loomed at the foot of the stairway, a frown stretched beneath his carved cheekbones.

Alice changed direction in mid-air. She landed lightly on her toes. The dripping ice pack thumped against Connor's chest as she stomped out of the room.

"I think that's about enough." Nate glowered at the crowd.

His audience dissolved, suddenly finding that they had other, more urgent matters to attend to. Connor shot Louisa one last hate-filled scowl before he disappeared through an open doorway.

Alone in the room, Jack smiled brightly at her shocked face.

"So... lunch?"

A LARGE HAND gripped her elbow and propelled her to her feet. Louisa blinked at the empty room. That growly guy had cleared the room faster than yelling "FIRE!" Maybe she should learn how to roar.

Jack beamed in front of her. What about that whole shit show could have possibly made him so happy? She probably should have paid more attention, but for survival's sake, Louisa's mind had clouded over sometime around when the suggestion of eating her had been tossed around.

"Now Lou, I'm sure you have a boatload of questions. But you haven't eaten since last night, so I think lunch should be our first order of business."

Louisa's stomach rumbled in agreement. It had been an awfully long time since she'd eaten anything. Normally, she didn't like to go an hour between snacks, let alone hours, plural.

She nodded at the suggestion. Besides, she needed to

keep up her strength; another avenue of escape had to be around here somewhere.

Jack's eyes danced with satisfaction as he tugged her along after him. He led her through one of the doorways on the left of the cavernous hall. Pushing her through a swinging door, Louisa stepped into the most beautiful kitchen she had ever seen.

Warm, worn butcher block counters graced cream-colored cabinets. An old-timey brick fireplace took up the majority of the far wall. Even though there wasn't a cookie in sight, an aura of warmth and chocolate chip cookies filled the room. Enormous, yet cozy.

Not that she could cook ramen, but Louisa could still appreciate art.

"Wow," she breathed.

"I know." Jack shook his head. "Nate designed it himself. Whenever I step foot in here, I expect a trio of grannies to pop out and ply me with baked goods."

Jack nudged her toward a stool at the giant island. Louisa padded barefoot across the tile and climbed into her seat. Glancing at the bottoms of her grass-stained feet, she winced. The world's best kitchen and she was probably leaving gross footprints everywhere.

Jack bounced around the kitchen with more confidence than she could ever hope to have near a stove. Flipping open cabinets like a tornado, he settled a large pot of water on the stovetop and a dumped a jar of marinara into a smaller pot beside it.

Her chin propped in her hands, Louisa admired Jack's shoulders as he moved around the kitchen. She was probably going to die soon, but at least she could enjoy the view first. As kidnappers go, she could do a lot worse. Louisa studied the way the denim stretched over his ass. Yeah, a lot worse.

It's not like anyone here had even been all that terrible to her. Except that douchebag, Connor. Louisa didn't feel a shred of guilt for bashing him over the head. In fact, she hoped it hurt a lot.

Now Jack, on the other hand...she might feel a little bad if she had to hit him over the head with household objects. He was a kidnapping jackass, but at least he hadn't threatened to eat her. And the way he kept eyeballing her chest? Louisa could do worse.

She jerked back in her seat. Oh no. Was this Stockholm Syndrome? Was being attracted to your captor the first symptom? Did it work that fast?

Worrying at her lower lip, Louisa's mind whirred out of control. Jack was just so damn handsome, and really, he hadn't been that terrible to her. With the exception of the damn lamp, of course.

"I hope you like spaghetti," Jack told her over his shoulder. "It's one of, like, three things I can make."

"I love spaghetti," Louisa whispered, her lip trembling.

Fat tears rolled down her cheeks. Jack turned, the smile on his face evaporating as she buried her face in her hands.

"Shit."

7

"Shit, shit, shit."

Jack hurried around the island and took the seat beside Louisa. Tears dripped between her fingers, splashing on the countertop. He could hear her heartbeat hammering in her chest from two feet away.

Jack wrapped his fingers around her wrists to pull them away from her face. Louisa's arms refused to move. Crap. He gripped her knees and spun her on the stool. Jack grasped her arms again. Louisa clamped her fingers to her tear-streaked face, resisting his gentle tugging.

"Hey, hey," Jack whispered soothingly. "It's okay. Everything is going to be okay."

Her hands abruptly dropped away from her face.

"Everything is not okay," Louisa yelled at him. "DON'T TELL ME EVERYTHING IS OKAY!"

"You're right," Jack backpedaled, leaning away from her. "Everything is not okay... um, which part specifically?"

"Oh, I don't know," Louisa drawled sarcastically, tears dripping down her face. "I've had a really stressful month. My boyfriend fucked my boss and emptied out my savings. I got fired and moved to this crappy little town where everyone treats me like a leper!"

Louisa's voice grew louder and louder until she was verbally jabbing him. "I've been kidnapped by what I can only assume is a cult, and I'm probably going to be murdered in some stupid ritual sacrifice! And now the cute, crazy guy who kidnapped me is making me SPAGHETTI! That is not okay, NONE OF THIS IS OKAY!"

"I can make something else, it doesn't have to be spaghetti," Jack muttered.

Louisa grabbed a stack of napkins from the counter and hurled them at him. They fluttered weakly to the floor between them.

"THE SPAGHETTI IS NOT THE PROBLEM, MORON!" she yelled, her face turning pink. "I HAVE BEEN KIDNAPPED BY A BUNCH OF WEIRDOS!"

"Oh is that all?" Jack winced. Scrubbing a hand over his ear, he tried to stop the ringing that had followed Louisa's angry shrieking.

"No, I also have a head injury and my favorite pajama pants have been ruined with grass stains," she sniffled. Louisa eyed the knife block on the counter, no doubt trying to figure out if she could reach it before Jack.

"Well, uh, let's work backward, okay?" Jack said nervously. He really didn't want to get stabbed today. "We can wash your pants—"

"They're ruined." Louisa glared at him, her lashes damp and shining.

"Okay, yeah. The pants are probably ruined," Jack agreed, studying the green patches on her knees. "But we can replace them with newer, better pajama pants."

"With penguins," Louisa sniffed. "These ones have penguins."

Furbidden Attraction

"Absolutely," Jack nodded. "With penguins."

"And?" She watched him through narrowed eyes.

Right, what else had she said? Jack scrambled to replay her rant in his head.

"The head injury? I had someone look at it, no problems there. We're agreed that spaghetti isn't really a problem; neither is you thinking I'm cute. Thanks, by the way." Jack forced himself not to smile. She thought he was cute. And as a human, no less.

"And the kidnapping?" Louisa's tears were beginning to dry on her cheeks.

"Oh, right. Well, I can't really fix that just yet." Jack cringed as her eyes flashed dangerously. "But we're not going to murder you?" he added quickly.

Louisa reared back. "Why did that sound like a question?"

Shit. Jack held up his hands. "It wasn't I swear. We are *not* going to murder you."

"Now you're emphasizing *not* like you're looking for a loophole!" Louisa's eyes welled up again. Her voice dropped, mimicking Jack's deeper growl. "Well, we're not going to murder you, but we are going to sell your organs on the black market. You might die in the process but we are *not* going to murder you."

Jack winced as fat tears dripped down her nose. She'd been here less than a day and he'd broken her with spaghetti. Jack thrust his fingers through his hair. *How do I fix tears?*

The animal inside howled his disapproval. He'd never made a girl cry before. Maybe he could get Louisa yelling again. It looked like she enjoyed it.

"Moving past the kidnappy part, I could offer to kill your ex if you'd like? Or your ex-boss? I really can't do anything about your savings, but maybe some meticulously planned manslaughter?" Jack tried desperately. "Of course, he cheated on *you*. And you seem pretty great, minus the yelling, so he's obviously an idiot, and I mean, isn't his stupidity punishment enough?"

Louisa stared at him for a long moment. Jack shifted nervously in his seat. Doubling over, she burst out laughing. Okay, laughing was good. Laughing was better than crying.

She rested her head on the counter, hiccupping softly. Louisa sat up and wiped at her face. Her hands, still damp with tears, only spread the wetness around.

"Here, let me." Jack wrapped the edge of his damp shirt around his hand and dabbed at her face. "There. All done."

A loud hiss snapped their attention to the stove.

"My noodles!"

Jack darted around the counter to rescue the overboiling pot. Turning his back to Louisa, he gave her a little time to compose herself. He'd really messed up.

Jack had felt in his gut that bringing her here was the right move, but logic was rearing its ugly head. Of course this was overwhelming. Who wouldn't be upset by being kidnapped by a naked stranger? Thinking back on it, he was actually surprised Louisa hadn't lost it much earlier.

She'd had been such a strong, sassy force while she'd taken care of him that it hadn't even occurred to Jack to expect anything less. He needed to question her and get her home, as much as the idea made his stomach churn.

Jack didn't want her to leave. And how the hell was he going to question her in a non-stressful way? Because frankly, he didn't want to get yelled at again. His eardrums were still ringing.

He really needed a vacation from his job—one he would actually remember.

Jack drained the pot in the sink and scooped pasta into two bowls. He ladled sauce over the pasta and placed one in front of Louisa.

A sudden rush of nerves swelled inside of him. What if she didn't like it? Would Louisa think that he couldn't take care of her? Jack shook his head, confounded. Where the hell had that come from? He was taking her home as soon as possible. Right?

Jack watched Louisa from the corner of his eye as he took a seat. She stared into her bowl, the remnants of her tears drying on her cheeks. Picking up her fork, she neatly twirled noodles around her fork.

He held his breath as her mouth closed around the pasta. A faint smile tugged at her lips. Fighting a smile of his own, Jack's insides twisted gleefully.

As Louisa raised a second forkful to her mouth, a large barn owl swooped through the door and landed on the counter. Jack cursed under his breath. So much for reducing her stress.

He glared at the bird preening next to the cookie jar. She couldn't give them ten minutes to themselves? Nosy brat.

Louisa's fork clattered in her bowl.

"There's an owl in your kitchen," she whispered out of the corner of her mouth.

"Yes."

"There is an owl. In. Your. Kitchen" Louisa said more slowly, as though Jack hadn't heard her the first time.

"Yes," he repeated. "She likes spaghetti."

Louisa stared at him. He continued scooping pasta into his mouth at a leisurely pace. If he was calm, maybe she wouldn't freak out again. Because who the hell wouldn't panic if a big-ass bird swooped into their kitchen. Jack twirled his pasta, the picture of serenity. *Please don't start crying again.*

"The owl likes spaghetti," she mumbled under her breath. "Because that's super normal. Who doesn't like spaghetti? Not owls, apparently."

Giving her head a firm shake, Louisa turned back to her food.

The owl started to grow. Pale-auburn feathers melted into skin, turning Jack's stomach. The spaghetti soured in his belly. No matter how many times he watched her shift, it never got any easier. Bird shifters were just... gross.

Jack sighed. The nice, peaceful lunch he had envisioned was slipping further and further out of reach.

Alice sat primly on the edge of the counter, stark naked. She hopped off the counter and stumbled across the kitchen. She rifled through a bin, her blind eyes squinting.

Louisa turned to Jack, her eyes wide.

"What the hell did you put in this spaghetti?" She poked at her noodles with her fork. "Am I hallucinating?"

"Is there enough to share?" Alice called, elbow-deep in the bin. She fished out an oversized T-shirt and dragged it over her head. Stepping into a pair of sweatpants, she raised her eyebrows at him.

"Help yourself," Jack grumbled around a mouthful of pasta. Stupid bird.

Alice padded barefoot across the kitchen to a cookie jar. Reaching inside, she pulled out a set of glasses and balanced them on her nose. She snagged a bowl and scooped herself up some spaghetti. Alice perched on the edge of the counter, cutting her pasta with a knife.

Jack shook his head—as if she weren't weird enough. She watched Louisa, a curious expression on her face, as she scooped noodles into her mouth.

He glared at her over the top of his bowl. Louisa had been abruptly thrust into their world and didn't need showy little birdbrains making it even harder for her.

Go away, he mouthed at her.

Alice ignored his steely gaze and continued taking dainty bites of spaghetti.

Jack glanced at Louisa. Calmly shoveling pasta into her mouth, she steadily ignored the glares being traded back and forth beside her.

He nudged her. "Slow down; you're going to make yourself sick."

"If I'm going to die in a hole in your backyard, I'm going to enjoy whatever hallucinogens you put in my food, thanks."

Alice carefully placed her bowl on the counter and turned to Louisa.

"Do you have a history of mental illness?" she asked primly.

Louisa blinked at the sudden breach of silence. A growl started to build in Jack's chest. He fully intended to wring Alice's neck when this little charade was over.

"Excuse me?"

"Do you have a history of mental illness?" Alice repeated.

"You were a bird five minutes ago," Louisa said slowly. "I think you have your own problems to worry about."

Jack chuckled. Inside, he was cheering. Alice was fighting well outside her weight class, and she hadn't even realized it yet.

"Ms. Miller. Louisa," Alice started impatiently. "May I call you Louisa?"

"No," she said shortly, her arms crossing over her chest. The wobble in her voice had turned to razor-sharp steel.

"I've been kidnapped—and drugged apparently—so we are not on a first-name basis."

Alice sighed. This was going to be the shortest interrogation in history. Louisa's earlier vulnerability was gone, replaced by well-worn armor. Jack sat on the edge of his stool, ready to leap up if Alice went for Louisa's throat.

"Ms. Miller," Alice started again. "I need to assess if you're a threat to the Den. Your cooperation would be appreciated."

"Well, I would appreciate not being kidnapped," Louisa said icily. "Yet here I am. Though apparently I will *not* be murdered."

"Why are you emphasizing *not* like that?" Alice puzzled.

Louisa turned to Jack and raised her eyebrows.

"Fine!" He threw his hands in the air. "You win. It sounds like a murdery loophole."

"The sooner you answer my questions, the sooner you get to go home," Alice reminded them.

Jack cleared his throat.

"Right, the sooner you answer *our* questions, the sooner you get to go home," Alice corrected.

"Oh, well in that case, fire away, Bird Lady," Louisa waved her on with her fork. "Though if I end up murdered by the end of the interrogation, I will be incredibly disappointed in the both of you."

"Noted. Do you intend to tell anyone what you've seen here?" Alice huffed, her feathers no doubt bunched uncomfortably. "The police? The government? Your mailman?"

"I'm not an idiot." Louisa raised an eyebrow. "I go around spouting off about animal people, and I'll end up in a straightjacket. Or I'll find myself in a dark alley, getting my head ripped off by some dude who turns into a goat or something. That's assuming I'm not having a nervous breakdown right now, of course."

"You're not having a nervous breakdown and you're not hallucinating." Jack sighed into his bowl. All he'd wanted was to feed her lunch and take a damn nap.

"What a relief," she said drily. "I'm not crazy, and monsters are real."

"And you're just okay with that?" Alice frowned, her head cocked to the side. "You're not freaking out?"

"No, I'm not okay with that. But I've already lost my shit over being kidnapped today. I don't think I have the emotional energy to consider the implications of your existence right now."

"Humor me."

Jack scooped up her empty bowl as she mulled over her answer. Serving up a second helping, his insides twisted nervously as he waited for Lou's response. The direction of these questions was suddenly insanely important to him.

"I'd say I'm somewhere in the middle with it." Louisa frowned. "I mean, on one hand, you do you. It's not my business. Be the best animal-person-thing that you can be..."

"And on the other?" Jack asked hesitantly as he placed her bowl in front of her.

"On the other hand"—Louisa's frown intensified—"it means that there are people who turn into animals who have chosen to kidnap me for no apparent reason. And I have a BIG problem with that, being the kidnappee, even if my kidnapper is ridiculously hot.

"And if animal-people-things are real, what else is real?! Vampires? Demons? The Loch Ness monster?! How much have I walked around my entire life completely oblivious to?"

Oh no, she was starting to yell again. Louisa was already

a bit brittle after that last outburst, and she was dangerously close to spiraling into another one. Jack held up a hand to slow her tirade.

"Let's rewind a bit...you think I'm hot?" he asked, turning the conversation. A satisfied grin played with the corners of his mouth.

"I don't think I said 'hot'." Louisa prickled, the angry tone evaporating.

"You're right," Jack said solemnly. "You said *ridiculously* hot."

Alice rolled her eyes as Louisa's cheeks glowed pink. Not that he was about to apologize, not when something in his chest was hopping around in delight. Cute, little Lou thought he was hot AND he'd successfully pulled her back from the edge. Win-win.

"ANYWAY," Alice shot him a nasty look. "It's still new and scary right now, but we need to know if you'll be okay with this knowledge long-term?"

Jack's fingers twitched to reach across the island and strangle Alice. If everyone in the Den was going to be this dumb, he was going to need a miracle to keep Louisa's sanity intact.

Louisa twirled pasta around her fork, her shoulders shrugging.

"I'll probably need an hour or two to curl up in a ball and hyperventilate... but otherwise, yeah. I should be fine."

"Just like that?" Alice raised her eyebrows. "You're not going to run screaming or anything? Make a few more escape attempts?"

"The way I grew up, you learn to adapt. And I am exceptional at adapting." Louisa stared coldly into Alice's eyes. "As for the escape attempts, as long as I have your word that I get to go home and won't end up in some dark cell in your basement when this is over, I'll put them on hold for now."

"Where did you grow up?" Jack watched her apprehensively.

Louisa waved her fork. "None of your business, Mr. Kidnapper."

"Until further notice, you will tentatively be considered an ally to the clan," Alice informed her, ignoring their interruption. "If you betray that trust...uh, bad things will happen. Understood?"

"Understood." Louisa snapped a salute with her fork. "Though I'm still not convinced this isn't all a dream," she added under her breath.

"This isn't a dream," Jack said softly.

"We'll see," Louisa sighed. "Is the interrogation over?"

He winced. Maybe he could wait a bit longer? Surely, tomorrow was better. Alice shot him a stern look across the island. Bossy bird.

"I need to know what happened to me when I was stuck in my other form," Jack sighed. "If you don't mind."

Louisa twirled her fork, her brow crinkled in thought.

"There's not much to tell." She shook her head. "You were brought in with a gunshot wound in your shoulder. We removed the bullet and patched you up. That's pretty much it."

"How did I get to the clinic?" Jack asked.

"You don't remember?" she blinked in surprise.

"I don't remember anything from the week before I woke up in your clinic."

"Whoa. No wonder you have questions," Louisa breathed. "Some teenagers brought you in. They said they had found you bleeding in the middle of the road. In fact, they almost hit you with their car."

"Did they say what road?" he pressed.

"No, just that it was in the middle of nowhere."

"And they didn't mention seeing anyone else there? Just me?"

"They were teenagers," Louisa laughed. "I practically had to waterboard them to get that much information."

"And no one came to the clinic asking about me?" Jack questioned.

"Not while I was there." She shook her head again. "I'm sorry, I know that's not much to go on."

The kitchen fell silent except for the quiet clinking of cutlery against china. Jack had nothing to go on. The only move he could see was to go back to square one and start the original investigation over. His sigh cut through the quiet kitchen. This week just kept getting worse and worse.

Louisa put her fork down and turned on her stool. A nervous energy danced through her hands, twisting in her lap. Jack raised his eyebrows.

"I think I need to see it again to really believe it," she stumbled anxiously over her words. "If you don't mind, that is."

"See...what?" Jack stared back into her round eyes.

"I need to see you do... the thing," Louisa gestured at him.

Jack and Alice looked at each other. He shrugged. If it made her more comfortable being here, it couldn't hurt.

"Animal or half-form?"

"Uh...half-form?" Louisa shrugged her shoulders. Right, like she knew the difference.

Jack stood up and pushed his stool in. Nudging his shoes off, he took a few steps back. Here goes nothing.

Jack's face started to boil, his tan skin giving way to pale brown fur. His hair shortened. His nose elongated into a snout. Arms and legs lengthened and shrouded themselves in slabs of muscle. Razor sharp claws grew from the end of his fingers. His clothing fluttered to the ground in pieces as seams burst open.

Louisa stared at him standing bashfully in front of her. Sandy fur covered his seven-foot-tall frame of uninterrupted muscle. A seamless meld of man and beast hovered in front of her, claws clicking nervously against the tile floor. He watched her worriedly.

A mouth of razor sharp teeth opened.

"Lou?" he garbled out.

Louisa swallowed. Her eyes wide, air frozen in her lungs. Every primal instinct still lingering from man's early days of surviving in caves no doubt screamed for her to run away as fast as her legs could carry her. She stood frozen in place.

"Louisa?" Alice called quietly from across the kitchen.

Louisa choked on a scream.

"Right," she whispered.

Her eyes rolled back into her head as she dropped to the floor. Alice stared down at her unconscious body. Looking back up at Jack, she smiled brightly.

"I think that went well, all things considered."

Jack pulled at his fur in frustration. Dropping his head back, a frustrated howl shook the house. He stalked around the counter. Bending at the waist, Jack scooped Louisa off the floor. He pulled her tight to his chest and inhaled the sweet vanilla of her hair.

He'd really fucked this one up.

8

A steady ache radiated through Louisa's forehead. She groaned. First the lamp, which frankly she'd never particularly cared for, and now... now what? The last thing she remembered was sitting in the kitchen eating spaghetti with Alice and... Jack.

Jack, who had transformed into a towering monster right before her eyes. Sure, Alice had been an owl for a bit, but it's not like she had teeth that could rip out Louisa's throat. Maybe if she were persistent enough, she could peck her to death.

Louisa cracked open her eyes, wincing as the light impaled her. She wiped the tears from her eyes and looked around. A familiar afghan lay across her lap. Aw, back in her "cell." Good thing she knew where the toolbox was.

The pale glow of the window caught Louisa's eye. The daylight faded behind the tree line as evening fell. Dinner had come and gone while she lay unconscious. How long had she been out? That couldn't be good for her battered brain.

Something to her left shifted, making a soft rustling

noise. The thought of brain damage slipped out of her head as she jumped. Alice sat balanced on a chair, feet resting on the bed beside Louisa's arm. An enormous, leather-bound book rested in her lap. Alice flipped the pages, her glasses balanced precariously on the tip of her freckled nose.

A wild panic ignited in Louisa. A thousand questions and worries flooded her mind at once. Was she ever going to be allowed to leave now that she knew their secret? Was she a prisoner for life? Were they going to turn her into one of them? Was that even possible?

Her heart pounding in her ears, Louisa closed her eyes and opted to ignore the redhead entirely. Peeking under her lashes, she forced herself to breathe evenly. She'd already had one freak-out in the last twenty-four-hours, bringing her total up to two was not a good idea.

"I can hear your heartbeat speeding up," Alice informed her, her eyes never leaving the page. "Take your time. I'm not going anywhere."

"Thanks, that's really disconcerting," Louisa sighed.

She popped her eyes open and pushed herself upright. Prodding at her forehead, Louisa winced at the dull ache in her skull. Two head injuries in one day. One more and she might just set some kind of moronic record.

"You fainted," Alice said, turning the page in her giant tome.

"Of course I did," Louisa grumbled. "It's not like I had a seven-foot monster spring up in front of me or anything."

Alice closed the book and set her feet on the floor. Louisa shivered under the full attention of her gray-eyed gaze. She wasn't about to turn into an owl again, right? Her stomach churned wildly.

"I know this has been a bit overwhelming for you, and you probably have a lot of questions." Alice tried to smile comfortingly at her, but Louisa couldn't help but cringe away. Every time she closed her eyes, the image of feathers melting into skin made her stomach heave. "Jack thought I would be the least-threatening option for this, but I can still smell your fear."

Louisa didn't bother to deny it. She was afraid. In fact, she was terrified. The last twenty-four hours had been the worst of her life, and the next twenty-four weren't exactly looking up.

"Come with me." Alice abruptly stood up and tucked the large book under her arm. "I have a better idea."

She moved to offer Louisa a hand up, but thought better of it, tucking her arm at her side. Alice crossed the room and opened the door. Dazed at the sudden change in plan, Louisa stayed curled on the large bed.

Alice turned back to her. "Come on. This won't be scary, I promise."

Yeah, well you turn into an owl. What do you know? Louisa pushed herself out of bed, dragging the soft blanket with her. She curled it around her thin pajamas, turning herself into a scaredy-burrito.

Following Alice, Louisa shuffled down the hall. The décor was lovely. She'd been so keen on escaping this morning that she hadn't had a chance to appreciate it. Tasteful, expensive, yet simple. The whole house was, in fact. It was like some weird antebellum mansion from an old movie that someone had felt needed updating. Louisa was pretty sure she couldn't afford a single floorboard in the whole damn place.

Alice led her up a short flight of stairs and stopped in front of a white door covered in sparkly, pink hearts. Knocking swiftly, she stepped back beside Louisa. A man with a serious face opened the door.

Louisa blinked. He had a face that would be at home on the covers of magazines. Sharp cheekbones underscored eyes so brown they looked black. He had the most beautiful skin Louisa had ever seen. Several shades darker than her own caramel coloring, he glowed like a stunning, bronze statue. Some type of Native American, if she had to guess.

"Yes?" His deep growl sparked a flare of recognition in Louisa. He was the guy from this morning, the one who had cleared the room with a single roar.

Oh great, he was probably going to turn into a giant lion-man or some shit.

A shiver of fear danced along Louisa's spine. He might have a face that would make women beg, but the severe glower made her blood run cold. Alice clearly had no idea what "not scary" meant.

"I need to borrow Abby." Alice answered his scowl with a secretive smile.

"Borrow her for what?" His sharp eyes scanned Louisa from head to toe. Doing her best to shrink behind the tiny redhead, she cringed away from him.

"For a bedtime story." Alice pulled the heavy tome from under her arm.

"You and Abby are one step away from sworn enemies, and you want to read her a bedtime story?" His dark eyes narrowed.

"Yes," Alice said firmly.

The two of them stared at each other for a long moment. Louisa glanced between them as the silence dragged on. Maybe she should just go back to the room and... what, hide under the covers? Wait for someone to drag her out? No, thank you. Louisa hugged the afghan tighter around her, her hands fisting in the woven yarn.

The small movement drew the eye of tall, dark, and

scary. His gaze lingered on the colorful afghan for a brief second before studying her face again.

"Fine." His eyes remained locked on Louisa's. "For Jack."

He turned abruptly and threw open the sparkly door. Louisa blinked, her eyes watering as she stepped into the room. Color exploded from every corner. It was like stepping inside a rainbow.

Louisa zeroed in on a small bed against the wall. The dark-eyed man dropped a kiss on top of a tiny head of dark curls. He turned abruptly to Alice.

"I hold you responsible for her safety," he growled, his words holding a weight that made Louisa shudder. He strode out of the room without a second glance.

"Louisa, this is Abby." Alice gestured toward the bed. "Abby, this is Louisa."

A pair of bright-blue eyes shone from a small, round face. The solemn look in her eye struck Louisa as familiar. She noted the bronzey tone in the golden face poking out of a pile of stuffed animals. So Tall, Dark, and Scary had a daughter.

Louisa blinked at the jarring thought. Even monsters get to have families.

"You're Uncle Jack's friend," a tiny voice squeaked out.

"Uh, yeah. I guess we're friends." Louisa looked helplessly at Alice.

Abby scooched some of her animals out of the way and looked pointedly at Louisa. A tiny hand patted the clear space beside her. Clearly being a friend of "Uncle Jack's" had earned her some kind of bump in status.

Louisa glanced at Alice. She gave her a small nod and turned to pull up a red, child-sized chair for herself. Climb into the tiny monster's bed...right.

She crawled up on the bed and wiggled into the nest of

stuffed toys. Tugging the blankets over their laps, she settled in. What a weird day. A chill ran up Louisa's spine. A weird day, indeed.

Abby offered her a stuffed pig. Louisa took it in shaking hands and hugged the soft toy to her chest. The little girl leaned against her side, a well-worn teddy bear curled in her arms. Louisa exhaled the pent-up breath in her chest. She smiled down at the dark head pressed against her ribs. Maybe Alice knew what she was doing after all.

Alice lowered herself onto the tiny chair and laid her giant book across her lap. Hiding a snicker, Louisa coughed. The big, bad owl looked ridiculous perched precariously on the baby chair.

"Did your daddy tell you why we're here?" Alice asked.

"You're going to tell me and Ms. Louisa a bedtime story." Abby beamed up at Louisa. Oh man, those big, blue eyes were killing her.

"That's right, except I need your help telling the story."

Abby clapped her hands together in delight. "What story are we telling, Ms. Alice?"

"We're going to tell Ms. Louisa the story of the Five Clans." Alice opened the book. "You're going to tell the scary bits so that she doesn't get scared before bed, okay?" she stage-whispered.

Abby nodded seriously. One of her little hands untangled from the beat-up teddy bear to rest on Louisa's. She patted her hand and whispered, "It's okay. I won't use scary voices."

"Thanks," Louisa whispered back.

Alice cleared her throat. "Thousands of years ago, there was a chain of islands. The islands were inhabited by a holy order of witches called the Divine Unity—"

"What was the name of the islands?" Abby interrupted.

"Nobody knows." Alice wiggled her fingers mysteriously at them. "The name was stricken from every record after the great curse."

Abby giggled. The corner of Louisa's mouth turned up slightly. She had to give Alice kudos. Throw a baby monster at the strange lady and watch her drown in cuteness overload. Pretty damn clever.

For the first time since she had woken up in the strange house, Louisa was relaxed...even though they were talking about witches, which exist, apparently. She sighed.

"The witches were a peaceful order, seeking harmony and balance in all things. Now, their islands were part of a small sea that was plagued by storms. That made trade from one side to the other incredibly difficult. The only option was to send caravans by land through enemy territory or risk crossing during the short summer season."

"But the islands were in the middle!" Abby piped up.

"That's right," Alice nodded. "And that made them the perfect halfway point for traders. The clans from the five surrounding coastal nations were constantly at war and all of them wanted access to the islands."

"And the witches said no!" she squeaked.

"They wouldn't risk creating an imbalance by giving one clan the advantage over the other, so they told them to come to an agreement among themselves. They refused, of course. So they kept right on fighting." Alice pointed at Abby. "Can you take it from here?"

"Yep!" Abby gave Louisa's hand a little squeeze. "Squeeze Porkchop if you get scared."

Louisa looked down at the stuffed piglet lying in her lap.

"Porkchop?" she giggled.

"Mr. Connor named him," Abby giggled back. She

scooted closer, her little, pajama-clad legs tossed over Louisa's beneath the bright comforter.

"What happened next, Abby?" Alice asked, drawing them back to the story.

"The fighting made the witches mad, so they wanted them to do a, uh, I don't remember the word?" Abby frowned. "They wanted them to be nice, so they needed to say sorry."

"Mediation?" Louisa guessed.

Abby shrugged. "I don't remember. The witches had a meeting with the clans but they started fighting and someone died."

"The high priestess of the Divine Unity," Alice supplied.

"Yeah, her." Abby squeezed her teddy bear tight. "They got really mad and used bad magic to punish the clans." She shivered.

Louisa wrapped an arm around her little shoulders. Inching a little further into her lap, Abby went on with the story.

"The witches cursed everybody in the clans. They made all of their important things bad."

"Important things?" Louisa puzzled.

"Our cultures and values," Alice supplied. "Our clan trained the fastest horses, the best hunting dogs, the most loyal pets. So they turned our ancestors into the animals that they loved. Now a shifter can't get within ten feet of an animal without them going mad with fear."

How awful. Louisa loved animals, usually more than she did people. That's why she'd become a veterinary assistant. She hadn't been allowed to have a pet as a kid, so she would sneak over and play with the neighbor's dogs after they'd gone to work. The thought of never getting to cuddle a puppy or pet a cat's soft ears again made her heart hurt.

"That's horrible." Louisa shuddered.

"When I'm bad, Daddy doesn't let me watch TV," Abby whispered to her. "But the witches were even bigger meanies."

"Yes, they were." Louisa gave her a little squeeze. "What happened next?"

"The bad magic made the islands sink. They had to run away."

"Wow, that's a big curse."

"Think of it like a magical atom bomb." Alice winced. "They didn't just kill their islands, they destroyed the sea and everything surrounding it. The amount of power they used caused the sea to dry up. The land followed after. Crops withered, rivers turned to dust, animals starved. Nations died."

Alice waved at a colorful map hanging on the bedroom wall. "Even now, the area is basically a desert, a barren wasteland that can't support life. I think Abby had Nate put a pin in the spot."

"It's pink!" Abby pointed at a tiny spot on the map.

"Keep going, Abby." Alice smiled sadly. "The story isn't over."

"Right, the mean witches disappeared, but everyone was mad at them. So they spent a long time looking for them. It took a really long time, but they found most of them."

Louisa cringed behind her dark head. She didn't need Alice's careful wince to read between the lines. The witches had been hunted down and killed by the monsters they had created.

"And then the king—is there a picture in the book?" Abby stopped and frowned at the big book.

"Yes, there is." Alice turned the book, propping it on her knees for Louisa to see. "This was our king, Cern."

"The king said, 'No. Leave the meanies alone.' So they let the last witches go and we started moving away to hide with the humans."

Louisa studied the ink drawing. A man with antlers stood surrounded by animals creeping out of the forest. The closer the animals got to the king, the more humanlike they appeared, until those closest stood as humans beside him.

"He was king of the five clans?" Louisa asked.

"Nope, just the shifters." Abby yawned in her lap.

"The curse didn't make all of the clans shifters?" Louisa locked eyes with Alice over her head. Red hair shook side to side.

"There's shifters, wolfs, ummm... banjos, and I don't remember the rest," Abby listed sleepily. Eyes closed, she curled into a ball in Louisa's lap, her teddy still tucked tight to her chest.

"Banshees, not banjos." Alice quietly corrected her. "The others are succubi and ghouls."

Gaping, Louisa's jaw dropped open. Seriously? She was just coming to terms with shifters and now there were more things that go bump in the night to worry about?!

Abby's fingers tightened around Louisa's as she drifted off to sleep. The tension drained from Louisa's shoulders as she looked down at the peaceful face.

Well, maybe it really wasn't such a huge leap. Once the idea of shapeshifters had forcibly settled itself in her brain, the thought of werewolves and ghouls wasn't quite as shocking.

She stared at the colorful walls for a few minutes, allowing her turbulent thoughts to settle. Abby's quiet snore huffed quietly in the silent room.

"Okay," Louisa whispered to the wall. She could do this.

Alice closed the book quietly. "I'll take you back to your room."

Louisa carefully lifted Abby off of her lap and slid out of the pile of animals. Tucking the blankets around the sleeping girl, she dropped a light kiss on her dark head. Louisa followed Alice out the door, giving Abby one last look before she eased the door closed.

They walked in silence down the stairs. The house was quiet around them, everyone going their separate ways to settle in for the night.

"You don't smell afraid anymore." Alice fixed her stormy, gray eyes on her. She studied her with a faint smile. "I guess Abby did the trick."

Louisa nodded. Meeting Abby had done the trick, but not like Alice thought. Seeing her, adored and loved, was all the confirmation that she had needed to know that they weren't quite the monsters they appeared to be. Truthfully, she hadn't even needed the story.

9

The sky turned dark as Louisa curled in bed, studying the illustrations in the book Alice had left with her. Including some disturbing depictions of shifters mid-turn. She had shivered when she stumbled across those. Her tired eyes burned.

A soft knock at the door startled her out of her cozy cocoon. She sat up straight as a familiar head poked around the door.

"Can I come in?" Jack asked quietly.

"Sure." Color flushed her cheeks.

She still couldn't believe she had fainted. As far as her badass status was concerned, Louisa was one case of the vapors away from having it permanently revoked.

Jack hovered awkwardly beside the bed, shifting nervously from foot to foot. He avoided her eyes, his gaze locked on the afghan. His mouth opened and closed a few times before Louisa took pity on him.

Poor guy was probably as embarrassed as she was after the kitchen incident. At least he hadn't fainted.

"Sit down," Louisa patted the bed beside her.

Jack balanced on the edge of the bed, his hands folded in his lap.

"Okay..." She threaded her fingers through the weave of the blanket. "I'll admit that there is a slight possibility that you can turn into a dog."

A bark of laughter burst out of Jack, taking them both by surprise.

"A possibility, huh?" His smile was hesitant. "I can work with a possibility... I'm sorry I scared you."

"It's okay, I've had all evening to come to terms with it... and I get it," Louisa patted his knee. "You were taking care of your people."

Jack shifted on the bed. He still wasn't meeting her eyes. Louisa waited. He would get to whatever was bothering him eventually.

"I need to apologize."

She waited. Jack had quite a few things he could apologize for... she just didn't know which one he meant.

"I shouldn't have given you the option of choosing half-form in the kitchen. You didn't know what it meant." He ran a hand over his face. "I should have realized how terrifying it would be."

Oh, yeah. Louisa winced. She'd nearly wet her pants when the sweet, fluffy dog had turned out to be a seven-foot demon.

"Why didn't you?" she blurted. "I mean, don't people normally freak out when they see it?"

Jack laughed. "It's not like I grocery shop in that form." He shrugged. "I'm a shifter. I was born a shifter and raised by shifters and I live in a house with a bunch of shifters. It never occurred to me that it would be scary for you."

Furbidden Attraction

She blinked. Oh, well that would do it. She fell silent as more questions rolled around, trying to figure out which one wanted answered most.

Jack took her hand in his, playing with her fingers while he waited. Callused fingers wrapped around her own; his rough thumb traced circles on the back of her hand.

A steady warmth curled in her chest. Her brow wrinkled, pulling her heart-shaped face in a soft frown. How did he do that? He was barely touching her, and every inch of her was tingling in anticipation. Was it some kind of shifter magic?

Louisa studied his tanned face. No, Alice didn't do anything for her and she was a shifter. It was Jack. Something about him drew her like a moth to a flame and set all of her bits on fire.

She wondered what would happen if they kissed. Would she spontaneously combust? Only one way to find out.

Gripping the back of Jack's neck with her free hand, Louisa dragged his head down. She caught a glimpse of his wide eyes as their lips met.

Louisa nearly groaned when she tasted his lips. Soft, yet firm, with a faint taste of mint and something that was uniquely Jack. Heat rushed over her, igniting her prickling skin. She slanted her mouth across his. Jack growled against her mouth and took the reins. Oh, lord.

He gripped Louisa's hips and dragged her into his lap, blankets falling away. Burying his hands in her curls, he pulled her deeper into the kiss. His tongue traced along the seam of her lips, invading her mouth as she opened for him.

Jack's tongue brushed against Louisa's in soft thrusts. She moaned. Her knees parted to straddle his lap. Rational thought fled as the kiss took on a life of its own. Louisa ground her hips against Jack's, the thin fabric of her stained pajama pants practically nonexistent between them.

Jack groaned as she rubbed against him. The ache between her legs intensified. Why were they still wearing pants? Louisa froze as she started to slip her fingertips under Jack's waistband. What the hell was she doing? This was just supposed to be a quick kiss, a test of this weird pull between them.

Feeling her tense up, Jack pulled back. He dropped one last peck on her mouth and pressed his forehead against hers. They leaned into each other, their gasping breaths and hammering heartbeats the only sound in the room.

Freeing themselves from her curls, Jack's hands trailed down her spine. Louisa closed her eyes and breathed in his scent. That was something, alright. Maybe not spontaneous combustion, but pretty damn close.

"Finally giving in to my charms?" Jack smiled.

"Just testing something," Louisa whispered back. The dance of his fingertips down her spine was doing nothing to cool the flames flaring in her belly.

"Did I pass?"

"With flying colors." Louisa pulled back, her arms still draped over Jack's shoulders. Warm green eyes studied her face. She had to ask. Louisa hated to ruin... whatever that just was, but she had to know.

"Why did you bring me here?"

Jack reared back, the humor in his eyes replaced by something else. Something she didn't recognize.

"I've been thinking about it all day. You could have left me in my apartment, but you didn't."

It didn't make any sense. Jack could have walked away without a backward glance. He could have gone on with his life and never thought about her again. Hell, he could have gone home with Connor and Alice when they showed up at the clinic... but he hadn't. He'd stayed with her. He'd brought Louisa home and taken care of her.

Jack looked down. Avoiding her eyes yet again. She gave his shoulders a gentle shake.

"Jack?"

"I don't know," he murmured.

"Jack."

His eyes shot up to study her face. Taking a deep breath, he nodded slowly.

"I couldn't leave. It felt...wrong."

Confused eyes met her own. Vulnerability. That's what she hadn't recognized. He wasn't handling the violent tug of their attraction any better than she was. Her eyes softened.

"You smelled nice," Jack murmured quietly.

"You kidnapped me because I smelled nice?" Louisa teased.

His arms squeezed her waist. "Really nice."

"What do I smell like?" She looked down at her tattered pajamas. Her nose wrinkled. "Grass and spaghetti?"

Louisa squeaked when Jack buried his nose in the crook of her neck. He inhaled deeply, making her squirm. He pulled back with a smile.

"Peanut butter and vanilla."

"So... a peanut butter cookie?" Louisa deadpanned. "You brought me home because I smell like a cookie?"

The grave expression cracked as she burst out laughing. Louisa buried her face in his shirt as she howled with laughter. A cookie?

This beautiful specimen of masculinity had kidnapped her, actually kidnapped her, because he thought she smelled liked baked goods. And here Louisa had thought *she* was hard up for sex.

"Uh, peanut butter cookies are delicious," Jack huffed.

"Oh my god, you're ridiculous!" Louisa yawned into his shoulder.

Jack growled and pulled her close for another quick kiss. He pulled back abruptly and scooched her off his lap. Climbing off the bed, he tucked the afghan around Louisa's legs.

"Bedtime," he announced.

Jack dropped a quick kiss on the top of her head before she could protest. Louisa scowled and lay back against the pillows. Rude. You don't just kiss and ditch.

Clearly, the whole lot of them needed more interaction with regular humans and human guidelines. Of course, the warm feeling that washed over Louisa from her heart to her toes every time he smiled at her had nothing to do with it.

Jack turned away and started pulling his shirt off over his head. Ummm...?

"What are you doing?"

Jack turned around. Louisa forced her eyes to stay on his face. If she focused on the carved muscles of his abs for too long, she wouldn't be able to stop...cause damn. She had seen fitness models on Instagram with less definition. She nearly groaned. Why had she pulled back earlier?

Right, because she shouldn't be kissing kidnap-y strangers. Let alone climbing into their laps.

"Getting ready for bed," Jack said slowly, as though it were the most obvious thing in the world.

His hands moved lower to unbutton his jeans. Louisa's eyes followed his hands as his thumbs slipped under his waistband. The waist of his jeans started to slip lower.

Jack cleared his throat expectantly, a sly smirk on his

face. Louisa dragged her eyes away. Heat rose up her chest to the roots of her hair. Probably red as a damn fire truck.

"You're not sleeping in here," she finally choked out.

His pants hit the ground with a muffled thump. Nope, this was not happening. Jack was not naked...again. You will not look, Louisa told herself. Really, *it* couldn't be as magnificent as she remembered from their brief tussle in her living room. Even magic had its limits.

Jack laughed at the pained expression on her face.

"Like I'm going to leave you in here alone." He crossed the room and flicked the light switch, bathing them in darkness. "The last time I did that, you climbed out the damn window."

Louisa stiffened as the bed dipped. She held her breath when a firm weight pressed against her side. Something cold and wet poked her neck, eliciting a surprised shriek.

She reached out hesitantly. Her hand connected with familiar fluffy ears. Louisa breathed a sigh of relief as Jack gave her a reassuring lick on the chin. He laid his paws across her stomach and tucked his head under her arm.

Sleep came quickly as his warmth enveloped her. Her fingers stroked his soft ears. Louisa's eyes drifted closed as the weight of the day slipped away.

LOUISA BLINKED HER EYES OPEN. The morning sun was bathing the room in a soft glow. She let her eyelids drop closed and cuddled deeper into the nest of blankets. An arm tightened around her waist.

Her eyes flew open. The fuck? She slowly raised the edge of the blankets. A tanned, muscular arm curled around her hips and slipped beneath the edge of her shirt. Louisa lifted the hem of her shirt to find a large, callused hand resting on her bare stomach.

She dropped the blankets and looked over her shoulder. Jack, very human and very naked… again, curled against her back. His sandy hair hung over his face, relaxed in sleep. Sleeping as a dog didn't go well, apparently.

Louisa snorted under her breath. Did she want to try and wiggle out? Not really. She surrendered to the mattress, Jack's naked body plastered to hers. Oh well, at least he was warm. Relaxing back against Jack's chest, her eyes drifted closed.

A curl fluttered across her face. Louisa flicked her head as another curl joined its friend. With every exhale, Jack blew more curls into her face. She shoved them back with a grimace.

So much for being the little spoon. Another curl puffed across her face. Son of a bitch.

Louisa tilted her head away from him, her hips shifting back against his. He groaned softly in her ear. She rolled her eyes and settled down to wait out her prison sentence. Within minutes, Louisa was shifting uncomfortably as she became increasingly aware of her full bladder.

Gently gripping Jack's wrist, she tried to wiggle out from under the weight of his arm. It slipped out of her grip and curled back around her. Jack sighed into her hair and pulled her tighter against his hard chest.

"Jack?" she whispered.

Something poked against her butt. Jack shifted and poked her again. Seriously? Trapped yet again, with his boner pressing against her ass… not that there weren't worse places to be. Any other time, Louisa might be interested but her bladder was leaving no room for improvisation.

Jack growled, his face pressed into her tangled bedhead.

She elbowed him lightly in the ribs as her bladder situation intensified.

"Jack?" Her voice got sharper.

He grumbled in his sleep and cuddled her closer. Louisa's teeth clenched as the pressure on her bladder grew.

"Jack!" Louisa slammed her elbow into his ribs.

"Eh?" he growled, his eyes refusing to open.

"I need to use the bathroom," she answered in a rush.

"Then go."

"Release your death grip and I will." She rolled her eyes.

Jack grunted and pulled back his arm. Louisa rolled out of bed as Jack turned onto his stomach and buried his head under the pillows. She stumbled into the bathroom, the door clicking shut behind her.

JACK SHIFTED UNCOMFORTABLY. The hell? He groaned. He had a fair idea what had sparked his raging erection. She had soft, honey-colored skin and a cloud of dark curls floating around her head and had thoroughly kissed the hell out of him last night.

Jack ran a hand over his face. He'd practically had Louisa underneath him by the time she'd elbowed him awake. There was no way she hadn't been fully aware of his appreciative little friend. Fuck.

"Jack?" a soft voice filled the room. "Can I take a shower?"

A shower. Naked. Louisa was going to be naked in. his. shower. The throbbing between his legs intensified as the image of soap trailing down her generous curves flashed through his head.

Jack kept his head firmly planted beneath the stack of pillows. Heat crept up the back of his neck as he blushed furiously. If he wished for it hard enough, maybe he could just disappear.

"Go ahead. Towels are in the cabinet," Jack mumbled into the mattress.

"Can I borrow a change of clothes?"

Oh god. Louisa. Naked. In his clothes. He breathed the warm scent that was uniquely Louisa on the sheets. If she didn't take her tantalizing scent and walk away, he was going to start humping the mattress.

"There's a bag of your clothes by the door," he gritted out.

Jack listened as she padded barefoot across the room.

"Thanks!" Louisa called, disappearing back into the bathroom.

"Kill me."

The sound of the shower turning on sent Jack into a shudder. He had to get the fuck out of here before he decided to use his rock hard cock to beat down the bathroom door and join her.

Jack rolled off the bed and snagged a pair of sweatpants off the floor. Yanking them up his legs, he glared at his tented crotch. It was too early for this kind of bullshit.

Lurching out the door, Jack shuffled down the hall to Connor's room. Thank heavens, he worked the early shift today. He ripped open the bathroom door and flipped on the shower. Seams groaned as he tore the sweatpants away in a hurry.

He stumbled into the shower and grabbed the bottle of shampoo. Thinking of naked grannies wasn't going to make a dent in the rampant horniness that had plagued Jack since he first caught sight of Louisa's luscious ass.

That kiss last night? He'd nearly come in his pants right

then and there. But no, the little voice in his head had warned him to step back and be a gentleman instead.

Slicking his hand with soap, Jack grasped his dick. He pumped his arm in languid strokes. His Lou was wet and naked in his shower, and he was here, in another man's bathroom, taking care of business himself.

Jack should be there with her, pressing her up against the tile, his tongue tasting her sweet skin. Louisa's legs would part as she arched her back for him, the water dripping from her curls to run down her perky, delectable butt. Oh, that sweet, round ass.

His dick ached to be inside of her. Jack could almost hear the moan he would tear from her lips as he gripped her hips and pushed between her folds. She would take every solid inch of him as he thrust inside of her. Harder and harder until Louisa was lifted onto her toes, her voice screaming out his name as she came on his cock.

Jack's frustrated groan echoed through the bathroom as his hand glided faster. Fuck, he was so close. Was Louisa touching herself? Was she imagining how good he would feel inside of her? The thought of Louisa's delicate fingers dipping inside of her pussy pushed him over the edge. Cum spilled over his clenched fist, ripping another groan from his throat.

Gasping for air, Jack pressed his forehead to the cool tile and let the water wash over him. He stood beneath the spray and bumped his head against the wall. Louisa was not his and if he didn't get his shit together, she never would be.

But Jack wanted her to be his, so very badly. Over the course of just a few days, admittedly most of which had been spent as a dog, he'd already come to regard her as a permanent fixture in his life.

So do what you have to do to make her stay, dumbass.

Jack straightened. That's exactly what he was going to do. Sure, he had a couple disappearances to solve, including his own, but that didn't mean he couldn't charm Louisa at the same time. If last night's kiss was anything to go by, she wouldn't need much convincing.

A grin spread across his face. By the time he was done, his Lou would be begging him to let her stay. Well, maybe not begging. It was Louisa after all.

Jack shut off the shower and dried off. Yanking his sweats back on, he strode out of the room on a mission. He'd had two days as a dog to study her life; it would have to be enough. Jack beelined for the kitchen.

Alice sat at the table, groggily picking at a bowl of cereal, when he entered the room. Without looking away from her bowl, she slid a folded piece of paper across the table.

"Nate left this for you."

Jack swiped the note off the table, his eyebrows raised.

"He actually left the house? Nate never leaves the house."

Alice shrugged. "Abby conned him into taking her out for breakfast. Something about how pancakes are good for growing children." She waved her empty mug around. "It was pre-coffee so I may have missed a few details."

Jack unfolded the paper and scanned the brief line of text.

Don't screw it up. Abby likes her.

He barked out a laugh. That was as close to a blessing as he was going to get from his Alpha. As long as Abby liked Louisa, Nate would tolerate her presence.

Ever since his ex-wife had taken off and abandoned him and Abby a few years back, Nate had doted on her, desperate to fill the roles of two parents.

Jack had warned him not to marry Kate, but Nate had

lost his head and made the one and only impulsive decision of his life. Oh well, at least they had gotten Abby from the mess.

Shoving the note into the pocket of his sweats, Jack started hunting through the kitchen for breakfast. Preferably something sweet; Lou liked sweets. His nose twitched as he followed the light scent of butter and sugar to a pink box tucked away in a cupboard.

He flipped open the top and smiled. Muffins—perfect. Alice's voice cut through the silent kitchen.

"Those are mine, Jack. I bought them specially from the new bakery in town."

"I'm confiscating two." He clutched the box to his chest.

Alice swirled her spoon in her bowl. "Go buy your own muffins, moron."

"I need to feed Louisa," Jack explained slowly. "It's my duty to the clan to maintain good relations with our guest."

Ha, argue your way out of that one, bird.

Alice's face softened. "Fine. For Louisa." She pointed her spoon at him. "I like her. Don't fuck this up."

"So everyone keeps telling me," Jack sighed. "Don't worry, I'm going to win her over."

"She'll be gone by dinnertime," Alice snorted into her bowl.

Jack scowled at her. "Don't even joke, Alice. I need her to stay."

The idea of Louisa walking away made his stomach hurt. Every cell in his body screamed for him to keep her right beside him. Now he just needed to convince her that she felt the same way.

Alice's head shot up, her eyes searching his own. Jack squirmed under her perceptive gaze. He hated when she did that.

"Do you think she's your mate?" she asked curiously.

"Shifters don't have mates." Jack shook his head. "You know that."

"Magic is constantly changing and evolving, even our curse." Alice shrugged her petite shoulders. "Never say never, Jack. If Louisa feels important to you, listen to that instinct. It could lead you somewhere we've never been."

10

"That son of a bitch!" Louisa was going to murder him.

She pawed through the overstuffed duffel bag. Clothes spilled out, the bag practically groaning in relief. Her comb and toothbrush, though bent and abused, had made the journey from her apartment. But apparently, underwear had not.

Louisa flipped the bag over and shook out the contents. Pants, shirts, a sundress, a handful of mismatched socks... and not a single pair of underwear. Six bras. She hadn't even been aware that she *owned* six bras.

She glared toward the heavens. Men, ugh.

Digging through the pile, Louisa liberated a pair of leggings. No way in hell was she going commando in jeans. Jack might be hot and jeans did great things for her ass, but no man was worth that level of chafing. She threw on the rest of her clothes and tossed her destroyed pajamas in the trashcan.

Louisa sighed. She'd really liked those pants. Stepping

over her pile of clothes, she crossed back into the bedroom, comb in hand. The bed was empty.

She scrubbed her knuckles at the disappointed ache in her chest. Louisa had known Jack for only a day and already she missed him when he left. Groaning, she dropped down on the bed. Louisa was in deep.

She never should have kissed him. Already, Louisa could see that Jack was like a drug. One she'd rapidly become addicted to.

Pull it together, girl. Stop thinking with your vagina.

Spine straightened, Louisa set her shoulders back and took a deep breath. She was a grown-ass woman; she could handle being around a good looking man for longer than a few hours without turning into a complete hussy.

Louisa tugged the comb through her damp curls with determination. Of course he had forgotten her hair products. Didn't he realize how much work goes into maintaining curls like hers?

The door opened as she hissed at the tangles. Jack strolled through the door, a tray in his hands. Her eyes dropped to his bare chest. An aching heat pooled between her legs.

Setting the tray on the nightstand, Jack offered her a steaming cup. Louisa took it from his hand, her eyes locked on the swells of his bicep. She sipped at her cup absently. Louisa's eyes dropped shut with a groan.

Oh, sweet caffeine, thou art an angel.

Now all she needed was some food. A sweet note of butter hit her nose. Louisa cracked open her eyes to find a blueberry muffin floating in front of her face.

"Breakfast." Jack smiled at her.

Louisa stared at him. Her earlier self-admonishments fell right out of her head. First coffee, then muffins? She'd throw the sexy bastard on the floor and ravage him on the spot if he could scrounge her up a single pair of underwear.

"Here, I'll handle that." Jack swapped the comb in her hand for one of the muffins. "You eat."

He crawled up on the bed behind her, his legs framing Louisa's hips. She turned her attention to the muffin. Mmmm, blueberries.

Working gently through each knot, Jack combed through the tangled curls. His hard thighs warmed Louisa through her thin leggings. Suddenly, she was painfully aware of her lack of panties.

Louisa cleared her throat. "Thank you. This is delicious."

"You're welcome," Jack said, his fingers still patiently working their way through her hair. "They're from some bakery that just opened. Alice has a serious sweet tooth; she haunts the place a couple times a week."

"The Rainbow Bakery? I haven't been there yet."

He lapsed into silence as she sipped her coffee. Two sugars, perfect. How in the world did Jack know how she took her coffee? Louisa's eyes dropped shut as the comb ran through her damp curls.

The feeling of Jack's fingers twisting through her hair was oddly comforting. She had no memory of anyone doing this for her before. Growing up, her hair had been a constant inconvenience to an endless string of foster mothers. Louisa had had to learn early on how to manage it for herself.

Not even her string of ex-boyfriends had shown her hair this much attention. The only time any of them had bothered to notice it was when they had a complaint about finding it somewhere they didn't want. The shower drain, their laundry, even one memorable incident with a toaster strudel.

Louisa's eyes watered. A kidnapper who turned into a monster was treating her better than anyone else ever had. She sniffled softly, determined not to cry.

Jack paused. "Did I pull too hard?"

She stuffed her self pity back into a box and cleared her throat.

"No, that was great." She took the comb from his hand and patted him on the knee. "Thank you."

Louisa clambered off the bed and tossed the comb on the nightstand. Winding her hair into a bun, she twisted a hair band around it. She turned to Jack, a mask of cheer plastered on her face.

"So...what are we doing today? Assuming I don't get to go home yet, of course."

Jack rose from the bed. He eyed Louisa suspiciously. Clearly, he wasn't buying the cheerful routine. They'd been having a nice moment and she'd ruined it with her emotional baggage.

Louisa opened her mouth to apologize.

"I need to start my investigation over today." Jack cut her off. "You're coming with." He grinned at her. "Unless, of course, you'd like to sit in the library all day with Alice."

Louisa blanched. "Uh, hell no."

She'd probably talk her ear off with endless amounts of terrifying monster knowledge. No fucking thank you. Louisa had managed to escape the previous night without any nightmares. That was probably thanks to Jack, but she wasn't about to look a gift horse in the mouth.

Whatever happened today was probably going to change that. Hide or embrace it? She wasn't much for hiding.

"Is this going to be dangerous?"

Jack opened and closed his mouth. "No."

"Jack."

"Okay, possibly," he admitted. "But I'm not going to let anything happen to you."

"I need you to promise me something," Louisa said.

"What?" He blinked.

"I need you to tell me everything, no matter how scary. I don't want you trying to sugarcoat it, like you just did." She sighed. "No more secrets, no more lies. I can't do *this* if I don't know what's going on."

Jack hesitated for a second, clearly turning her request over in his head.

"Please," Louisa whispered. "This is important to me."

"Okay," he said slowly, nodding. "No, lies. I promise."

Jack dug through the dresser for some clothes while Louisa fished some flats out of the pile of her clothes. Toes safely covered, she swept back into the room.

She stopped dead as Jack pulled a T-shirt over his head. Watching the muscles in his back ripple, Louisa nibbled her lip.

They really should talk about the kiss. He buttoned the jeans hugging his narrow hips, the denim curving over his tight ass. Or not. They could just skip right over the awkward bit and go back to kissing.

Jack tugged on his boots and grabbed a set of keys off the dresser.

"Ready?"

"Waiting on you, grandma." Louisa winked and sashayed out the door.

The deep rumble of his growl followed her down the hall. She wondered how many times she could poke at him before he snapped. Maybe he would bend her over his knee and spank her.

Louisa shook her head clear as Jack caught up to her. She needed to get her head in the game. *This place is too dangerous to be walking around with your head in your panties.* She glanced at Jack from under her dark lashes. *Or in his.*

Their footsteps echoed down the empty hall. Louisa looked around as they started down the staircase. It was so quiet.

"Where is everyone?"

Jack glanced around the foyer and shrugged. "Probably at work."

She stopped on the bottom step. "Work? You have jobs?"

He looked at the shock on her face and burst out laughing. Well, it wasn't that funny, Louisa bristled.

"What did you think we did?" he laughed. "Hung out in our lair all day?"

Her face flushed. Honestly, that was exactly what she'd been thinking. "Well, excuse me, but I thought there might be some perks to being a monster." She huffed and pushed past him.

Howling laughter rang out behind her. Infuriating man. Jack jogged up beside Louisa and spun her around. Her shoulders bumped the wall behind her. Leaning in close, he kissed the end of her nose.

"I'm sorry I laughed," he teased, his grin still turning his mouth up. "You're just so damn cute."

She was cute? Louisa's stomach fluttered. Damn it.

"You're forgiven," she sniffed.

Jack tucked her arm in his and led them down the hallway.

"So what does a supernatural creature do to bring home the bacon?" Louisa asked as they stepped into a cavernous garage. Holy crap, it was as big as the house. How had she missed it during her trek through the rosebushes?

"Most of the garage is under the house," Jack smiled at her confused face. "And to answer your question, we do what everyone else does."

He held open the passenger door of a massive truck. Louisa looked up at the truck bench. It may as well have been Everest. Strong hands gripped her hips and lifted her onto the seat.

"I just can't picture any of you as an accountant or something generic, you know?"

"Actually, Nate was an accountant before he became our Alpha. Now he just handles all our investments, retirements, that type of thing."

Louisa stared at Jack as he crossed the front of the truck to climb into the driver's seat. Tall, dark, and scary was an accountant? An honest-to-god, pocket protector-wearing accountant?

Jack climbed up and buckled himself in. His smile faded as he turned to Louisa and saw the shock on her frozen face.

"What? What is it?"

She swallowed. "It's just... I can handle the whole turning into pets and monsters thing. I get it."

"But?" Jack nudged her, worry twisting his face.

"But it's a little different when the monsters are your neighbors or, like, your dentist, ya know?"

Jack laughed. "My neighbors and my dentist *are* monsters. Yours probably are too."

Louisa sighed. "I think I just expected you to have really cool paranormal type jobs, and this is a bit of a letdown."

"I'm sorry we're not living up to your expectations." He chuckled and backed the truck out of the garage.

"I'll survive," she grumbled. She turned to look out the

window as trees whipped by. Louisa froze and replayed the conversation in her head. "Wait, what do you mean, mine probably are too?"

"Uh..." Jack winced. "Is there any way you can forget I said that?"

"No. You promised me no lies, Jack."

"I can't tell you," he shook his head. "I just...can't."

Anger boiled under Louisa's skin. He had deceived her, kidnapped her, and used his magical shifter magnetism to make her all hot and horny for him. Now her world had shapeshifters, and ghouls, and witches, and all kinds of other bullshit she couldn't even imagine.

He'd *promised* her not even an hour ago. Already, this was Jack's line in the sand? Telling her whether or not the stockboy at the supermarket could turn into a giant hell-beast? Well, now it was Louisa's line in the sand.

"Jack, you will tell me right now or I will end this stupid adventure right here and walk home," she said, her voice devoid of emotion.

Louisa unbuckled her seatbelt and crossed her arms over her chest. She had no urge to be covered head to toe in road rash, but she'd make good on that promise, damn it.

His eyes narrowed at the road. "You wouldn't."

Louisa glared right back. "Try me." She dropped her hand to the door handle.

Pulling over to the side of the road, Jack jerked the truck to a stop.

"Fine," he growled. "Go ahead and walk."

Louisa jerked the door open and jumped down to the ground. Flipping him the bird, she slammed the door shut and set off down the side of the road. Uh, which direction was town?

Fuck it, Louisa would rather wander around the damn

wilderness than get back in the truck with that infuriating man. She stumbled through the gravel, refusing to look back.

Jack's door opened and slammed behind her.

"Damn it, damn it, damn it," Jack muttered as he followed. "Louisa just wait—"

"Fuck off," she called over her shoulder.

She'd kissed him. Louisa had actually kissed him the other night. For a brief, glorious moment, it had felt like maybe this whole shit-show was happening for a reason. And then along came reality, crashing the party to punch her in the teeth.

"You're an ally to the clan, Louisa," she mimicked under her breath. "We trust you, Louisa. No more lies, Louisa. Just keep making out with me and don't ask questions, Louisa."

JACK WATCHED Louisa trudge down the road, her flats sliding on the uneven gravel. Just this morning, he had resolved to find a way to keep her. How long had he made it, an hour and a half?

"Damn it." Jack jogged up beside her. "Will you just hold on a moment?"

"No." Louisa ignored him. "I'm done with secrets, Jack. I'm done with half-truths. I'm done with feeling like an outsider in the place that's supposed to be home. I'm done with not belonging," her voice cracked.

Shit, Jack wanted to tell her, but it was against the rules in a big way. It was one of their most important laws, right next to not revealing their existence at all.

Of course, Jack had already fucked that one up. Nate was already planning on setting him an appropriate punishment when the investigation was over. Maybe he could just roll that one into the next one?

He couldn't let it end like this, not before they knew what *it* was. He couldn't.

"Just stop for a second, damn it." Jack grabbed her by the shoulders and pulled her to a stop. "I can't. This is a big rule."

Her muscles were tense under his hands. She stared straight ahead, refusing to look at him. Her curls twisted in the light breeze, drowning him in a cloud of her scent.

"Bigger than telling a human about shifters?" Louisa asked, her voice dead.

Fuck it.

"Two-thirds of the town is made up of supes." Jack gritted his teeth. He was so dead. Nate was literally going to kill him. "The leaders of the local clans made a pact to share the town. No one outside of the clans is supposed to know."

Jack dropped his hands from her shoulders. "You can continue storming off now if you want," he sighed. He'd kept his promise.

Without looking at her, Jack turned and walked back to the truck. He climbed in and shut the door. Staring at the steering wheel, he refused to look up and watch her walk away.

The beast inside clawed at Jack's chest. Every instinct inside of him screamed for him to run after her. To put her back in the truck and never let her leave again.

It had to be her choice. Jack tapped his forehead against the wheel. This was absolutely not how he saw this day going.

He bolted upright as the passenger door swung open. Louisa climbed into the truck and shut the door. Jack barely breathed as she buckled her seatbelt.

Furbidden Attraction

"Two-thirds?" She stared straight ahead.

"Two-thirds."

Louisa turned to stare directly into his eyes. Her coffee-brown eyes were somber. "Start the truck, Jack."

Jack reached for the ignition and hesitated. Well, he'd already broken two sacred laws, what was one more?

"In the spirit of honesty... we're on our way to a Blight hive."

"Great," Louisa sighed. "What's a Blight hive?"

"A Blight hive is where Blighted supes live." Jack winced. Rip it off like a bandage. "The Blight are the worst of us. They either allow the curse to take over or they're too weak of mind to control it on their own. They live according to their basic urges, raping, killing, and eating flesh indiscriminately. Once someone goes Blight, there's no going back."

Jack turned in his seat to look at Louisa. She watched him, wide-eyed. Now for the really bad bit.

"The Pact the local clans made also stipulates that all Blight must be put down before they can endanger our existence. Each clan has a member that acts as Executioner in the event that one of theirs goes off the reservation..."

"And you're the Executioner for your clan?" Louisa whispered.

"Yes." Jack turned to stare out the windshield. He couldn't look at her right now. "That's everything, no more secrets. If you choose to go, I won't stop you."

Louisa watched him for a long moment. She chewed her lip before nodding and turning back to the road.

"Start the truck, Jack."

The knot in his chest eased incrementally. He reached for the keys and paused, his hand poised to turn the ignition. He needed to hear it.

"Are we good?" Jack winced at the note of desperation in

his voice, but he was desperate. Desperate to know that she wasn't going to disappear on him.

Louisa turned, her hand snaking out to grab Jack by the back of the neck. She dragged his head down to press her lips against his. Eyes closing, Jack tasted her. The tense set of his shoulders relaxed under Louisa's hands.

She pulled back, her hand landing on the hand still lingering on the keys. The engine roared to life as she twisted his hand.

"We're good."

11

A half hour later, Jack pulled the truck off the road, slipping between two trees in the wide expanse of forest. They rumbled down a narrow path into a small clearing.

Louisa looked around at the shadowy forest. It looked the same in every direction and soon they were going to be trudging through it, the tension between them still sharper than she'd like.

She had forgiven him for trying to lie. Once Jack had dropped the knowledge bomb in her lap, she'd understood. Her presence was putting him in a hell of a position. He was trying to balance protecting his people and making her happy, and she wasn't making it easy on him at all.

Clearly this clan Pact thing was a big deal. Louisa winced. Yes, she had wanted the truth, but she would feel horrible if Jack got himself in trouble to give it to her.

She'd just have to find a way to make it up to him. Probably by taking her pants off; Louisa had a feeling that would be his preference.

Jack killed the engine and turned to look at her.

"We need to disguise you. This—" Jack gestured at her dark curls and caramel skin—"is too memorable."

"Please tell me I get a fake mustache..." Louisa smiled softly.

He snorted. Leaning over and reaching between her knees, Jack shot her a mischievous wink as he flipped open the glove box. A worn baseball cap and a large bottle of air freshener landed in her lap. She held up the bottle quizzically.

"What happened to smelling like a cookie?" Louisa sniffed at the heady scent of artificial flowers. Holy crap, it was strong.

"Your scent is as memorable as your hair." Jack grinned at the silky, black curls springing out of her bun. A single curl ran between his fingers, springing back into place when he released it. "And sadly, this is as close to a fake mustache as you can get for this kind of thing."

He plunked the hat on top of her head and raised the bottle. Louisa winced as the first cloying notes assaulted her nose. The scent rapidly filled the tiny space, enveloping the two of them in a cloud of perfume. Choking beside her, Jack cringed back in his seat with every spritz.

"Are you sure about this?" she coughed. The nauseating mixture of artificial gardens and hairspray burned her nostrils as she choked.

"Trust me, spray enough of this crap, and a supe won't be able to smell anything but Summer Mist for days."

And neither would Louisa at this rate. She sputtered as a poorly aimed spritz caught her mouth, drowning her tastebuds in a wash of bitter chemicals. Gagging, she scrabbled for her door handle.

Jack leaned across her and held the door shut. A glower

creased her face. Forget I'm-Sorry sex; she was going to soak his entire fucking room in Febreze when they got home.

"We can't open any doors or windows until your scent is completely gone," he gasped out.

Every few sprays, Jack would stop and sniff her hesitantly. He wouldn't declare Louisa "properly cloaked" until tears were pouring from both their eyes.

Jack opened his door and leapt out. Bending at the waist, he propped his elbows on his knees and dry-heaved the cloud of air freshener that had settled in his lungs. Louisa scrambled out of the truck and gulped fresh air beside him. At least they were knee-deep in suffering together.

"Okay." Louisa straightened, finally getting a look at the clearing. Frankly, it looked like an endless stretch of identical trees to her. "Where are we going?"

Trees grew in every direction. Thorny-looking bushes grew wild, forcing Louisa to look down at her thin leggings with a wince. The jeans might have been worth the chafing just to avoid a brush with thorns in her nether region.

"*We* are not going anywhere yet." Jack caught her around the waist. Louisa's butt hit the driver's seat before she had time to realize he was moving. "Wait here."

Jack shut the door over her protests. He set off through the woods, his feet landing silently in the heavy brush. Within seconds, she had lost sight of his broad back weaving through the trees.

First he had put this ridiculous hat on her head. Then he had practically drowned her in air freshener, and now she was stuck in the truck, ready to choke to death on it.

"What the hell was the point of dragging me along if I have to stay in the truck?" She smacked her hand on the dash.

Didn't he say that this was supposed to be dangerous?

The only thing Louisa was in danger of was her lungs collapsing under the weight of chemical potpourri.

Minutes ticked by slowly. Louisa kept her eyes on the stretch of trees Jack had disappeared into. Within minutes, her eyes were burning from the fumes. Ten minutes, and her sweaty hair had plastered itself to her face.

Fuck it.

She climbed out of the truck and took a deep breath of untainted air. Stinging eyes blinked, the cool breeze a balm against the burn. Louisa closed the door. She whipped off her hat and used it to fan her sweaty face. Leaning against the side of the truck, her eyes dropped closed as she let the sun shine down on her face. Mmmmm.

An eerie rustling of bushes smashed through her reverie.

"And maybe it's time to get back in the truck," she mumbled under her breath.

Louisa turned around and fumbled for the door handle. Fuuuuuck. The truck was locked. With the keys still hanging in the ignition.

If whatever the hell was out there didn't murder her, Jack would. She glanced around the clearing. There was no way she could stay here in the open. Louisa moved hesitantly away from the truck, shooting longing glances over her shoulder.

What she wouldn't give to be back in that hot, cloying coffin.

"Bad day to wear flats," she grumbled at the uneven ground.

Louisa plodded in the direction Jack had gone. He couldn't have gone too far. Sharp, prickly bushes scratched at her ankles. She grumbled under her breath as she shredded her hands batting them away.

Barely a dozen steps away from the truck and already she could barely discern its shape among the trees. A stick cracked loudly somewhere off to Louisa's left.

This was how the dumb girl always died in the movies.

The fine hairs on the back of her neck prickled uncomfortably. Was someone, or something, watching her? She picked up speed, her feet tripping over the uneven ground. Louisa forced the panic bubbling in her chest to settle. It was just the shadows making her uneasy.

Stumbling even farther into the trees, she jumped at each falling leaf. Jack was nowhere in sight. Louisa stopped dead. What the hell was she doing? She didn't even like camping.

"I am a city girl!" she growled at the looming trees.

Unless she magically stumbled upon a convenience store, she was going to end up wandering in circles until she died of dehydration.

Screw this. Louisa shook her head, disgusted with her helplessness. Drop her in any city and she could adapt. But the wilderness? Fuck the forest; fuck Jack. This city girl was out. She'd take her chances at the truck.

Louisa spun in a circle, a frown blossoming. Wait, which way was the truck?

Trees shadowed her as far as the eye could see. In every single direction. She looked down at the ground. The spongy undergrowth had absorbed her footprints. It seemed even the damn plant life was out to get her.

"Are you fucking kidding me?!" she shouted at the sliver of sky mocking her through the treetops.

A branch rustled behind her. Louisa whirled. A weight slammed into her side, clasping her tightly around the rib cage. She managed a shriek before a hand clapped over her mouth.

"I don't think you understand the meaning of stealth," Jack chuckled in her ear. His arm squeezed her chest, pushing her breasts towards her chin. "And for the record, you were going the wrong way."

Louisa tugged at his sleeve. The hand slid off her mouth, dropping to curl against her collarbone.

"You're an ass," she grouched at him. She leaned back against his chest, her heart still pounding wildly in her chest.

"So you repeatedly tell me." Jack gave her another gentle squeeze. "Why didn't you stay in the truck?"

"I was suffocating in a cloud of Summer Mist."

He sighed. "You could have cracked a window."

Jack spun her around and gripped her arms. All the humor had slipped from his face, leaving behind a grim mask.

"Next time, you will follow orders. I need you to understand how important this is, Louisa," he stressed, his eyes solemn. "If I tell you to stay, or to run, I need to know that you are going to listen. Otherwise, I will leave you at the Den and sort this out on my own. Do you understand?"

The grave expression on Jack's face killed the sassy retort on the edge of her lips. If he thought it was dangerous enough to actually admonish her, she needed to listen. Louisa nodded. A thin tendril of fear curled in her stomach.

Jack pulled her against his chest. Louisa relaxed against him as he pressed his face against her hair. Letting his masculine scent tickle her nose, she closed her eyes and breathed him in. Wrapped in his strong arms, there was no doubt in her mind that she was as safe as she could possibly be.

He leaned back and dropped a kiss on her forehead. Louisa melted into him. So much for her emotional walls.

Jack wasn't so much worming his way around them as he was barreling through.

"Stay close," he murmured.

Arms dropping to his sides, Jack turned and set off into the trees. He was utterly silent as he walked. Twigs bent beneath his careful footsteps; even rustling leaves seemed to still as he passed by. Beside him, Louisa clomped along like an errant toddler. Stealthy, she was not.

Jack kept throwing odd grimaces in her direction as they wove between trees. Twisting to look over her shoulder, Louisa studied the woods apprehensively.

"What is it?" she whispered to him. "You're making me nervous."

"Can you walk a bit more downwind?" He winced.

"What?" Louisa shifted closer to him. "Do you smell something?"

"Yeah, air freshener." Jack coughed. "Seriously, it's making my eyes burn."

Louisa's hands curled into fists. If she thought it would make her feel any better about trudging through the forest from hell, she would've clocked him then and there.

"Well, maybe you should've thought of that before you dumped a whole bottle on me," Louisa growled.

She stomped ahead of him. The warm feelings swirling in her chest refused to budge when she angrily poked at them. Apparently, they were there to stay, no matter how annoying Jack was.

"That's the opposite of downwind," he muttered to himself.

Louisa flashed her middle finger over her shoulder. One more little side comment and she was going to drown his ass in air freshener.

They stumbled out of the trees into a wide clearing. A

dilapidated house crumbled amidst knee-high weeds, the stench of rotting wood floating on the wind.

"Nice place isn't it?" Jack grimaced at the shack.

Louisa studied the building. Shutters hung on broken hinges, every single window appeared to be shattered. Enormous holes in the roof gaped open to the elements. A shiver danced up her spine. Long, winding claw marks trailed along peeling siding.

Every instinct screamed for her to turn and run as fast and as far as her legs could carry her. This was not a good place.

"Do we have to go in there?" She swallowed, her throat suddenly bone dry.

"Unfortunately," Jack sighed behind her. "I've already run the property and checked inside. There's no one here." He gripped Louisa's shoulders and turned her around. "Are you sure you want to do this?"

"No..." Louisa looked between the house and his face. "But I think I need to do it anyway."

"Stay close," he reminded her.

Jack's hands dropped from her shoulders. Wading through the overgrown grass, they closed the distance to the crumbling ruin. The closer they got, the more her skin prickled uncomfortably. Jack stopped in front of a set of crumbling steps. She moved beside him and recoiled.

A sour stench floated from the gaping front door. Louisa bent at the waist, gagging as the odor coated the back of her throat. Goose bumps skittered along her arms as she dry-heaved. She glanced at Jack, standing tall and stoic beside her.

Oh sure, but Febreze he whined about. Louisa shook her head. She should have taken his offer to go back to the truck, or home. Whichever smelled better.

"After you," he said, gesturing gallantly.

"Not a chance in hell." Louisa smiled sweetly.

"Worth a shot."

Jack leapt over the stairs and paused in the doorway, his hand extended. Louisa swallowed thickly. This was undoubtedly the stupidest thing she had ever done. She placed her hand in his.

"For the record, if anything chases us, I will trip you and run away."

"Not if I trip you first." He grinned.

Jack lifted her through the front door. Glancing over his shoulder into the enveloping darkness that waited, Louisa shuddered. She was brave. She could do this. The mantra started to repeat on a loop. Was she brave? Hell yes. Could she do this? Damn straight.

She shadowed Jack as they stepped into the darkness. Slipping his phone from his pocket, he lit the room with the screen.

Decaying floorboards creaked ominously beneath their feet. Exposed insulation poked out of the yellowing wallpaper hanging off the wall in ragged sheets. What was once an ornate, grand staircase rotted across the hall.

With every step, Louisa forced herself to breathe through her mouth. A whiff of peppermint cut the sour odor leeching through her senses.

"Is that... mint?" she took a deeper sniff, prompting a new fit of dry heaving.

Jack rubbed her shoulders, his own nose wrinkling. His arm remained draped over her shoulders as she straightened up.

"I've picked up six different Blight scents so far, but in certain spots there's nothing but the stench of peppermint. It's almost like they're trying to cover someone's scent. That's green magic." He frowned at the decaying room. "I think they might have a witch."

Jack turned his phone toward his face to type a quick update for the Den. He wasn't taking any chances after his first disappearance.

"A witch? An actual, honest-to-god witch?" Louisa asked, shocked. "Alice said they'd been hunted down?"

"Only two bloodlines that we know of were left alive by the end," he said, shooting off a text to Nate. "One was spared because the only surviving members were children, and the other was simply exceptional at covering their tracks."

"And they're doing...what?" She stared at him. "Running around, dousing the Blight in peppermint tea?"

"I don't know." Jack shook his head. "But whoever they are, they're helping cloak someone's scent. Someone doesn't want anyone to know they were here."

Once again, Louisa found herself wondering how she managed to put herself in these situations. Her eyes landed on the broad expanse of Jack's shoulders. Right. This one wasn't such a mystery after all.

Despite her careful steps, her foot punched straight through a particularly nasty stretch of rotten flooring. She pitched sideways, sinking all the way up to her knee. Jack spun at her surprised squeak.

An amused smile lifted the corners of his mouth. He bit his lip to keep his chuckles to himself. If he laughed, she was out. Louisa only had so much patience reserved for this little adventure and it was rapidly running thin.

"Don't," she said sharply. "Just... don't."

Jack mimed zipping his lips. Hooking Louisa under the arms, he lifted her out of the hole. He brushed the molding wood chips off of her leggings, his hands lingering a little too long.

Louisa cleared her throat. He met her raised eyebrow with an unrepentant grin. Grasping her hand, Jack turned and slipped her fingers through his belt loop.

"Try to step where I step," he told her over his shoulder.

They continued their trek through the ruined house, searching each floor room by room, each as dilapidated and neglected as the next. The stench grew more powerful the deeper into the house they ventured, the center of which turned out to be a library on the second floor. It was filled to the brim with damp, molding books and piles of half-eaten animal corpses. After the toe of her shoe squished through the head of a rotting squirrel, Louisa excused herself to vomit her breakfast in the hallway.

"Please tell me we can burn this pit to the ground on our way out?" she asked, wiping her mouth with the back of her hand.

"When the investigation is over, we can come back with torches in hand," Jack assured her. The sooner, the better.

"Can we go now?" Louisa begged.

The house had slowly sucked the warmth from her bones, leaving every inch of her cold and clammy. Louisa's bravery had long ago circled the drain. Now all she wanted was a hot chocolate and a blanket to curl up in.

"Yes." Jack gave the decomposing second floor one final, studying look before turning away.

He lifted Louisa onto his back like a koala, carrying her down the treacherous staircase in the hall. She clung to Jack's shoulders as he carried her towards the front door. From her vantage point on his back, Louisa caught something shining in the corner of her eye.

"Stop." She tapped his shoulder.

He froze in place. Louisa studied the room for the source of the gleam. A mound of shredded insulation and broken furniture stacked against the wall caught her eye.

The whole house was in shambles... so why was this crap pushed to the side?

Louisa wiggled down off Jack's back and picked her way across the room. Jack held his phone higher, illuminating the pile for her. The light reflected off a doorknob poking out from behind a fallen sheet of insulation at the back of the pile.

Louisa waved at the debris. "I think... there's a door behind all of this?"

12

Jack handed Louisa his phone and attacked the pile of junk. Heaving items over his shoulder, he cleared the spot in record time. He stepped back beside Louisa to regard the door.

Compared to the rest of the house, the door was in good condition, a shiny, new doorknob and lock gleaming against the dark wood. And he had completely missed it.

He glanced at Louisa. She eyed the door apprehensively, shifting from foot to foot. Pride swelled in Jack's chest. Lou was doing so well. He had been able to scent the fear and apprehension pouring off of her as they had stood outside regarding the house earlier, and still she had followed him inside without hesitation. His girl wasn't just beautiful and smart, she was courageous as hell.

"What do you think is in there?" Louisa asked him.

"Based on the rest of the house, probably not cleaning supplies."

She snorted. Jack stepped forward and tried the knob. Locked. He twisted his hand, ripping the doorknob and lock out of the door. Lou watched him wide-eyed as he tossed it over his shoulder.

"Well, that answers one question." Jack ripped open the door.

"What question?" she asked, shining the light into the darkness. A set of solid stairs crept down into the dark void.

"Whether the lock was to keep someone out... or to keep something in."

Louisa shoved his shoulder.

"Are you kidding me right now?" She stared at Jack like he was a simpleton. "You don't say shit like that right before you go skipping off into a creepy basement."

She shook her head.

"I've seen this movie," she muttered under her breath. "He is definitely going to get eaten."

Jack chuckled as he took the first few steps down. He slipped the phone from her hand and shined it down the stairs.

"Stay here," he ordered without looking back.

Jack ghosted down the stairs, his feet silent on the creaking wood. A maelstrom of scents assaulted his nose the further he walked. Humans, shifters, ghoul, Blight, and was that...wolf?. What the hell were they keeping down here?

He stepped off the bottom stair onto a stone floor. Holding the phone above his head, he lit the room. Rows of large, metal cells lined the stone walls. The fuck?

Jack moved closer to the nearest cell and doubled over, gagging. The stench of fear filled every corner of the room, coating his throat in a sour film. He pinched his nose. He'd been around the Blight long enough not to be affected by the scent of wrongness that poured off of them, but this... this was evil.

He reached out and brushed his fingertips against the

metal bars. A hiss whistled between his teeth. Jack looked down at his skin. Raw blisters dotted his fingers where the metal had destroyed his skin cells.

"Some kind of silver composite," Jack murmured, careful not to brush against them.

He walked the room, peeking in each cell. The cells were identical to the last; stone floor and back wall, metal bars on three sides. Not even enough room to lie down. Was this where the missing women had been kept?

He growled under his breath. Until Jack could get ahold of some of their possessions, he couldn't compare scents to confirm. More questions, and not enough answers to go around.

A soft thud sounded from the top of the stairs. He looked up at the ceiling. Louisa. Jack spun and leapt toward the stairs. As his feet ate up the distance, he heard a voice. Was she...singing?

"This house is really scary," Louisa murmured in a singsongy voice as she took a few steps down the staircase. "I'm probably going to die here. Which would really suuuuuck."

Jack doubled in silent laughter as Louisa continued inching down the stairs, singing nervously with each tentative step.

"I'm getting really tired of the dark," she sang. "I'd really like to go home nooooow."

He could hear the rapid staccato of her heart from the bottom of the stairs. Oh no. Jack bound up the stairs and out of the shadows. Louisa clapped a hand over her mouth as a small squeak escaped.

"That's the opposite of staying upstairs, you know," he said, smiling at her.

Louisa lunged forward and wrapped her arms around

his waist. His arms closed around her shaking body. Shit, she really was terrified.

"It's okay," Jack murmured. "Everything's fine."

They stood in the middle of the hellish staircase, holding each other. Jack pressed his face into her hair. The sweet scent of her curls chased away the lingering odor of fear from the cages below.

Louisa weakly smacked her balled up fist against his chest. She mumbled into his shirt. Leaning back, he looked at her face.

"Hmm?"

"Don't. Do. That. Again." She glowered at him.

Jack tugged on a curl. So fierce.

"No promises." He gave it another tug.

Louisa smacked his hand away and stepped out of his arms. Jack sighed. Already, he missed the warm scent floating off her skin. He turned back toward the darkness.

"It's okay." He squeezed her hand. "There's no one down here."

Jack placed her small hand on his shoulder. Louisa's fingers fisted in his shirt as they stepped back into the shadows. Cringing at his back, she shrank closer until her breasts were grazing his shoulder blades.

Jack swallowed a groan. Now was definitely not a good time to be aroused; he needed all the blood in his brain to stay exactly where it was.

"Jack...I can't see in the dark?" she whispered in his ear.

"Whoops." Jack whipped out the phone he had hastily stuffed in his pocket. The screen lit up, illuminating the steps in front of them. They shuffled back down the staircase.

Louisa stared around the room, her eyes round. Her face paled as she studied the cells lining the walls.

"Are those...cages?" she whispered into his shirt.

"Yes." Jack slipped his hand around hers. It was ice against his palm. "The bars contain silver. They were made to trap supes."

Louisa stepped forward, her hand slipping out of his. Jack's breath hitched in his chest as she stepped into a cell. Every instinct roared for him to throw her over his shoulder and get the hell out of there.

She studied the stone walls. Scratches crisscrossed over the back wall as though someone had tried to claw their way out. Pressing her fingertips to the wall, Louisa lined her hand up with the claw marks.

"Jack?"

He stepped into the cell behind her, the silver making his skin tingle as he passed through the door.

"I think that's a fingernail," she whispered, her face turning gray.

Jack leaned over her shoulder. A torn fingernail jutted out of a divot, the end stained brown with blood. It was painted a delicate pink.

Wrapping his arm around Louisa's waist, he nudged her behind him. Connor needed to see this. Jack fished a Ziploc bag out of his pocket and pulled at his magic until razor sharp claws extended from his fingers. He carefully gripped the torn nail between his claws and tugged it from the wall. Jack dropped it into the bag as his stomach churned.

Human. The blood smelled human.

Jack stepped out of the cell, Louisa shadowing his steps. He moved into the center of the room and closed his eyes. Inhaling deeply, he let the scents flood him.

A cacophony of smells swirled through his senses. Sixteen humans, four wolves, six ghouls, and three shifters. All female. And Blight. So many Blight, drenched in their sour stench, that he almost couldn't tell how many there were. Six, maybe seven? And the faintest hint of... peppermint.

"They weren't just caging supes," Jack growled. He glowered at the dark room. "There were over a dozen humans in here at one point."

"Why?" Louisa asked. "Why take anyone at all?"

"Any other time, I'd say the Blight took them for food... and other things." He winced. "But the cages? They don't have the capability for that kind of rational thought. The curse erodes their control until they're less than animals."

Jack fisted his fingers in his hair. A dull ache was settling in his head. Somehow, he knew that he'd been here before. He'd seen this already. No how matter how hard he concentrated, he couldn't bring the memory forward.

"I have no idea what they're doing." Jack sighed, dropping his fists to his sides. "But there are four unmated wolf scents in this room. If someone is taking wolves, they're either desperate or stupid."

"Unmated?"

"Wolves have mates. It's sort of an extra whammy in their part of the curse. They each have one person that is destined to be their other half," Jack answered distractedly.

"That sounds kind of nice," Louisa murmured.

"It's not. Imagine every other relationship feeling unnatural until you find your mate. A lot of them never manage to find theirs at all."

"I take it back." She winced. "That sounds awful."

"It is. That's why it's part of their punishment for starting the fight that got us all cursed in the first place."

"What's the other part?" She shivered.

Jack sighed. "They turn into giant werewolf killing machines."

"Riiiiight." Louisa nodded slowly. "And that's why taking wolves is such a big deal."

"Yes. Wolves prize family above all. They are pack creatures, and their packs contain dozens of families. If even one of theirs went missing, a call would go out to every Wolf pack across the nation to be on alert. And when they find the person responsible..." Jack surveyed the room, his glower growing darker. "Four wolves? That's unheard of."

There was no reason for the Blight to keep one person in their basement, let alone several dozen. They lacked the control not to just kill them outright and eat the bodies. Whatever was happening was bad, very bad. Jack sighed. And now he'd have to involve the wolves *AND* the ghouls, as if this weren't complicated enough.

Louisa shivered. "We should go." She pressed closer to him. "This place is making my skin crawl."

Placing his hand on her lower back, he led her toward the stairs. They jogged up the stairs and out the door. The light of the afternoon sun warmed their faces.

The faintest breath of a familiar scent drifted across Jack's senses. He spun in a circle, studying the overgrown yard. Sniffing the wind, Jack picked up nothing. Surely, he'd just imagined it? There was no reason for *him* to be anywhere near here.

"How long were we in there?" Louisa asked, her eyes closed as the sun shone brightly on her face. One eye cracked open at his silence. "What's wrong?"

"I thought I smelled something," Jack sniffed at the breeze.

"What is it?" Louisa gave the ruins a queasy look. "We're not going back in there, right?"

Her face was utterly gray. So much for taking care of her.

Day one and he had dragged her into a hell house and shown her what the worst of his kind were capable of.

"No, we're not." Jack's stomach growled. "And we missed lunch."

He tugged the bottom of his shirt up. "Can you see my ribcage yet? I can feel myself wasting away."

Louisa nodded gravely, her brown eyes regaining their wicked twinkle.

"You poor thing." She patted his arm sympathetically. "Are you strong enough to make it back to the truck, or will I need to carry you?"

Jack dropped his shirt. "I shall endure," he huffed dramatically.

The knot in his chest loosened at the sound of her giggle. The dark look in her eyes had begun to worry him. He'd tell Nate about picking up Carter's scent when they got home. No reason to worry Lou. They trudged through the trees, hand in hand.

Louisa stared off into the woods, her thoughts wandering. Jack watched her from the corner of his eye. The sunlight slipped through the trees, lighting up bronze strands hidden in her dark curls.

Trudging through that pit of evil with her had been tolerable, if not even a little enjoyable. And Louisa had handled it better than some supes he knew. She belonged here, in this world. Now all he had to do was make her see it.

Jack turned to her as they entered the clearing with the truck. "Toss me the keys."

Louisa froze. "Keys?" she asked innocently. Jack eyed her suspiciously.

"The keys?" He repeated slowly. "That we will use to start the truck?"

Furbidden Attraction

She cleared her throat. "I believe you left them in the ignition."

Jack watched her shift nervously from foot to foot. What in the world was she up to? He crossed to the truck and tugged on the door handle. No. No fucking way.

"Please tell me you didn't." Jack turned to her, eyes wide.

"I didn't *not* lock the keys in the truck," she hedged. Louisa nibbled at her lip.

Jack closed his eyes and leaned his forehead against the glass. Gently banging his head against the window, he counted down from ten. He would be calm. He would *not* yell. Forcing the breath out from his nose, Jack opened his eyes and straightened up.

Only one thing to do.

"Right," he sighed. "Rip it off like a BAND-AID."

Jack wrapped his hand in the hem of his T-shirt. He raised his fist and slammed it through the glass. Louisa jumped back as small pieces of glass rained down at their feet. Reaching through the window, Jack popped the lock.

He opened the door and swept off his seat. Jack stepped back, his mouth set in a tight line. Silent, he gestured for her to climb in.

Louisa slipped past him and clambered into the truck. It was a good thing it was Lou who had made him hurt his baby. If anyone else had locked the keys in the truck, they'd be walking home.

Jack climbed in and slammed the door. The engine roared as they backed down the road. After twenty minutes of him silently glowering at the road, Louisa cracked.

"I'm really sorry," she yelled over the wind howling through the cab.

Jack raised a hand to silence her. No, he wasn't ready.

"It's too soon," he grumbled. "I need more time to mourn."

Louisa blinked. "Mourn a window?"

Jack continued his quiet stare. Women. He wasn't ready to be friendly yet; he was too busy calculating the cost of a new window.

Wind blew through the cab, twisting and tangling Louisa's hair. She spit another curl out of her mouth. Jack's cap still sat firmly on her head, doing absolutely nothing to stop the barrage.

Louisa smiled beside him. Her small smile turned into a quiet giggle that Jack's sensitive ears just barely picked up over the wind. Giggles turning into all-out laughter, she buried her face in her hands.

Jack looked at her, askance. Seriously? She was laughing? He'd just shattered a window out of a truck that was his pride and joy and she was *laughing?*

"I'm sorry," she gasped out. "But at least we can't smell the air freshener anymore."

"You're not sorry," Jack sniffed. "You did this on purpose."

Louisa choked on her laughter. "On purpose?"

He nodded. "This was revenge for the air freshener." He turned to her, his face stone-cold. "You're jealous of our love."

"Jealous... of the truck?" she snickered.

"I get it. I'm a desirable man." Jack stroked the steering wheel. "But you'll never be able to come between us."

When she burst out laughing, he patted the dashboard and cooed sweet nothings. Poor baby. "She doesn't mean it," he whispered. Jack pointedly ignored her as she howled with laughter.

Furbidden Attraction

"I'm so sorry," Louisa said, unable to hide her grin. "I had no idea your affection ran so deep."

Shaking her head, she reached over and tucked his hand in hers. Her slender fingers squeezed his. Jack struggled to hide his own creeping smile. Her soft palm felt right at home against his calloused hand.

"Damn right, woman," Jack growled. He tightened his hand in hers. She rolled her eyes at him and returned the squeeze.

13

Jack winked at Louisa as he pulled into the drive-thru. The breath caught in her throat. Fuck, he was good looking. Louisa had convinced herself in the Blight house that she was becoming immune to his charms, but apparently it only took one cheeky wink to set her on fire.

Louisa fanned herself while he studied the menu through the broken window. His face was twisted in single-minded concentration, all trace of humor replaced by a solemn mask. She could respect that; food was life. The late afternoon sun lit the golden stubble on Jack's jaw from behind. She caught the moan trying to fight its way free.

The only thing keeping her from ripping at his clothes was her self-control. Louisa had no doubt that if she said the word, Jack would tear out of this drive-thru and find a deserted parking lot where he could bend her over the truck bench and help her out with the ache between her legs. But he was hungry; well, so was Louisa if she were being honest, and that would just be selfish.

Not that Jack would give a damn, based on the erection

he had been sporting just that morning. Heat pooled in her belly as she remembered the way he been grinding against her. No, Louisa could control herself, damn it. She was a grown ass woman, with bills and everything.

Jack turned away from the menu. "What would you like?"

She stared at him in horror. Could he read minds? Did he know that the only thing she was considering on the menu was between his legs?

"What?"

"To eat? What do you want to order?" Jack wrinkled his brow.

"Oh, right." Louisa flushed. Maybe an asteroid would drop from the sky and take her out, right here and now. No such luck. She sighed. "A cheeseburger and fries, with lemonade."

Jack turned back to the speaker and placed her order followed by his own order for a veritable mountain of food. Louisa eyed him suspiciously. How the hell did he eat that much and still have abs that could cut glass? Magic. It had to be magic.

He jerked back as he caught sight of her narrow-eyed scrutiny. "What?"

"How are you possibly going to eat all that?" she laughed. "That's like four people's worth of food. You can't possibly be that hungry!"

The tips of his ears turned bright red. He mumbled something indecipherable under his breath. Louisa poked him in the ribcage.

"I was worried you didn't order enough." Jack rubbed at the back of his neck, his ears flaming bright red. "I didn't want you to be hungry."

Louisa stared at him. Clearing her throat, she turned away.

"Thank you," she whispered. Louisa fixed her eyes straight ahead. Her eyes prickled uncomfortably. She wasn't going to cry, damn it.

Her entire childhood had been spent in the foster care system, bouncing from home to home. Maybe the system worked for some kids and they ended up in warm, friendly homes, but Louisa hadn't. Each one had been a special hell unique unto itself. And not in a single one had anyone ever worried whether Louisa had had enough to eat.

Not even her exes had cared all that much. If anything, they complained that she ate too much, not understanding that her deep appreciation of food had come from her constant worry as a child about where the next meal would come from. Certainly, none of them would go out of their to way order her extra just in case.

Jack pulled forward to collect their food, chatting amiably with the guy in the window. A small smile spread across Louisa's face as she blinked away her welling eyes. Yes, he was handsome, but Jack was also kind and thoughtful and a lot of other things that she was still discovering.

Pulling out into the road, he placed the bags of food between them and fished for a handful of fries. Louisa giggled as he tried to jam a fistful into his mouth at once. Stealing a few of her own, she liberated the fries and passed them to him, one at a time.

Jack pulled off the road beside a stretch of shady trees and parked the truck. Grabbing all the bags in his arms, he hopped out of the truck. Louisa scrambled after him. The tailgate dropped with a thump. Jack hopped up on the end and dropped the bags by his hip. He patted the spot beside him.

Two embarrassing attempts later, Louisa sat next to him as he tore open the food. Her legs dangled in the breeze. After the hellish morning spent trudging through the Blight house, it was nice to sit out in the sunshine. The charming man beside her, picking her out the choicest French fries, probably had something to do with it.

Stuffed with food, Louisa lay back and watched clouds drift by. What a weird day. Even in her wildest dreams, she never could have imagined spending the day exploring a creepy, demon house with a hot man who grew fur and could probably smell every perfume she'd ever used on her skin.

Which reminded her...

"Hey, what did you smell?" Louisa asked, turning her head to stare at the back of Jack's head.

"What?" Jack mumbled around a bite of burger.

"When we were leaving, you looked really tense." She sat up and folded her legs in a pretzel. "You never said what it was that you smelled."

"I'm not even sure it was really there." Jack shook his head. "It was just a flash."

Louisa tossed a balled-up napkin at him. "What. Was. It?"

He sighed. "My brother."

She stared at him. Jack had a brother? She wasn't quite sure what was worse, that he had a brother who was potentially skulking around a den of unhinged monsters... or that she didn't even know he had a brother.

Suddenly, the overwhelming knowledge that she knew next to nothing about the man beside her cracked Louisa over the head. She'd made out with him and she didn't even know his last name. Or what he did for a living. Or how old he was.

"I haven't seen him in two years," Jack said, interrupting Louisa's internal panic. "We don't get along."

"Then how can you be sure it was him?"

"Scents never really change that much. You can change your hair products and your laundry detergent, but the base scent? The bit that's who you are—that doesn't change much."

"You said you barely picked it up? Are you sure that's even what it was?"

"No," Jack growled.

Louisa could feel the waves of frustration pouring off of him. Her hand moved of its own accord, settling on his back. Jack leaned into her touch, his muscles relaxing against her palm.

"Why don't you get along?" Louisa asked, leaning her head against his shoulder.

"I don't get along with any of my family." A dark look crossed over his face.

"Why not?" she pressed. If Louisa had family, she'd be damn sure to make it work, whether they "got along" or not. Some things shouldn't be tossed aside so lightly.

"Nothing in common," Jack said vaguely. "What about you? Do you get along with your family?"

The reminder of their brief acquaintance still ringing in her head, she made a noncommittal noise under her breath. If he wasn't ready to unpack that kind of baggage, neither was she.

Jack ignored her evasive noise, lost in his own worries. Clearly his brother's unlikely presence was bothering him more than he let on.

He crumpled up their empty wrappers and tossed them

in a bag. Hopping out of the back of the truck, he offered Louisa his hand. She put her hand in his and let Jack lift her off the tailgate.

They drove home in silence, Jack's somber mood filling the cab. Louisa's uneasiness grew. Somehow, this big adventure of theirs was becoming alarmingly bigger. Ghouls? Wolves? Just how much more of this could she take?

His hand left the wheel and scooped up Louisa's. She looked down at their entwined hands as her mind eased. Turning to look at the trees whipping by, she gave her head the faintest shake.

She was amazed at how easily he could drive back the shadows creeping in her mind. A lifetime of trust issues screamed for Louisa to run and with a squeeze of his hand, Jack had her smiling.

She liked him, she realized. Not just to look at. Louisa shot him a sideways look from behind long lashes. Of course, his looks didn't hurt either. This would never work, she sighed.

Oh god, work. She hadn't even thought about work since this whole shit storm had started. And she wasn't sad about it at all. Louisa was unsettled. Who the hell was she becoming... or maybe she was just finally realizing who she'd always been?

Jack pulled the truck into the garage. Crossing to her side, he scooped her out of her seat and set her carefully on the ground. They lingered for a moment, his hands hugging her hips. Today had been both one of the worst and the best days of Louisa's life.

"I need to update Nate," Jack said against her hair.

"Right." Louisa stepped back. "I'll wait... in the kitchen?"

"I'll walk you up there." Jack threaded his fingers

through hers, a growing habit that she had no intention of putting a stop to.

Jack deposited her in the kitchen along with a stern warning not to wander. Yeah, talk about wasted breath. She had no urge to get tackled across the lawn again.

Louisa took a seat at the long, wooden table dominating half the room. She looked around the room, not really sure what to do. What she wouldn't give to have her phone back. Louisa tapped her fingers against the worn wood.

Alice breezed into the room, her head in a book. She stumbled around the kitchen opening cabinets, her eyes firmly glued to the page.

"Hi, Alice."

She jumped, her book clutched to her chest. Eyes wide behind her glasses, Alice looked around the room. Her eyes lit on Louisa. Clearly, situational awareness wasn't one of her super-human skills.

"How long have you been sitting there?"

"Since you walked in." Louisa smiled kindly at her.

"Oh..." Alice snagged a pink box out of a cabinet filled with cleaning supplies. She crossed to Louisa and folded herself into a chair. Flipping open the box, Alice nudged it across the table. "Cookie?"

"Sure." Louisa fished a chocolate chip cookie the size of a small dinner plate out of the box. Hot damn, now *that* was a cookie. "Why do you keep your cookies with the oven cleaner?" she asked curiously.

"Because the savages will eat them all if I leave them somewhere easy to find." Alice paused her chewing and sniffed, her nostrils flaring. "Did you bathe in fabric softener?"

Louisa sighed. God damn him.

"It's Febreze." She glared forlornly at her cookie. "Jack was trying to hide my scent."

"Well, he succeeded." Alice giggled. "Why did he need you to smell like... I wanna say hibiscus and hairspray?"

"He took me to a Blight house." Louisa winced. "Though it didn't do much to make a dent in the stench coming off that hole."

Alice straightened in her chair, her half-eaten cookie forgotten in her hand.

"Jack took you to a Blight hive?" Her eyes gleamed with excitement.

"Yeah, it was awful."

"I've only been inside one once." A shadow passed over Alice's face. "I was sick for a week after. The smell—" She shuddered. "It took me days before I could smell properly again."

"If I never step foot in there again, it will still be too soon."

Alice grinned at her. "Your second day in our world and you're already Nancy Drew-ing your way through a Blight hive. You don't do things halfway, do you?"

Louisa laughed. "I guess not."

Nibbling at her cookie, Alice watched her. "So what else did you and Jack do today?"

She winced. "Well, I locked the keys in his truck and Jack had to bust out a window and then he bought me lunch."

Alice dropped her cookie. She grabbed Louisa's wrist.

"Jack had to break the window? On his truck?"

"Yeeees," Louisa said slowly, tugging at her captive wrist.

Alice ignored her attempts at freedom. "And then he bought you lunch? Jack? Who loves his truck with a passion that everyone else finds disturbing? *Jack?*"

"Yep."

Alice dropped her wrist. She stared, her gray eyes round as quarters.

"Jack would've murdered anyone else." She shook her head. "Either he's in love with you or his little trauma caused more than memory loss. Insanity, maybe?"

"Maybe it knocked a new personality into him?" Louisa snorted.

"Or a little common sense," Alice mumbled under her breath. "No one should love a truck that much. It's a truck."

Louisa giggled. It was nice to have someone to talk to. Frankly, Raven Falls had been feeling lonely as hell since she'd moved. Of course, now that she knew that two-thirds of the town was made up of supernatural creatures in hiding, it made a bit more sense.

"Louisa." Alice's face sobered. "If you decide that you're ready to go home, I'll take you. No matter what anyone else says."

"Thank you." Louisa patted her hand. "But I don't think I'm quite ready for that yet. I want to see how this all plays out."

Alice stood, collecting her box of giant cookies.

"The offer is there should you need it," she told her as she left the kitchen.

Louisa appreciated it, she did. But she wasn't quite ready to say goodbye to this new world. Or to the green-eyed man who was dragging her through it.

14

Jack left Nate's office two hours later. The whole investigation was still a mysterious void in his pounding skull, and listening to Nate dissect every detail of the Blight house for hours had made the throbbing that much worse.

Of course, that was after Nate had yelled himself hoarse when Jack had informed him that he'd told Louisa about the Raven Falls Pact. He'd promised Jack a suitable punishment, which might or might not include outright death. He had zoned out of the lecture shortly before that bit.

All he wanted was to drop into bed and sleep for a week. The comforting smell of roasting chicken floated down the hallway. Jack inhaled, his eyes dropping closed. Mmmm. Maybe he could grab a plate and eat in his room before passing out. Louisa would probably prefer that to a giant dinner with the whole Den.

Jack's eyes snapped open. Louisa—oh, fuck. He'd left her in the kitchen hours ago. Setting off for the kitchen at a run, he silently berated himself.

How could he have forgotten her like that? Lou was

going to be pissed off enough without the entire Den converging on her. Jack was going to have to make it up to her. Was he above groveling? Reflecting on the passionate kiss they had shared last night, Jack decided that no, he was definitely not above groveling for forgiveness.

Bursting into the kitchen, he pulled up short. Sandwiched between Dorothea and Agnes at the kitchen island, Louisa chopped vegetables, a smile on her face. Oh no—maybe he could back out slowly? The three women blinked as Jack skidded to a stop. Nope, too late.

"Uh...hi?"

Louisa giggled as the two older women gave him stern looks. He swallowed nervously. Lou was flanked by two frowning lionesses and she was *smiling*.

"Dot and Agnes are teaching me how to cook." Her smile wilted a bit. "It's not going well. I've been demoted to chopping."

"I told you, call us Aunt Dot and Aunt Aggie. Everyone does." Dot patted her hand. "And you're doing just fine, dear."

Agnes's glare was still focused in Jack's direction. He squirmed under her flat, yellow gaze. He always felt like a disobedient toddler in the Aunts' presence.

"We were quite surprised to find your Louisa twiddling her thumbs in our kitchen," Agnes said flatly. "It's a pity we weren't introduced to her earlier."

Jack winced. Oh yeah, they were in fine form today.

Dorothea added her own yellow stare to the collective.

"Yes, a pity."

Jack sighed. "I was getting around to it, ladies." Lie. Total lie. He would rather eat glass than watch Louisa team up with the old cats.

Furbidden Attraction

"Am I doing this right?" Louisa interrupted, staring in dismay at her mismatched chunks of vegetables.

"Try to cut them a little more evenly, dear." Agnes lovingly tucked an errant curl behind Louisa's ear. "Such a delightful girl."

Oh god. They were already bonding with her.

The wrinkled sisters loved mothering each creature that passed their way, much to the chagrin of the less-friendly members of the clan. Not that that deterred the Aunts. From the moment they'd shown up unannounced at the Den two years ago, Dot and Agnes had managed to browbeat every single resident into begrudgingly accepting their unwanted affection.

Nate had been no help whatsoever. Whatever the Aunts had said to him when they strolled into his office off the street must have been pretty damn convincing. The two old ladies had grabbed their bags and made themselves at home in an empty bedroom.

Jack growled a warning. The interfering old bats were pushing their luck. He was not in the mood for this.

The women ignored his growls and kept right on cooking.

Agnes shot him a wink over Lou's shoulder.

"She's been such a help." Dot smiled, her eyes crinkling. The calculating gleam in her dark eyes, combined with her flyaway white hair, gave her the look of an evil dandelion. "I hope you stay a while longer, dear. Cooking for all of our little monsters can be so taxing. It would be nice to have another set of hands."

Agnes shot a narrowed-eyed warning in Jack's direction when he snorted. The dotty old hags had once gone on strike for three days because they had considered Alice's offer to help with Sunday brunch an affront to their honor.

"I should be here a few more days at least." Louisa smiled at her. Turning her attention to Jack, she asked, "How did the meeting go?"

A handful of people flooded through the door as Jack opened his mouth to answer. "Not great," he said shortly.

Connor sauntered up to the island and snagged a chunk of carrot. Dot made a move to smack his fingers, but he blurred, avoiding the sting of her palm.

"If it isn't my favorite old crones." Connor grinned at them. "What's for dinner?"

"Nothing, if you don't go set the table, you insufferable child." Agnes shook her head, her white braid stark against her walnut-brown skin. "That goes for all of you."

Connor backed away, snagging a stack of plates off the edge of the counter.

"Mean old dinosaurs," he muttered as he turned away.

"No appreciation," Dot sighed.

"None," Agnes agreed.

"Maybe they should cook for themselves for a few days..."

The kitchen erupted into a flurry of motion as everyone scrambled to gather plates and cutlery. Within minutes, the banquet table on the other side of the kitchen had been decked out for dinner.

"Oh, look at that," Dot deadpanned. "I guess the little monsters are hungry."

Louisa chuckled. Dot and Agnes exchanged quick looks. The scheming set to their dark, wrinkled faces made Jack uneasy.

"Jack, dear, why don't you and Louisa go get settled at the table." Aunt Aggie nudged Louisa in his direction. "We've got it from here."

"Are you sure?" Louisa looked between them.

Furbidden Attraction

"Oh yes, dear." Dot shot Louisa's mangled vegetables a sideways glance. "You're a guest after all."

Jack gripped her elbow and steered her to the table.

"It's best not to argue with them," he whispered in Lou's ear. "It's like screaming into a rampaging tornado."

"I gathered that when they started interrogating me over an hour ago," she giggled back.

Jack winced and pulled out a chair for her. Nosy cats.

The kitchen broke down into quiet conversations as everyone took their seats. Alice waved at Louisa from the other end of the table. Abby came skipping into the kitchen, her tiny hand clutching Nate's.

"Ms. Louisa!" she shrieked in delight. "Daddy, can I sit by Ms. Louisa?"

Nate scanned the table, eyes lighting on Jack and Louisa. Jack gave a small nod. Anything to take her attention away from the Aunts.

"Yes, you may." He led her to the empty chair beside Louisa and lifted her up. "Be polite. Best manners, okay?" Nate added seriously.

"Okay, Daddy." Abby nodded, her face just as serious. Her face brightened as she turned to Louisa. "Hi, Ms. Louisa!"

"Hello, Abby." Lou smiled back at the shining face.

Nate dropped into the chair beside his daughter, shaking his head. He closed his eyes, enjoying the reprieve from Abby's boundless energy, at least for a little while.

Dot and Agnes appeared, laden down with platters of food. They arranged piles of food up and down the table before taking the empty seats across from Jack and Louisa. He nearly groaned.

Everyone dug in, scooping piles of roasted chicken and potatoes onto their plates. Abby chatted, waving her hands animatedly as she shoveled food into her mouth. Lou nodded along silently, an amused smile on her face.

The Aunts watched her like birds of prey circling an unsuspecting rodent.

"Louisa, dear, you are so good with children," Dot said proudly.

She blinked at the sudden interruption. "Thank you?"

"So is Jack, of course." Agnes nodded. "He adores little Abigail."

His eyes narrowed. So that was their play.

"Butt out, cat," he hissed almost silently, knowing their enhanced hearing would pick it up.

Dot glared at him as she chewed a bite of chicken.

"You two make the most lovely couple," Agnes added.

Yep, he was going to die alone. Louisa stared open-mouthed at the sisters. Those seated around them were falling silent to watch the disaster unfold.

"I suppose," Louisa said hesitantly. She shot Jack a desperate look. He hurriedly glanced around the table, his eyes falling on Connor and Alice. The Aunts would need just the right nudge...

He turned to Alice who was laughing into her plate.

Help me, Jack mouthed down the table.

Fuck. No, she mouthed back.

Jack widened his eyes, begging for an assist. Looking pointedly at Louisa, he folded his hands in a silent prayer.

Please?

Her gaze flickered to Louisa. Alice's eyes softened for a second before she threw a glare in his direction. Nodding slowly, she waved him on.

"I think this chicken might be a bit dry," Jack loudly announced.

Furbidden Attraction

The Aunts turned in unison to glare daggers at him. All conversation died as everyone stared in horror.

"You know, I couldn't quite put my finger on it earlier," Alice drawled as she poked at her plate. "But Jack nailed it. Bone. Dry."

The two old ladies sputtered indignantly. A grin spread across Connor's face. As one of the most outspoken opponents to the Aunts' unwanted meddling, he predictably wouldn't be able to pass up the opportunity to pile on.

Jack casually reached behind Louisa and nudged Abby's chair back a few feet. Just in case.

"Maybe tomorrow we should order pizza." Connor sighed at his plate. "If you're feeling a bit off your game, ya know?"

Dot and Aggie hissed in unison.

"How dare you!" Dot screeched.

"Utterly ungrateful!" Agnes howled.

Nate stood up, his hands held out peacefully. He stepped in front of Abby's chair, shielding her from the angry old cats. Not that anyone would lay a whisker on the kid. Nobody here was that stupid.

"I'm sure they didn't mean anything by it," Nate soothed.

"I did," Connor smirked. "Maybe old age is slowing them down?"

The table exploded in an uproar as Agnes hurled her chair at Connor. Jack grabbed Louisa's hand and snagged the back of Abby's overalls. He dragged them across the kitchen, setting Abby on a stool at the kitchen island.

Jack darted back into the fray and snagged two plates. Dropping one in front of Abby, he kissed the top of her pigtails.

"Sorry, kiddo. We've got to go." Jack watched her dig into her food with a supernatural abandon. She ignored the wrestling match and screams echoing in the kitchen as she speared chicken into her mouth.

Jack handed the second plate to the horrified Louisa. His hand at the small of her back, he pushed her toward the door.

"Night, Ms. Louisa!" Abby waved goodbye with her fork.

Louisa was silent all the way up to Jack's bedroom. As soon as the door clicked shut behind them, she turned to him.

"What the fuck?" Lou hissed. "What. The. Fuck?!"

Jack winced. "Sorry, about that. We needed a quick exit and I couldn't think of anything better."

"She threw a chair!" She stared at him, wild-eyed. "The old lady THREW A CHAIR!"

"Yeah, Aunt Aggie gets a bit excitable." Jack took the clattering plate from her shaking hands. "That's why I moved Abby to the island. No one there would ever hurt her, but I didn't want her accidentally getting squished by flying furniture."

Lou stared at him. "Does this type of thing happen often?"

He shrugged. "Once a week, maybe?"

"You're all insane," Louisa breathed.

It took Jack a half an hour to calm her down enough to get her to finish dinner. The poor thing was so exhausted, she fell asleep before he had even tugged the plate from her hand.

Stripping his clothes, Jack shifted to his animal form. He jumped up on the bed and curled around Louisa. Giving her cheek a quick lick, he whined softly. He'd started a riot for her and he hadn't even gotten a bedtime kiss. Jack sighed. Maybe tomorrow.

. . .

LOUISA WOKE WITH A START. Jack shook her shoulder gently. Staring at him with bleary eyes, she was disappointed to note that he was fully dressed. Damn.

"We need to get going early today." Jack tugged on one of her curls. "We have an appointment to keep."

She buried her head under the pillow. "Go away."

"Out of bed, little sloth." He swatted her butt.

Louisa sputtered as she swung the pillow at him. Laughing, Jack danced out of her reach.

"You'll have to get up if you want to hit me." He grinned at her.

Louisa pushed herself upright. "I hate you." She scrubbed a hand over her crusty eyes and glared at his disgusting perkiness.

"Caffeine, get me caffeine."

Jack snapped her a salute and darted close to plant a quick peck on her cheek. She swung the pillow. He laughed his way down the hall.

Louisa pressed her fingers against her cheek. It tingled softly where his lips had brushed. Tired *and* turned on. Awesome.

Twenty minutes later, she was buckled into Jack's truck, an enormous, sloshing canteen of coffee clutched to her chest. When her man delivered, he *delivered*.

They drove in silence until Louisa had downed half of her bucket of coffee.

"Where are we going?" she yawned at Jack.

"Connor hunted down our Good Samaritan teens and found out where they picked me up." He snagged her canteen and stole a sip. "We're meeting him there to take a look around."

"We couldn't have done that after breakfast?" Louisa

yanked her coffee away and curled it possessively in her arms.

Jack dug around under his seat and pulled out a Tupperware container. He yanked off the lid and dropped it in her lap.

"The Aunts send their regards," he said drily.

Louisa blanched at the rows of buttery Danishes.

"They're not poisoned, right?" She gave one a suspicious poke.

Jack laughed. "No, they're not too happy with me, but I'm pretty sure they've informally adopted you as their own. If anything, the Aunts are preparing to secretly poison Connor or Alice."

"Eh." Louisa scooped one out and took a bite. She moaned. "Worth the risk."

When they rolled up besides Connor's patrol car miles outside of town, Louisa was still brushing crumbs off of her shirt. Stupid, perfectly flaky pastries.

Jack helped her out of the truck and took her hand. Connor rolled his eyes at their entwined fingers, his badge glinting on his tidy uniform. Louisa calmly flipped him the bird. She still hadn't quite forgiven him for that bullshit about eating her.

"Precious," he deadpanned.

Jack rolled his eyes and started sniffing. Pulling Louisa along behind him, he led them down the road.

"Here." Jack stopped at a patch of pavement identical to the stretch beside it.

"You're sure?" She raised an eyebrow.

"It's what he does, human." Connor scoffed at her.

Louisa stared coldly at him. "You're an exceedingly unpleasant man."

"Shhh." Jack shushed them. "It's rained, but there's still a faint trace."

He sniffed and zigzagged down the road, pulling away from Louisa and Connor. Great, she was stuck with the antisocial moron while her maybe-boyfriend sniffed his way to the scene of the crime.

"So...what do you turn into?" Louisa asked.

"None of your business." Connor stared straight ahead.

"He's a parrot," Jack called over his shoulder.

"Dude!"

She snickered. "A parrot? Really?"

"Shut up." Connor gritted his teeth.

"No wonder you didn't want to say." Louisa smirked at him. Served the jerk right. A parrot, ha.

"We should have left you passed out in your apartment," he growled quietly, so that Jack wouldn't overhear.

"And I should have hit you harder with that wrench," Louisa whispered back. "I guess we all make mistakes."

Jack veered off the road ahead of them and vaulted over the guardrail. Connor and Louisa watched him slide down the embankment and walk into the trees.

"Seriously?" She groaned. Why didn't anyone pack her some damn hiking boots?

"Feel free to stay here, *human*." Connor launched himself over the rail, landing lightly on his toes at the bottom of the slope. He stood at the bottom, his smirk challenging.

I hope he gets dirt on his pretty, little uniform.

Louisa carefully boosted herself over the guardrail and said a prayer as she shuffled slowly down the hill. She walked right past him, flipping him off again over her shoulder.

"Keep up, Birdbrain."

Louisa heard him chuckle quietly over her shoulder. Oh yeah, she was winning. Resisting the urge to fist-pump, she jogged after Jack.

He crouched at the edge of a narrow dirt road. Jack straightened as they walked up beside him.

"The trail ends here," he nodded at the stretch of dirt. "I'm guessing I jumped out of a car."

"Or someone threw you out," Louisa muttered.

Connor and Jack turned to her, eyebrows raised. Heat flooded her cheeks. Whoops, shifter hearing.

"I'm just saying, he's... you know?"

Connor started laughing at Jack's bewildered expression.

"I like her," he announced, clapping Jack on the shoulder. Connor turned and walked back toward their vehicles, leaving them beside the road.

"I'm what, exactly?" Jack sputtered.

Louisa tugged at her curls. "You're just a bit difficult, is all. Especially as a dog."

"Difficult? *I'M* difficult?" Jack shook his head. He turned back to the road, muttering under his breath. "Multiple escape attempts, sassing everyone in the vicinity, bashing interlopers over the head with tools, but yeah, *I'M* difficult."

"I mean... I like you anyways?"

"You're the worst," he grumbled, rising to his feet.

Louisa grinned at him. "And *you* like me anyways."

"Somebody's confident." He rolled his eyes. "Come on, let's get back to the truck."

Jack gripped her hand and led them through the trees. Louisa smiled at the trees towering over them. This was much more pleasant than her last stroll through the forest.

Jack wrapped an arm around her waist and carried her up the embankment. He lifted her carefully over the rail and hopped over beside her. His phone rang, cutting through the quiet morning, as they walked back to the truck.

Louisa leaned against the patrol car beside Connor while Jack finished his conversation. She glanced at his stoic face under her lashes.

"So... a parrot?" Louisa forced herself not to smile. "Like a big parrot? Or a parakeet?"

Connor glowered at the gravel under their feet. "Big parrot. Blue and yellow macaw."

"Oh, cool cool. Coooool."

"No, I will not show you," he sighed.

Louisa held up her hands and took a step back. "Hey, man. No one said anything about showing off their 'big parrot.' Keep that shit in your pants."

Connor laughed, his wide shoulders shaking. "Maybe he didn't choose terribly, after all."

Tucking his phone into his pocket, Jack jogged over to them. He eyed them suspiciously.

"Do I want to know what you two are cackling about?"

Louisa and Connor exchanged a look. "Nope."

Jack shook his head at them. "I have a quick work thing to take care of," he told her. "Would you rather have Connor drop you off at the Den or do you want to come with me?"

"Thanks for volunteering me." Connor rolled his eyes.

"And get struck by association when the Aunts murder him?" Louisa laughed. "No, thanks. You're stuck with me, pal."

Louisa took his hand and headed toward the truck. Ride an hour back to the monster hut with Grouchy Pants when she could be sneaking kisses with Jack? Pass.

"Later, Feathers!" she called over her shoulder.

Jack laughed as his angry curses followed them

15

Jack led Louisa up the steps of a two-story colonial. Studying the front porch, Louisa looked around while Jack flipped through his work keys.

"Why are we breaking into someone's house?" she asked him.

"We're not breaking in. One of these keys should fit." Jack rattled the ring of keys in his hand. "We're on a tight deadline, and the client changed his mind about the doorknob style, and now I have to run around and collect the old ones so the crew can go straight to installing the new ones tomorrow."

Louisa wrinkled her brow as he fit a key in the lock. Jack wiggled it around and frowned when it refused to turn. Damn it, he really need a better system for marking these things.

"I'm sorry, but what exactly is your job?"

"I own a construction company," he mumbled as he flipped through the keys. "This is a remodel we're working on."

"How did everything keep running when you disappeared?"

"Nate." Jack opened the door. Success! "He does most of my paperwork anyways, so it wasn't a huge stretch for him."

He tugged her through the door and nudged it shut. Louisa froze in the entryway and turned in a slow circle. Her mouth gaped open as she studied the room. Jack shifted nervously.

"Wow...you did all this?" Louisa waved her hands at the glowing wood floors and ornate wainscoting.

Jack felt his ears flush pink. "Uh, I designed it. And I did the bathrooms, but my crew did most of the rest."

She beamed at him. "You're *really* good. This is...amazing."

The rest of his face burned as hot as his ears. "Thanks," he mumbled.

Jack darted through the house, removing a pile of doorknobs while Louisa shadowed behind him, admiring the rest of the house. Peeking under his eyelashes, he snuck quick glances at her awed face.

Her breathy "oohs" and "ahhs" were driving him up a wall. Jack was one "ooh" away from pushing her up against a wall and really giving her something to lose her breath over.

"Can I help with anything?" she asked, popping up over his shoulder.

Jack gritted his teeth as her scent washed over him. He was dying a slow, agonizing death.

"Can you drag the box a little closer?" Jack grunted.

"Sure." Louisa bent over the box of doorknobs and scooted it toward him. The shoulder of her sweater drooped lower, giving him a clear view of her breasts hugged tight in her bright pink, lacy bra.

In a rush, all the blood whooshed out of Jack's brain.

The screwdriver in his hand clattered to the floor. Louisa glanced up at the sound. Her lips parted as she caught sight of the hungry look in his eye. The tip of her pink tongue slipped out, wetting her lips. A new scent swirled between them, a mix of Louisa's sweetness combining with her arousal.

Jack's brain short-circuited as the scent fried his senses. Before she could blink, he was across the room, his hands catching her hips. Fingers weaving through his hair, Louisa dragged his lips to her mouth for a crushing kiss. They swayed on the spot, mouths pressed desperately against each other.

She pulled back. Jack groaned. He didn't want it to stop, not this time. Dark lashes fluttered against his cheek as Louisa leaned in. Thank god; Jack had been waiting for this since the day he'd met her. Her pink lips brushed the length of his mouth and his mind went blank.

His groin ignited as she traced the corner of his mouth along the length of his jaw. The tip of Louisa's tongue painted tiny circles down Jack's neck. His dick surged painfully against the zipper of his pants.

Large hands traced along the curve of her hips to cup the generous ass he'd been admiring for days. Louisa groaned against his ear. A satisfied, masculine growl rumbled from his chest.

Spots danced in Jack's eyes as his erection tested the limits of his jeans. He gripped Louisa's ass and lifted her to him. Slim legs locked around his hips.

He spun and pressed her into the wall. She rolled her hips, grinding herself against the hard bulge between them. Jack moaned. He was pretty sure the pressure in his dick was going to kill him, but damn, what a way to go.

"Don't stop," he groaned into her hair.

"I couldn't if I tried," Louisa panted, her white teeth flashing in a grin.

He buried his face in her hair, inhaling Louisa's sweet scent as she greedily rubbed against him. The soft, feminine sound of her groans set his skin on fire. He need more. Jack needed to feel her. To taste her.

His lips pressed against her neck. His tongue brushed her skin. He nearly groaned when the first salty-sweet notes hit his tongue. Better than he could have imagined.

Suckling gently on her skin, Jack nibbled his way down her throat. He gently nipped her collarbone with the edge of his teeth.

Louisa moaned. Her fingers released their tight grip on Jack's hair and trailed down his spine. The light touches made his skin prickle with flames of pleasure. Fingers hooking under the hem, she tugged his shirt up his chest.

Jack leaned back, his hips pinning her to the wall. He dragged the T-shirt over his head and tossed it to the side. Stroking the planes of his chest, Louisa's fingernails dragged lightly across Jack's nipples. Molten heat raced behind her touches, the pressure steadily building. How the hell was she doing that?

"Fuck, it's like you're carved out of marble," she groaned.

Jack ground his hips harder between her legs. He had something marble for her, alright. The painful erection between his legs was hard as steel. Another wave of Louisa's sweet arousal washed over him. He was fucking drowning in the lusty scent.

Louisa's head dropped back against the wall. His eyes traced the graceful line of her neck down to the hint of cleavage poking out her sweater. The neck of her sweater teased even lower as she gasped for air. Jack needed to see her. Now.

"Take your sweater off," he growled, his hands kneading her ass.

She leaned away and tried to wiggle out it. Grasping the collar of Louisa's sweater, Jack tore it down the middle. The pieces fluttered to the ground at their feet. Whoops.

"Hey!" Louisa yanked a lock of his hair. "I liked that sweater," she growled at him.

"I'll buy you a new one." Jack planted a quick kiss on her swollen lips.

He groaned as his eyes dropped to the swell of her breasts peeking from behind pink lace. His sweet Lou had been built to torture him, every inch of her curvy body designed to bring him to his knees.

Seizing the edge of the lace, Jack jerked one cup down. Louisa's breast sprung out. Caramel skin stretched tight over her pert breasts. Tipped with delicate brown nipples, they were no bigger than a handful. Jack palmed her breast, the curve fitting perfectly in his hand, exactly as he'd imagined so many times.

Jack swallowed Louisa's surprised squeak. He traced along the seam of her mouth with his tongue, teasing at her lips. Their tongues danced in rhythm as his rough thumb swept across her sensitive nipple. Back arching, she pressed her breast into his palm.

"Yes," Louisa gasped against his mouth.

"You're so beautiful," Jack whispered in her ear, his hips rolling in tight circles.

She reached between them. Her hands trailed down his abs and slipped beneath the waistband of his pants. Jack's eyes rolled back as her soft fingertips brushed the root of his swollen cock.

Louisa grinned as he growled into her shoulder. Saucy little temptress.

Jack couldn't wait any longer. Crossing the room, he clutched Louisa to his chest. Her teeth nipped at his throat, sending fiery waves through his core.

Jack grabbed the large roll of carpet leaning against the wall and dragged it to the floor with one hand. Laying her back against the carpet, Jack paused to look at Louisa.

Fuck, she was so much better than he ever could have imagined. And he'd imagined this moment quite a bit over the last few days, every image in his head paling in comparison to the reality.

Louisa's breasts heaved as she panted, her bra still askew. Jack's eyes trailed down her body, her flat, honey-colored stretch of belly flaring into wide hips encased in black leggings.

He growled and yanked the leggings down her slim legs. Much better.

"Don't rip those," Louisa giggled.

Jack blinked at the dark curls between her legs. She wasn't wearing any panties. He swallowed the lump in his throat. Wide green eyes met her smiling brown ones.

Louisa blushed pink, squirming under his gaze. "You didn't pack me any underwear."

"You've been running around for two days without panties?" he groaned.

"Yes?"

Black crept along Jack's vision. His knuckles whitened against his clenched fists. Control was rapidly slipping from his grasp. He was a hairsbreadth from flipping Louisa onto her knees and burying himself between her legs.

No, he shook his head. Not before he'd tasted her. Jack had been aching to bury his face between her legs since that first clumsy, seductive escape attempt on the front lawn.

He lowered himself to cover Louisa's slim, curvy body.

Her legs widened to frame his hips. Louisa's hands worked at the button of his jeans as Jack kissed the small freckles peppering her shoulders.

He paused, his eyes softening as he caught sight of the pink flush on her heart shaped face. Sipping at her lips, he kissed her long and slow. Jack nipped at Louisa's kiss-swollen lips, reveling in the taste that was so uniquely hers. Fifty years from now, he would still remember the way Louisa's sweet taste flowed across his tongue.

Dropping fluttering kisses down her collarbone, Jack tasted his way down her body. He nibbled at the curve of her hip, his hands dropping beneath her to squeeze her round ass.

"What are you doing?" she asked, raising her head.

"Tasting you," Jack grinned.

Her eyes widened. "No one's ever done that before."

A growl rumbled in Jack's chest. He was going to be the first. He might not be her first lover, but he would get to be first at something. And her last, if he had anything say about it.

Kisses trailed down her thighs. Jack gripped her knees and spread her further apart. He groaned against Louisa's thigh as waves of her arousal flooded his senses. She squirmed against him in anticipation.

His tongue traced along her inner thighs, inching closer and closer. A quiet whimper squeaked from her throat as the distance closed. Jack nudged her legs over his shoulders and lifted her hips. He met Louisa's gleaming brown eyes with a grin and lowered his mouth.

. . .

HOLY FUCKING FUCK. Louisa arched off the carpet as Jack's tongue met her aching pussy. Forget the shifter bullshit; his mouth was the real magic.

He lapped at the wetness pooling between her legs. Louisa's bits had been damp since she'd first watched him bend over and start fiddling with those doorknobs. She'd been silently groaning every time those damn jeans had stretched tight, cupping his muscular ass.

Soft tendrils of heat blossomed where Jack's mouth brushed. Tight pleasure built in her belly. His thumbs pushed forward, gently pulling her folds further apart.

Oh god. Louisa's hands slid down her belly to fist in Jack's short hair. She mentally cursed herself. Why hadn't they been doing this the whole damn time?

His tongue dipped inside of her, tasting her wet heat. Jack raised his head and met her eyes as he slid one thick finger into her core. Louisa moaned. Her body pulsed around him. A second finger joined the first, thrusting gently.

Jack watched her face, his green eyes glowing with wild power. A third finger pushed inside, stretching Louisa to her limits. Groaning, her head dropped back as his rough hands rubbed against every tiny, deliciously sensitive spot inside of her.

A quiet voice in the back of her mind reminded her that this was probably a terrible idea. Louisa didn't care. Even if it was the worst mistake she ever made in her life, it would be well worth it. She closed her eyes and let the swells of bliss drag her under.

Her head swam as Jack's tongue traced teasing circles around her clit. Louisa's hips bucked. He held her hips in place, his hand on her belly. Ecstasy swelled, setting her on fire from head to toe.

Furbidden Attraction

The pressure built until Louisa was squirming in his hands. She wasn't sure how much more torture she could take. The pulsing ache in her pussy was dancing on the edge of pain.

Louisa gripped his hair tighter. The desperate whimper streaming from her throat grew in volume. Jack chuckled against her sensitive flesh.

"Jack," she groaned.

Fuck it, I'll do it myself. One hand unwound from his hair and drifted between her legs. Jack caught Louisa's hand and placed a light kiss on the inside of her wrist.

"No." He nipped at her fingertips.

His head dropped back between her legs. Jack sucked her clit and the universe exploded.

Her pussy clenched around his fingers as he gently coaxed the orgasm from her. Louisa panted, her heart hammering in her chest. Towering waves crashed through her. Jack kissed his way back up her writhing body, her muscles relaxing under his lips.

"I think you're going to have to take your own pants off," Louisa gasped, her body still drowning in aftershocks. "I don't think I can move yet."

Jack laughed into her shoulder. He dropped a kiss on the curve of her neck and shifted back to drag his jeans down his legs.

Louisa raised her head and let it thump back against the carpet. "Nope."

"Nope?" He arched a brow.

She shook her head. "*That* is not going to fit."

There was no way in hell Jack's dick was going to fit inside of her. To say the man was blessed was a gross understatement. Admittedly, her sexual experiences were limited, but Louisa was pretty sure perfect cocks didn't exist in nature.

"Do you trust me?"

Louisa bit her lip. Damn it. "Yes."

Jack hooked his hands behind her knees and dragged her closer. He stroked the sensitive bud of her clit with his rough thumb. Circling his cock, he pumped his hand once before feeding the first inch into her slit.

She groaned as the faint twinge from being stretched mixed with the pleasure coiling in her belly. Jack dropped soft kisses along her collarbone as he thrust gently, feeding inch after inch into her wet heat. She wiggled her hips, pulling him deeper inside.

"Good girl," he groaned against her ear. "Take all of me."

He captured Louisa's nipple, drawing it into his mouth. She arched up as Jack nipped the sensitive nub with his teeth. Turning his attention to the other nipple, he buried himself deep.

Jack stilled at her sharp inhale. He searched her face carefully. "Okay?"

Louisa twined her legs around his waist, pushing him in a little deeper. "Yes."

His hips rolled. Louisa gasped as every inch of him stroked her walls. She arched her hips to meet his thrusts, taking him even deeper. He growled, his chest vibrating against hers. The wild glow was back in his eyes.

Louisa swiveled her hips, her hands dropping to clutch his ass. Jack pumped faster. His thrusts lost their polished edge as he drove into her again and again.

"Yeeesss," she moaned. "Don't stop."

His mouth met hers in a fervent kiss. Jack swallowed her moans, his hips hammering between hers.

The storm building in her center swelled. Their eyes

met and Louisa shattered. Ecstasy roared through her as her scream echoed through the empty house. Her pussy pulsed, muscles tightening around his cock.

Jack groaned and bucked faster. His body shook under Louisa's hands as he came. Warmth flooded her core as he rocked gently, drawing the last convulsions from them both.

Her body weaker than a melted marshmallow, Louisa lay beneath his warm weight, his cock still buried inside of her. They lay there together, spent and tangled.

Jack carefully rolled them over, slipping from between her legs. Louisa winced at the emptiness. Well, he'd fit alright, but she was pretty sure her vagina was never going to be the same again. She curled on his chest, his hand stroking her hair.

Had that really just happened? Did she really just have sex with Jack, shapeshifting, carved-from-marble, JACK? Louisa didn't know whether to groan or high-five herself.

That had been a really bad idea. How was she going to walk away when this was over if he was going to destroy her like that? *Could* she even walk away anymore?

Louisa hated to admit it, but he had wormed his way through her admittedly impressive walls and set up camp. She wasn't sure exactly what the scary tangle of emotions in her chest meant, but she knew that she had inched past "like" quite some time ago.

Jack sighed into her hair. "You're silently freaking out, aren't you?"

"Yeeeessss," Louisa groaned, scrubbing her palms over her face. "I just had hot sex with the guy who kidnapped me. That's like the first rule of getting kidnapped: don't get attached to the kidnapper!"

"Are you still on that?" He tightened his arms around her. "I thought we were past the whole 'kidnapping' thing?"

Louisa laughed into his shoulder. "Did you just finger quote the word kidnap? As though it was subjective?"

"I just think that 'kidnap' is a little harsh." Jack stroked the length of her spine, his hand coming to rest on her ass cheek. "And frankly, since I gave you multiple orgasms, I think I should be forgiven."

She snorted. "Of course you do."

"Besides, it's not like you're having sex with any of your other 'kidnappers,' right?"

Connor and Alice's faces flitted through her mind. Yeah, definitely not.

Jack grinned at her wrinkled nose. "See? So you didn't have hot sex with your kidnapper, you had hot sex with *me*."

"You are literally the worst," Louisa huffed. Damn it if he hadn't just killed all her concerns with a laugh and some questionable reasoning. Apparently, his superpowers included soothing her anxiety *and* providing earth-shattering orgasms.

His face sobered. "In all seriousness, you know that you're allowed to walk away at any point, right?"

Louisa face softened at the earnest concern in his eyes. "I know." She kissed him gently on the lips. "Alice already told me that she would take me home when I was ready."

A phone rang, cutting through their warm glow.

"Damn it," Jack groaned against her ear and rolled her onto her back.

He rolled to the side, his arms flailing as he misjudged the height. Jack dropped to the ground with a thump. Louisa giggled into her hands.

Jack's head popped up beside her, a cross look darkening his face. He struggled to his feet, grumbling as he pushed himself upright. He picked up his abandoned jeans and fished through the pockets. Rescuing his wailing phone, Jack held it to his ear.

Louisa propped her chin on her elbow and watched him pace the room. Something was definitely wrong. The good natured scowl that had blessed Jack's face was gone, replaced by a blank mask.

"I'll be there tonight," he finished, ending the call.

Louisa pushed herself up. A prickle rolled down her butt to the backs of her thighs. Ow. She stood and glanced over her shoulder. Pale pink streaks ran down her caramel skin. Louisa glared at the rolled up carpet.

"We need to go," Jack called as he pulled his jeans up his legs.

Louisa tore her eyes away from the marks on her ass. The blank mask was long gone, now replaced with brow-wrinkling worry.

"What's wrong?" She fished through the scattered clothes for her leggings.

"A body just turned up at the morgue." Jack pulled his shirt over his head. "My contact says it looks like an animal attack."

"Why do you care about an animal attack?" she asked as she held up the shreds of her sweater. "We're surrounded by woods; they can't be all that uncommon. Also, I hope you have an extra shirt in the truck."

He yanked his shirt off and tossed it to her. She slipped his shirt over her head, a small smile lighting her lips as it draped over her like a tent. Jack sat down and shoved his feet into his boots. He paused and scrubbed a hand through his hair.

"They're not," he finally said. "But they're pretty sure that it's one of the women who went missing."

"So…we're heading to the morgue?" Louisa's stomach rolled.

She could handle wolfmen and people who turned into animals. She was even prepared for vampires. But a dead body? Louisa was pretty sure that danced pretty close to her "Nope" line.

"No, I need to go back to the Den and report to Nate," Jack said, offering her his hand. "Tonight, we're visiting the morgue."

"Oh good. I was worried it wouldn't be unsettling enough in the daylight," Louisa sighed.

Jack laughed as he locked the door behind him.

16

An hour later, and Louisa still wasn't sure how she felt about their earlier tryst... or visiting a corpse. And quite frankly, after those orgasms, the corpse felt like the more alarming issue.

She was prepared, so it wasn't like it was something she would just stumble upon. But did she really want that in her nightmares?

Louisa shook her head. She'd been going back and forth the whole car ride home. Even now, perched on a squishy armchair outside of Nathan's office, she wasn't sure if she should tap out.

Louisa shot a glance at the office Jack had disappeared into. Twenty minutes, and she hadn't heard a peep through the heavy, wooden door. Her leg tapped as she forced herself not to jump up and press her ear to the door, straining for any sound.

Stretching her legs, she stood up and paced. Her stomach growled audibly, seemingly deafening in the quiet stretch of hall. Even Louisa's stomach agreed; she needed chocolate to settle her mind. Maybe she could find the kitchen?

She snorted. Yeah, right. She couldn't even find the garage Jack had led her from just a few minutes ago. The place was a damn maze.

A small shadow came whipping around the corner and crashed into Louisa's knees. Her arms windmilled as she struggled to remain upright. What the hell?

A dark headed little girl lay sprawled across the ground. Abby and Louisa stared at each other in shock.

"Are you okay?" Louisa asked, hooking her hands beneath Abby's skinny arms.

Louisa propped her upright and straightened her little polka-dot dress.

"I'm okay," Abby squeaked back.

As Louisa opened her mouth, Alice came tearing around the corner, eyes wild. She skidded to a stop in front of them and glared at the small shape now attempting to hide herself behind Louisa's knees.

"Not cool!" Alice growled, pointing a finger at the small face.

"Is everything okay?" Louisa asked, puzzled.

"*Somebody* wanted to skip their history lesson today and decided to glue the pages of a priceless history of the clan to make sure it wouldn't happen."

"Oh," she breathed. "That is not good."

"Mr. Connor said it was okay!" Abby's small voice squeaked behind her.

"Mr. Connor also said that it was okay to replace all the sugar with salt. Mr. Connor also said that it was okay to put fake spiders in the cookie jar. *Mr. Connor* also said that it was okay to steal all of my left shoes," Alice hissed, her face as

Furbidden Attraction

red as her hair. "And what happened when you did all of those things?"

"I lost my TV priviges," she sighed.

"Privileges," Louisa whispered.

"Right, privileges."

"And what do you think you're going to lose this time?"

"Uh..." her eyes flicked from side to side, no doubt hunting for some means of escape.

"Maybe I should go?" Louisa said, stepping hesitantly to the side.

"No, please stay," Alice growled, her eyes never leaving the little polka-dotted body. "Your presence will keep me from getting rid of Abigail once and for all."

Alice met Louisa's wide eyes, her own shining with rage.

"It was a *very* important book," she explained.

Abigail inched backward. Eyeing her like the owl she housed inside of her, Alice lunged forward and snagged her by the arm.

Abby shrieked like a banshee and kicked at her ankles. Louisa stood a few feet back, frozen in shock at the scuffle in front of her. These people were so weird.

The office door flew open. Alice and Abby froze beside her in a tangle of limbs. Jack and Nathan leaned out the doorway, scanning the hall for danger. Their eyes widened simultaneously as they caught sight of the brawl taking place on what looked to be a very expensive rug.

"Alice...why are you wrestling with my five-year-old?" Nate rumbled.

Alice straightened and dropped Abigail in front of her. She trembled with barely controlled rage.

"Ask. Her," she hissed.

The men turned their eyes to the little girl shifting from

foot to foot. Her lip poked out, trembling pitifully. Abby sniffed back tears.

"Stop faking and just tell me what you did this time," Nate sighed.

Abby straightened her tiny shoulders, her sniffle disappearing in a flash.

"I didn't want to have history today." She glowered at Alice.

"And...?" Jack prompted, his lip trembling as he struggled not to laugh.

"And...I glued Ms. Alice's history book."

Nate stared at his daughter with a hopeless expression. Louisa met Jack's eye over his shoulder and forced herself not to giggle. She could imagine the emotions running through Nathan at the moment. Anger, astonishment, a little bit of pride.

Hell, she'd had only known the kid for a day, and even she was a little proud of her ingenuity. Where does a five-year-old even get that much glue?

Finally, Nate broke the silence.

"You've already lost your TV privileges..." He looked sternly at her. "I think the dessert privileges should be the next to go—"

Abby's jaw dropped in shock.

"But...but," she sputtered indignantly.

"For two weeks," Nate finished with grave finality.

Her tiny shoulders slumped dramatically.

"And we will be discussing your actions tonight," Nate added as he stepped back into his office. "Oh, and Alice?"

Her red head snapped to attention.

"Bring me Connor."

Alice smiled maliciously and stalked down the hall. She

moved gracefully, her limbs gliding like a silent predator on the hunt.

"In one piece, Alice!" Nathan called at her retreating back. "One piece!"

Nate closed his office door, leaving Louisa and Jack with his defeated daughter.

"So... did you glue every single page?" Jack asked curiously.

Abby looked up, the mischievous glint back in her eye. She nodded.

"You're lucky Alice didn't make a rug out of your furry little hide," he laughed.

"You guys are so weird," Louisa said, voicing the thought that had been bouncing around her head since this whole adventure had begun.

"Why does Ms. Louisa smell like you, Uncle Jack?" Abby looked curiously between them.

"Uh..." Jack glanced at Louisa in alarm.

Oh, hell no. She was *not* explaining the birds and the bees to a baby. Louisa liked Jack, sure. But she would never like him that much.

"Um... I used his shampoo earlier," Louisa stalled. "That's probably it."

"No, that's not it." Abby shook her head.

"So, two weeks without dessert?" Jack interrupted loudly. "That's a bummer."

"Yeah," Abby sighed. "Wait—"

Jack and Louisa exchanged nervous glances. Please don't ask about sex, please, dear god, do not ask about sex.

"You promised me ice cream!" Abby moaned.

Louisa sighed in relief. Close, too close.

"I guess it will have to wait until after your punishment," Jack said sadly.

"But... can't we have it now?" she pleaded.

He crouched in front of Abby, his eyes serious.

"Your dad is the Alpha," he said firmly. "We have to follow his rules."

Her tiny face scowled. Abby's foot began to tap as she thought through her options.

"Daddy said no dessert, not no sweets. But it's not dessert time, right? Dessert comes after dinner." Abby's nose wrinkled. "And since we haven't had dinner yet, it wouldn't count as dessert!"

Her face brightened as she reasoned proudly. Jack's gaping mouth snapped shut with a click. He turned to Louisa, raising his hands imploringly.

"Don't look at me," Louisa smirked. "This one is on you."

"I can't argue with this kind of logic." Jack shook his head. "She's going to rule the world before she reaches puberty."

Louisa snorted. "You just want ice cream."

Jack ignored her and turned back to Abby. He studied her seriously, his arms crossed over his chest.

"Alright," he sighed. "You've won me over with your foolproof argument."

Abby shrieked in delight. She hurtled across the hall and launched herself into his arms. He kissed her cheek and lifted her to balance on his shoulder.

"To the car!" Jack cried dramatically.

"To the car!" Abby echoed in her own high-pitched squeak.

Louisa followed behind them, shaking her head as they skipped along.

"You're such a sucker," she sighed at his back. "Nate is gonna be pissed."

"I'll explain it to him." Jack waved his hand. "He'll

understand. Frankly, he'll probably be thrilled that she has a promising future as a lawyer."

"Oh, and what about Alice?"

Jack's face blanched. He glanced quickly around and picked up his pace. Abigail bobbed on his shoulder, her small hands clutching the sides of his head for balance. They were so cute, it was slowly killing Louisa and her ovaries.

"Yeah, we'd better move faster," he flinched. "She might actually maim us."

"I believe she called the book 'priceless,' " Louisa informed him bemusedly.

"Did I say maim? I meant kill," he winced.

She giggled, shaking her head behind them all the way to the car.

Jack led them to an unfamiliar black sedan and opened the door so that Abby could scramble into the back.

"Car seat," Jack explained as they climbed in.

Louisa nodded, the car backing out of the garage.

THE DRIVE PASSED QUICKLY as they all sang along to the radio, Abby's squeaky voice soaring above their own on the chorus. Jack parked down the street from the ice cream shop.

Abby skipped between them, hanging off their arms like a tiny, polka-dotted monkey. They swung her back and forth, laughing down the street.

Warmth flooded Jack's chest. They were just like any little family, walking around on a sunny afternoon, stopping for a some ice cream. He liked this. Jack glanced at Louisa's laughing face. He liked this a lot.

They ordered their ice cream, Jack and Abby appropriately wrinkling their noses at Louisa's choice of black licorice. Yuck.

They settled into a booth and dipped their spoons. Small, satisfied noises were the only sounds breaking the silence for the first few minutes as the sweetness hit their tongues.

"Soooo... Uncle Jack." Abby stabbed her spoon into her scoop of strawberry. "When are you and Ms. Louisa going to have babies?"

Jack choked on his ice cream. Louisa thumped him on the back as he violently coughed. Where the hell had that come from?

"Who said anything about babies?" he finally choked out.

"There aren't any kids in the Den besides me," Abby said sadly. "I want baby friends. And you like Ms. Louisa, don't you?"

Louisa put her hand over her mouth, hiding a smile. Of course she thought this was funny. She wasn't being interrogated by a kindergartner.

"I do like Ms. Louisa," Jack said slowly. "But—"

"Good, then she can be Aunt Louisa, and you can have pretty babies." Abigail nodded decisively. "Would they turn into little bears?"

Her question drew an eyebrow raise from Louisa. He nodded subtly. Yes, Abby and Nate were bears. She shook her head.

"No." Jack sighed, defeated. "My babies will be puppies like me."

Abigail pursed her lips in thought.

"I'm okay with that." She nodded slowly.

He snorted. "I'm glad to hear it."

"So when are you going to have puppies?" Abby

questioned.

Jack's face burned. Someday, she would bring her prom date home and he would kindly remind her of this moment before enacting swift vengeance.

"How about we take our ice cream outside and walk around a bit?" Louisa interrupted.

"Yes," Jack said gratefully.

Strolling in the sunshine, he wished that he could shake Abby's questions from his mind. Would Louisa stick around when this was all over? He wanted her to. Jack knew that with more surety than he knew his own name. She needed to be in his life, smiling and laughing and brightening everything with that sharp wit.

Did she want that? Did she want him and the unexpected future that would come with it? And would Louisa even want his babies, knowing that they would shift into little, fluffy puppies?

But what beautiful babies they would be. Jack could see them in his head, clear as day. Dark curls springing all over their little heads, her chocolatey brown eyes smiling up at him. Oh, he could picture them all right. He just didn't know if Louisa could.

What if she didn't even want kids? Could he live without them as long as he had her?

Jack's stomach cramped as he worried himself in circles. When the girls stopped to throw away their empty cups, he threw his away half-eaten. The ice cream had soured on his tongue.

"Can we enjoy the sun for a bit longer?" Louisa turned her face into the warmth.

"Sure," he said distractedly.

They strolled along the sidewalk under the warmth of

the afternoon sun. A bead of sweat rolled down his back. It wasn't that hot.

Jack glanced around uneasily. The delicate hair at the back of his neck stood on end. He tensed, his hand tightening around Abby's.

Beside him, Abigail growled softly. She looked around, scanning shadows just like he was. Someone, or something, was watching them.

Louisa looked at the two of them, her brow wrinkled in confusion. The ominous feeling had yet to hit her weaker human senses.

Abby practically vibrated with tension between them. She looked up at Jack, her eyes wide and glowing a vibrant blue. Shit. She was going to shift.

"We need to get to the car," he told Louisa quietly.

She nodded. She might not be able to tell exactly what was wrong, but the worried energy pouring off the two of them was palpable.

They picked up their pace, Abby sandwiched between them. Jack scanned their surroundings, looking for anything that might be alarming his senses. He inhaled deeply. Nothing. Every few paces he inhaled again.

Abby moved gracefully, her knees bent low to the ground. The predator inside of her was on high alert and mere seconds from bursting out of her skin.

Jack unlocked the car. The girls scrambled into the front passenger seat. He took one last deep inhale and froze.

There was something familiar... again. But why would Carter be here of all places? This was miles outside of his preferred neighborhood.

"Uh, Jack?" Louisa called from inside the safety of the car.

He climbed into the driver's seat and locked the doors.

Her limbs shaking as she struggled for control, Abigail hunched in Louisa's lap. Louisa stroked her hair, her brown eyes worried.

"Can you hold it until we get home?" he asked Abby softly.

"I don't think so." Sweat dripped down her pale face.

"Go ahead and shift, but be careful," Jack warned. "Ms. Louisa doesn't heal like we do, so you need to watch your claws."

Abby nodded and closed her eyes.

"Won't people see her?" Louisa whispered as fur sprouted along Abby's arms and legs.

"Tinted windows." Jack watched her shift. "Nate had them installed for this very reason. It's harder to control the animal when you're as young as she is."

Louisa stroked shaking fingertips over the fluffy head propped on her arm. In a flash, Abby had completed her change and a small, brown bear cub lay curled, exhausted in her lap.

"She's beautiful," Louisa whispered and cuddled her closer. "What kind of bear is she?"

Abby sneezed and tucked her fuzzy nose into Louisa's elbow. She closed her eyes and settled in for a nap.

"North American Grizzly." Jack petted her furry head.

He smiled at the look of wonder on Louisa's face. Up until now, the only shift she had seen had been his terrifying change into half-form and Alice's unsettling shift to human.

Jack started the car and pulled onto the street. It wasn't until they pulled into the Den's garage that he remembered the scent he had picked up by the car. Why was Carter following him?

17

"It's not funny!" Louisa shouted into the pillows.

Jack's lips trembled as he forced his laughter down. Balancing the bottle on his knee, he squeezed another dollop of aloe into his hand.

"I can tell you're laughing," she growled.

"I would never." Jack grinned at the back of her head.

He looked down at the red, painful patches on Louisa's bare ass. Her face buried in pillows in despair, she lay flopped across the bed. He rubbed aloe onto the abused skin in gentle, sticky circles. He studied her butt with an appraising eye. Even marked up, it was a great ass.

Louisa mumbled into her pillow fort.

"What was that?" Jack lifted the edge of a pillow off her head.

"My butt is ruined." She glared at him. "All because of you and those damn dimples."

"You have carpet burn on your ass…because I have dimples?"

"Yes!" Louisa growled and jerked the pillow back down.

"You and your stupid, sexy dimples and 'come hither' looks have ruined my ass."

His shoulders shook with silent laughter. She was too precious.

"Stop laughing!"

" 'Come hither' looks?" he asked innocently.

Louisa turned on her side and whacked him across the head with a pillow liberated from her pile. The pillow smacked into him again and again as he dissolved into howls of laughter.

"Your supernatural sexual magnetism has scarred my ass forever!"

"Your butt is not scarred," he choked. "It's just a little carpet burn."

"When your butt is burning, you can have an opinion." She firmly slapped the bottle of aloe back into his hand. "Until then, keep rubbing."

"Yes, ma'am," Jack grinned as she flopped back onto her stomach.

Louisa shifted uncomfortably in her seat and stared up at the flickering light casting eerie shadows in the parking lot.

"Why do we have to meet your friend so late at night?" she whispered.

"Because she works the night shift." Jack looked at her oddly. "And why are you whispering?"

Louisa shrugged. "I don't know. People always whisper in movies when they go to make shady, backdoor deals in dark alleys."

He stared blankly at her. And she thought he was weird. He shook his head.

"So...who are we meeting?" she pressed.

"A friend." Jack checked his watch. "Okay, she should be alone in the building by now."

He started to reach for the car door and stopped. Shit. What if she figured out Iris wasn't quite human? The promise of honesty rang in his head.

Iris's kind tended to be a bit sensitive about their appearance, especially her. Jack didn't think Louisa would say anything, but...?

Jack turned back to her. She frowned at the serious expression on his face.

"What's wrong?"

"Nothing." He hesitated. "I just don't want you to be surprised when you meet Iris."

"Surprised? What, is she an ex-girlfriend or something?" Louisa quirked an eyebrow.

"Uh, not quite," Jack winced. "Iris is a ghoul."

She blinked. "A ghoul?"

"A ghoul," he affirmed. "She mostly looks human, but I've realized over the past couple of days that you are scary perceptive. I didn't want you picking up on it and being surprised."

"Okay, I get to meet a ghoul." A small smile stretched her full lips.

"Full disclosure...ghouls eat dead people."

"WHAT?!" Louisa's shriek rang through the car.

He wiggled a finger in his ear. "Yeah, they worshipped their ancestors and honored their dead, so that's their curse."

Louisa stared blankly at him. Maybe he shouldn't have told her... right before they were about to go in...

"Just, uh, maybe don't bring it up if she doesn't," Jack warned. "Ghallu tend to be touchy about what they are. The whole digging-up-corpses thing can be kind of a downer."

"Oh yeah, because those were going to be the first words out of my mouth." Louisa rolled her eyes. "I heard you like dead people. Eat anyone good lately?"

Jack shook his head, his own grin fighting his lips. Warmth spread through his chest as her eyes sparkled with laughter. His Lou was gorgeous and warm and worth every twinge in his absent memories.

He slipped a hand around the back of her neck and pulled her against him. His lips brushed hers in soft pecks, once, twice. Nipping her bottom lip, Jack sucked it gently between his teeth. Louisa gasped against his lips. Her fingers trailed up his chest and slipped deep into his hair. She pulled him closer, deepening the kiss.

His tongue slipped between her lips and stroked against hers. Warm notes of vanilla burst in his mouth. She groaned against him. Fingers clenching in his hair, her tongue danced with his. Delicious pain sparked against his scalp.

Jack's hand ran down her spine, pulling shivers from her as she pressed against him. They were supposed to be doing something…right? But how was he supposed to remember when Lou's tongue was tracing slow circles around his own?

Louisa gripped his shoulders and straddled his lap. Jack swallowed her moans as she rubbed herself against the hard erection straining his zipper. She jerked back against the steering wheel.

"Someone is staring at us," she whispered into his ear.

Jack struggled to untangle his thoughts as he waited for the blood to rush back to his brain. Some peeping tom couldn't wait fifteen minutes? Fucking universe.

"What do they look like?" Jack pressed his nose into her curls.

"Short, brunette, big glasses."

"Iris," he groaned, leaning his forehead against hers.

"I guess she got tired of waiting for us," Louisa giggled.

Jack pecked her lips one last time and growled. Gripping her hips, he moved her back into her own seat. He glared down at his erection.

"Later," she said, giving his bulge a comforting pat.

Jack groaned as she climbed out of the truck and shut the door behind her.

"Fucking universe."

Louisa started across the parking lot as Jack clambered out of the truck. His feet ate up the pavement as he strode quickly behind her and wrapped his arm around her waist. She glanced nervously at the pale figure waiting illuminated by the light of the open door.

Would she say something about their little tryst in the truck? How much could she actually see from all the way over here?

Jack adjusted his jeans with a tug, dragging her eye to the obvious bulge between his legs. Louisa groaned internally. Her first time meeting a ghoul and she was about to make the worst first impression in the history of the supernatural world.

As the distance between them closed, Iris cocked her head to the side and studied them from the shadows. Jack slowed to a stop in front of her. His hand squeezed Louisa's hip in silent warning.

Louisa squinted at the bright light pouring through the open door. Iris waved them inside. Jack nudged her into the light, following closely behind.

Louisa spun in a slow circle. She grimaced at the sharp, antiseptic smell saturating the small space. Empty and unfeeling, the hall sent shivers up her spine. Somewhere in these walls, dead bodies waited.

She froze when Iris stepped inside, the door swinging shut behind her. The ghoul was...wrong. It was subtle but still painfully obvious. Her grayish skin glowed in the fluorescent lighting. Overly large, owlish eyes flitted nervously between Louisa and Jack.

Iris looked human, but only in the way that a wolf resembled a house pet. It was as though whatever power had designed ghouls had tried to recreate a human blindfolded; all the components were there but the proportions were off.

Jack poked her in the ribs. Louisa quickly closed her gaping mouth. Shit, she was being rude.

Iris slipped a pair of tinted glasses off the top of her head and settled them on her nose. She stared at Louisa from behind her shadowed lenses. Leaning closer to give Louisa a sniff, her delicate nostrils flared.

Louisa glanced at Jack nervously. Did she smell? He would have told her if she smelled, right?

"Why do you smell like you bathed in air freshener?" Her soft voice tinkled like a bell.

Louisa's mouth dropped open as she rounded on Jack.

"You said you couldn't smell it anymore!" she glowered at him.

"I can't, I swear!" He held up his hands. "Her kind have a very powerful sense of smell."

Louisa scrubbed a hand over her face. Worst first impression, ever.

"You're human," Iris continued, her eyes never leaving Louisa's face.

"Last time I checked," she sighed.

Iris turned to Jack. Her gray eyes studied him intently,

pulling him apart like a particularly bewildering puzzle. He shifted uncomfortably under her scrutiny.

"You've never brought someone to me before, Hound."

His jaw tightened. A glower met Iris's perceptive gaze. Louisa's eyebrows rose as she watched Jack subtly shift himself in front of her. Unless ghouls could grow claws, she doubted the tiny woman could do much damage.

"Is that a question?" Jack growled, his voice cold.

"No." Iris smiled kindly at Louisa. "Simply an observation."

Without another word, she turned and walked down the hallway. Jack frowned at her back. He curled an arm around Louisa's shoulders and started after her.

"What was that about?" She poked him in the ribs.

"I don't like her noticing you like that," he muttered.

Louisa stared at him. Why was he being so paranoid? She knew he was still on edge after what had happened when they were out with Abigail. Someone was following them, but surely not Iris?

"I don't think she meant anything by it." Louisa patted the hand on her shoulder.

Iris stopped in front of an elevator and nudged the down button. Jack growled softly as the distance between them closed.

"He doesn't like another predator this close to someone that's his," Iris called over her shoulder. "Especially a predator that isn't part of his clan."

She smiled at Louisa as they drew even with her.

"We've known each other a long time; I don't take it personally," she said. "I would probably do the same thing in his shoes."

Now that the shock from her striking features had faded, Louisa could see the beauty in the lines of Iris's face. Dark, sooty lashes framed her molten-gold irises behind her heavy pink frames. Her full lips pouted beneath a delicate nose dusted with dark freckles. And her hair—Louisa would kill for those soft, brown sugar waves.

They stepped into the elevator as the doors slid open. Louisa turned to see Jack standing just outside of the elevator doors, glaring. What was his deal today? She caught his eye and raised a brow.

He shook his head and stepped lightly inside. His fists clenched tightly as the doors slid closed. Louisa peeked at him from beneath her lashes.

The lines of his jaw strained, his teeth grinding together. Jack took slow, even breaths through his nose and blew them loudly from his mouth. Sweat began to bead on his forehead. The big bad shifter was... afraid?

Sympathy welled inside her chest. Her eyes softened as she pulled his clenched fist into her small hands. She rubbed her thumb gently over his white, straining knuckles.

Jack shot Louisa a grateful look before flitting back to stare hopelessly at the descending floor numbers. His foot tapped impatiently as the elevator crept downward. Iris stared dutifully ahead, politely ignoring the tense man between them.

"So, Iris... why did you call Jack 'The Hound' earlier?" Louisa asked in a hopeless attempt to distract them all.

Jack groaned beside her. Maybe that was the wrong question to ask...

"That's his nickname amongst the clans," Iris smirked.

"The Hound?" Louisa wrinkled her nose.

"Because there's no escape when The Hound begins the hunt," she said, grinning at Jack. He stood tense between them, trying to glare a hole through Iris's head.

"I hate that name," he growled.

"I don't know." Louisa winked at him. "I think it's kind of badass."

Jack shook his head and went back to growling at the doors. As soon as they slid open, he bolted from the small box. He stopped just outside and bent at the waist, taking slow, calming breaths.

Louisa stepped out beside him. Poor guy. She rested her hand between his shoulder blades as he pulled himself together.

Iris slipped past them. She walked down the hall, giving them a moment to themselves. Louisa smiled at her back. The ghoul was quickly growing on her.

"Are you okay?" Louisa whispered. Her hand moved in soothing circles on his back.

Jack straightened with a nod. "I'm good."

Gripping Louisa's hand in his clammy palm, he pulled her after Iris. Jack led her confidently down the hall and through a swinging door. Louisa followed him into a room filled with gleaming metal and the powerful scent of antiseptic chemicals.

Iris hovered next to a wall of shining little doors. That's where they kept the bodies in the movies. Louisa shuddered.

When she had wished for some acceptance in this little town, bonding with monsters over corpses was NOT what she had had in mind.

Iris rolled out one of the drawers and unzipped the body bag. Louisa's eyes darted to the ceiling. Nope, she was not going to look. She did not need more nightmares from this little adventure.

"Some locals out rafting the river found her draped over the riverbank," Iris said. "Looks like she was too far gone to pull herself out."

Don't look, don't look, Louisa chanted to herself. She dutifully studied the ceiling tiles. How did she end up in these situations?

"I see why you called me. These are obviously claw marks," Jack noted.

Iris flipped through a clipboard for notes, her eyes flitting from side to side as she scanned the text.

"I didn't do the autopsy, but the examiner on shift thought they were consistent with scrapes from the rocks," she said drily.

Jack stared at her. "Scrapes? In even, parallel lines? Tearing apart the stomach and chest?"

"The daytime examiner is an idiot," she snorted. "But what does poor, lowly night shift know?"

"Why do you work night shift if you're the better medical examiner?" Louisa asked the ceiling.

Her stomach churned as Jack slipped on a pair of latex gloves and started poking and prodding the body. She was pretty sure Iris wouldn't want to be her friend if she vomited all over her shiny, clean morgue.

"I'm a ghoul," Iris said as though it explained everything.

"Pretend I know nothing about ghouls," Louisa said, studying a particularly alarming stain on the ceiling tile. "Because I don't."

"Ghouls can't go out in sunlight," Jack murmured distractedly.

"Hey, are you Ghallu? No?" Iris chided. "Focus on the body."

Louisa rolled her eyes at his snort.

"Anyway, ghouls can't go out in sunlight," she told Louisa.

Jack huffed beside her. Louisa giggled, the noise painfully at odds with the somber surroundings.

"We get severe burns if we don't paint ourselves in copious amounts of sunblock. It won't kill us, but it's extremely painful. Besides, this"—Iris gestured at her face—"is far more noticeable in decent lighting. Over time, we just accepted that it was easier to be nocturnal."

Louisa rolled that over in her mind. How... sad. Iris would never enjoy a sunny day strolling through the park. Or lounge on the beach, working on her tan. Or impulsively stop for ice cream on a sweltering afternoon.

"That's awful," she said.

"It's not great," Iris agreed. "But we'd been nocturnal for generations by the time I was born. It's all I really know."

"How did you get through medical school, then?" Louisa frowned at the ceiling. "I can't imagine they have many night courses."

"I would get up early and drown myself in a couple of bottles of sunblock before class and carry a giant umbrella," Iris laughed. "I'm pretty sure my fellow students thought I was total weirdo."

"I can imagine," Louisa said, smiling. "Jack mentioned that ghouls eat human remains? Was that why you chose this particular profession?"

The smiled faded from Iris's face. Pain flashed in her gold eyes before she shut it away. Louisa tried not to wince. Jack was right, she did ask too many questions.

"Yes, Ghallu have to consume human flesh to survive." Iris said softly. "Most of my kind work in the death industry. Morgues, funeral homes, cemeteries. It's easier than grave-robbing."

Louisa could smack herself right now. Iris had been nothing but kind to her, a human. What had Jack said? That the Ghallu culture had revered the dead. And here she was, interrogating Iris on her eating habits. Could she be any more offensive.

"So... your sense of smell?" she asked, desperately grasping for a new subject.

"For finding fresh meat."

Louisa tried not to groan. Oh god, she was just digging herself deeper into the hole.

"Are there any other physical differences between ghouls and humans?" she asked hesitantly. There, that had to be safer ground, right?

"Well, our claws flatten into spades to help us dig up graves, and we have razor-sharp teeth since we only consume raw meat," Iris answered with a raised brow. "Those of us that work with humans hide them with custom dentures."

Louisa could practically see her life flashing before her eyes. This was worse than that time she'd walked into high school calculus with her skirt stuck in the back of her panties. At least the people laughing at her hadn't been in danger of murdering and eating her.

Maybe Iris could see the distress painted across her face, because she took pity on her and continued on.

"Our eyes are larger to take in more light and see better in the darkness. See the pupil?" She tipped her glasses to the end of her nose. "The larger the pupil, the more light you take in. We can see clear as day in the darkness, but we don't see in quite as many colors. Similar to owls, actually."

Louisa jumped as Jack held up a hand. In the wake of the spiraling conversation, she'd almost forgotten that he was still beside her... poking at a corpse. Her stomach rolled again.

"Not to interrupt the anatomy lesson, but do you know the girl's identity?" he asked Iris.

As Iris started to flip through her clipboard, Louisa's eyes dropped to the pale, lifeless face. Cursing her impulse, she grit her teeth as bile rose in her throat. She quickly glanced around for a trashcan and froze. Nausea forgotten, Louisa turned to stare at the body.

"It looks like they're waiting on a family member or dental records to confirm, but her name is Daisy Lincoln."

"Her picture was in the newspaper." Louisa said softly. "She went missing... I don't remember... maybe two weeks ago?"

She glanced down and groaned. Her eyes fixed on the shredded flesh of Daisy's stomach and ribcage. No wonder she hadn't had the strength to drag herself up the riverbank. The poor woman had probably bled out in the river.

Iris nodded across the open drawer, her frown matching Louisa's.

"Now that you say it, I see the resemblance to the photo the newspaper ran. I didn't recognize her until you pointed it out."

"So she was one of the missing women," Jack murmured thoughtfully. Louisa could practically see the gears whirring in his brain. She suddenly wished that she could read minds. Whatever conclusions he was drawing were probably both fascinating and horrifying.

"And she's the only one who has turned up so far?" Jack looked at Iris.

She nodded. "Ms. Lincoln is the only one to turn up on a slab."

"Have any of your people gone missing?"

Iris stiffened. "Just what are you implying?"

"We investigated an abandoned Blight hive yesterday." Louisa winced at the memory. Jack carried on. "There was a basement filled with cages built for supes. I was able to pick up six separate Ghallu scents, all female, none Blight."

Iris's eye widened. "You think they were taken, like the human women?"

"I think so. There were traces of wolves and shifters as well."

"Wolves? Why would anyone take a female wolf? That's asking for violent, bloody death," Iris gaped.

"I have no idea. And the wolves won't tell us anything. Their people are missing, and they're circling the wagons." Jack sighed.

"I don't know of any of my clan that are missing... but if they came from another Ghallu clan?" Iris straightened, her face grave. "I'll send out feelers among my people. I'll let you know as soon I hear anything."

Jack peeled off his gloves. He tossed them in a trashcan and offered her his hand.

"Thank you, Iris. Stay safe."

Iris shook his hand, her fingers barely touching his skin.

"We'll see ourselves out," Jack said, putting his hand on the small of Louisa's back. He gave her a subtle nudge toward the door. She acquiesced, eager to put the room that made her skin crawl far behind her.

"You'll keep me updated as the investigation progresses, Hound?" Iris called. She watched them walk away as she pushed Daisy back into her cabinet, closing the drawer with a sharp click.

"I'll let you know as soon as I find anything solid."

Iris's nodded. She flashed Louisa a quick smile.

"Give me a call sometime, Louisa," she called at their backs. "We'll go out for drinks."

Louisa shot her a thumbs up over her shoulder as Jack moved faster, shuffling her through the swinging doors.

"I like her," she grinned.

"You're going to give me an ulcer," he sighed. "Stop playing nice with big, scary monsters."

"But you're a monster?" Louisa poked at him. She liked him all surly and protective. It was both endearing and entertaining.

"I'm *your* big, scary monster," he smiled. "Big difference."

The smile disappeared in a flash as they stopped in front of the elevator. He glared at the gleaming doors. Louisa hid a small smile behind her hand. Big, scary monster. Right.

"Maybe we should take the stairs?" she said innocently.

18

"So where do we go from here?" Louisa asked the next morning, swirling a spoon through her yogurt.

"I'm not sure," Jack sighed. "I'm stuck."

He scrubbed a hand through his hair and sighed again. She grit her teeth. If he sighed one more time, she was going to launch her yogurt at him. Louisa had gotten far too little sleep and not nearly enough coffee to listen to his dramatics.

"What are your options?" Alice asked, bleary-eyed.

Jack chewed his toast absently.

"We could go back to the Blight hive and see if we missed anything," he mused. "Or we could go out to the river where the girl was found and try to sniff out a trail. But with the water masking her scent, that's probably another dead end."

"We could question her family and friends?" Louisa added hopefully.

"With the cops and press swarming?" Alice said, dropping another bag of tea in her cup. "You'll never even get within ten feet of them."

"What about the fingernail from the basement?"

Jack shook his head. "Connor said it didn't match any of the missing women, so it's probably from one of the supes."

"I can try to parlay with the other clans, see if they've heard anything," Nate offered.

"Will they actually tell you anything?" Alice snorted skeptically.

"The Ghallu, maybe," Nate shrugged. "But if the wolves are anything to go by, the others won't say a word."

"I thought you guys were supposed to have some nifty Pact with all the clans?" Louisa yawned.

Nate shot a glare at Jack before turning to her. "We agreed to use the town as a haven, not to share sensitive information about our clans."

"How's that working out for you now?"

Alice snorted into her tea. Eyes narrowing, Nate turned to Jack.

"Remind me why she's here."

Jack's frustrated grimace was rapidly evolving into a scowl. He banged his fist against the table, sending the silverware rattling. Louisa raised her eyebrows. It seemed nobody was enjoying their morning today.

"None of this is going to help us figure out who is targeting us," he growled.

Nate narrowed his eyes, a rumble purring from his chest. Jack lowered his eyes to his plate and choked off his growl.

Louisa stumbled away from the table to refill her coffee cup.

"What about the bullet?" she called over her shoulder as she hunted for the sugar. "Can't you have Bird Boy analyze it or something?"

Who the hell had moved the sugar? Not Nate; the freak drank his coffee black. Louisa shuddered. She turned to ask Jack what he'd done with the sugar and froze as the collective gaze of the room settled on her.

Jack, Nate, and Alice all stared at her. Alice's head dropped back as she burst out laughing. The boys jumped in their seats at the unexpected outburst.

"We're idiots," she told them between chuckles. "We heal so fast, it never occurred to us to actually find the weapon."

"I told you she would be useful," Jack smugly informed Nate.

"Yeah, she's great," Nate dismissed. "But how are we going to get the bullet back?"

"I guess... Louisa is going to have to steal it," Jack said, shooting her a worried glance.

Louisa waved her hand dismissively.

"Sure—where the hell is the sugar?"

"I AGREED TO DO THIS?" Louisa stared bewildered at the veterinary clinic. "When did I agree to do this?"

"This morning," Jack patted her shoulder.

She glared at the building from the shadows of the alley. Surely she would remember agreeing to break into her own place of employment to pilfer a bullet and some medical records? Right?

"Wait a minute—had I had my coffee yet?" She squinted suspiciously at Jack. "Because it doesn't count without caffeine."

He sighed and rubbed a hand over his eyes. She wasn't going to make this easy for him, and frankly, he should have thought of that before he extracted promises from her before her morning coffee.

"Look, I would do it myself, but I don't know what I'm looking for... and a dog stealing paperwork might be worth some notice."

"Right," Louisa mumbled. "Right, I got this."

She shook the nervous trembles out of her arms. Louisa tugged at her sleeves and fidgeted from side to side.

"You have ten minutes," Jack warned. "Any longer and I'll cause a nice, big scene."

Louisa nodded and started inching toward the clinic's side door. Jack caught her arm and spun her around. He kissed her hard, his lips bruising against hers. He pulled back with a loud smack.

"Be careful," Jack whispered, giving one of her curls a gentle tug. "Go in there, get the file, and then I'll buy you lunch."

She turned back to the door and squared her shoulders. She could do this. Louisa opened the door and slipped inside.

She crept down the hall, padding silently on the balls of her feet. If she was lucky and Jessica, the receptionist, hadn't been feeling productive, which she usually wasn't, then Jack's records should still be on Louisa's desk.

All she had to do was creep across the lobby and back behind the reception desk, hunt down the files, and ninja back out. All without being noticed.

Right, a walk in the park. Glancing over her shoulder, Louisa skirted the edge of the lobby and slipped behind an overgrown fern, her eyes never leaving the reception desk.

Jessica sat, flipping her hair idly and sipping her coffee. A graveyard of discarded paper cups surrounded her. Any minute now she would disappear for her midmorning bathroom break.

Louisa waited, peeking through untended greenery. She glanced at the clock uneasily. Her time was quickly slipping away.

"Come on, come on, come oooon," Louisa hissed quietly.

She breathed a sigh of relief as Jessica finally slipped out of her chair and disappeared into the bathroom. Louisa crawled out from behind the fern and darted across the lobby. Approaching her desk, she couldn't help but cast anxious glances over her shoulder at the bathroom door. James Bond, she was not.

Louisa stared at her desk and shook her head. Three days she'd been gone and it was completely undisturbed. She whipped open drawers, shuffling through files. Please be here, please be here.

She silently thanked the heavens as she slipped the file out. Flipping through it quickly, she made sure the baggie with the bullet was firmly clipped inside.

Sharp footsteps cut through the silent lobby. Louisa's eyes flicked to the bathroom door, still firmly shut. She caught a glimpse of bottle-blond hair coming around the corner before she dropped to the floor behind the desk.

Louisa crawled around her chair and folded herself beneath her desk. Oh god, this was it. This was how she was going to die. It wouldn't be the monsters, but Dr. Adler who finally succeeded in murdering her.

She clutched the file to her chest. Fire spread through her lungs as she held her breath. Dr. Adler flipped languidly through the paperwork on Louisa's desk.

Louisa stared at Dr. Adler's garish orange stiletto, willing her to walk away. At least she knew that the hag couldn't smell her. Jack had assured her that he hadn't scented any other supernatural creatures in the building.

She'd been surprised. Louisa had been sure that Dr. Adler's evil was the byproduct of something unnatural.

"Where did that moron put it?" she muttered, the papers shuffling around.

Moron? Rude. Louisa rolled her eyes under the desk. It *so* was not the time.

"JESSICA!" her shrill scream echoed through the office. "Where is that little twit? JESSICA!"

Her orange stiletto stomped lightly on the carpet.

"Utterly inept," Dr. Adler growled under her breath. "Why would federal agents even want the stupid file?" Stomping out of the reception area, her shoes disappeared into the back office.

Louisa winced at the sound of filing cabinets slamming. She needed to get the hell out of there before the dragon came back.

She tucked the file into her waistband and crawled out from under the desk. Hopping to her feet, she scrambled out of the reception area and sprinted towards the backdoor.

Louisa burst out of the door and into Jack's arms. He rocked back on his feet as she slammed into his chest.

"Are you being chased?" he growled. Jack started to nudge her behind him.

Louisa locked her hand around his wrist. "No, but we need to go. NOW."

"Did you get the file?" He snagged her hand and pulled her down the alley.

She fished it out of her waistband. "Yes."

They leapt into the truck and locked the doors. As Jack went for the ignition, Louisa grabbed his wrist.

"Jack, I overheard Dr. Adler talking to herself. She was

looking for your file, she said the feds wanted it?"

Jack stared at her, wide-eyed. "The feds? Like federal agents?"

"I guess?" she shrugged.

"What kind of feds? FBI? CIA?"

Seriously? "Dude, she muttered it in passing. I was lucky to get that much."

"Right. Shit." He smacked his hand against the steering wheel. "Do you know if they're here? Are they in the clinic?"

Louisa shook her head. "I don't know." Her mind whirred. "But there shouldn't be any patients in the building. The dragon always schedules herself a half-day on Mondays because she gets her nails done before lunch."

"So if there are any cars in the parking lot..." Jack said slowly.

"They're probably your feds." Louisa nodded.

The engine roared as they rolled past the parking lot. An unremarkable black car sat tucked in the corner of the lot.

"Son of a bitch," he murmured.

"You'd better call Nate. Get someone to follow them around."

Jack grinned at her. "I could seriously kiss you right now."

"Get us out of here, and I might just take you up on that," Louisa giggled.

LOUISA PEERED around Jack as they pulled up outside the police station.

"We should've brought donuts."

Jack snorted. "Yeah, that would've gone over well."

"You're such a spoilsport," she muttered, jumping out of the truck. "It would've been hilarious."

He crossed to her, the bag with the bullet tucked into his pocket. Catching her around the waist, Jack pecked her on the lips.

"Once the whole investigation/feds thing is over, we can come back and deliver dozens of 'Fuck You' donuts to Connor."

Louisa's lips twitched. "Promise?"

Solemnly pressing a hand to his heart, he vowed: "My word as a shifter."

"It's a date then." She kissed him. Stepping back, she grinned. "Let's go fuck up Connor's day."

Throwing his head back, Jack laughed. He snagged her elbow and tugged her into the police station. Louisa leaned into his side as they walked. His muscular arm wrapped around her shoulders.

Mmmmm. He smelled nice. Maybe they could revisit their fun from the remodel later... without the carpet burn, of course. In the truck would be fun, if a little cramped.

Jack led her through the building, weaving around desks. Connor hovered across the room in a knot of uniforms. His back stiffened as he watched them close the distance.

He waved for them to stop. They froze between the desks, waiting for him to untangle himself from his fellow officers. He crossed the room and seized their elbows. Dragging them down the hall, he shushed their protests.

"You can't be here," Connor said, shoving them into a quiet alcove.

Jack and Louisa glanced at each other. "What's wrong?" he asked.

"Some FBI agent called the station and submitted a missing person's report." Connor glanced around behind him. He leaned in and whispered, "The report was for you."

"Me?" Jack raised his eyebrows.

"No, dumbass." He shook his head. "It was for her."

"Who the hell would report me missing?" Louisa stared at him. "I don't have any family, and my coworkers wouldn't hand me a glass of water if I were on fire. I'm nobody."

"I don't know but some agent is very interested in your whereabouts right now." He glanced nervously over his shoulder again. "Which means that you can't be here. They distributed your picture a half hour ago. I already warned the fellow supes in the department not to look too hard for you, but there are still several humans who will be on the hunt."

Jack cursed under his breath. Louisa just stared between them. Why the hell was the FBI after her? She was literally nobody. Hell, she had never even had a parking ticket.

"Seriously, I'm a nobody." Louisa repeated. "What the fuck is going on?"

Connor ran a hand over his short hair. "I don't know. I'll keep an eye on things here, but you two need to go. Now."

Jack pulled the bullet from his pocket and smacked it against Connor's chest.

"This is the bullet they pulled from my shoulder. Nate wants you to check it out, but keep it quiet. Especially with all of this—" he twirled his finger at the bustling police station—"going on."

Connor nodded and tucked it in his pocket. He checked the hall and waved them away. Jack dropped an arm around Louisa's shoulders and led her toward the door.

"Keep your eyes down," he whispered in her ear.

Louisa buried her face in Jack's shoulder. As he led her back to the truck, she couldn't help but wonder what the fuck had happened to her quiet life.

19

"The government is looking for me. THE GOVERNMENT IS LOOKING FOR ME!"

"I'm aware, Lou," Jack sighed.

She rounded on him. "Why are you not freaking out more?!"

"Honey, I think you're freaking out enough for the both of us." He patted her knee. "Besides, I promised you lunch. You have my word that I will appropriately freak out *after* we eat."

Louisa grumbled quietly to herself as Jack drove them to a nearby restaurant that he promised had great milkshakes. Those shakes had better be amazing because she was one shitty meal away from a breakdown.

They parked down the street from the restaurant and hurried in to find a table before the lunch rush descended. Louisa studied her menu, her feet propped in Jack's lap across the booth.

Their waitress hovered at the edge of the table, blowing bubbles with her gum. Louisa winced at the incessant popping as she tried to read the menu.

"I'll have the chicken tenders, double fries, and a chocolate shake... and a strawberry shake."

She closed her menu with a snap and passed it to the waitress. Jack watched her with a bemused expression.

"Hungry?"

"I eat when I'm stressed." She grimaced at him. He stroked her ankles resting on his thigh.

The waitress popped her hip provocatively. She blinked her wide eyes, fluttering her impossibly long lashes.

"What can I get you, handsome?"

"The same," Jack said, his eyes never leaving Louisa's morose expression.

Leaning in close to sweep away the menus, the waitress thrust her chest out. She lingered awkwardly for a few seconds before swishing her sheet of blond hair over her shoulder and strutting away.

Louisa watched the swaying motion of her hips as she disappeared around the corner. "How does she do that without dislocating a hip?"

Jack frowned and stared bewildered around the room. "Do what?"

"I can't tell if you're being sweet or if you're really just that oblivious," she laughed.

Jack reached across the table and tucked her fingers into his. He grinned as she grumbled into her water.

"Don't be jealous." He squeezed her hand. "She's not my type. I mean, she doesn't even have curls."

Louisa flushed pink. Little flutters kicked off in her belly every time he slipped her a compliment. Still trying to remain a little prickly, she made sure to roll her eyes.

"Now, Lou. I know that I am undeniably gorgeous, but you can't get jealous every time some... *Jezebel* makes eyes at me." Jack told her solemnly. "They can look, but only you get to touch."

She choked on a sip of water. "Jezebel?"

He shrugged. "The Aunts say it all the time. It felt right in the moment."

Louisa giggled. Her belly fluttered again. Silly man.

Their food arrived with another hip pop and hair swish. This time, as the waitress walked away, they both dissolved into laughter.

Louisa sipped at her shake. Mmmm, chocolate. Jack wrinkled his nose in disgust as she swirled a fry through the ice cream. He shook his head, a smile playing at his lips.

They ate in comfortable silence, Jack reaching down every so often to pat at her ankles. Louisa wasn't usually all that touchy-feely in relationships, but with Jack it didn't feel so awkward. Plus, it seemed to soothe him.

He tossed a fry down and cleared his throat. "You said something at the police station, and it's been bothering me."

Louisa ran through the conversation they had had with Connor, but nothing stuck out at her as remotely upsetting. You know, besides the whole wanted-by-the-federal-government bit.

"What did I say?" she asked, puzzled.

"You said that you didn't have a family." Jack leaned back in his seat, his hands resting on her ankles.

Oh great, he'd picked that bit up from her tiny freakout. She poked at her food. He'd promised her complete honesty; didn't he deserve the same? Louisa sighed. Fuck.

"I don't have a family." She popped a fry in her mouth and chewed slowly. She needed to phrase this in a way that wouldn't make Jack pity her. "I was abandoned at a hospital in Ohio as a baby. I grew up in the foster care system, and none of the homes really stuck, so I guess I don't really have anyone I would consider family."

He watched her, his face utterly blank. "Do you know who your family is? Have you ever tried to track them down?"

"No. Supposedly, my birth mother walked out after having me, and when the nurses tried to contact her, it turned out that all the info she'd written on the forms was fake." Louisa stared down at her plate. She hated this bit. "Even if I wanted to find her, I wouldn't know where to start. She didn't even hang around long enough to name me. My first and last names were assigned by the state. Just randomly picked off of a list."

She hated how bitter her voice sounded. Twenty-five years and it hadn't gotten any easier to tell that story. Maybe in the next twenty-five, she'd find a way to come to terms with it.

"I'm sorry that you had to go through that." He reached across the table and squeezed her hand. "That can't have been an easy childhood."

She shrugged. "It could have been worse. I prefer not to dwell on it."

"That's why you don't have any pictures in your apartment." Jack nodded, his face twisted in thought. "You had one photo in your living room, of a barbecue. It looks like it was ripped from a magazine..."

Louisa blinked up at him. He remembered that? "It was an ad for grills." She winced. "I found it in one of my foster mom's magazines when I was a kid. Everyone just seemed so happy and loved and... I guess I wanted that for myself. I ended up carrying it around with me for years. Pretty pathetic, right?"

Jack squeezed her hand. "I don't think that's pathetic at

all," he said quietly. "Now the Pez dispensers... those were a little weird."

Louisa laughed. "One of my caseworkers gave me one of those every year on my birthday, and I just sort of kept collecting them after."

"At least they're more interesting than stamps," he said, winking at her.

"Much harder to store though," she giggled.

They finished up their food, Louisa's dark mood dissipating with their banter. Somehow, her shitty childhood felt a little less shitty in his presence.

Jack threw some cash on the table, and they made their way out into the sunshine. Louisa tucked her hand in his elbow and turned her face up to the sky to let the light warm her skin.

Strolling down the sidewalk, enjoying the afternoon, Louisa was almost able to forget that her whole world was upside down. As long as she didn't think about being a missing person...or whether or not Jack could get fleas, or how Ghouls stored their leftovers, or if wolves chased cats.

But most importantly, she wouldn't think about how Jack's hands had felt on her naked skin. Or the carpet rubbing against her back, her legs wrapped around his waist.

A shiver ran down her spine. Yeah, definitely don't dwell on that... or how badly she was aching to do it again. She looked up at him, the sun making his hair glow gold. Jack caught her studying him and smiled down at her. He leaned down to plant a kiss on her mouth.

"Jackson!" a voice called, shattering the moment.

The smile vanished from his lips as he snapped upright. His face glacially cold, he turned to face the interloper. A slim woman glided down the sidewalk after them.

Louisa looked back and forth between them. There was something familiar about her... yet she was positive that she had never laid eyes on the woman before. They certainly hadn't run into each other shopping, she thought as she eyed the expensive handbag clutched in the woman's grasp.

Jack's expression could've been carved from granite as he addressed the haughty woman attempting to air-kiss his cheek.

"Blair."

She rocked back on her sharp heels. "You never come around for dinner anymore," she purred at him. "I haven't seen you in ages."

"I've been busy," he said coldly.

"There's always time for family, Jackson." Her voice gained a razor-sharp edge. "Try harder."

Louisa studied the woman reprimanding Jack. She had a sharp, white-blond bob. Her skin was as clear and pale as porcelain. There was a delicate air about her... no, not delicate. Brittle. Blair was sharp and brittle like a broken blade.

She and Jack looked nothing alike. Where he was the sun, warm and shining on everyone around him, she was as cold and barren as the moon... except for the eyes. The shape, the color, they were a perfect reflection of Jack's.

"Oh my, who is your precious little friend?" Blair asked, her frosty gaze landing on Louisa.

"None of your concern," Jack said firmly. He shifted in front of her, masking her with his bulk.

"Don't be rude, Jackson." Her eyes never left Louisa's as she peered around his shoulder.

"If I agree to dinner, will you leave right now?" he asked wearily.

Blair grinned, her even, white teeth flashing. "Mother

and Father will be so pleased!" She clapped her hands together. "We'll see you tonight."

She spun on her spiked heels, pausing to throw one last remark over her slim shoulder. "Don't forget to bring your friend. The family will be dying to meet her."

Jack growled low in his chest. Louisa watched the woman slip into a sleek, black town car and disappeared into the afternoon traffic. She shivered under the warm sun. That bitch was bad news.

SHIT. Jack watched his sister drive off down the street and roared internally. First the FBI and now his...*family*. He'd rather walk into a Blight hive naked then spend an evening with his relatives.

He glanced down at the curly head at his shoulder. Someday he was going to take Lou on a date that didn't involve a decrepit hell house, or a visit to the morgue, or demonic hellbeasts. But apparently, it wasn't going to be today.

"Soooo...what was that about?" Louisa tilted her head to look up at him.

The sunlight shone down, lighting up her golden skin. He stared down at her curious face. Her chocolate-brown eyes were round, her dark eyebrows raised in question.

Yeah, there was no way in fucking hell that she was coming with him.

"We'll talk in the truck." Jack gripped her hand and tugged her down the street. He lifted her into the truck and shut the door. Closing his eyes, he paused and breathed deeply. No suspicious scents. Good.

He ran around the truck and jumped in. How the shit was he going to explain this to her? His Lou didn't have a family; she'd literally told him that half an hour ago. There was no way she'd understand *why* he hated them without a full explanation.

Louisa sat turned in her seat, waiting for an explanation. It was so much easier when he could just knock her unconscious, damn it.

"Blair is my sister," Jack sighed.

"Yeeeeah, I gathered that much for myself," she said slowly. She waved a hand in front of her face. "It's the eyes."

"Well, remember when I said that I don't have much in common with my family?"

"Yes?" Louisa scooched closer, her face turned up to study his expressions.

Jack winced. "That may have been a bit of an understatement."

Her head quirked to the side. "How so?"

"Well, they hate me."

"They hate you?" Louisa reared back, her eyebrows soaring. "Why would they hate you?"

"They hate me because I'm not really one of them," he said, expression tight. How exactly was he supposed to explain this?

"What do you mean, not one of them?"

"The shifter curse is hereditary, right?" Jack said. "Our animals get passed down generation to generation. They're Bengal tigers. I'm a dog."

"But how...?" Louisa's eyebrows rose as the realization hit her. "Either you picked up some obscure recessive gene... or one of your parents isn't really your parent."

"I've heard it was quite the nasty shock for dear old dad when I shifted into a puppy at my second birthday party," Jack said grimly. He didn't really remember the occasion, first shift being traumatic and all, but Nate's mom had said that it was a sight to behold. Tables flying, tigers roaring, good times.

"Holy shit," Louisa breathed. "That's some soap opera drama, right there."

"Naturally, he's hated me and my mother from that day forward. And then mother blames me for not being a tiger, as if I were the one who had an affair," he rolled his eyes. "They didn't exactly try to hide their feelings about the matter, which meant Blair and Carter knew all about it and made my life hell."

"Do you know who your biological father is?" Louisa asked.

"Not a clue," Jack shrugged his massive shoulders. "She won't talk about it at all. Honestly, I don't really care."

Did he wonder sometimes? Sure, but not enough to go hunting for the guy.

Her eyebrows shot up. "You're not even a little curious who he was?"

"Nope." He shook his head. "Nate's parents pretty much raised me after the infamous birthday party incident. I always considered them my real mom and dad."

Louisa squeezed his knee. "Good. Your family sucks."

Jack laughed humorlessly. He patted the hand resting on his leg.

"You have no idea how right you are," he said. "They're monsters."

"Hate to break it to you, but you're all kind of monsters," she giggled.

Jack flashed her a grin that quickly disappeared off his face. He sighed into the steering wheel. She was going to just love the next part.

"Really, you need to be prepared. They are Monsters, capital M."

Louisa waited as he weighed his words carefully. He could already see the hate brewing in her face; she definitely wasn't going to be a fan for long. Jack sure wasn't.

"There's a certain class of supernaturals that consider humans to be... less than." Jack winced. "They view humans as little better than animals. They even consider shifters with less impressive animals to be lower class."

"You've got to be kidding me," Louisa stared at him.

"I really wish I was," he sighed. "They're like the supernatural version of Nazis. If they had their way, humans would be rounded up and enslaved."

Jack turned to stare at her, his eyes sad. "Which is why you won't be going."

Her eyes narrowed. Oh shit.

"Pump the brakes, buddy. If you're going, I'm going."

"Lou—"

"I'm going," Louisa said firmly.

His expression hardened. "When I was six, my sister trapped me in an old, abandoned well on our property because she thought it would be funny. I was in there for almost two days before Nate found me. No one in my family even noticed that I was gone."

"Is that why you don't like small spaces?" she asked gently. "Like the elevator at the morgue?"

"Yes." Jack cringed. Just the thought of climbing back into that coffin made him queasy. "I'm not telling you this for pity. I'm telling you this so that you fully understand what kind of people they are. My family is a horrible stain on the supernatural community. I could have died in that hole, and they wouldn't have lost a minute of sleep. And I'm family; imagine how they're going to feel about you."

"All the more reason why you shouldn't go alone."

Frustration boiled through him as their argument ran in

circles. He just wanted to keep her safe. Couldn't she see that?

"Louisa, you're not—"

Her hand clapped over his mouth, stifling his words. "If you think for one second that you're going to face these shitheads without me, then you're seriously deluded. I'm going because we're a team. Team Kickass."

Jack lifted her hand a few centimeters off his face. "Team Kickass?"

"Yes, I'm going to have hats made," she sniffed.

His resigned sigh filled the truck. Goddammit. "This is going to be a truly unpleasant evening for both of us."

"Why?" Louisa quipped. "Because they despise your existence and consider me equal to a house pet?"

Jack chuckled, some of the shadows leaving his eyes. The hard knot that had formed in his stomach at Blair's arrival started to loosen. This dinner was going to be a shit-show, but at least he'd have decent company.

"But seriously... this is going to be the worst 'meet the parents' in the history of the world." She grinned at him.

"At least you're not related to them," he grumbled. "Oh, and there's one more thing."

"There's more?" Louisa groaned. "What is your aunt the Loch Ness monster or something?"

"No..." Jack hesitated. "They're also ridiculously wealthy and will consider you poor if your net worth is less than a couple of million."

"So they're rich, monster Nazis?" she groaned. "This just keeps getting better and better. Are you sure you don't want to skip this whole catastrophe?"

"You can stay home, but I have to go and get a look at Carter. Well, a sniff really. His scent keeps turning up, and frankly he's an asshole. I wouldn't put it past him to be neck deep in this whole mess."

"So, what you're saying… is that kidnapping women might be a family trait?"

She looked up at him innocently, her eyes wide. A tremble shook her lips as Louisa tried not to smile.

"Laugh it up, house pet." Jack rolled his eyes.

20

Jack lay on his bed, staring at the ceiling. This dinner was going to be a disaster, and they were going to walk straight into it. How had he let her talk him into this?

His head dropped to the side to stare into the bathroom. Dancing around on her tiptoes, Louisa worked her curls into an elegant knot at the back of her neck. She hummed softly under her breath as she twisted each curl back.

Jack studied the graceful lines of her bare legs. Her small feet arched as she swayed from foot to foot to her quiet tune. She glanced at him over her shoulder and winked. A gentle flutter warmed his chest.

He wasn't taking her. Not a chance in hell. Shit, Jack didn't want to go either. Maybe he could just get someone to tail his idiot brother and save them both the humiliating evening.

"I don't know what to wear," Louisa announced. "What says 'I might be screwing your son, but I'm not about to take shit from a pompous jungle cat'? A dress, right?"

Jack eyed her from head to toe. His oversized T-shirt

hung from her narrow shoulders, draping over her to brush tops of her thighs. Louisa pawed through her duffel, bent at the waist. The edge of the shirt hitched up, revealing the bottom curve of her ass.

"I like what you're wearing now," he said, admiring the view.

She peeked around her hip at the sound of his hungry growl.

"We don't have time for that." Louisa straightened, her hands settling on her hips. Her words flew over Jack's head as the motion inched the hem of the shirt higher up her thighs.

"We have a little time," he growled.

She pointed her finger at him. "No. Stop the sexy growling."

The rumble in his chest grew. She shivered, her teeth dropping to nibble her lip. The scent of her arousal drifted across the room.

"Are you really going to deny your poor, suffering man a quickie before he has to go eat a three-course meal with his overbearing, abomination of a family?"

His lip jutted into a pout. "Heartless," he muttered bitterly.

Louisa shifted her weight, her hip popping provocatively.

"Well, when you put it like that."

She crossed the room, her hips swinging. The bed sank under their combined weight as Louisa crawled up and straddled his hips.

Slipping beneath the hem of his shirt, her fingers traced the lines of his abs. She peeled the shirt up his chest. He sucked in a breath as she bent to trace the path of her fingers with her tongue.

"Fuck," Jack cursed low as her teeth scraped gently across his nipple.

Heat pooled between his legs. The bulge straining his jeans grew, pressing tight against the bare flesh between her legs. Louisa groaned and rolled her hips.

Jack's hands grazed her soft thighs and slipped beneath her shirt. Louisa stretched to capture his lips. Her tongue brushed his as he stroked his hands down the length of her spine.

Thoughts scattered as Louisa's kisses traveled down his throat. Wasn't there something he was supposed to be doing...something important? Right, dinner.

"We should just stay here," he groaned against her ear. "Order food and hide up here...naked."

"Tempting," Louisa murmured into his neck.

"Seriously. You, me, some pizza, a lot of sex."

She reared back, her eyes narrowed. "You're trying to distract me, aren't you?"

"What?" Shit. He'd overplayed his hand.

"You're trying to get out of this dinner." Her jaw dropped. "What were you going to do? Fuck me and disappear while I was in some... post-coital bliss? Unbelievable."

Louisa climbed off of him and crossed to the bedroom door.

"Where are you going?" Jack asked, sitting up.

"To borrow a dress from Alice. I suggest you get dressed. I'm already going to make a bad impression; I'd prefer not to be late as well."

His head dropped back to the mattress. Damn it. That had *not* gone according to plan. His erection pulsed painfully against his zipper. Definitely not according to plan.

Twenty minutes later, Jack was grumbling in the cab of

his truck. His fingers tapped on the wheel. How much longer was she going to be? He checked his watch again. Five minutes behind schedule.

Horny and late. Awesome.

At least Nate had had time to hire someone to fix his window. Horny, late, AND windblown? His mother would keel over in shock.

Jack's eyes lifted as the garage door swung open. His jaw landed in his lap. Louisa swept through the door on sky-high heels. A dress of silky midnight-blue wrapped around her waist, hugging her breasts tight. The skirt flared at her hips, swishing to mid-thigh. Red lips twisted into a smile as she caught a glimpse of his shocked face through the windshield.

She climbed into the truck and buckled her seatbelt. Louisa leaned across the bench and closed his mouth for him. He swallowed and backed the truck out of the garage. He was a goner.

Jack snuck glances at her from the corner of his eye. He wasn't sure what was worse, spending an evening with people who hated him or doing it knowing that Louisa was inches away and not wearing panties?

He groaned.

Louisa snickered quietly to herself. There was a certain level of satisfaction achieved in going to an effort to look hot... but when you literally render a man speechless? Poor Jack had been sneaking less-than-subtle looks the entire drive.

She should feel bad for leaving him hard up earlier, but it was his own fault for trying to be tricky. Besides, she was going to take pity on him after this whole fiasco was over. Sooner if Jack didn't stop shooting her heated glances.

He cleared his throat. "You look, um, really nice."

"Really nice?" Louisa raised an eyebrow.

Truthfully, she wasn't all that comfortable, but he didn't need to know that. Alice was several inches shorter and less curvy than Louisa, the borrowed dress was bordering on scandalously short, and she was going to split a seam if she breathed too deep. But damn it, if she was going to be treated like a second-class citizen all night, she was going to be a *hot* second-class citizen.

"Well, it was that or pull over and have my way with you," Jack shrugged. "But you were adamant that we not be late."

Louisa laughed as the truck weaved its way through town. He fidgeted, his muscles tensing, as the houses started to grow. Children's toys scattered on the lawn were being replaced by manicured hedges and fountains.

A faint whine built in his chest the longer they drove. Louisa put her hand on his thigh. Poor guy. This wasn't even her family and she was queasy and terrified. She couldn't even imagine how he felt.

Jack gripped her hand and squeezed. They slowed in front of a large, gated mansion surrounded by towering trees. His face paled as the gate swung open at their approach.

He steered them down a tidy, brick driveway and pulled to a stop directly in front of the grand front entry. He killed the engine and glared at the ornate house.

Turning to her, he gave her hand another squeeze.

"You might not like the guy I have to be in there," Jack warned.

"Is that guy a racist shifter planning to enslave me?"

"No." He shook his head vehemently.

Louisa smiled. "Then we're good."

As Jack reached for the door handle, she hooked her hand in his buttoned collar and dragged him down for a blistering kiss. Louisa pulled back, her lips parting with a faint smack.

"For luck," she winked at him.

As she moved to unbuckle, Jack jumped out of the truck and ran around to open her door. He gripped her waist and set her carefully on her stilettos. Louisa tucked her hand into his elbow.

Jack led her up the front steps and reached for the doorbell. A blank mask settled on his features. The warmth vanished from his eyes as the door swung open.

An unsmiling bald man ushered them down the hall and into the dining room. His family sat silently at table. Louisa nearly stepped back when they turned in unison to stare at the two of them.

Jack's hand dropped to her lower back. Without a word, he steered her to an empty seat at the far end of the table. He pulled out her chair as she studied their faces.

Blair sat at the other end of the table, her expression as sharp as it had been that afternoon. Her pale hair glowed under the sparkling chandelier. Beside her sat a younger man, equally blond and unpleasant-looking. He sprawled sideways in his chair, his hair artfully sticking up in a messy, windblown look. This must be Carter.

He was handsome, but his eyes were utterly cold. Maybe Louisa was biased, but Jack was better looking by far. Of course, a huge part of that could just be that he didn't have Carter's serial killer eyes.

Louisa eyed their silent parents as Jack took his seat beside her. His father looked nothing like him, of course. He was shorter and sallow, his pale hair thinning. His mother was delicate-boned and slender like Blair and Carter. Jack's green eyes winced behind her dark lashes.

Maybe it was just because she already knew the history, but it was clear that the two wanted nothing to do with each other. Where Jack's hand had already drifted to her knee, they leaned away from each other, a careful distance operating between them.

"You're late," Jack's father said, his voice empty of emotion.

"It's good to see you too, *Father*," Jack answered just as coldly. "Louisa, these are my parents, Alistair and Camille Halliday."

"It's a pleasure to meet you," Louisa lied through her teeth.

Camille waved non-committally, her eyes focused on her plate. Louisa could only imagine how horrible this had to be for her, sitting across from the son who wore the weight of her sin across his face. She might actually feel bad for her... if she wasn't a horrible person.

"So this is your little pet," Carter drawled. His eyes burned across the table. Her skin prickled at the greasy trail his eyes painted up her body.

Louisa steeled her spine and stared back. A smirk stretched across his mouth.

"Oh, she's fun."

Jack growled low in his throat, his narrowed eyes burning a hole through Carter.

"Relax, dog." He turned his smirk on Jack. "She's all yours. I don't have the time to house-train her."

"Children," their mother sighed.

Louisa waited as Jack and his family settled into the

world's longest staring contest. He sat stonily beside her, his glower aimed across the table.

After an eternity, Blair propped her chin on her hand and smiled at them.

"So, what is it you do now, Jack? Some sort of manual labor?"

Her brittle, glassy veneer sharpened. Louisa could picture the bitch as a child, just as cold and hateful, pushing poor little Jack into a well for laughs.

Jack's jaw tightened. "I'm a contractor."

Louisa could almost hear his teeth grinding together. Fuck this noise.

"Don't be so modest!" she smiled, fake cheer infusing her voice. "I saw one of the houses he's renovating. It's absolutely gorgeous."

She smiled at him, her eyes glinting. Anger burned in her chest. Louisa turned her blinding smile on his parents.

"I'm sure Jack would have no trouble fitting you in, when you finally decide to redo this old place. He's got an amazing eye. He really makes old houses shine."

Jack choked on his sip of water. Blair blinked slowly, her large eyes glittering.

"Is that so?"

"Oh yes, he's amazing." Louisa patted Jack's arm. "He's got that kind of talent that runs in the blood, you know?"

Jack closed his eyes and started counting down under his breath. The rest of the family stared at her. Carter's face was turning red as he struggled not to laugh.

Louisa squeezed his hand under the table. She was going to show the monsters just how awful humans could really be.

"Well, um, I think it's nice that Jackson has found a hobby," Camille said blankly.

"Does being an errand boy for our mongrel overlord not pay well enough?" Alistair drawled, his sallow face wrinkling in disgust.

"Putting down monsters pays very well," Jack said coldly. "But everyone needs a hobby."

As Blair opened her mouth to spit back something scathing, the door swung open. A small, pale man wheeled a cart laden with plates into the room. The room was silent as dinner was served.

Louisa raised an eyebrow at their stony silence. It must be beneath them to air their drama to the help. The pale man shot her a surprised look as he placed a bowl in front of her.

That's right, buddy. Their shifterly magnificence is deigning to eat with a lowly human. Scandalous.

Louisa saluted him with her fork as he sidestepped out of the dining room. The sound of cutlery clinking echoed between them.

"Sooooo, how did you two meet?" Carter crooned across the table.

Louisa shot Jack a sideways look. He smiled and squeezed her knee. Oh boy, this was going to be good.

"I kidnapped her," he said, swirling his spoon through his soup.

"Kidnapped?!" Camille sputtered. "Jackson, *we* do not kidnap... humans."

"I did," Jack turned his eerie grin on her. "Best decision I've ever made, in fact."

"Awww, babe." Louisa fluttered her lashes at him. "That's so sweet."

"We've really bonded during her captivity." He smiled down at her, his eyes laughing.

"Yeah, once that concussion you gave me cleared up... sparks."

The shifters across the table stared in horror. Eyes wide, Camille clapped a hand dramatically over her gaping mouth. Carter propped his chin his hand, watching them with obvious delight.

"You're an odd human." Alistair shook his head.

"Why do you keep calling me human?" Louisa's ribs were aching from containing her laughter.

The shifters recoiled as though she had slapped them. Finally cracking, Jack burst out laughing. Tears ran down her cheeks as she joined him. She was damn well going to make them rethink any future dinner invitations.

"I'm just fucking with you, Al," Louisa hiccuped. "I already know you guys turn into house cats."

"Tigers," Blair said tightly.

"Pardon? I didn't quite catch that." Maybe she was enjoying this a little too much, but at least she had Jack smiling again.

"We. Are. Tigers," Blair said slowly, enunciating each syllable.

"Right, a cat. Like I said," Louisa waved her spoon dismissively.

Blair's pale face started to flush red. Knuckles cracked as her fists clenched on either side of her bowl. Oh dear, the ice queen was feeling the heat.

"You should muzzle your pet, Jackson." Alistair glared across the table.

The smile on Jack's face vanished behind stone. He turned slowly to stare at his father. Alistair leaned away and turned his face toward the table.

It was cute when he got all protective like that. Louisa stroked his hand. No worries though; she had this.

"Pet, Al? If anything, I think I'm the one doing all the petting."

Camille blanched. "Jackson! Surely, you wouldn't...*sully* yourself like that?"

Jack's spoon clattered in his bowl. His chair screeched back. Rising, he gripped Louisa's hand and pulled her to her feet.

"I've tolerated your bullshit tonight out of necessity, but I will not sit here and listen to you malign my Louisa." Jack pulled her toward the door.

"You're a disgrace to our name," Alistair growled under his breath.

Jack didn't even pause. "The feeling is mutual!" He yelled over his shoulder as they walked into the hall.

21

Jack pulled Louisa out the front door and down the front steps. The door slammed behind them, sealing the prejudice and bitterness in the house.

"So... that was fun." She gripped his wrist and checked his watch. "Fourteen minutes—I think the next time I can shave another two and a half minutes off our time."

He stopped abruptly and pulled her into his arms. Pressing his face into her curls, he breathed in her scent. The tightness in his shoulders eased with each breath.

"I'm sorry," he murmured into her hair. "They shouldn't have said that shit."

Louisa pulled back. Her small hands gripped the sides of his face. She looked him in the eye and smiled.

"It wasn't so bad." Standing on her tiptoes, she kissed him on the nose.

Jack could hardly believe his ears. "Not so bad? They called you a pet."

"The horror!" Louisa laughed. Her face calmed at the sadness twisting his mouth. "Hey, it seriously wasn't that bad. You told me ahead of time how horrible they are, remember? I was prepared."

He rested his forehead against hers. She was... amazing.

"I don't deserve you," Jack murmured.

Louisa twined her arms around his neck. "Probably not, but I guess I can settle for your six-pack abs and gorgeous smile. I'm selfless like that."

"Yes, you're such a giver," he chuckled. "Ready to go home?"

"No, I need food. You dragged me out of there before we were even done with the soup course."

Jack laughed. "You and your stomach." He pulled back and looped his arm around her shoulders. "You're going to eat the Den out of house and home."

"Bite me." Louisa pinched his arm. Ouch.

"Let's get you a burger before you start biting *me*."

"A burger? Camille would positively faint at the indecency," she giggled. "How did you grow up so wonderful when *they* are so damn awful?"

Jack lurched to a stop. A warm glow grew in his chest. There was something important she needed to see. No, that he wanted her to see.

"Can the burger wait a bit?" he asked nervously.

"Why?" Louisa arched an eyebrow. "I can't imagine that you want to go back in there and finish up dinner."

"I want to show you something."

"Okaaaay." She trailed behind him. "It's not your dick is it? Because I've already been suitably awed."

He snorted. "No, it's nothing in my pants."

"Bummer," she murmured under her breath.

Jack turned away from the truck and led her down a path that wound around the side of the house. The cobblestones snaked through the trees into a knot of heavy, green foliage. They passed under an archway of flowers and emerged into a lush garden oasis.

"Whoa," Louisa breathed, spinning in a slow circle.

Jack watched her. Wonder spread across her face as she admired the vibrant flowers spilling from every corner of the garden. She turned to him, her eyes gleaming.

"It's beautiful," Louisa smiled at him.

"*This* is where I grew up." He crossed to her and spun with her in a careful circle. "After the infamous birthday shift, Nate's parents did most of the raising. Nate's dad was the groundskeeper."

"Did he create… this?" She waved her hands at the delicate waterfall of flowers pouring over a stone birdbath.

"He did… with my and Nate's begrudging help." Jack smiled ruefully. "John didn't let us get away with shit."

"Tell me about them." Louisa leaned back against his chest. He curled his arms around her shoulders and cuddled her against him.

Jack opened and closed his mouth. A stone settled in his stomach. He both loved and hated talking about the couple he considered his real parents. It just… hurt.

They would have adored Louisa and her feisty attitude. They would have been thrilled that he had found someone like her. And yet they would never have a chance to meet her.

"They would have loved you." Jack smiled into her hair. "Martha, my mom, was warmth and joy. They lived in a house on the back of the property and every time I came stumbling in, traumatized by some shit Carter and Blair had pulled, she would be waiting with a hug and cookies in the oven. She was the one who bandaged up my skinned knees and hung my scribbles on the fridge."

"She sounds like a great mom," Louisa murmured to the flowers.

"She was," he agreed. "That blanket on my bed? She made that for me when I was twelve. It's my favorite thing in the world."

"What happened to her?"

"Mom died in a car accident when Nate and I were fourteen. Drunk driver. It was our freshman year in high school."

Louisa hugged the arms wrapped around her chest. "That must have been awful."

Jack swallowed the lump in his throat. "It was. I moved into their home after the funeral. It was easier to mourn with Nate and Dad then it was to stay in the house, surrounded by people who didn't care."

That had been a dark time. The little cottage had felt cold and empty for months. It had been nearly a year before he heard Nate laugh again. The only place he'd ever felt welcome up until that point had felt like the home of strangers.

"What was your dad like?" She nudged, pulling him back from the shadows. Jack nuzzled her hair, absorbing her delicate scent.

"He was a lot like Nate." He smiled. "Quiet, serious. He smiled a lot less after Mom died. When I was little, I would follow him around when he'd work the grounds, like a tiny, persistent shadow. He never complained; he'd just walk slower and admire the flowers so that my little legs could keep up.

"I remember the first time I called him Dad. It was an accident. He didn't say a word, he just passed me the watering can and pointed at the hydrangeas."

Jack kept talking, the story unraveling itself out of his control.

"The day I turned eighteen, Nate and I came home to a house filled with moving boxes. I was terrified that they were going to leave me behind, but Dad packed up the boxes and put Nate and me in the car. He walked up to the house and rang the bell. Ten minutes later, we could hear my parents screeching from the driveway. Dad came strolling out like it was nothing. He got in the truck and drove us out of here.

"He worked here for twenty years, built his life and his family in the little house out back. But the second Dad could legally get me out of this hell, he turned his back on the place and drove me out of here."

"He must have loved you so much," Louisa whispered. Jack caught the hint of envy in her voice. She'd never had that. She'd never had someone kiss her boo-boos or frame her macaroni masterpieces.

"He died five years ago," he said sadly. "Dad formed the Den; he made us a place where our kind could go when they had nowhere else. Some shifters, the type that saw eye to eye with my parents, didn't particularly like that. They made a deal with some rogue wolves. He was killed when the wolves stormed the house, trying to hold them off while the others escaped with the kids.

Jack swallowed the lump in his throat. "Nate was out of town on business and I was in the city, picking up some building supplies. We came home and made them pay for what they'd done. Shifters, wolves, we killed every last one of them and Nate took over the clan. We established the Pact with the other clans after that, so that it would never happen again."

Louisa turned in his arms to wrap herself around him.

Her hands clutched at his shoulders as she drew him tight against her. She didn't apologize or offer condolences, she just held him.

Jack's aching heart eased. Louisa pressed her lips lightly against his collarbone. His nose dropped into her hair, inhaling deeply. The soft scent washed over him and soothed the howling monster in his chest.

He leaned back and hooked his finger under Louisa's chin. Tilting her head up, he dropped a kiss on her lips. His hands trailed down her back to rest on the swell of her hips.

She twined her fingers behind Jack's neck and leaned back to look him in the face. Her somber expression cracked into a lopsided smile.

"Clever move." Louisa winked at him. "Bring a girl to your amazing garden, get her all emotional, and then try to get in her pants."

Jack threw his head back and laughed. "Is it working?"

She pursed her lips. "It might be."

He bent and hooked his hands behind her thighs. Lifting her to him, Jack carried her along the rocky path. If he was remembering right, there was a stone bench around here somewhere?

Louisa nibbled at his neck. A growl purred in his chest as he scanned the lush garden. Spotting the ivy-covered bench, Jack strode down the path and perched her on the edge.

Slim legs locked around his waist. He captured her lips, his tongue invading her mouth. Louisa ripped at his starched collar, her fingers trailing across his collarbone. Each soft brush against his skin sent little zings of pleasure straight to his dick.

She rolled her hips, a quiet whimper escaped as the sensitive flesh between her legs brushed against the fabric of his pants. He groaned as she rubbed herself against his growing erection. Louisa reached for his belt.

"Are we really doing this here?" Jack panted.

She grinned up at him. "Why not? It's more your garden than it is theirs."

The monster in his chest howled. She unhooked his belt, her fingers slipping down the front of his pants. Jack's eyes rolled back as her small hand circled him.

Louisa grinned at his white-knuckled grip on the edge of the stone bench. Stroking the steel cock between them, her fingers barely wrapped all the way around him.

Her soft hand gripped him tight, caressing his length from root to tip. Jack gritted his teeth as the pressure built in his cock. Just one little touch, and he was on the brink of spilling himself in his pants.

Wetness beaded at head of his cock. She dragged her thumb through it, circling his tip with the pad of her finger. Fuuuuuuuuuck. Stars danced in his eyes as he fought for control.

Easing his tight grip on her hips, he slipped his hand up the short skirt of her dress. His fingers stoked her dripping core. Already, Louisa's thighs were slick in anticipation. Jack buried his face in the crook of her neck with a groan.

He released his grip on the bench and pushed her skirt up. Louisa yelped. Jack jumped back at her surprised squeak, his claws at the ready. She flushed.

"Sorry, it's a little cold." She nudged the skirt between the frigid stone and her bare skin. His severe expression softened.

"Are you sure you want to do this here?" Jack unbuttoned his shirt, revealing a white T-shirt that hugged every curve of his abs. Tugging his button-up off his arms, he draped it over the cold stone.

He took long, even breaths until his claws sank back into his fingers. Control was a hard-fought battle. His monster wanted to feel Louisa sliding up and down on his cock as much as he did.

He slid his hands under her hips and lifted her off the back of the bench. Jack settled her carefully on the folded pad of his shirt.

A gentle smile crossed her face as he took care of her. Louisa gripped his chin and kissed him hard, their teeth clacking together. "Yes, take your pants off."

Jack pulled back. "I don't know if I can do slow and gentle right now..."

He didn't want to hurt her, not now, not ever. After the dinner fiasco, his control was already tenuous at best. He took a step back. Maybe they should go home, let the animal calm down a bit first.

Her legs tightened around his waist, stopping his retreat.

"I don't want slow. Take your pants off."

Any lingering doubts evaporated. He chuckled and dropped his zipper. As if his Lou would ever back down from a challenge.

His grip on her ass tightened as he tugged her to the edge of the bench. Louisa grasped him in her hand and slipped the tip of his cock into her opening. Rocking her hips, she drew him in inch by inch.

Air hissed from between his teeth as her tight pussy clamped down on him. Shit, she felt good. Jack watched her big, brown eyes flutter as she stretched around his cock.

"So tight," he groaned against her ear.

Jack rocked his hips, driving hard into her. Louisa moaned. Every desperate gasp coming from her lips pushed him a little further.

He bucked into her, his hips moving in a hard rhythm.

Gripping her ass, Jack drove her hips into his with a sharp slap. Louisa's head dropped back. Each powerful thrust of his hips dragged a needy moan from her throat.

God, she was driving him crazy. Jack's fingers tangled in her curls, dragging her mouth to his for a punishing kiss. The aroused scent pouring off of her was drowning his senses in pleasure.

Pressure built in his cock. He was close, too close. Louisa had to come first. He *needed* her to come first, needed to hear his name on her lips as she broke.

She writhed, her back arching as he thrust harder and faster. Jack looked down to where they met. His dick pounded into her, her greedy pussy swallowing every inch of him. The pressure between his legs grew to excruciating levels.

Reaching between them, he slipped his fingers between her folds and stroked her clit. Louisa shattered. She screamed into his shoulder, her core tightening around his aching cock. He thrust once, twice, and the dam broke.

Jack emptied himself inside of her, each pulse of her core dragging the pleasure out a little longer. Rocking his hips, he shuddered. Louisa leaned against his chest. They panted, their breath seesawing in rhythm.

They stood in silence a moment longer, the tranquil garden absorbing the passion from the air. Jack smiled at the top of her head. She was his, even if she didn't know it yet. They had a lot of years ahead for him to convince her of the fact, but Jack was a patient man. He would wait as long as it took for Lou to see how thoroughly she was caught.

Louisa looked up at his face and smiled. "So… about that burger?"

. . .

"You and your stomach," Jack laughed.

Zipping his pants, he moved to lift her off the bench. He froze, his nostrils flaring.

A steady clapping shattered the cloak of silence in the garden. Jack turned into a statue beneath her hands. Louisa peaked over his shoulder. Oh fuck.

Carter strode through the arched entrance, the light shining through his white-blond hair like a halo. He sauntered down the path, smirking.

A warning growl rumbled in Jack's chest. He turned, placing himself between Carter and Louisa. She slid off the back of the bench and balanced on her teetering heels. Tugging her skirt down in a hurry, she glared at Carter around Jack's shoulder.

"I figured you would have run off after that shitshow, yet here you are. Right where you always hid as a child," Carter leered. His nostrils flared, scenting the air. "And you even took the time to play with your pet."

Louisa cringed behind Jack. That wasn't a bit humiliating or anything.

"What do you want, Carter?" Jack rumbled, his arms crossed over his chest.

"Can't a guy just want to hang out with his little brother?"

"Not when that guy is you," he said shortly. ""Why have you been following me?"

A crooked grin twisted Carter's mouth. "What makes you think I've been following you?"

Jack tapped his nose. "You don't smell like Blight, so you're not looking to be put down. Which means you must want something?"

He snorted. "What could I possibly want from you, dog? Your girl? She can't be *worth* much."

"Keep talking and I'll show you *exactly* how much I think she's worth."

Jack's arms dropped to his sides. His claws extended, ready for blood. Louisa cringed. Degrading behavior, underhanded remarks, rude gestures? Sure, she'd been prepared for that. But bloodshed? No, fuck no.

Louisa sidestepped Jack. "Boys, this is dumb. You're both big and tough, but this isn't getting me any closer to a burger."

Carter looked her up and down. "I'm not here for your little friend, though I do find her rather entertaining."

"Then what are you doing out here?" A sharp voice interrupted.

Blair stepped through the arch. Carter tensed as Jack nudged Louisa back behind him. "Don't move," Jack whispered to her.

She sighed. Why had they left that awful dinner if they were all just going to end up arguing out here?

"Carter, I expect more from you," Blair purred as she stepped up beside him. "Surely, you aren't out here looking for a turn with Jack's new pet?"

Louisa closed her eyes and counted to ten. What was the point of stopping Jack from tearing them to pieces if they were really this stupid? Ridding the world of these idiots would probably count as community service.

Jack took a step forward. Her beautiful face twisted in a hateful sneer, Blair hissed. Carter looked between them nervously. He glanced at Louisa poking her head around Jack's elbow.

Hands held imploringly, Carter stepped toward them. Louisa winced. She knew it was a mistake before his foot had even landed. Jack blurred, grabbing Carter by the collar. He flew through the air to crash in a rhododendron bush.

Louisa blinked. Well, at least he hadn't just killed the twerp outright.

Carter lurched to his feet, hissing wildly. Jack stepped forward, moving the fight out of Louisa's reach. Eyes glowing orange, Carter's claws extended. Louisa gasped as he rushed at Jack.

Holding his ground, Jack calmly let his brother launch himself at him. His hands shot out at the last second to catch him in mid-air. Jack snagged his arm and spun, using his own momentum to whip Carter into a birdbath.

The decoration crumbled to pieces. Carter delicately brushed the dust from his lapel. He rose silently, razor-sharp teeth dropping into his mouth.

Louisa glanced at Blair. Illuminated by lanterns, her face was cast in shadows. Her eyes shone from the darkness, a satisfied glint blazing from the orange. Evil bitch.

As Carter moved to launch himself at Jack again, a slim figure stepped through the arch. Camille planted her feet and roared.

Carter skidded to a halt at the rolling thunder. Jack turned slowly to stare at his dark-haired mother. Silence descended on the garden as no one dared to breathe.

"Enough," the quiet woman hissed.

Blair turned and glided out of the garden. Camille motioned for Carter to follow. He glanced at them over his shoulder, regret plain on his face, before stomping after his sister.

Camille looked between Jack and Louisa, her face devoid of emotion.

"Get out," she said coldly.

22

Jack gripped the steering wheel so hard that he was surprised it hadn't snapped off already. Frankly, careening off into a ditch might be a welcome distraction from the maelstrom in his head.

He glanced at Louisa from the corner of his eye. Slumped against the door, she had nodded off on the drive home, a half-eaten burger still clutched in her hand. The knot in Jack's stomach tightened as he watched her chest rise and fall.

She was everything he had always wanted, and so much more. And tonight, he let her be in danger. No, it was so much worse than that. He had walked Lou, hand in hand, into that pit of vipers without a backup plan.

Never had it occurred to Jack that his family would actually attack them. Belittle, demean, or even threaten, sure. He should have known better.

He watched Louisa's curls twist in the air blowing from the vents. He should have known better about a lot of things. This was not a world for humans. Jack would never be able to keep her safe from what they were.

He had forgotten for a short, blissful week that at his core, he was a monster. Jack sighed. Maybe he was a monster, but Louisa hadn't seemed to mind.

He pulled the truck into the garage, his thoughts still twisting painfully. Brown eyes blinked open as the truck came to a stop. Louisa sat up and smiled sleepily.

She frowned at the burger in her hand. "Huh, I thought I finished that."

Louisa opened the door and continued nibbling at her burger. Jack watched her, bemused, as she stumbled sleepily around the truck, her shoes forgotten on the floor.

I love her.

The thought crashed through his skull like a ton of bricks. He caught a glimpse of his wide eyes reflecting in the windshield.

Jack had known that he felt something for Louisa, something powerful. But he hadn't been ready to call it *Love,* with a capital L. L-O-V-E.

What had he told Alice the other morning? Only wolves had mates. Jack thought of the pull that he had felt toward Louisa since the very beginning. Maybe their curse was evolving, like Alice had claimed.

He sat frozen in his seat. Mate or not, it changed nothing. He couldn't keep dragging Louisa along, tossing her into dangerous situations. Just being in the Den put a target on her back, as Dad had shown them five years ago.

Jack knew what he needed to do. He'd known from the moment Carter's claws had burst from his fingertips. He just hadn't wanted to admit it.

The monster in his chest roared, clawing to be free. Jack gritted his teeth and shoved back. He needed to be human for just a little longer, and then he could let the beast out to tear at its fur. The monster raged, furious at what had to come next.

Louisa paused at the door and turned to wait for him, absently chewing her scrap of food. Jack watched her through the windshield. Tonight, or else he would lose his nerve.

JACK CLIMBED out of the truck, her shoes in hand. Louisa glanced down at her bare toes. She frowned. When did she take her shoes off? She shrugged and took a bite of her cold burger.

Louisa turned her face up as Jack leaned past her to open the door. The smile evaporated from her lips. His face was alarmingly somber, more so than she had ever seen it. Had his family really bothered him that much?

She reached for his hand, but it slipped right out of her grasp as he trudged down the hall. Louisa stared at his tense shoulders. Hurt pinched at her chest. He had never pulled away from her like this—something was definitely wrong.

She trailed behind him, the tense silence sharpening between them. He led her to his bedroom, closing the door behind them. Still, Jack refused to meet her eyes. The worry eating at her belly crested.

"What's wrong?" Louisa nibbled at her lip.

Jack fished through his dresser, his back ramrod straight.

"Go get changed," he said without turning.

"Jack." She crossed the room and tentatively placed her hand on his hard shoulder. "What's wrong?"

He shuddered under her palm. "You need to get changed."

Louisa sighed. "Okay, I'll change my clothes. Then will you tell me why you're being this way?"

"It's time for you to go." Jack leaned away from her touch and spun out of her reach. Tossing his clothes on the bed, he stared out the window.

Shock crashed through her in turbulent waves. Go? As in... go *home*? Louisa hadn't thought about her empty apartment in days. Quite frankly, if she never saw the depressing little hole again, she wouldn't be heartbroken.

But why did he want to go there? Did he think there was some clue there that he had missed?

"Why are we going to my apartment?" Louisa puzzled.

"*We* aren't." Jack turned to look at her for the first time since they'd set foot in the house. His laughing eyes were flat and empty. She shivered. "*You* are going home."

Ice flooded her veins. Jack wasn't just benching her, he was getting rid of her. He didn't want her anymore. A knot tightened in her belly as her old insecurities scrabbled for purchase.

Louisa shook the crippling thought from her head. No. He cared about her. He had proven again and again that he had feelings for her.

"Why are you doing this?" she asked, hating the vulnerable tremble in her voice.

"This world isn't for you," Jack said, his voice flat. "I never should have pulled you into this."

Anger boiled to the surface, drowning the hurt.

"Bullshit," Louisa spat. She'd been doing just fine for herself. Hell, she was excelling at handling this mystical crap.

Jack raised a sandy eyebrow. "Bullshit? You're a human and you're playing with monsters that can, and will, snap you like a toothpick. You have no place here."

"You didn't feel that way a few days ago when you kidnapped me, or even a few hours ago when you were leading me into your prejudiced and mentally unhinged family's dinner party."

The muscle beneath Jack's eye jumped. Her eyes narrowed.

"That's it, isn't it?" She glared at him. "It was your family. You're the big, bad shifter and I'm the lowly, human pet who doesn't belong."

"Don't call yourself that," Jack growled.

"Why not? You said it yourself, I don't belong here."

He took a step forward and froze, his hand clenched at his sides.

"Do you even realize how close to death you were this evening?" he asked quietly.

"What? When your idiot brother was attacking you?" Louisa scoffed. "There's a reason I stood behind you and didn't rush out to shake his hand."

Jack turned and paced the room. His fingers thrust through his hair, leaving behind frustrated spikes.

"You don't get it." He shook his head.

"Then explain it to me," she said, her voice honed to a sharp edge by her anger.

Jack stopped in place and turned to face Louisa. "I can tear through Carter like tissue paper. It wouldn't have even been hard. But what if Blair had also attacked? And my mother? And my father? Yes, I would have won but one of them could have gotten past me and ripped your throat out. I'm good, but if all four had targeted you instead? I don't know that I would have been fast enough and that scares the shit out me.

"And just like that, you would be dead. No supernatural healing, no do-overs. You would. Be. Dead."

Louisa's frown softened. The doubts clamoring for attention settled to a dull roar. He was afraid… for her.

She stepped toward him and grabbed his hand. "Then we don't go there again. No more terrible dinners, no more hateful comments. They can't hurt me if I'm not there."

Jack's face shattered. His large hands cupped her face, his thumbs tracing the lines of her cheekbones. Louisa winced at the devastation in his eyes.

"It's not just them, Lou. Everyone in this house is a monster. Nate, Alice, me... even Abby. It only takes one slip, and you're crippled, or worse. You saw what happened at dinner the other night and that was over a meaningless comment about dry chicken."

Shaking his head, Jack dropped his hands and stepped back.

"I won't put you in danger like that," he said firmly.

Louisa looked away, her eyes welling with tears. She would not cry, she told herself. She would not. The pain in her chest pulsed.

"So that's it? I don't even get a say?" She bit her lip. "Even if I choose to stay, if I think you're worth the risk?"

"That's exactly why you don't get a say," Jack smiled sadly. "You're too brave for your own good."

She shook her head. "And you're a coward."

Turning her back on him, she stomped into the bathroom and jammed her scattered clothes into her empty duffel. Slinging it over her shoulder, Louisa walked to the bedroom door. She pulled it open and paused. She wouldn't look at him, she couldn't.

"Good-bye, Jack."

The door clicked shut behind her. An anguished howl echoed through the house, shaking the walls. Louisa blinked back tears as her heart howled with him.

Alice poked her head out her bedroom door. She took

one look at the bag over her shoulder and straightened. The corners of her mouth sank into a sad frown.

She crossed to Louisa and took the bag from her shoulder. "Come on. I'll take you home."

Louisa trailed after Alice, her bare feet silent on the polished wood floor. With each step the hope that Jack would change his mind shrunk. He was really quitting on whatever this was.

Anger and grief twisted inside of her. She wasn't sure which was going to win, but the ice cream tucked in the back of her freezer was prepared for either possibility.

Alice led her down the stairs toward the garage. A tiny figure darted out of the kitchen door and froze in front of them. Abby stared at them, her dark eyes wide. A smear of chocolate colored the corner of her mouth.

Alice raised a slim, red eyebrow. "Aren't you supposed to be in bed?"

Abby shifted from foot to foot. "I was thirsty."

"Thirsty for chocolate?"

Abby's eyes landed on the bag over Alice's shoulder. She ignored the question, eyes flitting between the bag and Louisa.

"You're leaving." Her bottom lip trembled.

Oh god, please don't cry. Louisa was holding on by a thread. If the kid cried, she was a goner.

"I'm sorry, Abby." Her eyes burned. "But it's time for me to go home."

Tears dripped down Abby's round cheeks. She sniffled and darted forward to wrap her arms around Louisa's knees.

"But you were going to give me puppy-friends," Abby sobbed into her legs. "You were gonna be Aunt Louisa."

Louisa took a deep breath and looked up at the ceiling. The misery clawing at her chest was nearly overwhelming.

"Alice?" her voice cracked.

She dropped Louisa's bag on the floor and gently unwrapped Abby's clinging limbs. Scooping her into her arms, Alice quickly carried the crying child up the stairs.

Goddamn Jack and his stupid, selfless bullshit. She forced the tears down as the air in her chest sawed painfully out of her lungs. The tightness in her chest constricted further as she breathed through the unshed tears.

Alice glided down the stairs, her arms empty. She snagged the duffel and gently gripped Louisa's elbow.

"If we're going, we need to go now," she whispered to her. "If the Aunts come to investigate, we're sunk."

Alice had Louisa down the hall and tucked into a car within minutes. They drove in silence. No prying questions, no careful condolences, just blessed silence.

Her heart was shattered to pieces. There would be no mashing it back together after this one. Jack, with his cheeky grins and kind eyes, had ruined her.

The car pulled up outside of her building. Louisa reached for her door handle and froze. How could she walk back in there like nothing had happened? Like her world hadn't just fallen apart?

Alice didn't say a word as the car idled. Louisa closed her eyes. Keep it together, just a little longer.

She looked at Alice, unable to muster even the saddest of smiles. "Thank you... for everything."

"No, thank you."

Louisa blinked. "For what?"

"He might be too stupid to realize what you are to him, but I'm not." Alice patted her knee. "You give me hope for the rest of us."

"Thanks... I think?"

Alice smiled sadly. "You're welcome. If you ever need

anything, don't hesitate to call the Den. We protect our own."

"I'm not one of you." Louisa shook her head. "I'm just human."

Alice's cool gray eyes stared back at her. "You're clan enough for me."

Louisa choked on her tears. In a hurry, she opened the door and slid out of the car. She ran up the stairs of her building and pounded on the super's door.

He ripped open the door, eyes red and ready to scream at whoever was disturbing his sleep. He took one look at the tears running down Louisa's cheeks and handed her a spare key.

She took the stairs two at a time and burst into her apartment. Swaying on the spot, Louisa stood in her living room. Same mystery stains on the carpet and discolored patches on the walls. Same secondhand furniture. But not the same Louisa.

Stumbling to the sagging couch, she collapsed into a pile and let herself break.

23

Louisa woke, shivering in her blankets. Where was Jack? Didn't he know that it was his job to keep her warm? She rolled over and patted the empty stretch of mattress beside her. When her hand hit empty air, she cracked open one eye.

She was home, in her own bed. Alone. Lying on sheets that still smelled like him. Jack's angry words crashed over her like a tidal wave. Her raw, tear-wrung eyes crashed shut as they welled up again.

No. She scrubbed the heels of her hands over her face. She was NOT going to cry again. Last night was for crying; today was for living.

Louisa whipped the blankets off of her and stumbled out of bed. Ripping the sheets off, she dragged the lump of bedding out the door and onto the couch. First laundry, then probably job-hunting, because there was no doubt in her mind that Dr. Adler was ready to give her the boot.

Two hours later, Louisa rolled up to the clinic, a tray of giant coffees clutched in her hand. A quick search online had showed her just how few available jobs

Raven Falls had at the ready. If she didn't want to bag groceries, she'd have to take her chances with the dragon.

Dr. Adler turned a brilliant shade of purple as she walked through the door. Louisa shoved an overpriced coffee into her hands and crossed to her desk without a word.

Nonplussed, the vet clutched the cup to her chest and stomped into her office. The door slammed with a resounding crash. Jessica turned in her chair, her eyes wide. Louisa dropped a cup in front of her.

"How did you do that?" she asked in shock.

"Do what?" Louisa snatched her own coffee and tossed the tray.

Jessica glanced nervously over her shoulder. "You disappeared for almost a week and she didn't even yell. How did you do it?"

"Not caring seems to help," she drawled as she sorted through the pile of debris that had accumulated on her desk.

"Where did you go?" Jessica scooted her chair closer.

"Nowhere," Louisa glared at the piles of papers. "Did you do ANY filing while I was gone?"

She sipped her coffee. "Uh, no."

"Great." Louisa shook her head. "Glad to see nothing's changed."

Her heart stopped as she shoved some papers aside. Lying on her desk, still sealed in a plastic bag, was Jack's collar. She glared at it suspiciously. Opening the bottom drawer, she swept it quickly off her desk. Louisa slammed the drawer shut. Stupid Jack.

Scooping up the small, white mountain, she trudged into the filing room. She wiled away the morning, stuffing paperwork into files and grumbling under her breath. Anything to keep her mind occupied and away from *him*.

Jessica poked her head through the door. "Yo, there's someone here to see you."

Louisa's heart leapt. Jack. She ran out of the office in a rush. Blinking, she skidded to a stop in front of two strangers in somber, black suits.

"In a hurry?" the taller of the two asked.

"Uh, no. Sorry," Louisa stammered. Who the hell were these guys? "I thought you were someone else."

Their focus sharpened. She squirmed under their intense stares.

"Who were you expecting, Ms. Miller?"

"I'm sorry, who are you?" Louisa frowned. "You did ask for me, yes?"

The short, blond man stepped forward. Reaching into his jacket, he pulled out a badge.

"Agents Marshall and Scott. FBI, Unnatural Occurrences Division." He slipped the badge back into his pocket. "We have a few questions for you, Ms. Miller."

Oh shit. With all of last night's drama, Louisa had completely forgotten about the federal agents looking for her. She schooled her face. Be cool, girl.

"Questions about what?" She crossed her arms over her chest and studied the pair.

Agent Marshall was shorter than Louisa. She couldn't even begin to guess his age due to the round, baby face he had been cursed with. He no doubt had problems being taken seriously as a federal agent.

Agent Scott, on the other hand, couldn't be taken as anything less than serious. The perpetual frown lining his face made him look like one of those wrinkly-faced dogs with a bad attitude. Louisa wasn't much for police procedurals, but if this wasn't a good-cop/bad-cop setup, she'd eat her shoes.

"About where you've been for the past week," Agent Scott growled. "Would you care to enlighten us?"

Louisa raised an eyebrow. "No."

"No?" he sputtered.

"No," she repeated firmly.

"Now, listen here, Ms. Mil-"

Louisa silenced him with a wave of her hand. A week ago, his pissy little growls might have scared her into cooperating, but in the past few days she had seen monsters that would make him wet his bed.

"Agent Scully-"

"It's Agent Scott," Marshall interjected.

"Right, Agent Scott. Whatever. Am I a suspect in a crime?"

"Well...no."

"Then why would you possibly need to know where I've been?" Louisa stared him down. He glared and took a step toward her.

Agent Marshall moved between them. "Perhaps we can take this somewhere more discreet?" His eyes flicked toward Jessica, her mouth hanging open.

"Right." Agent Scott straightened. "We'll take her down to the station."

Louisa bristled. "Am I being arrested?"

"Technically, no." Marshall winced.

"Then *technically*"—Louisa glared at his partner—"we can speak in an empty exam room."

Agent Scott opened his mouth to argue, but his partner waved him down.

"That'll be fine."

Smiling brightly, she gestured down the hall. "After you, gentlemen."

The suits filed awkwardly into the empty room and stood against the wall. Louisa closed the door behind her and perched on the rolling stool in the corner.

Agent Scott rounded on her the second her butt hit the seat.

"Where have you been this week, Ms. Miller?"

"Home." She smiled sweetly at him. "I've been under the weather."

"Is there anyone who can verify that?"

"No, I live alone."

Agent Marshall inserted himself into the conversation. "And you didn't call in sick?"

Louisa feigned confusion. "I could have sworn that I did. My fever was pretty high at one point; I might have just thought I did."

Marshall balanced a briefcase on the exam table and flipped it open. He snagged a file and pulled a series of photographs from inside.

"Do you recognize this man?"

A photo of Jack stared back at her. She took the photo and pretended to examine it. Were they watching Jack? Watching the Den? Louisa didn't recognize any of his surroundings; he seemed to be just walking down the street.

Careful to keep her face pleasantly neutral, she handed the photo back.

"No, I don't know him. Should I?"

Agent Scott leaned in, his eyes narrowed. "You didn't spend the past week with him?"

Louisa frowned. "I was sick. I already told you that."

The two agents looked at each other, the kind look slipping from Agent Marshall's face. They both turned to give her a hard stare. Oooh, bad cop/bad cop.

"You need to be truthful with us, Ms. Miller," Marshall said, his eyes cold.

"I am," she said, faking confusion.

"You worked on a patient the day before you disappeared," Agent Scott pulled a different photo from the file. Jack's fluffy animal form, again taken from a distance. "Where did you take him? Your boss wasn't sure."

Of course, Adler had sold her out. Louisa scrambled for a plausible lie.

"I didn't take him anywhere. He died."

"Dr. Adler says differently." Agent Scott ripped the photo out of her hand, his eyes narrowing triumphantly.

Louisa snorted. "Dr. Adler spends half the workday at the salon. Do you really think she has a clue what goes on here?"

"Why are you lying to us?" Agent Marshall hissed at her, his boyish face going red with anger. "You know what they are, don't you?"

"Are you okay? You're looking a bit flushed?" she asked pleasantly.

"You know where they are!" He screamed in her face.

Both Louisa and Agent Scott leaned back at the outburst.

"I don't know what you're talking about, Agent Marshall, but I think you might be unwell." Louisa stood, staring the little man coldly in the eye. "However, unwell or not, I do not appreciate being strong-armed in my place of work, and I like being called a liar even less. The dog in the photo died of surgical complications and without anyone to claim him, was promptly cremated."

"Do you have the paperwork verifying this?" Agent Scott asked over his partner's stammering.

"I do. You may wait in the lobby while I collect it," Louisa said firmly.

Without another word, she turned on her heel and marched back to the filing room. She scrambled to remember any other patients that had been cremated last week. A cat, there had been a cat.

Louisa glanced over her shoulder to check on the agents and started flipping through the unfiled paperwork. Whipping out the correct paper, she quickly scanned it. Unfinished, just like she had hoped. It didn't even have the species filled in.

Taking a deep breath, she walked out to the lobby.

"I'm sorry gentlemen, it looks like the paperwork is only half-finished." Louisa handed them the paperwork and winced. "Unfortunately, with my being out of the office, Jessica was too busy to get these completed. However, you can see the date in the corner and the order of cremation. That animal was the only one cremated that day. I'm sure Jessica would be willing to verify that."

Not *technically* a lie. Plus, Jessica would usually sign anything you put in front of her.

The men turned to the desk and frowned at her empty seat. Louisa choked on a snort. Good old Jessica. You could always count on her to disappear in your hour of need.

"I'm sure she'll be back soon."

Agent Marshall stomped out the door, slamming it behind him. His partner tucked the paperwork into his briefcase and frowned his wrinkly jowls at Louisa.

"They are dangerous, Ms. Miller. I suggest you keep that in mind."

Louisa watched his back disappear out the door. Panic

twisted her belly. They were hunting Jack and the Den. Maybe even all the supes. She had to warn them.

She walked back to her desk and opened the bottom drawer. Jack's collar glinted in the fluorescent lighting. Louisa squinted at the numbers and lifted the phone off the hook. She dropped it and took a step back.

They could have tapped the phones. Or god only knows what else. The two stooges were probably sitting in their car, right outside, just waiting for her to go running and lead them straight to him.

Louisa kicked the drawer closed and dropped into her seat. She would have to wait. A plan started to piece together in her mind. Lunch. She would only have to wait until her lunch break.

She watched the clock tick as seconds crawled by. At twenty to noon, she couldn't take it anymore. Close enough. Louisa ripped open the drawer and slipped the collar into her pocket. Grabbing her jacket, she tugged it to hide the bulge at her hip.

"I'll be back in a minute," Louisa called to Jessica, who had mysteriously drifted back in with another coffee. She waved one pink-tipped hand dismissively.

Louisa slipped out the back door and walked calmly down the street. A black car peeled out of the parking lot and shadowed her at a leisurely pace. Looked like Scully and Mulder were on the prowl.

She slowed her pace. Out for a nice, leisurely stroll in the sunshine, not suspicious at all. Louisa walked, beaming pleasantly at her surroundings. A vibrant explosion of color on the corner announced her destination.

Just a few more feet. Her face schooled into a peaceful, blank mask as she closed the distance.

A brilliant rainbow graced the large front window,

twinkle lights wrapped around the colorful door. Louisa waved at the agents creeping along in the car and stepped through the door.

Clouds of vanilla and chocolate wafted comfortingly around her. She took a deep breath and let the cheerful vibes wash over her. Louisa studied the interior.

A handful of customers sat cozily around mismatched tables, coffee and pastries in hand. Behind the counter, a willowy blonde frosted cupcakes. Her long hair was piled on top of her head, loose tendrils floating around her face. She looked up as Louisa crossed to the counter.

The blonde shot a frown at the FBI agents' car, parked right in front of her colorful window. Louisa made a show of perusing the baked goods neatly displayed behind the glass counter. Blondie leaned in, her face a mask of calm.

"Do you need me to call the police, honey?"

"No, thank you." Louisa smiled at her. "Just two chocolate cherry cupcakes... and a small favor."

She leaned back, a mischievous twinkle in her eyes. "What ever you need."

When she turned away to slip two cupcakes into a bright pink box, Louisa slipped the collar out of her pocket. She slid it onto the counter, hiding her movements by leaning into the counter.

Don't mind me, scary FBI men. Just getting a look at these lemon tarts.

Blondie slid the box in front of the collar. Louisa smiled and pulled a crumpled twenty-dollar bill from her pocket.

"If you could call that number"— she nodded toward the collar—"and let them know that their dog is still under observation, I would appreciate it."

Blondie slipped the collar off the counter and dropped it

into a deep pocket on her apron. Louisa scooped up her pink box and clutched it to her chest.

"Keep the change," Louisa said as she turned toward the door.

A slim hand brushed her arm. Blondie's sharp-blue eyes met her own.

"They're bad news; I can see it on their faces." She flicked her eyes at the car. "Do you want to slip out the back?"

"No, thank you. I'm going straight back to work, my cupcakes in plain view." She looked pointedly at her apron pocket. "Besides, I think my ride will be showing up soon."

"My name is Rainy." She grinned and dropped her hand. "Don't be a stranger."

24

Louisa waved at the scowling agents as she rounded the clinic, her pink box clutched to her chest. She walked down the alley to the side door and froze, her hand on the doorknob.

The hair on the back of her neck stood at attention. A shadow moved forward, casting her in darkness. Louisa turned slowly. A sour stench washed over her. She bent at the waist, gagging.

Choking, she looked up. Iris stood across the alley. She scrambled back, her shoulders bumping the door. What the fuck?

Louisa looked the figure up and down. No, not Iris, not even a female. But definitely a ghoul. A squat man, his shoulders broad and framing a barrel chest, loomed. His golden eyes stared blankly through her. Gray skin blistered in the afternoon sun.

"Do you need help?" she asked hesitantly.

The ghoul hissed, exposing a mouthful of razor-sharp, bloodstained teeth. Louisa recoiled as one arm reached for her. She leapt back, grasping behind her for the doorknob. A wave of his stench crashed over her as he inched forward.

In a rush, the ghoul lunged forward, wrapping an arm around her waist. Louisa beat at the arm with her free hand. She hurled the box of cupcakes to the ground and clawed at the arm.

He hissed again, his mouth a fraction of an inch from her ear. Louisa elbowed him in the throat. The ghoul dropped her, gagging.

She ran for the door. Her fingers closed around the doorknob as something crashed against the back of her head. Louisa's vision narrowed to a tiny tunnel of light.

Her last thought before slipping out of consciousness was of the uselessness of the FBI agents sitting in the parking lot just around the corner.

JACK RESTED his head on the table. The Aunts' piercing glare burned a hole through the back of his skull. Angrily stirring her yogurt, Alice kept making little, indignant noises under her breath. If he tried hard enough, maybe the morning would just reset itself.

"You're a fool," Aunt Aggie hissed from the stove. The pancake on the end of her spatula flipped with an angry splat.

"So we've established, Agnes," Jack mumbled.

"You sent our girl away," Dot spat as she wiped down the table.

He sighed into the stained wood of the kitchen table. The old bats had been at it for well over an hour now. Swooping into the kitchen, they had refused to acknowledge his presence until Alice had stumbled in, shooting daggers from her eyes.

"She wasn't your girl," he repeated for what felt like the thousandth time over breakfast. "She wasn't even mine."

"She could've been," Alice interjected. "But you fucked it up."

Jack lifted his head and glowered at the disapproving harpies. Not an ounce of compassion in the whole damn room. Did they just watch their soulmate walk out of their lives? That was a big, fat, fucking no.

Even Abby was refusing to speak to him now. She'd stomped her little feet into the kitchen, snagged a pile of pancakes and walked out with barely a glare in his direction. Nate at least had shot him a sympathetic shrug as he followed his trudging child out of the room.

"You need to eat something." Aunt Dot slid a plate of food across the table. "If you're going to be an idiot, you may as well be a well-fed idiot."

Jack's stomach curled uncomfortably. "No, thank you." He nudged the plate away.

"She's right. Just because you're a moron doesn't mean you don't deserve food," Alice added, spooning yogurt onto her pancakes.

Weird-ass bird.

"I'm not hungry," Jack grumbled. He rested his face on the table again.

How could he possibly think about food when his chest felt like there was a gaping hole in the center of it? Eat? When every whiff of vanilla made his stomach clench?

"Well, if you went and begged your mate to forgive you, maybe your appetite would come back!" Aggie banged her skillet against the stovetop.

"No." The table rattled as his fist crashed down. Jack raised his head, his eyes glowing green. "I am doing what I have to to keep Louisa safe. Now BUTT. OUT!"

The old cats hissed in unison. Dot opened her mouth to spit something scathing and was interrupted by the ringing of the house phone. Alice looked back and forth between their glowering faces.

"I'll get it." She rolled her eyes and pushed to her feet. Alice stumbled around the table, her fork still clutched in her hand.

"We want Louisa back." Aunt Aggie's eyes narrowed dangerously.

"Too damn bad, cat."

The Aunts scowled at him, their gold eyes flashing. They could glare and hiss all they wanted, but Jack wasn't going to drag Lou back into their shadowy world. She deserved better than that.

Alice's irate voice cut through the stare-down. "Listen lady, I'm looking at our only dog right now so I really don't know what you're talking about."

Jack and the old lionesses turned to stare at Alice as she grumbled into the phone. Her eyes widened and she spun to face Jack.

"Who brought you his collar?"

Whose collar? Wait, *his* collar? When had he even had it last, and why was some stranger calling about it? Jack wracked his brain. He had to have had it in the clinic or else Connor and Alice never would have known to come and get him.... Louisa.

Jack leapt from his seat and vaulted over the table. Snatching the phone from her hand, he pressed it to his ear.

"What did she look like?" he interrupted. "Dark curly hair, brown eyes?"

"Yes," a musical voice answered.

"What exactly did she say?"

"She said to call this number and to let whoever answers know that their dog is still under observation."

"That's it? Nothing else?" Disappointment settled like a dumbbell in his chest.

The woman on the phone hesitated. "She didn't say anything else... but there were two men following her. Dark car, mean eyes. The whole thing was giving me bad vibes."

Jack's stomach dropped. "Did they follow her when she left?"

Alice's face paled. The Aunts exchanged worried glances and leaned in to listen to her answer.

"Yes," she said firmly. "I offered to let her sneak out the back but she said she was going straight back to work and that someone would be along to pick her up... are you that someone?"

Jack tossed the phone back to Alice and ran for the door. Dark car, mean eyes? He would bet every cent in his bank account that it was the same car that had been parked outside the clinic, the same car that belonged to their mystery agents.

Shit, hadn't Nate put someone on the car? Jack skidded to a halt as Nate himself appeared next to him. He grabbed him by the shoulders.

"Who did you have on the mystery agents?" Jack asked in a rush.

Nate blinked at his wild eyes. "What?"

Jack shook his shoulders. "Who's tracking the feds right now?"

"Uh, Tony. Why?"

Jack dropped his hands and darted around him. He sprinted down the hall for the garage. Tearing through the door, he searched his pockets for his keys.

Shit, shit, shit. He patted down his sweatpants. Where

were his goddamn keys? Alice burst into the garage, the phone still pressed to her ear. Nate followed right behind her.

"Rainbow Bakery! Down the street from the clinic—she left less than five minutes ago."

"I need keys!" Jack roared back.

Nate pushed past her and yanked his own keys out of his pocket. Jack lunged for them, his hand sailing back empty as he whipped them out of Jack's reach.

"I'll drive; you're too worked up."

Running around the front of the car, Jack ripped open the door and dropped into the passenger seat. Nate climbed into the driver's side and peeled out of the garage.

The blaring ring of Nate's phone cut through the tense silence. Eyes on the road, he fished it out of his pocket and held it to his ear. Jack stared at the trees whipping by, his leg bouncing. Couldn't he go any faster?

"You're sure? Thanks." Nate dropped the phone in his cup holder. "That was Tony, he says the feds followed her to the bakery and back to the clinic. They're still parked right out front."

The tangle in Jack's chest didn't ease. His skin prickled uncomfortably, screaming for them to get there. Something was wrong, and it wasn't the FBI agents babysitting the parking lot.

"Nate, drive faster."

"What?"

His fists clenched in his lap. "Something's wrong. Drive faster."

Nate glanced at the tight expression stretched across Jack's face and stomped on the gas. Trees blurred as the speed limit became a passing suggestion.

They screeched into the back alley eight minutes later,

half the time of the usual drive. Jack leapt from the car and burst through the side door.

The dozing receptionist's head shot up at the commotion.

"Where's Louisa?" Jack scanned the lobby, his eyes moving wildly from side to side.

"She left for lunch like thirty minutes ago," she yawned, giving her empty coffee cup a shake.

Jack spun and moved toward the front door, ready to tear the federal agents right out of their car. They had her. Tony must not have been paying attention. If anything had happened to Lou, Tony was next on his list.

Nate grabbed his arm and dragged him back. "No."

"Louisa should be here by now," he hissed. "*They* have her."

"No, they don't." Nate pulled him back down the hall to the alley. "You were in such a hurry that you completely missed it."

"Missed what?"

Nate shoved him out the door. Jack bent at the waist, choking. An overwhelming stench of bleach coated the alley. What the fuck?

"Even I can smell that." Nate shook his head. "Someone doused the whole alley before we got here."

He held his breath and pushed himself upright. There was only one reason to spray an entire alley with disinfectant. He stepped into the center and spun in a slow circle, scanning every inch of dirty pavement.

Eyes dropping closed, he gritted his teeth and breathed deeply. Jack gagged.

"There." He pointed to the dumpster a few feet back. Nausea rolled through him as bleach crashed across his senses.

Nate hurried across the alley and flipped open the lid. Dipping an arm inside, he pulled out something small. He turned slowly, a small pink box clutched in his hands.

Jack hurried to him and ripped the box out of his hands. Raising it to his nose, he sniffed. Chocolate and cherries and garbage danced through his nostrils. He sniffed along the edge. The faintest hint of vanilla and peanut butter, the scent that was so uniquely Louisa's, painted the cardboard where her small hands had clutched it.

"She made it back from the bakery." Jack stared at the little pink box, dread coiling in his belly. "Someone ambushed her here and cleaned their scent."

Nate cursed. Jack stared at a spot on the wall. He leaned in close and dabbed at it with his finger. Was that... blood? He raised it to his nose and inhaled.

The coppery scent of blood washed over his tongue. Someone had taken his Louisa and *hurt* her. Jack's skin boiled as he struggled to maintain control. All he had wanted was for her to be safe, and now she was gone.

His head dropped back. An ear-splitting howl echoed through the alleyway. Nate's hand clapped over his mouth.

"Stop," he hissed in his ear.

"She's gone," Jack whispered against his palm.

Nate's hand lifted and slapped the side of his head. "Pull it together."

He towed Jack along by the arm and stuffed him into the car. His mind reeled. Every investigative instinct vanished in the face of his panic. Louisa was gone and he didn't have a fucking clue how to find her.

"Breathe, Jack."

Breathe? Wasn't he breathing? Jack forced air in and out of his lungs. Some of the panic cleared enough to let him think.

He clenched his jaw. "The bakery—we need to talk to whoever called the Den."

Nate backed out of the alley, glancing around for their FBI friends.

"I will speak with the cupcake lady; *you* will stay in the car."

Jack growled at his Alpha. His girl was missing, and Nate actually thought that he would sit quietly in the car while Nate messed up interviewing the only witness?

"Your eyes are glowing, and your claws have been out ever since I dragged you out of that clinic. Plus, you're not wearing shoes."

Jack glanced at his feet. Sure enough, they were bare. Not much he could do about that. He glared at his hands. Two-inch-long claws poked out of his fingertips. He closed his eyes and focused. He cracked an eye open; still there. Damn it.

Nate parked the car and gave him a stern look.

"Do NOT get out of this car. That's an order."

A whine built in Jack's chest. "I can find Louisa faster by myself."

"How?" Nate challenged, his arms crossed over his chest.

"I'll... sniff her out."

He raised an eyebrow. "You're going to run around sniffing the whole town until you stumble across her scent? That would take a week."

Jack tore at his hair, his claws pricking at his scalp.

"What else can I do? I can't just sit here!"

"You can trust your clan to get the job done," Nate told him calmly. "Wait here."

25

Face pressed painfully into the stone floor, Louisa cracked her eyes open. Her head throbbed sharply. She hissed, her eyes snapping closed, as pain radiated from the lump on the back of her head.

She pushed herself up. Waves of nausea rolled through her, turning her stomach. A fresh burst of pain crashed into her skull. The contents of her stomach spilled across the cold stone.

"Another concussion. Fucking splendid." Louisa spit acid.

Propping herself against the wall at her back, she opened her eyes and saw nothing but darkness. Louisa raised a hand and waved it in front of her face. Air buffeted her face.

Either she'd gone blind... or she was in some serious shit. With her luck, both.

She stretched her legs out in front of her and bumped something with the toe of her shoe. A frown twisted her brow. She dragged her feet from side to side, listening to the clink of her flats against the metal. Bars?

"Oh... fuck," she groaned.

The damned Blight hive, with its rotting walls and sour stench. The Blight hive with its terrifying basement... filled with wall to wall cages.

Her heart pounded erratically as the darkness closed in. Putting her head between her knees, Louisa fought the tightness in her chest.

Pull it together. She was no stranger to kidnapping at this point. She'd nearly pulled off one successful escape attempt. What was one more, really?

Louisa forced herself to take deep, even breaths as the panic welled inside of her. Her arms wrapped around herself and held tight.

Jack would find her. They might have gotten in a fight, but he would never leave her here. Assuming he could track her after the blonde at the bakery had called. Hell, that was assuming that she had called at all.

Louisa inhaled deeply and blew it out in a whoosh. *Work the problem.*

Ignoring the dull roar in her head, she crouched in her tiny cell. She stretched her fingers and traced the edges of her cage. Cold metal stung her fingertips as she counted each bar. She made sure to give each one a shake for any sign of give. Not a single loose bar in the bunch.

A rattle echoed through the room as her fingers traced the lock. Louisa dropped her hand. The door at the top of the stairs opened, letting in a single beam of burning light.

Shit. She needed more time. Dropping to the ground, she closed her eyes and curled in on herself. Her breathing slowed. The stairs creaked under each footstep as someone moved down the stairs. The footsteps stopped outside of her cell.

Louisa forced herself to breathe evenly. Be unconscious.

Furbidden Attraction

You can do it, you've had enough practice this week. She waited, her mind whirring.

Go away, go away, go away.

A faint hint of peppermint tinged the air. She cracked an eye open and peeked from behind her dark lashes. Sharp stilettos tapped against stone.

"Stop pretending to sleep," an impatient voice sighed. "You're wasting both of our time."

Louisa winced and blinked her eyes open. Fucking monsters.

She pushed herself upright. A dim shaft of light lit the room from the top of the stairs. Tears welled in her eyes as light burned away the darkness. Louisa pressed her back against the wall. No fear, she steeled herself.

"Fancy meeting you here, Blair." She yawned.

Blair turned and waved into the shadows. A folding chair skidded out of the darkness and stopped at her feet. Oh shit, they weren't alone.

Settling it in front of the cell, Blair perched on the edge of her seat. Her slim ankles crossed in front of her as her hands folded in her lap.

Aw, the princess doesn't want to get her skirt dirty. Louisa blinked at her teetering heels.

"How exactly did you get through the house in those?"

"Ingenuity, dear." Blair flicked a speck of dirt off the hem of her skirt. "It's good that you've been here already. Saves me some time."

Louisa shivered as dark figures shifted around her in the shadows.

"I aim to please," she sighed.

Blair ignored her and studied her manicured nails. Maybe if she sat there quietly enough, the ice queen would just forget the little bug in the room.

"I was surprised when my people told me that Jackson was cavorting with a human." She shook her head, her short-blond hair swaying. "I've never had particularly high expectations for the little shit, but even I was surprised by how low he was willing to debase himself."

Louisa rolled her eyes. Yeah, Blair was abducting women and chucking them in cages, but *Jack* was the one debasing himself.

"What can I say; I have a great ass."

Blair's eyes flashed gold, narrowing dangerously. Her fingers clenched in her lap. A satisfied smirk spread across her face.

"Yes, you are lovely," Blair agreed. "And very soon, I think some very wealthy buyers will agree."

Dread pooled in her belly. "So that's what you're doing with the women. Why would a bunch of Blighted need money? I thought you guys were supposed to be mindless monsters?"

Blair's cold laughed echoed through the basement. The shadows shifted closer at the sound, their blurry features almost perceptible in the darkness.

"I'm not Blight, *they* are the Blight." Blair waved a hand at the shadows.

Shapes moved closer. Louisa gagged at the fresh wave of sour odor that washed over her. One by one, they stepped into the dim light.

She recoiled as their twisted features came into focus. The shifters were tall, their heads nearly brushing the ceiling. Their animals swirled on the surface, faces shifting like melted wax as features repeatedly twisted and rearranged in horrific melds of man and beast. Smaller shapes moved around the half-forms.

A lean man hissed at her from behind what looked to be

Furbidden Attraction

a badger shifter. His gray skin and round gold eyes told her he was yet another ghoul. Razor teeth lined his mouth. He hissed again, his face twisted in a feral grin. Not her ghoul from earlier.

Other monsters moved into the light, neither ghoul nor shifter. Their glowing eyes and grotesque snarls were the only indication that they weren't human. The other clans, banshees? Succubi?

"You should know that the ghoul who took you has been disposed of," Blair sniffed. "He was ordered not to harm you."

"You're working with them?" Louisa squeaked.

"They work for me, thanks to a little nudge from a magical acquaintance." Blair waved her hand, sending them back into the shadows. "And I work for the greater good."

"I think the women you sold would disagree on your definition of 'greater good,' " she said shortly.

Blair sighed. "I never said it was for *their* greater good."

"Well, then for who? Because it sure as shit isn't me."

Blair threw her arms open. "For all the clans! There are thousands of us spread across the world and instead of taking our rightful place, we hide in the shadows, dying out!"

"So, let me get this straight... your witchy 'acquaintance' enslaved your little Blight friends and you're using them to kidnap, and SELL, humans and supes." Louisa stared at her. "How does ANY OF THAT help supes take over the world?"

Blair's smile sharpened dangerously. "Who do you think I sold them to?"

Louisa gaped silently as she stood and folded her chair. Blair leaned it against the adjacent cell. She sighed at her askance face.

"Oh, don't be like that." She shook her head. "Our organization is saving our people from dying out. You should be honored to have been chosen to bear our future."

Blair turned her back and teetered her way back up the stairs, her heels clicking on the rough steps. Her shadows followed in her steps.

"He's coming for me," Louisa called at her back.

Blair paused at the top of the stairs. "I'm counting on it."

The door clicked shut, sealing Louisa back in darkness. She closed her eyes as the basement fell silent. Her head thunked back against the stone wall.

Shit. Super fucking shit *no*. She was going to be sold as some weird monster brood mare? Fear slid down her spine in a greasy trail. She would die first.

Louisa gritted her teeth as fear turned her rocking stomach. She was never going to leave this cell alive. Jack's eyes winked through her mind. She was never going to get to tell him that she loved him.

Her eyes flew open. Somehow, in the midst of this hurricane of weird she had stumbled into, she had fallen in love with the big, kind jerk and now she was going to die in this disgusting basement because of it.

Louisa felt the ghost of Jack's arms wrap around her, enveloping her with his warmth. He *would* come for her. She repeated it under her breath like a mantra. She had to believe it with every scrap of will she possessed.

Each memory of Jack's smile, his rumbling laugh, wrapped around her. The warmth of his kindness, his silly humor, enveloped her tightly. A cocoon of strength cloaked her, driving back the darkness. He would come.

JACK PACED the length of the kitchen. The Aunts jumped out of his path as he passed. He should be out there, searching

Blight hives for her. Passing him on his lap, he glared at the back of Nate's head.

"You can't kill me just by glaring," Nate said without looking up from the maps spread across the table.

"I can try," Jack hissed.

"I'll let you know if I feel so much as a twinge," he vowed. "Frankly, it would be a relief to let someone else inherit this headache."

Jack growled and continued his pacing. Glaring at the clock, he winced. Eight hours and counting. He never should have pushed Louisa to leave. How could he protect her if she wasn't right here in front of him, right where he could keep an eye on her?

Because you were the one endangering her, moron, a little voice reminded him. Fucking common sense. This is what happens when you don't trust your gut.

Jack scrubbed his knuckles across his chest. The monster was howling to be set free. It would find his Lou for sure, but it would leave a swathe of carnage behind him. If the other clans didn't finish scouring their territory soon, he was going to drop the reins and let the beast tear through the whole bloody town.

He clenched his fists as he rounded the table. Sharp pricks stabbed his palms. Jack stared at the blood beading on his rough hands. Fucking claws. He was so agitated he couldn't get the damn things to retract.

"It would be faster if I could search," he argued again. "I can scent her from a mile away."

"No." Nate looked up and glared at him. "And stop asking."

Jack dropped into the chair across from him at the table. "If it were Abby they had taken?"

A dark smile crossed Nate's face. "I would have burnt

Raven Falls to the ground already. Luckily, you have an Alpha capable of rational thought to stop you from doing the same."

Jack stood and raised his chair over his head. It crashed down on the table, splintering into shards of wood.

"Feel better?" Aunt Aggie popped up beside him.

"No." The monster howled for him to tear her to pieces.

She calmly handed him another chair. Jack spun and smashed it against the wall. The carnage continued as chairs were passed down the line.

"We're running out of chairs," someone whispered.

Connor sprinted through the door, a phone in his hand. The room fell silent as he passed it to Nate. He listened for a moment and disconnected.

"Tony says the Ghouls' territory is clear." He picked up a marker and crossed off another section of town. "That only leaves the banshees' and the north-western quadrant of our territory to check in."

Jack shoved Nate's chair sideways and bent over the map. His blood turned to ice. His claws grew another inch. Eyes glowing wildly, he turned to Nate.

"I know where she is."

He took the marker from Nate's hand and circled a spot on the edge of their territory. Everyone leaned over the table to study the map.

"It's a patch of forest," Aunt Dot murmured.

"No, it's a Blight hive," Nate breathed. "You said it was empty?"

Jack forced himself to take long, slow breaths. His claws dug furrows in the wooden table. "It was four days ago."

Nate spun on the room. "I want every scout on that location, now. We need a report on their numbers NOW!"

The room erupted in a flurry of activity, phones pressed to ears, people erupting in feathers and taking flight.

Jack's mind reeled. He was clutching to his control by the thinnest of tendrils. The growl in his chest had been thundering since he'd laid eyes on the map. She was going to disappear, just like the other women. His Lou was going to fucking disappear.

Jack threw his head back and howled.

Nate grabbed him by the shoulders and forced him to meet his eyes.

"Breathe," he ordered.

Air sawed in and out of his chest. Jack closed his eyes and made the monster a promise. It paced in his chest, calming enough to let him gain control.

He opened his glowing green eyes. "Every favor, Nate. I want them all."

"You'll have them."

Jack took a deep breath and stared into the eyes of each stunned face.

"I want their heads at my feet, their Hive ash by sunup."

26

Louisa's eyes snapped open. Blair loomed in front of her cell, her head cocked quizzically to the side.

"What?" she growled. "I'm trying to sleep."

"You're handling this much better than the others did." Blair waved at the surrounding cages. "The crying and screaming started to wear on the nerves after a day or two."

"Well, I'd hate to be a bother," Louisa deadpanned. Her head dropped back against the wall as her skull pounded. "Was that all? I've got a head injury to sleep off before my rescue shows up and tears this shithole apart."

Blair raised an eyebrow. "How my idiot brother hasn't snapped your neck by now truly escapes me."

A shiver crawled down her spine. She had no doubt that Blair wouldn't hesitate to reach through the bars and dig her acrylics into her throat if she thought it would make her life a little easier.

Louisa forced herself to shrug casually. "What can I say? He's a fan of my plucky attitude and sparkling wit."

Blair studied her from head to toe. Her skin pricked

uncomfortably as she was weighed and measured by the empty eyes of a monster.

"I wonder if you'd be worth more with or without your tongue?" Blair regarded her sparkling claws. "I did just get them done. It'd be a shame to ruin them."

Louisa stared at her. Her heart hammered in her chest.

"Yes, a shame," she choked.

"I brought you a present." Blair smiled, her teeth sharpening to fangs.

Polite pass, Louisa winced. She waved her manicured hand. A malformed shape appeared out of the shadows. Louisa squinted. It wasn't one pathetically shaped supe, but three. The two on the outside dragged the sagging form of the third.

They stopped beside Blair. She gripped the limp man's bloody hair and dragged his face up. Louisa recoiled at the pained, green eyes staring back at her.

"My dear little brother was sniffing around where he didn't belong." Blair dropped his head. "I never would have pegged him for a blood traitor, though. That position belongs to Jackson."

She waved at the cell across from Louisa's. Her minions dragged Carter inside, careful not to touch the bars. He lay still on the floor, his breathing ragged.

Blair popped up with a camera tripod. She carefully unfolded it and pointed the camera at Louisa. Stepping back to admire her handiwork, she gave her a quick once-over.

Frowning, she waved at the shadows. An expensive handbag materialized beside her. Blair fished through it and pulled out a comb. It clattered at Louisa's feet.

She raised her eyebrows. "Seriously?"

"The auction will begin in an hour." Blair snapped her

bag closed. "Try to look presentable. I'm trying to make a sale, after all."

She turned her back and clicked her way up the stairs, her shadows following along like little ducklings. Louisa glanced around quickly before the light disappeared. It was exactly how she remembered it from her explorations with Jack. Dark and grimy. A heavy stench of sweat and fear doused the room, no doubt some of it hers.

As the door closed and the light narrowed, a silver flash caught her eyes from the cell beside her. The door clicked shut, drowning her in darkness once again.

Louisa scooted up against the bars and stuck her arm through the cage. She stretched. Nope, not quite. Louisa lay flat on the hard ground, her legs scrunched against the bars. She stretched through every muscle to her fingertips and prodded the ground.

Carter groaned in his cell. She could hear him moving around in the darkness. Orange eyes glowed like pinpricks from the abyss.

"What are you doing?"

"Hush," Louisa shushed him. "I've almost. Got. It."

Her fingers brushed the edge of something. Damn it, she couldn't quite hook it. She sat up and patted the floor of her cell. Her fingers brushed over plastic. Thanks, Blair. She scooped up the comb and went back to her flailing.

"You look ridiculous," Carter snorted.

"And your face looks like raw hamburger right now, so fuck off."

Louisa heard the gentle scraping of plastic on metal. Got it. She flicked her wrist and dragged it closer. Sitting up, she clutched the mystery object to her chest.

A thin chain wrapped around her hand. She carefully unwound it and studied it with her fingertips. Her fingers traced over a narrow bar suspended on the delicate chain. It had some type of engraving.

O? An A for sure. Maybe an I? Definitely an S and a Y. Daisy. The poor girl stretched out in Iris's morgue. Louisa could see her lying cold and shredded on the shining, sterile tray, her flesh pale and waterlogged.

Louisa fingered the chain. It had flashed silver in the light. Hadn't Jack said the cages were made for shifters? Some kind of silver composite? Hopefully, Daisy didn't cheap out on the silver. She might need it to get out of here.

"We are so fucked," Louisa whispered to the dark.

Carter snorted. "No shit. At least you'll be sold to live another day. Knowing Blair, I won't be leaving this shithole alive."

"What are you even doing here, Carter?" she sighed. She had preferred the silence to this whiny schtick he had going on.

"I got caught on the boundary line with a crowbar."

"That literally tells me nothing." Louisa shook her head.

"I was going to bust you out."

She stared at the green glow through the bars. Carter? Save her? Frankly, she had had him pegged as more the sex-slave-purchasing type.

"Why?" she asked, bewildered.

"Because you're Jack's." Louisa heard a shuffle, followed by a hiss. Probably trying to shrug his battered shoulders.

"You hate Jack; you all do."

The silence dragged on as he considered his words. "Hate is a strong word. Maybe strongly dislike would be more apt?"

"And you're siding with him over Blair?"

"She traded him." His voice was cold in the darkness. "We don't betray our blood."

"Traded him?" Louisa leaned her head against the bars. "I need you to pretend that I've only known about monsters for a little less than a week and back up the explanation."

"Jack didn't explain?"

"Explain what?"

"How he got shot?"

Louisa stared into the darkness. She might not be able to see in the dark, but even money said that Carter could. Hopefully he could see the confusion on her face, or the middle finger she was going to send his way if he didn't start explaining properly.

"Jack doesn't remember how he got shot."

"You've got to be fucking kidding me?" A light tapping made Louisa squint in his direction. Was he... banging his head on the wall?

"We're deader than you realize, kitten," he laughed. "He's never going to find us if he doesn't have his memories."

"Carter, I'm getting closer to being sold as a monster incubator by the minute."

"Ah, right. Mind you, most of what I know is from eavesdropping on Blair's phone calls and following her minions around town. Monster incubators. I can't believe Blair got involved with this shit. She's pretty, but not the brightest.

"Kidnapping human women for some mysterious overlord? Might as well have painted a big, fat target on supes around the world. And they fucking did, idiots. The feds have been sniffing around Raven Falls for weeks."

"Ah, Mulder and Scully."

"Who?"

Louisa laughed. "The FBI agents, Marshall and Scott. They *really* don't like being called Mulder and Scully."

Carter laughed with her. "I bet you were oh-so-polite to them."

"Oh, I was a delight."

"I bet," he chuckled. "Your little friends managed to stumble on Blair's branch of the operation. So she hid the breach from her bosses and cut them a deal."

"Money?"

"No, worse. She gave them supes."

"What?"

"She gave them supes to take back to their little shadow organization and experiment on in exchange for silence."

Louisa's mind reeled. "What the fuck? WHAT THE FUCK? Like sex slaves weren't bad enough?"

"I was gathering information to shut this shit down before she helped destroy our existence, but then I overheard her most recent trade."

"Jack."

"Bingo. Turns out His Royal Fuzziness ordered little brother to poke around, and Jack is much better at this shit than I am. Within days, he was further along than I had gotten in weeks. Started throwing a real wrench in the works, so Blair had him ambushed and offered up to her little stooges."

"That fucking bitch," Louisa hissed.

"Oh, but it gets better," Carter laughed. "The little shit actually managed to escape. Led them on a merry chase through the woods. The feds have been trying to find him again ever since.

"I've been following Jack, trying to get close enough to warn him, but the bitch was on to me by then. Her flunkies have been tailing me for days.

"But since he doesn't remember any of this, he won't

know where we are, who he's up against, or how big the stakes are. Fucked, kitten. We. Are. Fucked."

"You're a really positive energy, Carter. I really appreciate that kind of optimism in this dark hole that we've found ourselves in."

"I should've just let them sell you."

"At least it would be quieter," Louisa grumbled.

JACK PACED at the edge of the trees. All around him, the glowing eyes of shifters shone like stars in the night as they climbed out of vehicles. A handful of forms sprinted into the trees to scout the hive, shifting as they glided over the ground.

Nate pored over a map, stretched across the hood of an SUV. Jack paced behind him. If his Alpha hadn't sternly, and rather loudly, ordered him to stay put, he would already be tearing the Hive apart with his bare hands. But even the monster inside couldn't escape the powerful magic of Nate's commands.

A set of headlights appeared, illuminating the shadowed road.

Jack paused and frowned at Nate. "I thought Connor set up a roadblock?"

"He did," Nate glowered at the flowing lights.

The suburban parked next to the Den's line of cars. Doors whipped open as a mass of pale bodies spilled out. The shifters froze, claws and teeth at the ready.

Iris rounded the car, a pack of ghouls at her back. Glasses and dentures gone, she looked like the monster that she was. Her eyes locked on Nate and Jack. She closed the distance, her entourage shadowing her.

Pausing in front of them, she inclined her head to Nate. "Alpha."

Iris straightened and addressed them both. "Our Elders offer their assistance. Our numbers may dwindle, but we still have twelve warriors to avenge our lost sisters."

Nate studied the knot of gray-skinned ghouls. "What can you do?"

Iris grinned, her pointed shark teeth glinting. "Whatever you need us to, Alpha."

Nate motioned her over to his map. Her ghouls huddled together against the evening chill. Jack shook his head. Going into battle with ghouls at his back—there seemed to be something exceedingly foolish about that.

He paced the treeline impatiently. Only a handful of days ago, he had trudged through these trees with Louisa at his back. Jack glowered at the shadows. He wasn't quite sure which was worse, the guilt gnawing at his stomach or the fear that they were wasting time Louisa couldn't afford.

Iris popped up beside him, her conversation with Nate finished. She nudged her elbow into his ribs.

"She's going to be fine."

"And if she isn't?" He turned his glowing gaze on her. "What if we're too late?"

Iris snorted. "Please. She's tough as nails. I know that and I only spent fifteen minutes with her. Hell, we probably need to rescue the Blight from *her*."

Jack chuckled, the sound dying in his throat as Alice swooped through the trees. Her pale, feathered face glowed in the moonlight. She twisted, shifting in mid-air. Dropping lightly to her toes in front of him, Alice hugged herself against the brisk wind. A shifter popped out of the darkness and draped a blanket around her bare shoulders.

Nate jogged over to them. "Report?"

"Eighteen Blight. Eight shifters, none I recognized. Plus six ghouls, three banshees, and one wolf," she panted.

"A wolf? A *Blighted* wolf?" Nate stared at her.

Jack cursed. They only had fifty-three battle-ready shifters and twelve ghouls. Each Blighted would take four or five of them to take it down. They might have just managed the other seventeen Blight by the skin of their teeth, but not the wolf. Maybe with twenty more bodies and a Gatling gun.

"Did you see her?" Jack cut in.

"No, we checked every doorway and window." Alice shook her head, her red hair drifting in the wind. "If Louisa's in there, she's in the basement."

Jack closed his eyes. The goddamn basement, filled with supe-proof cages. How the fuck was he going to get her out *AND* deal with a Blighted wolf?

His eyes popped open. "We go through the floor."

Nate raised his eyebrows. "Come again?"

Iris's eyes lit up. "You clever dog. We go through the floor." She turned and sprinted back to her troops.

Nate looked back and forth between them. Jack grinned, his teeth elongating into razors. The beast howled his approval.

"Ghouls are diggers, Nate. We go through the ceiling and the floor. Attack from both sides."

His eyes lit up. "Son of a bitch... we go through the floor."

Another set of headlights interrupted them.

"Is Connor actually bothering to keep anyone out?" Nate sighed.

Connor hadn't exactly been thrilled to be kept out of the fight, but tonight his uniform was more useful than his talons. The Aunts were sitting out as well, despite their incredibly loud displeasure. Someone had to be ready to bolt out of town with Abby if things went sideways, and the old cats were ferocious enough to keep her safe from pretty much anything on the planet.

Another suburban parked beside the ghouls'. Four towering men climbed out and strode toward them, each step oozing menace. Two of the wolves shared identical faces, They stopped in front Jack and Nate and inclined their heads.

"Alpha."

One of the dark haired twins in front raised his head. "Our Alpha sends his regards."

"Can you handle a Blighted wolf?" Nate asked, ignoring the formalities.

The man beside him raised his identical head, a ragged scar twisting along his cheek. Huh, not-so-identical twins. "We'll take care of our brother."

"How do you feel about small spaces?" Iris asked, drifting back to their group.

The scarred twin stumbled back, his eyes round and glowing. The twin on the right ignored him.

"We'll manage."

"Then welcome to the party."

Jack turned on Nate. "Now?" he begged.

"Now," he nodded. Nate looked at the crowd of monsters gathered amongst the trees. His head dropped back to face the sky.

"SHIFT!" he roared.

Clothing shredded and dropped to the dirt as fur and feathers, and in a few cases scales, burst through skin. Razor-sharp claws and talons grew from fingertips. Jack closed his eyes and let the monster out.

27

"I see you didn't take my advice," Blair sneered.

Louisa cracked her eyes open. Movement shuffled through the shadows. She squinted. Blair's minions were dragging some lights down the stairs to arrange around her cell. She blinked as the dim light became blinding. Oh goody, it was auction time.

"Don't listen to her, kitten," Carter called from his cage. "I think you look radiant."

"Kiss my ass," she yawned.

"Comb?" Blair held out her hand impatiently.

Louisa dropped the bent, twisted plastic into her hand. She held it up to the light and studied the broken teeth with raised brows.

"Did your hair do this?"

Louisa snorted. "Naw, tried to pick the lock."

Carter's chuckle echoed through the basement. "Now, that you should have filmed. It was fucking hilarious."

"You didn't do much better on your attempt, bud."

He waved a pale hand. "Details, kitten."

Blair looked between them and shook her head. Ignoring their banter, she started fiddling with the camera.

Carter rolled his eyes at her back. A giggle bubbled up in Louisa's throat. Stuffing her fist into her mouth, she stifled the sound. She would never admit it out loud, but his presence was making the hellish experience a little more tolerable.

He was no Jack, but he made for a halfway decent understudy.

"Alright, the auction will begin"—Blair glanced at her watch—"in six minutes."

"What a relief," Louisa deadpanned. "I was getting so tired of that nasty little thing called freedom."

Blair flashed her a shark smile. "Such a delightful woman."

A flash of irritation burned through her. She was fucking *done* with being condescended to by these furry dipshits.

"Better than a frigid ice queen," Louisa smirked at the back of her head.

Carter's eyebrows shot up as Blair turned in a slow circle.

"Excuse me?"

"Oh, I was saying that you're an icy bitch with all of the warmth of an arctic glacier. Are you planning on selling yourself next? Because I don't see how you could get a man by any other means."

Blair stepped up to her cell and leaned in close. She looked down her proud nose with hate in her eyes.

"You are dirt beneath my feet, little insect."

Carter waved his arms wildly behind his sister. Louisa watched him out of the corner of her eye, her glare matching Blair's. He gestured at his ears and... the walls? The ceiling? What?

Carter rolled his eyes and gestured for her to keep going. Oh, keep her distracted... so the walls could attack? Whatever. Distraction was Louisa's middle name.

"Better an insect than an unwanted pussycat. At least I've gotten laid recently. Can you say the same, Ice Queen?"

Louisa laughed at the incredulous look on Blair's face. She was trembling with rage by the time Louisa's laughter had slowed into gentle hiccups.

"Humans are nothing but prey to run down and trample beneath our feet," she started quietly. "I will sell you to the highest bidder to be raped again and again. You will bear them children to carry on our glorious gift."

Blair leered at Louisa, who carefully schooled her face into bored disinterest as a trickle of fear crawled along her spine. She feigned a wide yawn. Carter waved her on, still glancing at the ceiling.

Any second now, the bitch was going to tear through those bars and rip her to pieces. But sure, keep going. Plan B was not going to cut it if she was left to bleed out in her cage.

Blair continued. "When you're old and used up, and all that's left is an empty, bitter shell, I hope they tear you to pieces and leave you to be picked at by the crows."

"So, in that order?" Louisa muttered. "No room for improvisation?"

Blair swiped her hand through the cage, her eyes glowing madly. A sharp claw nicked Louisa's shirt, slicing through the fabric.

A howl cut through the air. Blair and Louisa looked up. The ceiling shook with muffled snarls and growls. An earsplitting shriek cut through the air. Blair frowned, withdrawing her arm from the cage. She took a step toward the stairs and froze.

"I told you he would come." Louisa smiled.

Jack crawled through the narrow tunnel, wincing every time a dirt clod rained from the fragile ceiling. Sweat poured down his face as the walls closed in. Fucking ghouls. Never again.

One of Iris's ghouls stopped, her ear pressed against the thin stone wall. She nodded at Jack and wiggled back beside him.

"The basement is on the other side," she whispered low in his ear. "You should be able to hear the signal through the stone."

She shimmied left, opening up another tunnel with her spade like claws. Her dark hair disappeared in a flutter of dirt.

Tunnel in? What the hell had he been thinking? Sure, it was great in theory. Not so much in practice. Jack wondered how the wolves were managing in their own tunnels. Too heavy for the bird shifters to drop through the wasted ceiling and too large to scale the outer walls of the houses with the other shifters, they were stuck down here with him. Wiggling along, praying that the dirt wouldn't become their graves.

Jack took a deep breath and squashed down his growing panic. Any second now, the signal would come and he would be out of the godforsaken tunnel. For Louisa, Jack reminded himself. He could do this for Louisa.

He crawled forward, his back brushing the dirt ceiling. He coiled his body, the power building in his legs to launch him through the wall. Pressing his ear against the stone, Jack listened for the signal. He breathed in and out slowly, trying to maintain his calm.

Alice's shrill bird call sounded through the stone. Now.

Jack burst through the stone. He landed in a crouch on hard floor, dirt raining from his fur. His eyes were drawn to Louisa with laser focus. She blinked at him from behind bars. Her hair stuck up in a wild mess, face alarmingly pale in the sharp light.

Fuck, he'd missed her. The raw ache in Jack's chest settled a bit as she smiled at him. Smiling was good. Smiles equaled alive.

Four men straightened beside their own gaping tunnels. Ghouls crawled out of the tunnels behind them. Two of the wolves had ended up side by side inside the silver cages. The other two changed, bones cracking and snapping until they stood well over eight feet tall, every inch of them covered in dark fur.

Ghouls leapt into the air and ripped into the ceiling, burrowing their way into the floor above. Iris gave Louisa a quick wave as she disappeared amid the flying debris.

One of the Wolves nodded at his sister hissing at them. "You good here?"

Jack glanced between Blair, her pale hair disheveled as she hissed angrily, and the bloodied and bruised Carter laughing in his own cell.

"Yeah, I got this."

The furry monsters calmly ripped the doors off their brothers' cages, growling as the silver composite burned their skin. They leapt into the air, snagging the wooden rafters above them, and clawed their way up through the floorboards. The remaining ghouls scurried after them, their golden eyes shining in the darkness. The last two wolves burst into fur and followed behind.

Jack turned calmly to Blair, the claws on his feet clicking against the stone floor. The stench of peppermint wafting off of her was nearly enough to gag him. He loomed over her, casting her pale head in shadow.

"I have to say, I'm surprised that it's you." Jack shook his muzzled head. "If anyone was going to puppet-master a bunch of Blight, my money was on Carter."

"Always underestimating me," Blair hissed.

"Well, you are awfully underwhelming," Carter drawled from his cell.

Blair snarled. Her skin began to melt and twist. She grew until she nearly matched Jack's own towering height. Designer clothes split, falling to the floor in tatters. Orange and black fur sheathed her slim arms and legs.

She bared her mouthful of razors at Jack. "I'm going to rip your heart out and feed it to your little girlfriend."

Jack smiled, his furry lips parting over his own set of razors. "Cute."

He waved at Louisa over Blair's shoulder. "Be with you in a minute, honey."

She waved dismissively. "Take your time. Carter and I can gossip for a bit while you take out the trash."

Blair hissed, her fur standing on end. Jack shook his head. "No manners whatsoever."

She roared and charged at Jack. They met with a crash, like a pair of mountains battling for the same space. His muscles strained as he tried to hold her back. Shit, she was way stronger than she should be. Must be an extra push from the mystery witch.

Fur flew as Jack raked his claws across her ribs. Spitting with fury, Blair hurled him back against the silver cages.

Sharp pain streaked up his back as the silver burned his fur away.

Jack lurched forward and snatched her wrist. He twisted, hurling her into the bars face-first. Blair yowled. She spun away. Raw, angry lines crossed her striped face. Her orange eyes burned with rage.

"Oh no, not so pretty now, Blair," Carter taunted from his spot on the floor.

Blair dropped her head back and screeched. When her bright gaze met Jack's, her eyes glowed with triumph. Loud scraping noises came from the ceiling. Shit, that was definitely bad.

A ghoul dropped through the torn ceiling, his grin feral. A twisted and bleeding shifter clawed its own way through the floorboards to land beside the ghoul. Blair laughed, her voice dripping with power.

"Kill them."

They were fucked. Jack met Louisa's terrified eyes. He couldn't take all three of them, not when two were Blight, and now his worst fear was going to play out right in front of him. He growled. They'd have to rip through his fucking corpse to lay a claw on his mate.

Jack grinned at them. "Well? I haven't got all night."

Carter pushed himself to his feet. He swayed on the spot, color draining from his face. "You just have to antagonize them," he sighed.

Claws shot out of his fingers. He wiggled his fingers. Carter waited, arms relaxed at his side, ready to shoot out between the bars. Hopefully, he wouldn't turn on him and rip out Jack's intestines while he was distracted by their new friends.

They launched at Jack in unison. He rolled the ghoul over his shoulder into the bars and took the shifter to the chest. The shifter jabbed his three-inch claws at his throat. He managed to grab one wrist and twist to take the other claws in his shoulder. Jack wrenched the hand sharply to the side, snapping bones. The shifter snarled. He hooked his claws into its shoulder and rolled it over his head into the lights surrounding Louisa's cell.

He caught a glimpse of Blair hurrying up the stairs as the shifter's weight cracked the stone floor. Cowardly bitch.

As he leapt to his feet, the ghoul scrabbled up his back, his spadelike claws burying themselves into his flesh. The sharp little talons tore at his spine. Jack spun and threw himself backward against the cages. The ghoul screeched as the bars burned through his flesh. Turns out a room filled with silver was a good defense against raging Blight.

The claws disappeared from his ribcage as it scrambled to crawl out of the middle of the ghoul sandwich. The shifter roared and rushed at Jack. He reared back and slammed a sharp kick into its chest. It stumbled sideways, right into Carter's waiting claws.

Carter hooked his claws through the back of its furry throat and gripped its spine. The Blighted monster thrashed. Carter roared as his arms were dragged up against the silver bars.

Jack ripped the ghoul off his back and smashed him into the bars again and again until he dropped at his feet, nothing but a bloody mess of pulp. He glanced at Carter. He curled against the wall of his cell, his raw, blistered arms in his lap. The shifter lay dead on the floor, his head lying three feet away in a bloody puddle.

Turning to Louisa's cell, Jack froze. Blair stood beside her cage, her arm through the bars, claws around Louisa's throat. A growl rumbled in his chest.

"Let her go, Blair."

"When there's no way out of this house? Your little friends are swarming the upper floors." Blair laughed. "I don't think so. Your girl is my ticket out of here."

"You hurt her, and your body will hit the floor before hers does," Jack growled.

"Shall we test your reflexes, dog?" Her hand tightened, claws digging into Louisa's throat. Small ribbons of blood ran down her skin.

Jack took a step forward and froze as her hand closed tighter. Louisa looked at him, her brown eyes shining, and smiled. A flash of silver in her hand caught his eye.

"It's okay, Jack," she choked. "This is going to hurt her a lot more than it hurts me."

Whipping her hand up, she slapped a silver chain to the hand digging into her throat. Blair howled as blisters erupted across her skin. She jerked her hand back. Her eyes widened as she realized her mistake.

Jack crossed the room in a leap. He grabbed his sister by the throat and slammed her against the bars of the cell. Blair hissed and clawed at his hands as he ground her against the silver.

"You think you can hurt my mate?" Jack slammed her against the bars, each word punctuated by another crash into the silver.

Louisa's small hands reached through the bars, the silver chain in her hands. She looped the necklace around Blair's throat. Her scream split the room as the silver bit into her neck.

Jack stared into Louisa's eyes as his sister thrashed between them, blood pouring down her throat. Blair's screams faded into whimpers as her writhing slowed. They waited, their eyes never leaving one another's, as the life left her body.

Blair stilled, her gold eyes unseeing. Jack unclenched his hand. Her body slid down the bars to slump on the floor. He ignored the blood pooling around his feet.

"Are you okay?"

"I'd really like to go home now," Louisa whispered.

Jack glanced around him. His eyes landed on the mangled remains of the floodlights. He grabbed one and wedged it into the door. With a sharp twist, he wrenched the door open.

Louisa stumbled forward into his arms. He clutched her against his chest. He rubbed her back and buried his furry face into her hair. Jack breathed in her sweet scent as she sobbed into his shoulder.

"It's over," he murmured. Jack closed his eyes and caged the power inside of him. His skin rippled, absorbing his sandy fur. "We can go home."

"Uh, I'd really like to go home too," Carter groaned from his cell.

Louisa snorted and stepped back. She froze when Jack started to lead her to the stairs. Looking back at the bleeding lump that had once been Blair, she stepped out of Jack's arms.

She stood trembling over the body. He blinked as she dropped a hard kick into Blair's oozing ribcage. Rage twisted her face. She kicked out again.

Jack glanced at Carter, his eyebrows raised. Carter just shook his head. Okaaaay, that told him absolutely nothing.

Louisa dropped into a crouch. Hand shaking, she tugged the silver chain from the bloody furrow she had carved into Blair's throat. She dropped the necklace into her pocket and kicked the bloody mass one more time.

She stumbled back to Jack, swaying drunkenly in front

of him. He scooped her into his arms and strode up the stairs, Carter's objections sounding behind them.

He looked down at her face. Tears streaked down her cheeks, cutting tracks through the patches of dirt. His brow pinched as familiar worry pooled in his belly.

Jack glanced at the basement door. "Close your eyes."

28

Jack tightened his grip on her and stepped through the door. The main room was a sea of blood. Compared to what his people had done to the rest of the Blight, he had been positively restrained. He stepped over the shredded mass of a severed hand and picked his way across the room.

Someone on his team had thoughtfully used some scraps of wood to create a walkway over the ruined floor for him. He walked down the path and out the front door.

Jack carried her to an SUV that someone had managed to navigate through the overgrowth. He opened the door and tucked her in the backseat. Hanging his head in his hands, he finally let himself breathe.

Nate walked up beside him. His large hand squeezed his shoulder. Thrusting them into his chest, he handed him boots and a change of clothes.

"She's alive," he reminded Jack. "Take her home."

He nodded, slowing his breathing. Jack straightened up and started to move around the SUV. He yanked on the clothes. Hand on the door handle, Jack paused.

"My brother is in the basement in a cage. Someone should probably let him out and give him a couple BAND-AIDS."

"What?" Nate stared as Jack climbed into the car.

"He can explain," Jack said, closing the door.

Louisa sat huddled in her seat, eyes still firmly closed. Jack scooped her into his lap. He buckled the two of them together, just like he had the first time.

She was utterly silent as the SUV took them home, her head buried in his shoulder. He stroked her hair and cuddled her to his chest.

Louisa didn't open her eyes until Jack had carried her through the garage and up to his room. He kicked open the bathroom door and balanced her gently on the sink.

Her warm brown eyes stared blankly over his shoulder. Jack winced. He turned away to turn on the shower and pull himself together.

Lifting her in his arms, he marched them into the shower fully clothed. They stood there, swaying under the water. Louisa still stared at the wall, her expressive eyes utterly empty.

Jack stripped her wet clothes off of her. The hot water loosened the sticky blood gluing the fabric to her skin. Louisa shivered under the spray, huddling against his body.

Careful of yet another head injury, he gently massaged soap through her tangled curls. He rinsed her off until the pink water running in rivulets down her skin cleared.

Turning off the water, Jack reached out and snagged a towel. He wrapped her carefully and balanced her back on the counter. Pulling a first aid kit from under the counter, he smeared antiseptic across the gouges on Louisa's throat. She didn't even twitch.

Jack smoothed a wide bandage over her neck and

carried her to the bed, his boots squelching with each step. Each silent breath was breaking his heart piece by piece.

He dragged a T-shirt over her head and tucked Louisa under the covers. Bending over her, he pressed a gentle kiss to her forehead.

"Let me grab a comb, and we'll take care of your hair," he whispered against her skin. Silence dogged his footsteps as he walked into the bathroom.

Jack stared at his reflection in the mirror. His wet hair was plastered to his skin, but it was his eyes, as empty and hopeless as Louisa's, that shook him.

He backed up until his shoulders bumped the wall. Sliding down the wall, Jack sat on the ground, his head in his hands. He didn't know how to help her, how to make the bad memories disappear.

The monster in his chest still hadn't settled. Louisa wasn't okay. Jack had pulled her out of hell, held her in his arms, but she wasn't okay. Not by a long shot.

Jack pushed his wet hair off his face. Pull it together, man. As long as Louisa was here, he would try. He would give her all of him... but he couldn't do that sitting on the bathroom floor, feeling sorry for himself.

Toeing off his wet boots, he pushed himself up. Jack stripped off his sopping clothes and tossed them on the shower floor. He tugged on a pair of sweats and grabbed a comb.

A silver glint caught his eye from the shower floor. Jack nudged Louisa's soaked clothes aside. A silver necklace crusted with blood curled on the tiles. He grabbed a pair of tweezers from the drawer below the sink and carefully picked it up.

Running it under the faucet, he rinsed the tacky blood from the chain links. Jack squinted at the name stamped into the small silver bar. DAISY... the girl from the morgue. His stomach churned. Louisa has been so close to ending up right beside her in Iris's shiny drawers.

He laid the necklace to dry on a hand towel and padded out of the bathroom. Jack stopped. Louisa lay where he'd tucked her in, a shapeless bulge under the blankets. So still. Swallowing the lump in his throat, he crossed the room and nudged her upright.

The silence swallowed them. Jack studied the empty look in her eyes. He had pulled her out of that cage, but he worried that a part of her had been left behind. He felt his rage bubbling up inside him once again, his helplessness driving him mad. The urge to tear his sister to pieces all over again made his fingers twitch.

He crawled up the bed behind Louisa and set to work on her curls. It had to be easier than watching her stare soullessly at the wall.

A TEAR STREAKED down Louisa's cheek. The comb dragged gently through her tangled hair. She had killed someone. She had actually killed someone. The thought repeated again and again in a loop.

A small voice in the back of her mind tried to scream over the endless circle. It wasn't her fault. To be fair, Jack had done most of the work, but she had definitely helped. Blair had been a freaking psychopath, and she'd deserved far worse than she got, but Louisa was shaken that she had been the one to do it.

At least no other women would suffer from Blair's greed. She stiffened, her guilt settling itself on the back burner. How could she have forgotten?

"Jack?" she croaked.

The comb froze in her hair. Jack exhaled, a relieved rush of air flowing from his lungs. His arms wrapped around her chest. Too tight. Louisa squeaked as her ribs groaned.

He loosened his hold. "Sorry, you were just so quiet. It was scaring the shit out of me."

Sympathy flooded her heart. Louisa had known that he would come for her, without a single doubt in her mind. Her only worry had been how long she was going to have to wait.

But Jack, poor, sweet Jack, didn't have that kind of surety to lean on. He must have been terrified that he wouldn't find her, or worse, that he wouldn't find her alive.

Louisa hugged his arms to her chest. "I'm okay. It's just... a lot."

"I'm sorry it took so long." He breathed against her hair. "We had to search the whole town."

Carter's dark revelation sparked in her mind. Louisa winced. There was a lot to tell him, and he wasn't going to like any bit of it.

"There's some stuff we need to talk about—"

"I'm sorry that I sent you away," Jack interrupted. "I was afraid and I let the fear make the decision for the both of us."

"Yeah, that wasn't what I was talking about..." Louisa yawned. "But we're definitely going to talk about that later."

"Oh..."

"The women are alive."

Jack gripped Louisa's hips and spun her around on the bed. Her aching head whirled. She put a hand to her skull, wincing at the pain. Too many head injuries in too few days.

"Run that by me again?" Jack pressed. His green eyes studied her face.

"The women that were taken, they're alive."

He cursed and leapt off the bed. Jack scooped her off the bed, blankets and all. He hurried out of the room. What the...?

"Jack, what are you doing?" Louisa squeaked.

"I need you to tell everything you know to Nate," he said, his eyes on the hall.

She closed her eyes. The nice, restful nap that she'd been looking forward to was getting further and further away. Brushing her half-combed hair out of her face, Louisa groaned. Couldn't he wait until after he'd finished her hair to be weird?

"Can't I just tell you?"

"No," Jack said, stopping outside of Nate's office.

"Why?" Louisa stared at him, exasperated.

He sighed. "Because once this is settled, we're not leaving my room for a week. You're going to stay where I can keep an eye on you until I'm good and reassured that you're not going to disappear on me."

Her heart fluttered. She didn't know whether to hug him or deliver a big, fat "I told you so". Maybe she could save that for later, to cheer her up when the guilt crept back in.

Jack nudged the door open and strode into the room, the bundled up Louisa still clutched tight to his chest. Everyone looked up. Nate frowned, a cut still healing across his cheekbone. Alice smiled, her lips tense, as she pointedly ignored the two identical dark-haired men across the desk.

Oh good, there were even more witnesses.

"Jack, we're having a meeting," Nate growled at the interruption. He glanced at Louisa. "Normally, you'd be in it, but extenuating circumstances."

"You're going to want to hear what she has to say." Jack glared at one of the men until he sighed and vacated his chair. Jack gently perched her in the sturdy armchair and stood behind her, his hands light on her shoulders.

"The women are alive," Louisa sighed. Couldn't she have just sent a damn email?

The twins leaned in, their eyes glowing an unnerving shade of blue. She blinked at the wide scar running down one of their faces. At least she'd be able to tell them apart.

Louisa squinted. Aw, the wolves from the basement. She had thought they looked growly and familiar.

"Where?" One of them rumbled.

"I don't know," she admitted. "But I do know that they were sold, auctioned off to other supes across the country."

"Sold?" a familiar voice sputtered. Iris stepped out of the shadows by the window. Her throat was collared with dark bruises. Louisa winced. That had to hurt like a bitch.

"Sold." She nodded. "Blair went on and on about how you guys were going to take your rightful place in the world but you're dying out."

"They're incubators." The scarred twin frowned. "They took them to produce children with the curse."

Louisa nodded. The wolf was a smart cookie. "It only gets worse from there."

They interrogated her for nearly an hour. Finally, Jack had snapped and picked her up like a blanket-swaddled burrito. He had stomped out of the room, informing them over his shoulder that any further questions would need to be submitted in writing... or wrung from Carter.

"I can't believe the bitch actually sold me." Jack shook his head. He stomped them back to his room, Louisa cuddled to his chest.

"Really?" Louisa drawled, exhaustion dragging her voice. "You can't believe your greedy, supremacist sister, who has never liked you, sold you out to save her own skin?"

"Hush, you're supposed to be tired."

"I am tired," she yawned. "What are we going to do about the FBI? They shot you, Jack."

"That's for Nate and other clan leaders to figure out. I imagine that they'll have a lot of tense meetings over the next few weeks. At least Connor can stop looking into where that bullet came from."

Jack carried her to the bed and caught her when she tried to slump sideways. He held up the forgotten comb as protests squawked in her throat. Louisa grumbled as he settled behind her and went back to work detangling her hair.

Eyes drifting shut, she relaxed against him.

"You can yell at me now, if you want," he murmured.

Louisa cracked an eye open. "Eh."

"Eh?" Jack snorted. "You, Louisa Miller, do not want to say snarky things to my face? You don't want to tell me how foolish and shortsighted I was? Or maybe how you're getting kidnapped *again* was all my fault?"

"Maybe tomorrow?"

He pressed his hand to her forehead.

"What are you doing?" she sighed.

"You look like Louisa, and you sound like my Louisa, but there must be something wrong with you. A fever? Maybe some kind of doppelganger impersonating my Lou?"

She rolled her eyes. "Jack... I'm going to start yelling."

He laughed and kissed the top of her head. Tossing the comb on the nightstand, he laid them down and spooned her blanket lump.

Jack reached across her and turned out the light. As the darkness settled over them, Louisa's heart thundered in her chest. The blanket cocoon tightened around her, cutting the air from her lungs. Her breath ripped in and out of her lungs in painful gasps.

Jack's arms gripped her tight. His lips pressed against her ear.

"It's okay," he whispered. "You're safe, in bed, with me."

"It's too dark," she choked. "It's like being back... there."

His arms disappeared and the bed dipped. Soft footfalls moved across the room. The bathroom light clicked on, giving Louisa just enough light to see Jack. He propped the door halfway open and crawled back into bed.

"See? You're home." Jack wrapped himself around her.

Louisa breathed, the comforting weight of his heavy limbs settling her racing heart. She stared into the shadows. Dresser, nightstand, lamp. No bars.

"Jack?"

"Yes?"

"I'm afraid to fall asleep," she whispered. "I don't want to live through it all over again."

Jack fingers stroked her cheek. She leaned into the touch, letting the caress warm her from outside in.

"If you have a nightmare, you'll wake up and still be right here with me," he soothed. "No more cages, no more darkness. Just me and you."

Louisa turned in his arms to rest her cheek against his bare chest. His hand petted her hair, while the other stroked long, soothing lines down her back. Her eyes drifted closed. She was safe.

29

Light stabbed Louisa in the eye. Hissing, she burrowed beneath Jack's arm into the safety of the pillows. His quiet chuckle warmed the room.

"It's too early to wake up," she growled into a pillow.

"It's almost noon."

Louisa groaned and pushed herself up. Curls blocked her vision. Hesitantly, she prodded at her hair. A frizzy cloud erupted from her scalp. Shit.

"Next time I try to go to bed with wet hair, stop me."

Jack laughed. "I think you can be forgiven after everything you've been through in the last few days... Besides, I kind of like it." He poked a finger into the frizzy tangles. "It's like a big cotton ball."

Louisa glowered at his cheery grin. "Remember how I said the yelling could wait until tomorrow... it's tomorrow."

Grin sliding off his face, he pushed himself up to sit across from her. Jack closed his eyes and took a deep breath. Blinking his eyes open, he met her stern gaze.

"Okay, I'm ready."

Louisa opened and closed her mouth. Huh. "I don't actually know where to start?"

Jack winced. "We can just skip to my begging for forgiveness if that's faster."

"No," Louisa snorted. "You're not getting off that easy."

She stared out the window for a moment. They did need to talk about what happened, but he had come for her. That was worth a lot more than words. What did she even need to hear from Jack at this point?

Louisa turned to meet the worry in his green eyes. "Can you promise me that it won't happen again?"

He cocked his head to the side. "What, specifically?"

"You can't force me to leave again without giving me a say. I know you were just trying to keep me safe, but all it did was hurt us both." Louisa hated how her voice trembled. "This isn't going to work if you don't treat me like an equal. I know I'm just human—"

"You're not just human," he interjected. "Not to me."

Louisa held up a hand to stop him.

"I appreciate that, but I am just a human. I don't have superpowers. I'm not some badass supernatural weapon, I'm just Louisa." She sighed and scrubbed her fingers through her wild mane. "You were afraid that you couldn't keep me safe here, so you sent me away. But now I'm back and nothing has changed. What's going to stop you from freaking out and trying to end this for my own good again?"

Jack stared at her for a second. In a rush, he leapt off the bed and jogged into the bathroom. She gaped after him. *Well, I guess that's where the conversation ends...*

He walked back into the room, a towel clutched in his hand. Louisa raised her eyebrows as he sat beside her. Wordlessly, Jack dropped the bunched up hand towel in her lap. Carefully gripping the edges, he unfolded the bundle.

Laying in the center was Daisy's silver necklace, cleaned of all evidence of Blair's death. Louisa looked between the necklace and Jack's face.

"I don't understand?"

Jack touched a single finger to the edge of the slim nameplate. He raised his finger for her to see. The outer layers of skin had been eaten away to a bloody blister. As she watched, it began to knit itself back together.

"I can't keep you safe from the monsters every second of every day and that's something that I'll just have to accept." Jack placed her hand over the curled chain. "But knowing you have some kind of weapon, that helps. It doesn't have to be this necklace. We can return this to the family and get you something new, if you want."

Fingers curling around the chain, Louisa blinked back tears. "Did you ever find out what happened to her?"

"She escaped," he said quietly. "We don't know how exactly, but one of our trackers found a sweater with her scent in the woods around the Hive. We think she made a run for it and ended up in the river."

"I'd like to keep it, if that's okay," she sniffed. Whether Daisy knew it or not, she had saved her life. Something Louisa wasn't about to forget anytime soon.

Jack's hands fluttered weakly in his lap. "I can't help you put it on."

She looped the necklace around her wrist into a bracelet. Tucking her hand in her lap, she kept it far away from Jack. A flutter ruffled her heart. He'd given her a weapon to keep her safe, even from him.

Louisa smiled. "I love you."

His eyes widened. Mouth gaping open, he struggled for words. She nibbled her lip nervously. Maybe he wasn't quite there yet.

"You don't have to say it back," Louisa rushed out. "I thought about it when I was... there, and I promised myself that I would tell you the next time I saw you."

"Damn," Jack murmured. Her heart sank. "I wanted to say it first."

He gripped her chin and kissed her gently on the mouth.

"I love you too," he whispered against her lips. "Even though I keep finding your hair all over my clothes."

Louisa giggled. "You're a dog—shouldn't you be the one who sheds?"

They both dissolved into laughter, the tension in the room evaporating. Jack's phone buzzed on the nightstand. He scooped it up while her giggles slowed. A grin spread across his face as he read the text.

"Looks like Nate decided on my punishment for revealing our existence to you," he chuckled.

"And?"

"Apparently, my punishment is that I have to keep you."

Louisa raised her eyebrows. "Excuse me?"

Jack's grin got bigger. "I have to, and I quote, 'Keep her from causing trouble by whatever means necessary.' "

"And that's a punishment?" she grouched.

"According to Nate," he laughed. "Oh, and I have to pay your tuition because apparently he's enrolled you in veterinary school."

Her mind went blank. But...what? Veterinary school?

"Wha—?"

"Oh look, he's written a contract and everything. Since you've undoubtedly lost your job at the clinic by now, the Den will be providing the seed money for your new clinic. Once you've graduated, of course." Jack continued skimming the text. "You'll be our lookout in case another shifter ends up injured."

She stared at him, her eyes round. "Did he just... puppet-master me a new career?"

"Yeah, he does shit like that."

"And the Den can afford to just buy me a clinic?" Louisa sputtered.

"Nate might be a shifter, but his real superpower is day trading." Jack's grin disappeared at the bewildered expression on her face. "Hey, if you don't want to do it, I can tell him where to stuff the contract."

She shook her head slowly, her mind still reeling. "No, I just never expected to have an opportunity like this. I wanted to go to vet school originally, but couldn't afford it. I always figured I would save up and go back later."

"Well, it looks like 'later' just became 'now.'"

Louisa's head spun with all the choices in front of her. A whole new career? A whole new life? Should she get rid of her apartment and move in here? What about her furniture? She'd have to sell it.

She looked at Jack and calmed. Everything was going to be okay. They would figure it out, together.

Her stomach grumbled loudly. Louisa blinked in surprise at her roaring belly. How long had it been since she'd last eaten? Two days ago? Three?

"I think you need food." Jack grinned.

He scooted off the bed. She silently cursed her traitorous stomach for ruining their cozy morning... er, afternoon, she corrected as bright sunlight poked through the shades.

Louisa propped her chin on her elbow and admired Jack's muscular back as he shuffled around the room. He winked over his shoulder at her sigh.

He stretched dramatically, every muscle in his back rippling at the motion. She giggled into her pillow. He was ridiculous... and completely hers.

Jack dropped a kiss on top of her head and strode out of the room, barefoot and shirtless.

"Put a shirt on!" Connor's muffled voice sounded from down the hall.

"Bite me, Bird Boy," she heard Jack growl.

Boys. Louisa shook her head, a grin stretching her lips. She rolled herself upright and pushed her frizzy mass of hair out of her face. She winced.

She really shouldn't have let herself fall asleep with wet hair last night. It would be utterly unmanageable until she washed it again.

Louisa grumbled as she tumbled out of bed. Might as well get it done with. She opened the curtains and let sunlight flood the room. She blinked into the brilliant afternoon sun. It was going to be a beautiful day, as though the universe was trying to burn away the dark horror of the last few days.

Louisa turned and stumbled into the bathroom, wincing at the ache in her muscles. Sleeping bunched up in that cell had done a number on her body.

Shivering, she shuffled into the shower. She wasn't ready to think about that hole yet. Louisa had buried it in the dark recesses of her mind. Maybe tomorrow... or never.

The hot water tore a groan from her chest as it beat against her sore muscles. She winced at the sting of the soap running down her bruised and scraped up legs.

Someone had lined her favorite brand of hair products along the shelf. She thanked the heavens for actual conditioner and rubbed a puddle of it through her curls.

Louisa hurried through her routine, not wanting to keep Jack waiting. She hopped out of the shower, taking a quick second to wrap a towel around herself. Poking her head out the bathroom door, she glanced around the empty room.

No Jack yet. He must be trying to cook again. Louisa shook her head, wet curls flying. One of them really needed to take cooking lessons, or there was a good chance their kids would be surviving on peanut butter and jelly sandwiches and ramen.

Louisa paused. Their kids? The thought made the corners of her mouth curl up. The smile died as she flashed back to Abby's demands for friends.

Jack had said the curse was genetic. Was she okay with her children shifting into tiny, fluffy puppies? A faint warmth flooded her chest. Yes, yes she was.

But was she really ready to think that far into the future? She'd never thought, no, *hoped* like that with any of her past boyfriends. When Louisa had closed her eyes and pictured that backyard bbq framed on her wall, none of them had quite fit before.

But Jack? She could see him there, as handsome and ridiculous as always. The sun would be bright and shining, lighting up his sandy head like a halo. He'd stand at the grill, flipping burgers, his head thrown back at some joke he had no doubt told. Alice and Connor would be there of course, probably arguing over something silly, like the proper ratio of condiments. Nate would sit in the corner, frowning at some snide remark of Carter's.

Louisa grinned at the image. The Aunts would chase around Abby and green-eyed toddlers with wild curls. And Abby would finally have the little monster friends she'd always wanted.

And Louisa would have the family she had always wanted. Maybe it wouldn't be quite what she had pictured. The clan was nosy and pushy and would probably drive her to drink at some point. There would be bickering, and certainly more fur than Louisa had imagined, but they would be hers.

All because of Jack. The silly man with the laughing eyes who made her stomach flutter with butterflies every time he flashed his brilliant smile at her or tugged her hand into his own enormous paw. He had come crashing into her quiet, lonely life and shattered it to pieces. He'd given her a family and friends and asked for nothing in return.

She heard the bedroom door click shut and hurriedly combed through her wet hair. Louisa wrapped herself in a fluffy, pink robe hanging on the back of the door. Probably an addition of Alice's.

Louisa opened the door and watched Jack quickly make the bed she'd left in disarray. She leaned against the doorjamb and smiled as he hummed to himself. He was so damn cute it made her heart skip a beat.

Jack turned around, his smile widening at the sight of her. He raised his eyebrows as her grin matched his.

"Why are you so happy?" he joked. "It's because you were checking out my butt, isn't it?"

"Just thinking about how much I love you... and your butt." Louisa winked.

Jack's smile softened tenderly. He padded across the room and folded her into a tight hug. Pressing his nose into Louisa's damp hair, he breathed her in.

"I don't think I'll ever get tired of hearing that," he rumbled against her ear.

They swayed together, lost in their jumble of arms.

Jack's stomach rumbled in concert with Louisa's. Chuckling into her hair, he dropped a kiss on top of her head and stepped back.

He nudged her toward the bed as he collected the food he had scavenged from the kitchen. Louisa climbed up, crisscrossing her legs in front of her. Jack placed a tray stacked with sandwiches in front of her, waving his arm with a dramatic flourish.

She picked up a sandwich as Jack sat across from her. She nibbled as he dived into his own. Turkey and cheddar, perfect.

"Excellent sandwich," she mumbled around her bite.

"I tried to make mac and cheese, but I burned it," he said, wincing. "I figured sandwiches would be a safer alternative."

"We really need to learn how to cook," Louisa said, hiding her smile as she tried not to think about her earlier daydreaming. She would tell him all about it, but not today.

"And bake," Jack agreed, regarding his sandwich thoughtfully. "Though I think that Alice accounts for about forty percent of Rainbow Bakery's profits, so maybe not."

He pointed at two chocolate cherry cupcakes tucked away to the side.

"The bakery delivered of couple dozen of those this morning. Apparently, they've called every hour to check up on you. Connor is grumbling about harassment."

She snorted into her sandwich. Blondie was tenacious. Louisa owed her one hell of a tip for calling in the cavalry when she did. She should stop by and thank her at the very least, and pick up Jack's collar while she was at it.

"For cupcakes as good as these, she can harass us as much as she wants," Louisa said.

"Connor and Nate will love that," Jack grinned. "They're already freaking about security since we have no idea how the bakery knew our address."

He scooped up a cupcake and started to peel off the wrapper. Louisa frowned. Could he...?

"Should you even eat chocolate?" she asked worriedly. "You know, being part dog?"

Jack froze, his mouth open to bite into the pastry. He looked between Louisa and the cupcake with wide eyes. His grin widened as he dissolved into howls of laughter.

EPILOGUE

A ripple of pain twisted along her spine. Louisa grimaced and scrubbed her knuckles down her back. Jack nudged her hand aside and massaged the offending ache. She shot him a grateful smile.

These stupid chairs were going to be the death of her. She knew they were expensive, as though Nate had spared any expense on the big day. For everyone else they were probably comfortable enough, but the spasms wracking Louisa's back were killing her.

She sighed into her punch. How soon could one feasibly leave a wedding reception without being rude... especially when the groom could transform into a twelve-foot grizzly? Maybe after the cake?

Louisa looked at Jack out of the corner of her eye. Handsome as ever in his tux, the jacket cast aside and the sleeves rolled to his elbows. His grin flashed as he laughed at something one of the Wolves had said. As if he would ever leave before cake. She snorted into her drink.

Jack leaned down, his lips brushing her ear.

"Maybe moving around would help?" he whispered.

He gave the dance floor a quick, hopeful glance. No doubt he'd been dying to get out there all evening. Instead, Jack had hovered at Louisa's side, plying her with food and drink, content to hum along with the music.

She stifled an exhausted sigh and nodded. One dance couldn't hurt.

He jumped up and offered her his hand. She shook her head ruefully. Even after nearly two years, she was still in awe of his enthusiasm. Louisa's eyes dropped to her hand, wedding band sparkling in the twinkling lights, as she placed it in his.

Jack pulled her to her feet and kissed her forehead, practically vibrating with excitement. His hand at the small of her back, he led them to an empty spot on the dance floor. She rested her hands around his neck, careful to keep the dainty silver necklace around her wrist away from his skin. She leaned into him and relaxed.

Jack swayed them side to side, still humming quietly in her ear. Louisa winced as a sharp pain rippled across her stomach. Feeling her tense, his hand slid along her side to cup the round belly pushing them apart.

"Is she giving you a lot of trouble tonight?" he worried.

"Unfortunately," Louisa sighed. "I don't think she's a fan of weddings."

"Not much longer now," Jack smiled, dropping a kiss on top of her head.

"Not soon enough, either," she grumbled.

"It hasn't been that long," he teased.

Louisa glared at his playful grin. He was the one who'd got her into this mess. If she'd known how awful this whole pregnancy bit was going to be, she would've taken one look at him that day in the clinic and run the other way.

"Thirty-nine weeks, Jack. Thirty. Nine," Louisa growled.

"When your feet have been swollen for thirty-nine weeks, then you can talk about the passing of time."

"I thought you were going to stab the doctor during that last ultrasound when he said it may take up to forty-two."

"If it takes another three weeks and this kid isn't the cutest thing on Earth, I'm demanding a refund," she grumbled.

Something small bumped against her hip, knocking her off balance. Jack steadied her and wrapped his arms around her a little more tightly. Louisa looked down at Abigail's dark head trying to squeeze between their legs.

"Sorry, baby!" she squeaked, patting her small hand against the side of Louisa's swollen stomach.

"Who are you hiding from?" Jack asked, hiding his smile.

"Ms. Alice said that it was a wedding tradition to hold the flower girl upside down and tickle her," she giggled. "Mr. Beau said he would distract her so that I could hide."

"As big as this belly is, I don't think it will hide you for long," Louisa giggled back. "Maybe try under the treat table?"

Abby's eyes lit up. She gave them a quick nod and took off, her flower crown askew as she darted between dancers.

The music faded away as a spoon clinked against a glass, announcing the coming toasts. Jack and Louisa turned toward the head table, where Nate stood, his arm around his willowy, blond bride.

"I'd just like to thank everyone for coming to celebrate my beautiful bride, Abigail, and myself becoming a family... speaking of, does anyone know where Abby ran off to?"

Jack and Louisa chuckled at one another. He would no doubt find her at the end of the night, passed out beneath the treat table and covered in chocolate.

Louisa squeaked as liquid trickled down her legs. Nate's

speech faded into background noise as she stared at the puddle forming around her shoes.

"Uh Jack?" she gasped. "I think it's time."

"I know," he said, rifling through his pockets. "I've got my notecards here somewhere. I'm gonna blow Nate's best man speech out of the water."

Louisa gripped his elbow and squeezed as wave of pain crashed through her. This evening's cramps had been... contractions. Great.

"No," she breathed. "It's TIME."

Louisa pointed at the floor. Jack's eyes widened as he followed her arm.

"It's time? Like... TIME? Are you sure?"

"Well, I've either peed myself or my water just broke," she rolled her eyes. "Either way, we should probably go."

"Right. Go, we should definitely go," Jack said, his eyes panicked.

He gripped Louisa around the waist and started steering her towards the door. She glanced back worriedly.

"Should we tell someone about that?" She glanced back at the puddle.

"Don't care." He shrugged.

Applause sounded throughout the room as Nathan finished up his speech.

"And now we'll have the best man come up and give a toast!"

Jack and Louisa stopped in their tracks and exchanged a look. The universe had always had bad timing.

"Go," she said, nudging him back. "Be quick."

Jack jogged across the room, weaving his way through guests. He took the microphone from Nate and swiped a glass of champagne off the table.

"Congratulations to the happy couple!"

He downed his glass and sped across the room.

"My Best Man's speech was way better than that!" Nate yelled at his back.

"We're having a baby!" Jack shouted over his shoulder.

He scooped the gaping Louisa into his arms and hurried out the door. Jack jogged across the parking lot to his truck. He settled her carefully into the passenger seat and buckled her in.

Louisa grabbed Jack's arm as he started to step back. His eyes were wide and shining with panic. She gripped his hair and gave him a quick peck.

"Are you ready to meet Daisy?"

"I've been ready for thirty-nine weeks," Jack grinned at her.

If you want a glimpse of Jack and Louisa's struggles as new parents, sign up for my newsletter!

CAN THEY RESIST THE TEMPTATION?

What's Next?

Chocolate is life. Rainy sighed at the delicate aroma swirling from her cutting board. Anyone who thought otherwise needed a priority-check.

Sweeping the dark shavings into the mixing bowl, she gave the buttercream a gentle stir. Her spoon scraped the edge of the bowl and disappeared into her mouth. Sweetness spread across her tongue.

"Yeeeessss," Rainy groaned. She'd really outdone herself with that one.

Scooping her pen off the table, she scribbled the final ratios in the battered notebook beside her. Tomorrow would be the first test run with customers, but there wasn't a doubt in her mind that they wouldn't go crazy over her latest experiment.

But what to pair it with? Rainy raised an eyebrow at the gleaming bowl. Chocolate fudge cupcakes? She shook her head, blond tendrils escaping her bun. Not special enough.

She turned in place to regard the racks against the wall filled with cooling cakes and cookies. What would shine beside the dark chocolate-flecked mascarpone masterpiece waiting patiently for adoring fans?

Brownies? "No." She snapped her fingers. "*Mudslide* brownies. Coffee, chocolate, mascarpone. Perfection."

Rainy's triumphant grin slipped away as she glanced around the empty kitchen. Right. All alone. What was the point of earth-shattering brilliance if no one was there to pat you on the back?

"I really need to hire an assistant," she told the empty kitchen.

Rainy snorted. She'd been telling herself that for months, but had rejected every resume that had landed in her lap. Not just anyone was allowed to step foot in *her* kitchen. She had worked far too hard—begging, borrowing, and scraping together every spare dollar—to let a stranger muck about with her baby.

Glancing at the clock on the wall, she yawned. Night was rapidly turning to morning and adding projects to her to-do list wasn't getting her any closer to her bed.

First thing tomorrow, brownies. Covering the bowl in cellophane, she tucked it away in the gleaming refrigerator and set about tidying up the pile of ingredients strewn across the worktable.

Rainy scraped dough scraps and the layer of flour that managed to blanket every free inch of workspace into the trash. Her elbow smacked against the edge of the table. Fireworks swam through her vision.

Hopping up and down, she waited for the sharp pain to settle into a dull ache. She glared at the offending table edge. Stupid worktable, always out to get her.

Rainy shook her blond head. She must really be tired if she was accusing the furniture of colluding against her. Eyeing the remains of the mess littered around her kitchen, she sighed.

It could wait until tomorrow—well, later today. She would finish tidying up before she flipped the glowing "OPEN" sign on. Morning would just have to come a little earlier than she'd planned.

Tugging free the knots in her apron, she hung it by the door. The bright kitchen lights glinted off the dog collar hanging beside it.

Wrapping it around her hand, she lifted it off the hook. The pad of her thumb ran across the name imprinted on the metal tag.

Rainy had no idea who "JACK" was but she had spent many quiet nights in the kitchen wondering if the curly-headed woman who had slipped her the collar was alright.

What's Next?

God knows Rainy had called the number on the tag enough times. And looked it up in the phonebook. And searched it on the internet. A little cyber-sleuthing and she had an address in the middle of nowhere to go along with the mystery number.

The grumbling voice on the other end of the phone had given her vague reassurances and then promptly threatened her with harassment if she kept calling. Naturally, she'd sent them a box of cupcakes.

If Rainy couldn't speak to Curls, as she had started to affectionately refer to the woman in her head, she could at least let her know that she was still here, ready to help her again if need be.

Too many people had been poking around after the poor girl. Those rude FBI agents had spent over an hour badgering her, asking her where she'd disappeared too. How was she supposed to know? It's not like the cupcakes she'd sold her had tracking devices mixed into the fudge ganache.

Of course, Rainy hadn't been paying much attention to their interrogation. She'd been too busy wondering how *he* was involved and whether Curls had already called dibs on him.

Less than a half hour after Curls had disappeared from her bakery, the man had burst through the door and rendered her speechless. Mortal men did not look like *that.*

Tall and heavily muscled, he'd seemed more carved statue than human. Bronzed cheekbones sharp enough to cut the glass of her display case loomed beneath dark serious eyes. He'd locked on her before he'd even crossed the threshold. As his long legs ate up the distance between the door and the counter, Rainy had nearly forgotten how to breathe.

And then he opened his mouth and ruined it.

"Where is she?" he had demanded.

Apparently blinking in wonder at the way his T-shirt stretched across his chest wasn't the answer he was looking for. He'd snapped questions at her until the sexy bubble around him was no more than an afterthought.

Talk about a buzzkill. The handsome creature might have had a face sent from heaven, but that personality was express delivered straight from hell.

Until the day she died, Rainy would never forget the look on his face when she'd told him to get lost. Respect, annoyance, and a surprising heat that had knocked her back a step.

He'd turned and disappeared the way he came without another word, leaving her with nothing but the image of his denim-clad backside seared into her brain. She'd wondered about him almost as much as she had Curls, if not more.

Rainy bit her lip and dropped the collar back on the hook. If she let that sexy grouch back in her head, he'd spend the rest of the night haunting her dreams. It wouldn't be the first time.

She shook her head and started for the door leading upstairs to her apartment. Her hand froze on the doorknob. The trash.

Tomorrow morning was trash pick-up. If the bags weren't in the dumpster in the next couple of hours, they would linger in the alley for another two days. And no amount of bribing her neighbors with treats would get her forgiven for missing yet another trash day.

Rainy groaned. Her hand dropped away from the door, delaying her meeting with a soft, inviting mattress. She crossed to the enormous trash and recycling bins by the back door with a grumble and tied the bags off.

What's Next?

She dragged the garbage bags behind her. Kicking the back door open with a yawn, she heaved them into the alley. A small tear opened in the top of one bag. She narrowed her tired eyes. That's what she got for buying discount bags in bulk. So much for shopping thrifty.

Faint shuffling noises echoed through the dark. A small tremor of fear skittered down her spine. Rainy squinted into the shadows at the opening of the narrow alley.

"Hello?" she called out nervously.

Probably just a stray cat. She frowned. What if it was injured? She'd never sleep knowing she left it there.

Rainy leaned the torn bag against the wall. She hugged the other trash bag to her chest like a shield and crept toward the street, cursing her soft heart with each tentative step. The shuffling noises grew louder as she moved closer. Dark shapes separated from the shadows and sprinted toward the streetlights.

A man dressed in vibrant rainbows ran one step ahead of them. No, not rainbows, feathers. As the light hit his face, Rainy froze in place. He wasn't a man at all.

"Holy sugar," she breathed.

Ready for more? Available on Amazon!

ALSO BY R. O'LEARY

Raven Falls Cursed Romances:

Furbidden Attraction

Unbearable Temptation

Howling Devotion

Deathly Desire

Bewitching Allure

Siren Craving

Screaming Sins

Wild Indulgence (2023)

Smoldering Seduction (2023)

Novellas:

Frosted Kiss (Christmas Novella)

Winter Caress (Christmas Novella)

Frozen Embrace (2023)

Prequels:

Deerly Beloved

Hexed Heart

Cursed Claim (2023)

Galactic Fairy Tales:

Vermilion Stars

Crystal Nebula

Bound Nova

Novellas:

Gilded Moon

ACKNOWLEDGMENTS

There are so many people without whom this book would not have been possible; most importantly my parents, who let me live in their basement and eat their food while I made this book a reality. They always told me that I could do it, even when I was ready to set the rough draft on fire.

A special thank you to my sister Sarah, who I forced to read nearly a dozen different drafts of the first chapter before I was finally happy. Thank you for not murdering me in my sleep, it probably would have been justified.

This book would've been an absolute disaster without Suzanne Johnson, my editor. She finished two weeks earlier than I expected and was wildly supportive from day one.

Sylvia and Dyani, you two are total bosses for dealing with my nitpicking and delivering a set of stunning covers! Thank you so much!

And lastly a special shout out to David's Tea who makes a crazy good tumbler. When I inevitably forget about my tea when I'm growling at my computer, it's still insanely hot when I remember it hours later.

ABOUT THE AUTHOR

R. O'Leary lives in North Pole, Alaska (no, really). When she's not spending half the year freezing to death, she's writing about shifters and aliens and anything else that strolls through her head. Most of her day is spent in pajama pants, chasing the pack of corgis that have claimed her living room as their own.

Furbidden Attraction is the first installment in R. O'Leary's Raven Falls shifter series.

For bonus content, cover reveals, giveaways, and other fun stuff, sign up for my **newsletter** or check out my **website!**

Made in the USA
Las Vegas, NV
13 December 2023